FROM BEN

The bare earth rippled again. This time Molly felt it as well as saw it. There was a definite undulating motion beneath her hand. Then, to her surprise and horror, the soil began to split apart.

Her cat sniffed at one of the cracks to investigate.

"No, Dinah, no!" Molly reached out for the animal, but too late.

The cat hissed and would have fled if the mass hadn't already spread toward it, first covering the front paw, then the limb and neck. Molly gaped, paralyzed with disbelief and horror. The tiny things that were spreading and rapidly covering her cat were like greenish-black maggots with wings that fluttered with blurred rapidity but did not fly. There were so many of them—hundreds, maybe thousands—and they moved in one rippling mass.

Other Leisure books by Edmund Plante:

SEED OF EVIL
TRANSFORMATION

GARDEN OF EVIL

Edmund Plante

LEISURE BOOKS ∞ NEW YORK CITY

For my mother and
In memory of my father
George A. Plante

A LEISURE BOOK

Published by

Dorchester Publishing Co., Inc.
6 East 39th Street
New York, NY 10016

Copyright©1988 by Edmund Plante

Printed in the United States of America

GARDEN OF EVIL

I force my gift on no one, but whoso is willing and worthy to receive it may with welcome take.

—Friar Roger Bacon

PROLOGUE

OXFORD, 1294

The assistant held the lantern high as he carefully made his way to his master's cell. Not permitted to enter, he stood at the aperture in the wall of stone and peered in. The friar was asleep—or was he dead? It was difficult for the assistant to tell, for the man had grown ancient and pitiful in such a short space of time. He seemed so pale, so frail. Yes, it would only be but a matter of days, the assistant was certain. A fortnight at the most.

Then to his surprise the friar stirred, opened one eye, then the other. He squinted in annoyance at the lantern's brilliance. Aware of his master's explosive temper, the assistant spoke quickly and softly. "It is I, Master. You requested my presence, did you not?"

The friar grunted, then struggled to a sitting position. "You arrive late, fool," he grumbled in a voice that was surprisingly strong from one who was so ill. He made an attempt to stand, failed, then made another attempt, this time succeeding. The assistant noted for the first time that there was a small metal box in the man's hand.

"I have something for you," the dying friar said, as he forced himself to the open window.

The assistant accepted the box, and with one hand tried to lift its lid, but it would not open.

"Only when ample time has passed," the friar

explained, in a raspy, almost inaudible voice. "Then, and not before, it shall open."

"What is in it, Master?"

"Seeds."

"Magic seeds?"

"Art!" the man corrected petulantly. "Not magic. Art!"

"But, Master," the assistant said, frowning, "I had come to believe you had shunned your . . . art."

"Different . . . an exception," the friar muttered, suddenly tired. In the flickering glow of the lantern his angular, pallid face glistened with perspiration.

"What do you wish me to do with the seeds?"

"Keep them safe . . . until it is time." The friar no longer had the strength to remain standing. Tottering, he returned to his bed. "Until . . . it is . . . time."

"Master?" the assistant asked, in a whisper.

There was no answer.

The assistant waited, just to be certain, then he quietly retreated from the cell. What was he to do with the seeds when it was time? he wondered. Plant them? He tried again to open the box; the lid still refused to yield. It was just as well, he thought, for he wanted no part of the friar's magic anymore. It had frightened him immensely in the past. If anything, he should destroy the seeds, but then he knew he could never do it. Magic—Art—was too precious to destroy.

What was he to do? Perhaps on the morrow he would discuss this extensively with the master. Perhaps, just perhaps, the man would have the strength to talk.

But he never saw his master again.

Part I: The East Garden

1

Steve Ludden thought the day was running smoothly, devoid of hassles and setbacks for a change, until he returned to his apartment. He caught the delicious aroma of broiled steak and smiled, suddenly remembering he was hungry. He even kept the smile as he peeked into the kitchen and saw his wife of eight months busily preparing dinner, her nine-year-old daughter in the room with her, setting the table. I'm the luckiest man alive, he thought. Then he saw the note near the phone in the small hallway—*Call Shelly*.

The smile vanished. He stared at the note for a long moment, his appetite as suddenly gone too. What did Shelly want? he wondered. She never called unless she wanted something. He picked up the receiver and started to dial, the number branded permanently in his mind, for it was the number of his childhood. The mother house, the house he didn't like to think about, *refused* to think about. It gave him vague, uneasy feelings, but Shelly, his twin sister, was still living there.

Before he could finish dialing, he changed his mind. The call could wait, he decided, replacing the receiver. There was plenty of time to talk to his sister, to contact the house, but first he wanted to hug his wife and have a drink.

"Hi, hon, I'm home!" he shouted, as though he'd just

come through the front door. He loosened his tie and stepped into the kitchen.

His wife, Lara, smiled and hurried toward him. Her daughter, Molly, wasn't aware of Steve's presence at first, for she hadn't heard him. The hearing aid on her right ear was turned down, and her left ear (the dead ear, she frequently called it, since the hearing loss was complete in that one) was in the direction of the door. But when she saw her mother rush by, she looked up from the table and spotted her stepfather. She smiled, also, especially when the couple hugged each other and kissed. She watched, her smile becoming wistful.

"Hey, look at her." Steve tilted his head toward the girl. "She thinks we're the perfect couple."

"And she's right, darling," Lara said. She gave him a quick last kiss, then extricated herself from his embrace. Together they looked over at Molly. Her pretty face flushed from the sudden attention. She quickly averted her gaze and resumed setting the table.

"Shy one, ain't she," Steve said in a low voice, not wanting the girl to hear him.

"She's still not used to having a man around the house," Lara said, keeping her voice low as well, and carefully turning her head so that her mouth could not be seen and read. "But she likes you, Steve. She told me so herself. It'll take time, but we'll be at ease with each other. We'll be a good family."

"I know that, hon. Never doubted it for a sec." He went into the bathroom, urinated, then studied his reflection in the mirrored medicine cabinet. The reflecting image made him frown. At 33 he was getting old. His walnut-colored hair was graying at the temples. Maybe he was working too hard. He wondered if his sister, who was the same age as he, was also turning gray.

He groaned inwardly, regretting the thought. *His sister. His goddamned sister who always wanted something. His sister, who always got what she wanted. What did she want now?*

Why couldn't she leave him alone? Didn't she know how he felt about the mother house, about that ancient, oversized monster?

Suddenly he felt tense, clammy.

"Damn her!" he cursed, then went back into the kitchen, poured himself a glass of Cutty Sark, and sat at the table. Lara watched him for a silent moment, as though trying to read his mind, to sense his mood. No longer needed in the kitchen, Molly had gone into the living room to return to a jigsaw puzzle she had set up on a card table. She had been working on it since school had let out for the summer, a little over two weeks.

"Hard day, darling?" Lara asked. She checked the steaks under the broiler in the oven, then sat opposite him.

"Actually, no," he said. "The restaurant's fine. The new manager I hired seems to know his stuff. The cooks get along with him—and that's a first!" He exaggerated relief and amazement, then took a sizable sip. "Instead of a drink to unwind, I'm having one to celebrate." He lifted his glass to prepare a half-hearted toast. "May there be more smooth days like this."

"Maybe you should take a little vacation," Lara suggested, solicitously studying his features. She could see that he was tired, pushing himself. Her eyes lingered on the gray hairs at his temples, until he self-consciously averted his head and took another long swallow of his drink. "You've been spending long hours at the restaurant," she said, "every day since we've come back from our honeymoon."

"I'll be spending more time home, now that I've got this new manager," he promised. "Think I'll be able to depend on him."

"Why don't you take tomorrow off? We could go somewhere, do something together," Lara said.

"Naw, not tomorrow." He shook his head firmly. "Tomorrow's Friday. The place'll be too busy. The manager's too new. Sorry, honey. Maybe Monday, though.''

Disappointed, Lara got up to check the steaks again. Steve watched her as she flipped the meat over with a long carving fork. He felt a rush of guilt, then reminded himself that Lara knew before she married him that it'd be like this sometimes. The restaurant, The Four Winds, was his baby, only two years old. Until recently he hadn't felt at ease with a manager, and had gone through three of them, in two years. None of them had seemed dedicated enough to suit him; all had seemed interested only in salary and title.

But someday the restaurant would pay off, he thought confidently, as his gaze absorbed the feminine curves of his wife's slender body. She was petite, not much taller and heavier than her nine-year-old daughter. But at 28 there was nothing childish about her, with the exception of her eyes, which were brown and huge, deceivingly innocent. Lara's life had been anything but that; she had been through difficult times, and he was glad he had found her, that he had "saved" her.

God, how he loved her.

"A few more minutes," she said. "By the way, your sister called."

The feeling of dread rushed back. He tried to ignore it, at least to keep it from showing on his face. "I saw the note." His voice was tight. "What does she want, do you know?"

"She refused to tell me. Said it did not concern me."

Steve sighed. That was something his sister would say, all right. The bitch!

"Why does she have to be like that?" Lara asked.

"Like what?"

"You know, so . . . unfriendly."

Steve shrugged. He wasn't sure why. His mother had always pampered her, especially after Dad died. Shelly's such a sensitive person, she had said. That's why she's such a successful writer and poet.

"I've never done anything bad to her," he heard Lara say.

"I know that."

"Well, then, why?" she asked.

He thought about it, then said, "She's a snob, pure and simple."

"Because she's had a bestseller?"

"She was always that way. Her makeup, I guess." He drained his glass and pushed himself away from the table. "Might as well find out what she wants."

He went into the living room, passing Molly at the card table. The girl looked up from her puzzle, and he gave her an affectionate wink. She blushed, smiled, then quickly dropped her head in search of a puzzle piece. Warmth and sympathy surged through him—warmth because he could see her eagerness to be accepted by him, and sympathy because she seemed so uncertain and insecure.

But this will change, Steve vowed. Soon he'd be home more and they'd become better acquainted. He'd work on her confidence. He'd make it grow until she was as confident and proud as her mother. Yes, someday soon.

He picked up the phone receiver in the small hallway and found his hand was actually white from clutching the instrument so tightly. *Get a hold of yourself. What the hell is the matter with you? You're just making a phone call . . . not making another visit to the house.*

Just a call. A long-distance call.

This time he dialed the complete number. After the third ring Shelly's crisp voice filled his ear. "Yes?"

"Hello, Shelly. What's up?"

"It's about time you returned my call."

"I just got home. Give me a break, will ya?"

There was a pause, and Steve suspected his sister was doing this deliberately to make him wait, as he had made her wait. Finally she said, "Momma is not well at all, Steve." There was a tearful quality in her voice. Whether it was sincere or not, Steve wasn't sure, for he knew his sister could be overly dramatic at times.

"What do you mean?" he asked.

"If you had come to visit more often you'd know what

I mean.'' The tears were gone and the crisp edge was back. ''She asks about you all the time, Steve. *All* the time,'' she repeated emphatically.

''What's wrong with her?'' Steve rephrased the question.

There was another deliberate pause. ''She has the big C.''

At first Steve didn't comprehend. He had heard what his sister said, and he knew that the big C meant cancer. But something, a strange shield of some kind, kept Shelly's words from penetrating his brain. He tightened his grip on the receiver and looked blankly around him. He saw Molly working on her jigsaw puzzle and his wife in the doorway to the kitchen, watching him.

''Steve?'' Shelly demanded. ''Steve, are you still there?''

Slowly, a bit at a time, it registered in his brain. *Big C. Killer C. Man's number one killer. Or was the automobile the biggest? Or heart disease?*

''Steve?'' Shelly sounded angry now. ''Speak to me! Did you hear what I—''

''I heard,'' he said finally. His eyes locked with his wife's; they held for a moment, then looked away and stared blankly at the wall. ''How serious?''

''If you'd visited recently you would know—''

''How serious!'' Steve demanded sharply.

''She's had chemotherapy, but it didn't work.''

''Chemotherapy?'' Steve said, feeling the beginning of anger boil inside him. ''Then you've known this for some time.''

''Well, yes. As I've already said, if you had visited—''

''You could've called and told me, dammit!''

He heard an audible intake of breath, then slow, controlled breathing. ''You don't have to shout. I didn't tell you soonei because . . . because it was Momma's wish.''

''What?''

''She didn't want you to know, Steve. She . . . well, she

really thought she could fight this. And she thought there would be no sense in worrying you, especially since she was sure she'd recover. But . . ." She fell silent, unable to finish.

"How long does she have?" Steve forced himself to ask.

"Not long. It could be two months . . . two weeks." The reply was soft, broken.

"Oh, God," Steve moaned, now feeling a mixture of grief and guilt overtake his burgeoning anger. "When *was* the last time I saw her?"

"Christmas."

That was six months ago, Steve realized. Why had he stayed away so long? Why had he let so much time slip by?

"She knew of the cancer then, but chose not to tell you," Shelly said, then added sarcastically, "Will we have the pleasure of your company now?"

"Yes. I'll be right down," he said. "I don't believe this." And before his sister could make another caustic remark, he hung up.

Lara was still watching him, and so was Molly, their eyes pleading for answers. But Steve's throat was painfully dry. He went into the kitchen and made himself another drink.

Lara hesitantly followed him back into the room. She waited until he had taken a swallow of Scotch, then said, "What happened, dear?"

Steve suddenly wanted to cry. He found himself wondering whether it was grief or guilt that was pushing tears behind his eyes. "My mother's in a bad way," he said at length. "She has cancer."

"Oh." Stunned, Lara sat down at the table, the carving fork still in her hand.

"She hasn't much time."

The silence grew and quickly thickened around them. Molly appeared in the doorway. She stared at Steve's lips, then, finding them motionless, turned to her mother.

"Whad's wrong?" she asked, her voice low, almost guttural.

Steve looked at her. It took him a moment to realize what she'd said. The girl's t's and g's sounded like d's. Sometimes she could speak quite well, but only if she concentrated. Her speech therapist told her to practice saying words with t's and g's in them as often as possible. Someday, the therapist had assured her, these consonants would come naturally.

"My mother's not feeling well," he said, lowering the glass from his face so that she could read his lips clearly. "She may be dying." Then he turned to Lara. "I haven't seen her since Christmas. And before that, when was the last time? Our wedding?"

"Let's not think about that now, darling," Lara said gently. "We definitely have to see her as soon as we can."

"Yes." He nodded quickly. "Right." He took a sizable swallow, as though to warm his stomach, which had suddenly grown cold.

"You seem . . . reluctant," Lara said, frowning in confusion.

"No, of course not." Steve forced a thin smile. "We'll start packing right away. We'll have to bring a lot, because we don't know how long we'll be gone. We don't know how long my mother . . ." His voice trailed off.

"You want to leave tonight?" Lara asked.

An unbidden image of his mother's house appeared in his mind. He saw it standing dark and tall against a night sky. He was reminded of the many spacious rooms that were unused except by spiders. Rooms collecting dust and webs. Rooms filled with shadows, shadows that were darker than the night itself.

And he was reminded of the cellar, that dark hole in the ground where . . . where . . .

God, how he hated that place!

"No, we'll . . . we'll go first thing in the morning," he said, straining to mask the dread he felt.

"But won't it be better if we travel when there's hardly any traffic, dear?"

"No," Steve replied too quickly, too sharply. Lara's frown returned. "No," he repeated, softer this time. "I'll have to work a few things out first with the restaurant. Can't just get up and leave it, you know."

2

After leaving The Four Winds Restaurant, where Steve made a quick stop to reassure himself that everything was and would be running smoothly, the Cutlass turned into 146 South and headed toward Rhode Island. It was a warm morning, the sky thick with clouds, but the sun frequently broke through, as though determined to push its way out and become the main attraction.

"It's going to burn off," Lara said of the clouds.

Steve gave her a small, distracted nod. Obviously his mind was on something else. The restaurant? she wondered. Or on his mother and her house? Lara studied her husband's profile for a moment, hoping to find something in his handsome features that would reveal his thoughts, but his face was grim, his lips compressed and chin resolute. So serious, so somber, she thought. Lighten up, sweetheart, you're only going to your mother's house.

Which was beautiful. Lara only had seen it a couple of times, the first being when Steve introduced her to his mother and sister. His mother, Margaret Abigail Ludden, had brightened like a lamp, and her frail, ancient body had hobbled over and hugged her with surprising strength. She had just turned 80 then, so that meant she was 82 now. She was a sweet woman. Lara now wished she had seen her more than on holidays.

And then there was Shelly, which was an entirely different story.

Shelly hadn't received her warmly on that day when Steve had introduced her to the family. From a slight distance Shelly had brazenly appraised her, then released a cold, polite smile. No gleaming eyes and warm hug from her. Later that day Shelly had spoken to her, and Lara remembered thinking with relief that the woman was trying to be sociable, perhaps friendly, but now she saw that this wasn't her intention at all. Shelly had had no interest in amicable conversation. She had questions she wanted answered. "What do you do for a living?" she had asked. "Where did you graduate from?" "Are your parents still alive?" "What do they do?" "Have you been married before?" "No? But isn't it true, darling, that you have a child?"

The questions had been delivered in a sweet—*too* sweet—tone, and Lara had fallen into the trap, innocently answering every question. It wasn't until much later that she realized that Shelly had interviewed her as though she were applying for a job and had subsequently rejected her. Now, whenever Lara thought about her sister-in-law, she would experience a heavy, cold feeling of resentment.

Lara again glanced over at Steve who seemed less tense. Maybe the monotonous highway was tranquilizing him, softening that hard profile. Impulsively, she leaned over and kissed his cheek. He blinked in surprise.

"What was that for?"

"I get these uncontrollable urges at times. Bad habit of mine. Sorry."

He smiled. "I like your bad habits. Want to see some of mine?"

"I'm not so sure."

"Got to pull over to the side of the road and get rid of Molly first."

"Never mind." She snuggled up closer to him. "We'll talk about our bad habits later. Tonight, maybe?"

He didn't answer but winked instead. Lara felt a

warmth grow inside her. She loved Steve so much. Finding and marrying him was one of the best things that had ever happened to her; having Molly was the other. It was hard to believe that he and Shelly were twins, for they were so different. He was so warm, whereas she was so cold.

Lara, smiling inwardly, leaned her head against his shoulder, careful not to impede his driving. Doing this made her feel like a teenager riding around with a boyfriend. She, herself, hadn't had a boyfriend until after she had graduated from high school. Her parents had been too strict and self-righteous. So when she graduated she bolted out of town, went to the Big Apple, and earned a living as a waitress. That was when everything began to move at a whirlwind speed.

She met a handsome actor at the restaurant where she worked. His name was Brad MacIntyre, and he introduced her to his agent who, in turn, got her a small part in a daytime soap opera. She thought she was dreaming, and because of this she did something foolish. Letting Brad convince her that she owed him one for introducing her to his agent, she slept with him.

Lara found herself pregnant after Brad had left for California in pursuit of a better career. She couldn't locate him anywhere; she didn't hear from him or about him until she saw his name in the papers in the obituary section. He had OD'd on heroin. She had cried copiously that night, not because she loved him, but because she was alone with his child.

Then she received bad news at the studio. The show she was in was losing its ratings, dropping every week at an alarming speed. The producer blamed it on her, claiming it was her character that was pulling them down, so they wrote her off, killing the character in a car crash. And Lara found herself unemployed and broke. She went promptly to her agent, but he had nothing new to offer her. So it was back to waitressing again.

She gave birth to a beautiful baby girl and named her Molly, after a favorite aunt who used to visit the family every Sunday, faithfully bringing a small brown bag of penny candy just for Lara. Lara went back home with the baby, and when she was strong enough, she enrolled in a business college.

After graduating, she opened a boutique. Ignoring everyone's warning that she was moving too fast, she was convinced that she was already too far behind in life. She wanted security now, wanted her own home. And she wanted her daughter far from her parents' stringent clutches.

Gradually she noticed that Molly was silent and withdrawn. A dreamer was her first thought, but a visit to a physician revealed that Molly had a hearing impairment —complete loss in one ear and 75 percent in the other. A hearing aid would be needed along with special, once-a-week schooling for the deaf. The child would learn to speak correctly and read lips. Sign language was not required, for the therapists at the school believed lip reading would be enough, especially since the child would still be going to a public school and would be surrounded by those who were not handicapped.

And then, as if this weren't enough, Lara's store went bankrupt.

She cursed her bad luck, and then miraculously, after she closed her store for the final time, she met Steve.

It was not love at first sight, but he had relentlessly insisted that he take her out to dinner. He knew all the best restaurants, for restaurants, he had told her, were his specialty. He had perservered until she finally accepted the dinner invitation. One date led to another, and now she was hopelessly in love with him.

Smiling, she looked over at her husband at the wheel. The sun, for the umpteenth time, broke through the gray clouds and now splashed light on his hair, accentuating the red highlights amid the dark brown, reminding her of polished wood. She found herself wondering if his hair had been redder in his youth. There was so much she didn't know about him, and so much she wanted to know —especially about his past and the house that they were going to. Why had he been so unwilling to talk about it? Did he have an unhappy childhood there?

Yes, there were so many secrets about him, but it must be just that he was a quiet man, a man who hid most of his emotions. He needed to be coaxed. He needed time.

Someday, she was certain, she would know him as well as she knew herself.

Filled with confidence, she closed her eyes and fell asleep. When she awoke they were near the Ludden House. Lara blinked away the blurry vision and straightened up, moving toward her side of the car. The house was at the end of a lengthy driveway, at the crest of a small hill. It seemed to be sitting with regal defiance, like a queen sitting on a throne, Lara found herself thinking.

Although she had seen this house twice before, she could not help whispering, "It's beautiful, Steve. Absolutely beautiful."

He did not answer. There was a glassy glaze in his eyes as he stared at the colonial mansion before him. He seemed to be shielding himself against the structure. The knuckles on his hands as he gripped the steering wheel were bloodless.

Lara looked at him, puzzled. He actually looked afraid. Why? she wondered. What happened here? He had been like this the last time they were here, too. Then her gaze returned to the house. It was ancient, perhaps built somewhere in the eighteenth century, and yet it was in perfect condition, gleaming with fresh white paint under the sun that had at last succeeded in banishing the clouds. As the car reached the end of the driveway Lara found herself craning her neck to take in its impressive height and the large gambrel roof. She counted five wide chimneys, two smaller ones, then began counting the many long windows that gazed back at her in three separate rows across the house. Each window was framed with gray-blue shutters, also recently painted.

"Fifty-six windows in all," Steve said, aware of what she was doing. "Eighteen in the front, eighteen in the

back, and ten on each side." He gave her a small smile.
"Used to count them all the time whenever I was bored.
Sometimes I'd count wrong and think a window had
disappeared or been added."

"And what did you think had caused the windows to
disappear or appear?" she asked, amused.

Steve shrugged. "Didn't think anything of it. Thought
the whole house was weird, so the windows were no big
deal."

Lara saw an opportunity to ask once more why he
found this house disturbing, but Molly's head appeared
between her and Steve from the back seat.

"Nice house," the girl said. "Are we doin' do live here
for a while?"

"Are we *going*, dear," Lara corrected automatically,
turning her face for her daughter to see her lips. "Don't
forget to pronounce your g's and t's."

Molly swallowed, then repeated slowly, "*Going*."

"Good." Lara gave her an encouraging smile. "Yes,
sweetheart, we'll be here for a little while. It all depends
on Steve's mother, on how sick she is."

"Nice house," she said again, her eyes absorbing its
imposing size as Lara had done a moment earlier. "How
many rooms?"

Lara looked over at Steve, waiting for him to supply
the answer.

"Twenty-seven," he said.

"Wow!" Molly's large brown eyes grew larger, as
though eager to take in more of the mansion.

"Why so many rooms when there were just you,
Shelly, and your mother?" Lara asked.

"You're forgetting my father," Steve reminded her.
"He's the one who bought the house. Maybe he had
plans to have a large family before he died. Who knows?
After Mom had Shelly and me, she had complications
and couldn't have any more children, but the house was
already bought. And besides, my father was never a
practical man. He had a successful printing business,
made a fortune, and when he saw this house he fell in

love with it and bought it. Just like that.'' He shrugged. ''He hired servants, but when he died Mom or Shelly got rid of them.''

''Does your mother like this house?'' Lara asked.

''I'm not sure. I think she keeps this place because it holds a lot of memories of Dad.''

Lara continued to admire the house, finding it almost impossible to look away. There seemed to be so much history in it. It seemed so mysterious, a house with secrets.

''I wouldn't mind having a home like this,'' she said wistfully.

Steve looked at her. ''Why? It's only an old house with too many rooms. Most of them were unused, and some of them are blocked off in the winter to keep out the drafts and conserve heat.''

''Oh, I don't know. There's something charming about it, Steve. It's . . . well, romantic. Something out of a romance novel.''

''You're beginning to sound like my sister.''

''You think she got some of her ideas for her books from this house?''

''Probably.''

''Does she like this house?''

Steve nodded. ''Like you, she things it's charming and romantic. That's why she still lives here.''

''But you . . .'' Lara began, then stopped, for someone had opened the large front door of the house. It was a tall, slender woman with shoulder-length hair, the same color and thickness as Steve's. Clad only in a thin, silk-like dress, she hugged herself against the outdoor air. She looked over at the car, waiting, not moving beyond the stoop. It was Shelly.

''What about me?'' Steve encouraged Lara to continue.

It took her a moment to remember what she had wanted to ask. ''You don't like this house,'' she finally said. ''You still haven't told me why.''

When he opened his mouth, Lara actually thought he

was going to tell her, but he changed his mind and emitted a sigh instead. "Shelly's waiting for us. Another time, okay?"

"Is that a promise?" Lara asked, disappointed.

He hesitated a beat, then nodded. "A promise."

Lara searched his face for a fleeting moment and saw that glassy gaze return to his eyes. A defense mechanism of some sort? she wondered. He certainly seemed to be steeling himself against the house. But why?

The family climbed out of the Cutlass and met Shelly at the door, who now seemed annoyed that she had been forced to wait so long. When Steve was close enough she offered him her cheek, which he dutifully kissed.

"It's been a long time," she sniffed.

"Christmas," he replied, feigning a no-big-deal tone.

"That is still a long time to stay away from your family."

"I've my own family now, Shelly," he reminded her.

"Of course." She cast a glance at Lara, then at Molly. "Hello." She gave each a plastic smile, her china-blue eyes remaining dull and impassive.

"Hi, Shelly," Molly responded, smiling, as though endeavoring to brighten the woman's eyes.

But Shelly returned her attention to her brother. "Momma is eager to see you, Steve. God knows you've kept her waiting long enough."

"How is she?" Lara asked.

"Not well at all," she said without looking at her. "Steve, go on up now. You can unpack later."

Steve nodded, then stepped aside to let Lara and Molly precede him into the house. When everyone was in the large foyer, Shelly closed the door and gestured with her eyes for Steve to climb the wide, mahogany staircase.

"She's in her room?" he asked.

"Of course. Where did you think she'd be in her condition?"

Steve paused, as though trying to think of a caustic reply. When none would come to mind, he set the suitcases down on the beige and brown Indian carpet and went up the staircase. Lara and Molly started to follow him, but Shelly intercepted them.

"Family only," she coldly stated. And before Lara could respond, she briskly turned on her heel and joined her brother on the stairs.

3

Steve began to protest, but his sister's arm slid into the crook of his and urged him onward up the stairs of Ludden House. Only a violent wrenching would stop her, and a scene would undoubtedly ensue, something he definitely wanted to avoid.

"Why did you do that?" he said in a low, angry voice.

"Do what, Stevie?" Her pencil-thin brows arched, affecting ignorance.

"You know damn well what. Why did you tell Lara and Molly they weren't family?"

"Well, they're not, actually. They aren't of my flesh and blood—nor of Momma's—and at this point, Momma is what matters. I do not think she wishes to have a roomful of faces watching her in agony."

"That still gives you no reason to treat my family the way you do."

"*Your* family is no concern of mine." Shelly's voice took on a sudden hard edge, her eyes flashing coldly at him. She paused to lift her hair from the back of her neck, then daintily shook her head to let it fall back in place. This was something she did whenever she was incensed, whenever she needed a moment for control. "Momma is dying right now," she continued, slowly and tightly. "That is my main concern. My only concern. If I had hurt your new bride's feelings, then please forgive

29

me, dear brother. But what about you? You haven't exactly been sensitive and compassionate. Why do you stay away for so long? Don't you realize what you're doing to poor Momma? Don't you realize you're breaking her heart? Well, don't you?''

''I realize you have a sickening tendency to overreact.''

Shelly stopped short, as though he had slapped her. She dropped her arm from his and glared at him. They were in the carpeted hallway, two doors away from their mother's. ''Overreact!'' she said incredulously. Then she lowered her voice to a harsh whisper. ''How dare you say I'm overreacting, Steve Ludden! Momma's dying! How do you expect me to act? Calm? Uncaring like you?''

''I'm not uncaring, Shelly,'' Steve quickly said defensively. ''You're being unfair.''

''Well then, where were you since Christmas, half a year ago?''

''I told you—busy.''

Shelly sniffed, then stiffly resumed walking toward her mother's room. ''You can use any excuse you wish, but I assure you none will be good enough to repair Momma's broken heart.''

Steve rolled his eyes heavenward. He couldn't believe his sister. ''No wonder you're a maudlin writer,'' he remarked before he could stop himself.

She swung toward him. ''What's that supposed to mean?''

Steve hesitated, debating whether or not to drop the issue or continue it. He decided on the latter; she hadn't been tactful with Lara, so why should he be with her? ''You overract and you overwrite,'' he said bluntly.

She lifted her hair off the back of her neck again. It was a moment before she could speak, and Steve suppressed a smug smile, knowing he had hit a nerve. ''For your information,'' she finally said, ''critics have praised my work. They have called them in-depth and profound, sensitive and realistic. And my last novel, may I remind you, reached number four on the New York Times list, neither a simple nor minor achievement, let me assure you, brother dear."

"Hey, take it easy. You're overreacting again."

For a fleeting instant Steve was certain she would slap him. Her nostrils flared, and her prominent cheekbones seemed even more severe. She glared wordlessly at him for a long moment, her hands small fists at her sides. Then she spun on her heel again and marched, as dignified as possible, toward her mother's bedroom door. Before she disappeared into the room, Steve heard her declare under her breath, "I do *not* overwrite!"

This time Steve let the smile surface on his face. He was now more amused than anything. Sometimes his sister was as cold and ruthless as frost, but there was also a soft side to her. Her concern for their mother was genuine. And her writing was definitely a sensitive subject. It did not take much to bruise her in this area. Maybe he'd gone too far criticizing something that was so important to her. Maybe he had fought too unfairly.

The smile faded as he reached his mother's bedroom door, which Shelly had left open for him. Now he felt a rush of guilt—guilt for hurting his sister and guilt for staying away so long from his mother. Why the hell hadn't Shelly told him about the cancer, damnit! He would have come immediately.

He braced himself, then entered the room.

What he saw in the fourposter canopied bed stunned him. An emaciated, skeletal head stared back at him from an incongruously overstuffed pillow. Pale blue, almost colorless eyes bulged from the small face, and the toothless mouth was pulled inward, nearly swallowed out of sight. There was scarcely any hair on the skull, only a white, gossamer halo. Steve couldn't even tell if this was a man or woman, for it seemed ancient, older than any person he had ever seen. The skin seemed incredibly dry with myriad cracks across each cheek and the forehead, like fissures in a desert, and the color was as pale as the pillow case under her.

He couldn't believe this was his mother. He *refused* to believe it.

His eyes hesitantly descended to the body, which was hidden under the patchwork coverlet. There was hardly anything to be seen. So thin was this person that the coverlet was almost flat. Only the head on the pillow confirmed that someone was lying in this bed. Steve repressed a shudder.

This was not his mother, he tried to tell himself. This was not the same woman he had seen six months ago. Nobody could change this much so fast.

The woman spoke, and there was no more doubting the truth. It *was* his mother.

"Steve, darling," she whispered in a faint voice. The toothless mouth smiled, and a stale breath permeated his nostrils, forcing him to repress another shudder. The breath had smelled of decay, of something old and mildewed, of . . .

Death?

Tears burned his eyes. "Oh, Mom," he blurted, his voice cracking. "I'm so sorry. I didn't know."

"Shush, shush." The smile widened, and the stench intensified. "Darling, I understand. Oh, yes, your father was just like you, and I admired him."

Steve choked back his tears, then in confusion glanced over at his sister on the opposite side of the bed. Why had she said that he'd broken his mother's heart? The woman seemed to harbor no resentment.

Shelly caught and read the glance. "She's not going to show her true feelings, fool!" she said, as though the woman wasn't even present.

The old woman, Margaret, lifted her gnarled, emaciated hand from under the covers in protest, then, as though finding it too heavy to keep aloft, let it drop. "You two are always fighting. You never stop. Never." She looked over at Shelly, then at Steve. She didn't seem to be complaining; if anything, she seemed amazed that her two children, after all these years, could still find something to quarrel about. "Never," she sighed.

"But, Mom, I really am sorry," Steve said, meaning it. He reached for the bony hand and held it in his. It felt so frail and small. One firm squeeze and the bones would crush, he was certain. Once more he felt the rush of guilt and tears, blinking back the latter. "If there's anything I can do, Mom. Anything."

Margaret shook her head again, maintaining the warm, although wan smile. Her eyes began to gleam with love as they searched his face. "You don't understand, dear. I admire one who has strong ambitions. You had a dream, and you went after it. Of course you were busy. You had a dream to fulfill. Your father, I said, was the same way. How do you think he became so successful? How do you think he was able to buy this house, this white elephant? Eh?"

Steve looked over at his sister again. Now he was certain his mother's heart wasn't broken. Shelly, standing rigid, chin tilting upward, avoided him.

"And speaking of this house, Steve, darling," Margaret went on, regaining his attention, "it is the reason that I asked you to come here. I fear I may not make it until next Christmas—"

"Oh, Mom—"

"That was not said with sarcasm," the woman quickly clarified. "No. I must discuss matters concerning this house with you and Shelly before it is too late."

"Mom, don't talk like this. We'll discuss the house when you're feeling better."

"Oh, Steve, you always were the optimistic one, but alas, not always realistic." She closed her eyes, as though suddenly too weary to keep them in focus. When she had garnered further strength, she reopened her eyes. "I'm not going to be feeling better, so the time to talk is now. First, I want to see how the two of you feel about what I have to say, then I'll have a lawyer draw up a will."

"Will?" Steve echoed dumbly. His hand inadvertently squeezed the fragile hand inside it. Quickly he released his grip. Why did his mother have to talk about death and a will like this? Why couldn't she instead inform him that she was going to fight her illness and win, no matter what?

"Yes, a will. We must discuss it," she insisted gently. "As you all know, your father left his business to me when he died, and rather than face the headaches of keeping it, I sold it. I sold everything he bought, except the house. Perhaps I should have sold this as well, for we certainly didn't need to live in anything as big as this, especially without the help of servants. But I love this house and couldn't bring myself to part with it. So with the money I'd received from the business I was able to maintain this house and at the same time raise you two comfortably and properly." She smiled proudly. "I managed quite fine, if I say so myself. You two were never in want of anything, were you?"

"No, Momma," Shelly said softly.

Steve shook his head in silent agreement.

"I thought not." Margaret's proud smile reached her pale eyes, lighting and watering them. "I even managed to send you both to the college you wanted. Yes, your father's fortune went a long ways. He provided for us all, long after he was gone." The watery eyes began to brim with tears and mat her lashes, but she made no move to wipe them. "Oh, I loved your father so much. And just think, I'll be seeing him very soon."

"Mom—" Steve cut in.

"Shush, darling. I want to talk. Now please let me." She waited to see if he would interrupt further, but he fell silent. "But I'm sorry to say your father's fortune is almost gone now. There'd been some bad investments. I so much wanted both of you to be financially secure after I'm gone, but I'm afraid there is not much left to bequeath."

"Oh, Momma," Shelly cut in, reaching for Margaret's other hand and patting it tenderly. "We don't need your money. We're getting along fine. Isn't that right, Steve?"

"Yes, Mom, we don't need—"

"But there is the house," the old woman broke in, "and I'm sure it can be sold for a handsome price."

"Sold?" Shelly gasped, as though finding the idea shocking and offensive. "Momma, we could never sell this house!"

"But it is all I have to give the both of you. I have only one house, one legacy, and loving you both equally, I must give equally. The house will belong to both of you . . . to do as you wish with it."

"But I love this house," Shelly added, a whine creeping into her voice. "It has supplied me the mood, even many ideas, for my novels. It is a part of me. It—"

"Then perhaps you can buy Steve's half," the woman suggested, her eyes sliding from her daughter to her son. "Do you wish to keep the house, too, dear? My God, I hope I haven't created a problem."

"No problem, Mom," Steve assured her, smiling to confirm this.

"You never did like this house, did you, dear?" Margaret said.

"Why do you say that?" Steve was surprised. He didn't realize his dislike toward the house was so obvious.

"It is just a feeling. But is it so? Do you not like this house?"

"Well . . . there are a lot of empty rooms," Steve hedged. "A lot of space to heat in the winter . . ."

"You used to be afraid to go into some of the rooms." Margaret smiled, as though this was something amusing from his childhood. "I could remember trying to convince you that there were no monsters in those rooms, no ghosts. Especially the room in the basement. Do you remember that, dear?"

Remember? Suddenly Steve was young again, remembering. *Nothing there, nothing there, nothing there*, seven-year-old Steve Ludden had repeatedly told himself as he turned the knob to the last bedroom on the north side of the house. *Nobody's in there. Nobody's in there*. The knob was cold in his hand, like gripping a ball of ice, instead of glass. He heard the door click, then he hesitated, feeling a sudden urge to pee. Then he opened the door and peeked inside. *Nothing there. Nope.*

Nobody's there. He forced himself one step forward. Then another. *No!* Cobwebs clung to him and he frantically peeled them off his face. Then he felt some-thing icy cold caress him. He tried to take another step, but the cold (draft, his mother later told him) reached and chilled his heart. He had spun around and fled the room, slamming the door shut behind him.

"Steve, dear?" His mother now demanded an answer.

"Wha—Oh yeah, I remember." Christ, did he ever!

"Well, the choice is yours to do whatever you wish. This house is all I have to give my children, and I do hope I haven't presented a problem," she said again, then sighed wearily. "Lord knows how you two can squabble over anything."

"There'll be no problem, Momma," Shelly assured her this time.

"That's right, Mom," Steve added. "I just want you to think about getting better, nothing else."

"Oh, Steve, I am *not* going to get better. You must accept this. Shelly and I have."

Steve glanced over at his sister, as though to see if this were true, but her face was a blank mask, eyes fixed on her mother, avoiding his. She fondly caressed and patted the old woman's gnarled hand.

"Where is your wife and that lovely child?" Margaret suddenly asked. Shelly visibly stiffened, but her hand continued stroking her mother's.

"Downstairs," Steve replied. "Would you like to see them, Mom?"

"Oh, yes, very much."

"Then I'll get them," he said, half-expecting Shelly to protest. But his sister seemed not to have heard, intent on keeping the woman in the bed tranquil and comfortable. Steve kissed his mother on the forehead, fighting back more tears as he felt the dry, lifeless skin. Then he turned away and went in search of Lara and Molly.

The house fascinated Lara. As though in a trance, she wandered in and out of spacious rooms, her daughter keeping in step with her. She let her hands wistfully touch the beautiful antiques that filled and adorned these rooms. The long windows were all hung with curtains, some with lace, some with heavy velvet. The house's interior was dim and shadowy, but Lara found this somewhat peaceful rather than dingy, as Steve had occasionally described the house. She did not like bright or stark colors that often accompanied contemporary homes. She was partial to dark, subdued colors and dim lights. She loved the deep mahogany staircase, the cherry inlaid grandfather clock in the alcove below, the cranberry-colored silk wallpaper, and the beige and brown Indian rug over the gleaming wooden floor. This was a house in which one could truly relax and sit in a winged chair by the fireplace, a book in one hand and brandy in the other.

This was a house out of the past, a house that demanded respect. It was elegant. It was lovely. It was a house that she would very much love to have.

Lara glanced behind her to see if her daughter was sharing the same feelings. To her surprise she found the girl kneeling on the floor, petting a large orange cat.

"Nice cad . . . Nice cad . . ." she said softly as she stroked the animal's fur. The cat purred, looking up at her.

Lara smiled and joined her daughter. The cat reminded her of a stray she had taken in once. The poor animal had been limping and starving when she had found it. She secretly adopted it and fattened it up, but the landlord eventually found out and demanded that the cat be thrown out, for no pets were allowed. Unable to do so, she had looked for another apartment instead. Her mother, she remembered, had accused her of being too soft and foolish. "You'd take in an axe murderer if he's pathetic enough!" she had told her.

"Friendly cat, isn't he?" Lara now said to Molly.

The girl nodded. Together, mother and daughter petted the cat, wordlessly sharing something that was binding them together. A loose strand of yellow hair fell across the girl's forehead and Lara instinctively swept the hair back, then kissed the forehead. She has her father's blonde hair, she reflected without any pain or regret. "Love you, sweetheart," she whispered, but the girl did not hear her.

Then her other love came into the room.

"Lara, Mom wants to see you and Molly."

The mood broken, due to the unexpected intrusion, the cat scampered off, disappearing into another room. Disappointment showed on Molly's face, then vanished when she realized she was wanted upstairs.

"I apologize for that lousy remark Shelly made earlier," Steve said as they mounted the stairs. "You *are* family, and don't you ever forget it."

Lara didn't want to talk about her sister-in-law. "I don't know why you don't like this house, darling," she said to change the subject. "It's marvelous. It's so charming, so . . ." Her voice trailed off, for she could tell he wasn't listening. "How is your mother?" she asked as they reached the second floor.

He shook his head slowly, unable to trust his voice, but the gesture said enough, and Lara found herself tensing. What would she say to the woman? *I'm terribly sorry you are dying. I'm terribly sorry I never did get to know you better, but you see, your son here has been very busy, and well, you know how it is . . .*

When Steve paused at the doorway and moved to the side to let her and Molly enter the room, she experienced an overwhelming urge to turn and run back down the hallway, but she fought it and willed herself to be tough. She got her smile ready and forced herself to enter the room. Molly followed closely behind.

Margaret struggled to a semi-sitting position, her eyes beaming for a quick moment, obviously delighted to see Lara and the girl. "Hello, dears," she said, grinning, but the energy was soon spent and the eyes and smile began to dim.

"Hello, Mrs. Ludden," Lara returned softly, as

though afraid a voice any louder would break and, yes, even kill this sickly woman.

"I've said it before and I'll say it again," Margaret said. "You are a beautiful woman. My Stevie couldn't have done better."

"Thank you." Embarrassed and flattered, Lara's face colored. She moved closer to the bed and kissed the woman's cheek. When she stepped back she found she'd done the right thing. The kiss had definitely pleased the woman, for she was beaming again.

"And you—Molly, is it?" The woman turned her head toward the girl, who nodded in confirmation. "I can see you are going to grow up to be as lovely as your mother. Yes, I am certain of it."

Molly's brow furrowed as she concentrated on the woman's lips, then smiled as she realized she'd been given a compliment. Carefully, she spoke, "Thank you."

The woman studied the girl for a lingering moment, as though admiring her, then she returned her gaze to Lara. "Lara, tell me, what do you think of this house?"

"Think? Why, I find it simply breathtaking. I love this house, Mrs. Ludden."

Pride glowed on her face until it exhausted itself. "Don't you find it too big? Or perhaps, too old?"

"I love old houses, especially one that is kept up so well. When I'm in here I feel like I'm in the past."

"And is that good?"

"Oh yes, I find it enchanting," Lara gushed. "The past is romantic, exciting with its mysteries and history. A house like this inspires the imagination."

"My, my, you and Shelly are so much alike."

Shelly, lifting her hair from the back of her neck, said nothing, but the tight, controlled countenance clearly revealed that the comparison had affronted her.

"Is something wrong, dear?" Margaret asked her daughter.

Shelly's face reddened as she realized she had failed to mask her annoyance. "N-no Momma," she answered.

"Why do you ask?"

"I know when my daughter is upset, and right now you are definitely upset. Is it something someone said? Something *I* said?"

"No, Momma, of course not," Shelly insisted, but she could see that her mother was not convinced. Her face flushed brighter. "I just remembered there's something cooking on the stove," she suddenly said. She kissed Margaret's forehead, nodded politely at Steve, Lara, and Molly, then left the room. She walked gracefully, chin high and shoulders back, but she fooled no one.

Nothing was cooking on the stove.

4

Like almost everything else that she did, Molly took her time unpacking her clothes. She let her eyes absorb the room that was to be hers for the duration of her stay. The room reminded her of something out of a dollhouse she had once owned. It was old-fashioned, complete with mahogany highboy and canopy bed. The lacy coverlet and matching canopy were a soft pink, her favorite color, and the wallpaper was pink too, with hundreds of tiny roses all over it.

But unlike her old dollhouse, this room had two breathtaking views. The multi-paned window on the north side overlooked an extensive, verdant lawn which was intermittently broken by various flower gardens that, in June, had just begun to grow. She could imagine how colorful and pretty these gardens would look in another month. They were like islands in an emerald sea. Who took care of these gardens and mowed the lawn? she wondered.

The window on the east side commanded a different view. The lawn, also broken by scattered flower beds, extended for about 100 yards then ended abruptly at a concrete, waist-high wall. Beyond this Molly could see an endless stretch of ocean, the water glittering under the sun. A sea gull swooped down from the sky, perched a moment on the wall, then flew away. Molly sighed wistfully. She would love to live here permanently. She would develop a dark tan, and her hair would get even lighter. Maybe she would be pretty like a Barbi doll. It would be fun.

Molly finished unpacking everything that was to go into the highboy and began hanging the rest of her clothes in a closet, which was surprisingly dark. She groped the inside wall for a light switch and even reached for the ceiling in search of a fixture, but it was too high. At length she gave up, searched and found the rod and hangers, and finished unpacking in darkness. She made a mental note to get a flashlight later, for the closet seemed awfully deep and she did not have the courage to explore its depths without light.

When the suitcase was empty Molly found herself suddenly tired, from the task of unpacking as well as from the long motor trip. The bed looked wonderfully enticing with its fluffy pillow and lacy coverlet. She sat on it, took off her hearing aid and carefully put it on the night stand. Then she lay back against the downy pillow and closed her eyes.

She welcomed the darkness and silence, for they fueled her imagination. Sometimes she loved the silence, allowing her to dream on and on. It pushed the real world away from her and permitted many fantasies to enter in its place. Right now she was a princess in a beautiful castle. The king and queen were deeply in love, and the king's sister was jealous, for she had no one to love her.

Yes, sometimes the silence was welcomed, and with a house like this to help the imagination soar, she could go far. She could pretend to be anybody. She could pretend each room in the house was a new place, a new planet even. She could . . .

Something heavy jumped onto the bed, startling her. Her eyes flew open, her heart leaping to her throat. Then she saw it was the fat orange cat that she had petted earlier.

"Jeez, you scared me," she said, then leaned against the pillow once more. She closed her eyes again and lazily began stroking the cat as it curled beside her. She continued to dream. Now she was a beautiful princess who had a beautiful white Persian cat with a beautiful diamond collar. Everybody in the kingdom admired and wanted this cat, but it was hers alone.

Molly smiled in the silence and darkness, dreaming her wonderful dreams.

Then she fell asleep.

Later that evening, two rooms away from Molly's, they made love. Somewhere in the vastness of the house came the muted clacking of a typewriter, a sound that at first annoyed Lara but gradually became a natural part of the background.

When they were done, Lara wrapped her arms tightly around Steve and buried her face in his neck and hair, loving the masculine smell of sweat and Brut. "I love you so much," she sighed contentedly.

He didn't return the words, instead giving her a kiss that said it all. He held the kiss as long as she held him in her arms, then he rolled off and lay beside her. Lara fought an urge for a cigarette, for she had given up the damn things with Steve on New Year's day.

The clacking noise of the typewriter was noticeable again. The sound came in spurts, and Lara found herself listening to it. Somehow it seemed to magnify the peace and silence around them, rather than break it.

"I'd think your sister, being so successful and all, would have a word processor for her writing," she said.

Steve, too, listened thoughtfully to the typewriter for a moment. "Shelly's old-fashioned in a lot of ways. I think her motto in life is: If you're happy with something, don't change it. She was never one for modern technology or progress. She likes simple things, would rather ride a horse than drive a car. Maybe that's why she's so good at writing historical romance; her heart is in the past."

"And that's why she loves this house," Lara added softly. Except for the moonlight slanting through a window, the room was in darkness.

"Yeah," he agreed, his voice equally low. "I guess it is."

"What were you talking about when Molly and I were shut out?"

"Don't let Shelly bother you, hon. Just let her remarks glance off you, like I do."

"Well, I do wish she'd be nicer to me."

"She will, in time. She's cold and detached with everyone at first. She'll thaw eventually, especially if you're warm to her."

Lara couldn't imagine that woman ever thawing, not with those severe features and hard eyes. "But what were you talking about when Molly and I were downstairs?" she repeated.

"Mom is having a will made. Apparently the only thing left of Dad's fortune is this house, and she's going to give it to both me and Shelly."

"To sell?"

"What else?"

"But it's such a lovely house," Lara protested, for a sudden image of bulldozers and wrecking crews filled her mind. She could envision the house being leveled, then carted away, and in its place a McDonald's or a shopping mall sprouting up. "It's too lovely," she said again.

He grunted, and she knew he didn't agree with her. "Anyway, my mother is still alive," he said, "so I don't think we should be talking about selling the house yet."

Lara listened some more to the clacking of the typewriter, thinking how strange her ears or mind could turn the sound on and off. It was something like a scent controlled by a breeze. Sometimes it reached you, sometimes it didn't. She listened for a long time, wondering how late Shelly usually worked. Then her mind returned to the house. Margaret Ludden had said that Lara and Shelly were alike, both finding this house charming, but Steve was different.

"Why do you dislike this house so?" she suddenly asked. "And this time don't avoid the question."

He must have been on the verge of sleep, for it took him a moment to answer. "You're not going to give up, are you?"

"No. You promised, remember?"

"Yeah, I remember." He fell silent as he gathered his thoughts. A minute passed and Lara began to think he'd fallen asleep. Then he said, "You might think it's silly or childish, but I was always uneasy about this place. It spooked me when I was a kid."

"You thought you saw a ghost?" she asked quietly, encouraging him to continue.

"No, I never saw anything like that, but . . ."

"Yes?"

"I could *feel* something. There was always a presence here, someone watching me . . . the family. I always thought there were too many shadows in this house, too many places for this person—this presence—to hide, to watch from."

"Are you saying you're psychic?"

"No, not really. I only got these feelings in this house."

"Maybe it was only the result of a wild imagination, darling," she suggested. "Maybe you'd read too many ghost stories when you were a child."

"Maybe. I remember watching a Vincent Price movie, 'House on Haunted Hill'. It scared the shit out of me. But . . ." His voice trailed off doubtfully.

"Then what was it?" Lara pressed gently.

"There were—are—stories concerning this house," he said slowly. "Stories about the original owners. No one is certain about them, and probably they were not at all what people around here claimed at that time."

Lara noticed the typewriter had stopped for a while. A part of her waited for it to start up again, but it never did. She glanced at a luminous clock on the night table. 1:15. The silence was complete now, but she wasn't sure if she liked it.

"How old is this house?" she asked.

"As far as I know it was built in 1722."

"And the original owners were—?"

"A carpenter, his wife and six children. Collins was the name. They were a mysterious family, kept to themselves. The townspeople thought they were strange and not to be trusted, but it was the wife, Dolly, that the stories were mostly about. It was believed that she possessed magic."

Lara frowned in the dark. "What do you mean?"

"Magic had been passed down from generation to generation. An uncle of Dolly's had given her this magic from Europe, and that, it was believed, was how it came over here from the old country."

"What magic are you talking about?" Lara looked over at her husband beside her. In the spectral moonlight beaming in through the window, she could dimly make out his profile and see that he was staring pensively up at the ceiling, up where it was much darker and seemingly depthless.

"Dark, evil magic," he answered after a long silence, his voice barely audible. "Magic that was used in the thirteenth century."

"You mean witchcraft and sorcery?"

"He did not call it that. He called it Art."

"He?" She wished he wouldn't be so cryptic. "Who, darling, is *he*?"

The profile turned to face her, his eyes glinting for a fleeting instant as they caught the light of the moon. "Friar Roger Bacon," he replied, as though surprised she hadn't guessed.

"Friar Roger Bacon," she echoed uncertainly, weighing the name in her mind.

"Yes. Haven't you heard of him?"

The name was vaguely familiar. She concentrated on it until it gradually surfaced from her brain's murky depths. "Yes . . . I remember reading someting about him in school. He was a monk, wasn't he?"

"A friar," he clarified. "A scholar at Oxford in the thirteenth century. A man who had vast knowledge of the world around him. He spent his life educating himself and others. He knew so much . . . *too* much.''

An image became vivid in Lara's head. She could see a tall, frail man in a gray hooded robe with cord and sandals. She could even see him hunched over at a wooden work table scribbling something down with a goose quill. Nearby was a human skull gaping at him.

"What has he to do with this house?'' she asked, confused.

"His Art,'' Steve reminded her. "He did not pass down all his knowledge to the academic world. He was believed to have some secret knowledge, knowledge which only a small few had attained. He had many books in his cell at Oxford that were destroyed, some that he, himself, had written, and some that he had collected and treasured until the end. It was believed they dealt with theology, astrology, and his Art.''

"Steve,'' Lara whispered sharply, now growing impatient with him, "exactly what do you mean by his Art?''

"He could perform magic.''

"Oh, illusions, you mean.''

"If you wish to call conjuring up the dead and demons illusions.''

Lara stared at his dark face and felt a chill, conveniently blaming it on a draft from one of the windows. "You don't really believe this, do you?''

"Yes, Lara. I do.''

"But . . . but no one can summon spirits or demons. This is only done in horror movies.''

Steve turned and resumed staring silently at the black ceiling.

"It's true. No one can,'' Lara insisted.

"Friar Bacon was a scholar who spent his life searching for knowledge,'' Steve said slowly, still staring upward into the darkness. "His chambers at Oxford were said to have been filled with ancient books, scrolls and charts. Some of these works were of magical Arabian theories. He had a manuscript copy of *The Key of Solomon*, which had formulas and spells that had been preserved for hundreds of years by the Arabs. It was with this book that he could conjure up demons and spirits. It was even said he had summoned the ghost of Julius Caesar, had confronted and outwitted Satan himself."

"What happened to this *Key of Solomon*?"

"He burnt it along with his other collections. Too many deaths had resulted from his magic, so he destroyed all his learnings in a big bonfire. He was a holy man foremost and did not want to harm anyone, but sometimes his magic—Art—went beyond his control."

"So you are saying these so-called books of magic no longer exist?"

"Yes."

"How did you find out about all this? I certainly never read about a Roger Bacon dealing with ancient magic, ghosts and demons."

"I did research on him and the legends about him."

"Legends," Lara repeated, clutching the word. "They were only legends, not truth, darling."

"They were truth," he said quietly and confidently.

"But the books are gone now, so there's no proof," Lara pointed out.

"The friar didn't burn everything. When he cleaned out his chambers at Oxford he gave away many things to his students. He had magic objects—a chair that could travel through the air at an incredible speed—"

"And that exists somewhere today?" she interrupted skeptically.

"I don't know. But there were other things that were passed down."

"A magic wand, perhaps?"

"Are you making fun of me?"

"Oh, darling, you take things too seriously." Lara moved closer, rested her head on his naked chest and began to stroke his smooth, hard skin. "Anyway, I still don't know what all this Roger Bacon stuff has to do with this house."

"Hey, you're the one who wanted to hear this."

"I'm sorry, dear." And to prove this, she kissed his

chest. "Go on. What else was passed down from his chambers?"

"A . . . mirror, for one."

"Oh?" She caught the hesitation and knew the reply had not come easily.

"Yes, I know for certain there was a mirror. One of Bacon's students had taken possession of it and later gave it to someone else. For generations it was passed down, and eventually it fell into Dolly's hand, the wife of the first owner of this house."

"What kind of mirror?" Lara asked, her interest suddenly renewed.

"It was a mirror that . . . that could see events within fifty miles."

"Reminds me of the magic mirror in *Snow White*."

"This is not a fairy tale, Lara!" Steve retorted sharply, startling her. There was a lengthy silence, and Lara contemplated sliding away from him. She didn't like how serious he was being. He was speaking of medieval legends with the same graveness that an anchorman would broadcast the 11:00 o'clock news.

"Didn't mean to snap at you, hon, but that mirror did exist, no matter how farfetched it may sound. Bacon, in his rage, smashed this mirror when two young men died because if it, but fragments and shards were collected when he wasn't looking, probably by his assistant. I know, because I found a piece of that mirror in this house when I was a kid."

"Are you serious?"

He didn't answer.

"Do you still have it?"

"No, I smashed it. Ground it out with my foot until there was nothing left of it."

"Why? What did you see in it?" Suddenly there were so many questions. Mainly, did she, herself, believe what he was telling her? "How big was this piece of glass? How old were you when you found it? Where in this house did you find it?"

When she was done, she was surprised to hear only

silence. "Well?"

"I don't want to talk about it anymore."

"But—"

"You don't believe anything I'm telling you, anyways."

"That's not true!" She bolted upright to a sitting position and glared down at his shadowy face. The truth was that she didn't know whether or not to believe. "I want to hear everything about this," she demanded. "You still haven't told me why you don't like this house, you know."

To her surprise he lifted his head and kissed her breast, then her nipple. "Rather talk about something else," he said in a deep, husky voice.

"No," she said, but did not pull herself away from his mouth. "I want to know more about this mirror and about Dolly. Was she a witch?"

"Hmmmm?" He was working on her other breast now.

Lara felt her body stir with renewed life. She was tempted to give in to him, but her curiosity had not been satisfied. "Was she a witch, Steve?" she repeated, louder this time.

"She had a piece of the friar's mirror," he finally replied, his voice muted against her skin. "Had inherited other things, too."

"But was she a witch?" Lara demanded for the third time. "Did she practice witchcraft?"

"It was said that the things she'd inherited gave her certain powers." His head rose to kiss her neck. "Don't want to talk about it."

"What kind of powers?" she insisted, at the same time pressing against his lips.

"They said . . . part of the house burnt down because of her powers."

"Part of this house is missing?"

"It was restored."

"Oh." The questions stopped. His mouth covered hers, and soon the taste of him was all that mattered. Her body responded, arching to meet him. She felt his erection and moaned as he entered her, then she clung to him as he carried her with him to a dizzying summit. The house around her was forgotten, as though the walls, floor, and ceiling had receded and vanished, leaving them alone in empty space. Then, when they were done, panting softly, the house rushed back. And so did the questions.

But Lara didn't want to destroy the peaceful moment, for Steve was still holding her. His body was wonderfully warm, and its warmth permeated her, made her close her eyes and smile.

"Now I really love this house," she said.

"Uh?"

"It seems to make you awfully horny, darling."

5

The sun streaming through the east window awoke Molly. When she opened her eyes she at first was startled to find herself staring up at a pink canopy, then she remembered and smiled. She was in the big dollhouse. And curled asleep at her knee was her new friend, the fat cat.

"Dood mornin' " Petting the animal until it stirred and stretched, she nuzzled her face into its fur, loving its silky softness. Then she reached for her hearing aid on the nightstand, wiggled the tiny, plastic device into her ear and snapped on the switch. There was still silence, but the silence seemed crisp and electrical now, which was the only way she knew how to describe it. The silence without the aid was deeper and cushiony. Sometimes the difference was so slight that she'd find herself purposely exhaling a gust of air just to hear something. With the aid she could hear this; without it she couldn't.

In her cotton nightshirt, which was many sizes too big and fell below to her knees, she looked out the east window. The ocean glinted in the horizon, nearly blinding her. She opened the window, wondering if she could hear the surf, but to her disappointment found herself only able to hear the wind. Wind, it seemed, always managed to coil around her head and slap against her hearing aid, blowing, cackling, and drowning out chances of anything else, anything better to be heard.

She closed the window, deciding it was time to get dressed and have breakfast. She was starving! But when she found her way to the kitchen, she discovered it empty. Everyone was still sleeping. The cat had followed her, so she gave it some milk. Then she searched through the cabinets until she found a box of Froot Loops. She ate a bowl of the cereal at a small pine table in a recessed corner of the room that was drenched with warm sunlight. Here, she pretended she was a robot being recharged for the day with solar energy.

When she was done with her breakfast, she rinsed out her bowl and spoon at the sink, then stood indecisively for a moment in the middle of the room. There were three doors. Three choices. Now she felt as if she were Alice in Wonderland. This was sure to be an adventure.

At length she decided on the second door, opened it and stepped into what looked like a storage room, for there were canned foods and paper goods. The cat followed her, and Molly looked down and smiled as the animal rubbed against her legs. Yes, she had a new friend.

"I dodda div you a name," she said. Then she remembered Alice from Wonderland had a cat, too. Now what was its name? After a moment of concentration it came to her. Dinah. "I'll call you Dinah," she announced, as though making it official. Then she looked around at the surrounding shelves that rose to a 10-foot ceiling. Most of these shelves were empty, coated with dust and framed with cobwebs. There was a sour smell, causing the girl to wrinkle her nose with distaste. It was an old smell and reminded her of how ancient this house was.

"Don'd like id," she said to the cat, then promptly retreated from the room and closed the door. "Maybe this one is bedder," she said of the third door, then opened it.

Darkness and silence engulfed her. Usually this was the stuff that launched her imagination, but this was not happening now. As Molly groped the walls, she frequently broke webs that clung to her fingers, forcing her to peel them off like stubborn gloves. Where was she? Then her hand found a railing which went downward. A cellar?

Tentatively she inched forward until her foot reached empty air. Holding the railing tightly, she allowed the foot to descend until it touched something solid. A step. She did the same with her other foot. Then she inched forward once more, found the edge of this step and proceeded to the next one below it.

She knew she shouldn't be doing this—it was too dark in here—but her desire for adventure was too strong. She'd be careful, that's all, she told herself. Then, still gripping the railing, she found another step, then another.

The stench that was in the storage room was here also, only it wasn't as strong, probably because the space wasn't as small. This is an old, old house, she thought. It smells old, like the way old people smell sometimes. Sour, no longer sweet.

"Dinah," she called, although she knew she'd never hear the cat cry out in return. Suddenly she didn't like being alone. With her foot she carefully swept the air below and around her, searching for the animal, but she felt nothing. She was alone.

Go back, dummy! Go back! her mind demanded. *At least get yourself a flashlight or something!*

But the urge to explore was still strong. She tried another step. Maybe this one will be the bottom, the floor. It wasn't. Her foot stepped down again.

This time there wasn't something solid under her. It was something spongy, like rotting wood, but this she realized too late. She let out a startled cry as her foot plunged through the step, splitting it. The stench was suddenly overwhelming, and she knew it was rot and decay she was smelling. She lost her balance and fell backwards onto the steps above her, her hand still clutching the railing.

Now that she knew she wasn't hurt, only scared, she let herself sob with relief. She wiped the tears from her eyes, then regretted doing so, for remnants of spiderwebs from her fingers adhered to her lashes. They felt like tiny strands of gum pulling and balling when she tried to remove them.

Molly sat on a step for a while and waited for the pain in her twisted arm and back to subside, then she stood up. She no longer wanted to continue her exploration. Another time, she told herself. She'd get a flashlight first, then she'd explore the house to her heart's content.

The day passed, then another, and another. Lara found herself enjoying the colonial mansion immensely. In her mind's eye she decorated many of the rooms. The hallway and the main foyer were papered cranberry-red, but she'd change that to gray-blue. She'd put an armchair here, add a butterfly table there, a bench here, a bureau with a vase of flowers there. Oh yes, she'd love to decorate this beautiful house. It was a shame that Steve did not feel the same way.

Repeatedly she was reminded of what her husband had said the first night in the house, and repeatedly she brushed it from her mind. Imagine! A magic mirror! Certainly he couldn't believe in such a thing now. Also, he had talked about witches and sorcery and about a friar conjuring up spirits and—she shuddered—devils.

How could Steve be so . . . so juvenile?

Lara refused to think about all that and concentrated on the house. She loved Steve and was not going to pick on his faults or idiosyncrasies. Lord knew, everybody had them. When the sun was bright and the sea breeze balmy, she went outside to the east grounds and sat on an ornate stone bench at the waist-high wall and gazed out at the ocean for a spell. There was no sandy beach here, only large rocks and boulders that the surf ruthlessly slammed into and smoothed to a slippery gray gloss. It was steep and treacherous. One would not have any chance to survive a fall here. But beyond this, the ocean enchanted Lara. It seemed endless, merging with the sky at the horizon. Scattered throughout were white specks, some in the water, some in the sky. They were far away, so it took her a moment to realize that what she was seeing were actually sailboats and sea gulls. Lovely, she thought, smiling as the salt air permeated her nostrils. Lovely view. Lovely yard. Lovely house.

Lovely!

Her heart ached that these things weren't hers.

Molly finally had got a flashlight, although it had taken some snooping to find one, and begun her investigation of the house. She could sense that her stepfather didn't like the house and was curious to learn why.

Was it because it was too big and creepy? For it certainly was that at times, especially at night when all the lights were out. She'd been thirsty one night when everyone else was sleeping and, with the flashlight, had headed for the kitchen. The darkness, she remembered, ate most of the light in her hand, leaving only a weak beam shining no more than two feet ahead of her. The darkness went on and on, and she felt as if she'd been walking forever. The hallway had seemed longer than usual, and the stairway seemed to have more steps, and the rooms she crossed seemed bigger. On and on she went, and the darkness darkened with each room. She had heard horrible sounds. A creak over there. A giggle. A hiss. Wind against the house, rattling the many windows. Footsteps in the room behind her, in the room ahead of her. At length her courage had vanished, and she'd fled back to her room where she'd locked her door and buried herself under the blanket.

Now she realized her ears could have never picked up those soft sounds. She had let her imagination frighten her. But Steve was a grownup, a man. He wouldn't be scared of noises in the dark, would he? Hearing noises wouldn't make him dislike this house, would it?

No, not a man like him. He was brave and strong. He was Mom's Prince Charming.

It had to be something else, Molly decided. Maybe there was a ghost in this house. Maybe he had seen one, and Shelly hadn't, which would explain why she still seemed to like the house. Now the question was if Molly was brave enough to prove this theory.

Nancy Drew would be brave enough, she reminded herself, and with that thought, she gripped her red plastic flashlight and continued her exploration of the house.

She had already seen most of it and had found several hidden stairways and passages, even a hidden room. Her bedroom closet was one of the passages, leading to a trap door in the floor, but the door was nailed shut. Probably another secret room. And the attic had been great fun, for it was filled with old clothes, toys and broken furniture. She had spent two whole days up there, indulging in one fantasy after another, ignoring the heat and dust. So the only place left to explore was the cellar, where the stairs leading down were so rotten.

She headed for the kitchen and the cellar door. When her hand touched the knob, she hesitated. She wasn't sure why, but there was something about the cellar that demanded more courage than usual. There was a bad feeling in her stomach, maybe because of that fall through the rotten steps.

Maybe she should forget about the cellar and go into the attic again. There was still a lot of stuff up there that she hadn't seen yet. But her hand ignored this logic and began to turn the knob, while the other hand got the flashlight ready to pierce the darkness.

Maybe the cellar's why Steve doesn't like this house, she thought. Gotta find out. Gotta solve the mystery.

Nothing would stop Nancy Drew, and right now she was Nancy Drew.

She drew in a deep breath to steel herself, then opened the door and carefully descended the stairs. In the weak, yellow light, the wooden steps disappeared into darkness. Molly clutched the railing with one hand and the plastic flashlight with the other. The cellar was incredibly deep and dark. She searched for a light switch, but couldn't find any.

She spotted the step that her foot had gone through, at the same time catching a whiff of the acrid smell of rot. She carefully skipped over the bad step and beamed the feeble light downward. At last she found the floor . . . and something scurrying away from the light. A mouse? Or worse, a rat?

Molly froze on the stairway. Maybe she shouldn't go on. Maybe it was too dangerous down here.

But you've a mystery to solve, she reminded herself. You gotta find out why Steve doesn't like this place.

She aimed the flashlight up at the kitchen door above her. It was lost in darkness, and suddenly she realized she was actually in the ground, that the cellar was deeper than a grave. And with this thought came a damp, earthy smell. Or was this only in her mind?

Molly forced herself to move onward, testing each step before applying her entire weight, and after what seemed like an eternity, she reached the solid, concrete floor.

She shivered, although the air was not cold. She swept the floor with light and relaxed a bit as she found no further creatures scurrying away into darkness. Then she scanned the walls, which were made of crude stones and flaking mortar. Garden tools and clay flowerpots were in a sloppy heap against one wall, and a wooden workbench was against another, long unused, for dust and cobwebs shrouded most of it like gray snow. Turning the light on the cellar itself, she illuminated thick, wooden poles that seemed to be everywhere, supporting the big house above. She tried to find the end of the cellar, but the light was too weak to reach it. Endless like space, she thought and shivered again.

She aimed the flashlight at the ceiling, but it was too far up. Were there bats sleeping up there on the beams? Were there snakes up there, too?

Jeez, why did she have to think of these horrible things!

She heard something.

No, that was dumb; she couldn't hear.

She turned her hearing aid up louder. Nothing. She had only imagined the sound. She wished she could stop doing this, because not only was it making her angry, it was scaring the hell out of her.

The word "hell" jumped out in her mind. Was this "Hell"?

Of course not, dummy!

She noticed something in the air, a strange thickness of some kind. It almost felt as if she'd just walked into a mist or fog, but of course she couldn't see much of anything—only the endless rows of wooden poles supporting the house, tools here and there, and darkness.

But she *had* walked into something. She was sure of it.

It was suddenly damper here. She told herself to stop walking and pause for a minute, but she ignored any sensible instinct. Curiosity was dominating fear. She proceeded onward, determined to explore the entire length of this . . . this underground world.

It was a world, she mused, a different kind of world. It was a world that was—she groped for the right word—*unnatural*. There was something that wasn't right down here, something that bothered her. There was something . . . something . . .

Magical?

This time she stopped. Yeah, magical! She could feel magic all around her. She had crossed over into something like . . .

The Twilight Zone?

"Damn!" she cursed aloud. She wished she could stop letting her imagination scare her all the time.

She continued forward. The end of the cellar had to be coming up soon.

As she haltingly walked on she began to understand why her stepfather didn't like this house. She didn't very much like it herself right now.

The mist seemed thicker. Molly still could not see any difference in the air; the darkness appeared to be exactly the same as when she'd first stepped through the kitchen door, and the yellow beam from her flashlight was no brighter or weaker. Also, the temperature had not changed, and the humidity remained the same, damp with an earthy stench. The smell of graves, she kept thinking, although she had never smelled one in her life. Nothing changed, and yet . . .

The air was heavier, turning to something palpable. She could sense something like arms protruding from this mist and coiling themselves around her. She could almost feel them pulling her, gently yet inexorably deeper into the cellar.

Go back . . . Go back . . .

The warning came from somewhere deep inside her brain, too faint and distant for her to pay any heed. The "arms" that were pulling her were all she could think about now. She was no longer afraid, only curious. Where were these "arms" taking her?

This was magic.

Like a leaf caught in the flow of a stream, she moved toward the north side of the house. She held the flashlight firmly ahead of her, letting it light the way.

At length she came to a wooden door. It was ancient with some of the boards missing, leaving a gap wide enough to fit a head through. Molly shined her flashlight through this gap, but again the light was too feeble to penetrate such darkness.

The magic "arms" urged her to open the door and enter this room, and after a brief hesitation, she complied. To her surprise, the door opened easily, resisting and scraping only once against the cement floor. When she stepped through the doorway the strange mist was markedly thicker. She knew now that she was entering the core of . . . something.

She pointed the flashlight at the door that was now behind her. Two wooden brackets flanked this door, and on the ground was a board. It did not take much to realize that this board had been used to bar the door. It looked as if whoever had used this room wanted privacy. But what kind of room was this? Molly wondered as she swept the flashlight across it.

The floor, she noted, was no longer concrete but rather packed earth. It was almost as if this room was separate from the rest of the cellar—or from the house itself, for that matter. The room somehow seemed, or rather, *felt* so much older.

Her light caught another creature, scurrying too fast into the dark for her to recognize it.

I'm going back, she thought. I've seen enough!

But she didn't move. Curiosity still controlled her. She could sense that this room was special, and she wanted to know why. The air was not only thicker here, but the temperature was lower, and the darkness darker—something that a minute ago she thought couldn't be possible.

Yes, this room was special.

She moved farther into it, searching for clues, but the room was devoid of furniture, empty except for a rotten board half buried in the ground here and a piece of broken glass there. Then, at last, she reached a wall and ran the light across it. Like the rest of the cellar, it was made of rocks and mortar.

Like a dungeon in a medieval castle. Yes, that's what it was. And a lovely princess must have been thrown down here to die when she refused to kiss the wicked king, but happily, a prince had heard her cries for help and rescued her.

Of course she knew this had never happened here, but it bolstered her courage. She searched for another wall and found it to be more of the same. Maybe this room wasn't special after all, she finally decided. Maybe this was just a wine cellar or something like that.

Maybe she was letting her imagination run wild again.

Then she felt the air close in on her, felt its "arms" hug her. No! she thought as her heart thundered. It's not my imagination. This room is special. And there's something in it!

She spotted a peculiar protrusion in the wall, one stone not quite even with the others surrounding it. Molly stared at it for a moment, curiosity mounting. She made sure there were no spiders or other insects near the stone, then she reached out for it.

At mere contact, the stone fell out onto the ground. Startled, Molly jumped back. When she realized that nothing had actually leaped out at her, and that the rock had probably been ready to fall anyway, she aimed her flashlight into the oval-shaped hole that was now in the wall. She'd expected to see sunlight winking back at her from the other side, but instead met a reddish glare that nearly blinded her. She jumped back a second time, somewhat stunned. What had she seen? A reflection of her own flashlight bouncing back at her? She stared dubiously at the hole, which was now black like the minature mouth of a cave.

Go back . . .

Molly peeked into the hole again and narrowed her eyes, as though to shield them from another red blast, but this time her flashlight picked up something silver. It took her a long moment to realize it was a box she was seeing. She reached into the hole, hesitated for a brief second, then touched the box. It was surprisingly warm. She hesitated again, then pulled the box out.

As she held it in her hand, the box gradually cooled. Had she only imagined that it was warm? She lifted the small box to eye level and shined the light on it. It was made of metal, dull and silver, and was surprisingly weighty for its small size. It seemed ornately carved, until she peered closer and saw that the carvings were actually letters engraved in the metal. The letters were worn, prompting Molly to move the flashlight closer and tilt the box at various angles.

Gradually, she made out the first letter. *S.* Then *E . . .* and . . . another *E . . .* then . . . *D . . .* and another *S.*

Seeds?

Blinking, she stared at the box. Should she open it? Suddenly she became aware of the deep hush surrounding her. Her first thought was that the battery for her hearing aid had run out, which it often did with little warning, but when she deliberately exhaled to test this, she easily heard the expulsion of her breath. So her hearing aid was still working, yet the silence *was* deeper.

It was as if the room were holding its breath, watching and waiting for her to open the box.

Molly stared at the metal object some more, stalling to muster up additional courage. Then she sat on the earth floor, placed the box on her lap, held the flashlight on it, and slowly, hesitantly, removed the lid.

Red light shot out at her, then beamed past until it disappeared in the dark. Molly let out a frightened gasp, almost knocking the box off her lap. She thought of jumping up and running out of this eerie room, but everything immediately seemed normal again, with no hint that something unusual had just occurred. She looked down at the box again, this time with the lid removed. There were four tiny cloth bags inside. With her thumb and forefinger, she lifted one out and held it up to her face, beaming the light on it. The bag was drawn shut with a thin cord. Carefully, she worked it open and looked inside.

Seeds. Tiny, black, pepperlike seeds.

Were they still good? she wondered, feeling strange excitement coursing through her body as questions filled her mind. Were these vegetable seeds? Flower seeds? Grass seeds?

She closed the bag tightly with the cord, returned it to the box, then picked up another. The seeds in this one were different, bigger and reddish-brown. The third bag contained yet a different batch—white and coarse, like grains of sand. And the fourth bag surprised her most of all; it held only one seed, which was woody and large, somewhat acornlike. She stared at it, mystified, wondering what it would grow into. Then she reverently put it back in the box and replaced the lid.

She kept the box in her lap for a long time, staring at it in fascination. So many questions were still popping into her mind. Not only did she wonder what kind of plants these seeds would produce, but also where did they come from? How long had they been hidden in the wall? Who had hidden them? Why?

When the questions finally abated, she became aware of her surroundings, as though for the first time. When she had first come here, curiosity and possibly another force, an unexplainable one, had driven her to this room, but now that these forces were gone, the dank darkness was alarming. Molly felt panic rising. The stairs to the kitchen were far, far away. Something would certainly leap out of the dark and attack her. A monster. A boogeyman. Anybody. Anything.

Molly was filled with an urge to cry out for help, but she fought it and forced herself to find her way back to the stairs. As she walked, gripping the flashlight with one hand and clutching the box of seeds against her chest with the other, she mumbled over and over, "I'm not afraid . . . I'm not afraid . . ."

When she reached the stairs she almost cried out with relief and joy.

And when she reached the brightness of the kitchen she forgot all about the horrible darkness below. That's how pretty and charming the big house really was.

6

Margaret Abigail Ludden died.

Shelly was hysterical, but Lara somehow felt that the woman's reaction to her mother's death was not sincere. Granted that the woman was grief-stricken, but did she have to sob so convulsively and frequently into her hankie and then rush out of the room, slamming the door after her? Yes, Lara had to agree with what Steve had said about her; Shelly had a tendency to overreact, almost to the point of being ludicrous.

Steve, on the other hand, mourned quietly, inwardly. He refused to talk about his mother, no matter how much Lara tried to convince him that expressing his sorrow would make him feel better. She even reminded him of her motto—communication kept a marriage alive and strong—but he kept insisting he wanted to be alone. He would take off in his car, check on his restaurant, then stop at a pub for several drinks. Then he'd come home, not to be with her but to spend a few hours in the library. Here, he'd sit by the cold fireplace, a book on his lap and a glass of Scotch in his hand. He did not read the books, for whenever Lara stealthily looked in on him, he'd be staring into the empty fireplace lost in thought. Once she had seen him break down, covering his face with his hands. She wanted to comfort him, but knowing her touch would only shame and infuriate him, she forced herself to retreat from the doorway and let him have his own way.

Lara suspected grief was only a small part of her husband's suffering. Guilt was the larger part. He had let foolish juvenile fears keep him away from his mother, and now it was too late.

A week passed and to Lara's relief Steve began to recover. His smiles returned and his eyes resumed their blue brilliance. When he came home sober from his restaurant, skipped the library, and pulled her into their bedroom to make wild, prolonged love, she knew she had her wonderful husband back.

Shelly also knew he had finally sprung back, for she chose this moment to make her move. She knocked at the door. "Stevie, dear, are you in there?" she called in a sweet voice.

She knows damn well he's in here! Lara thought as she reached for her clothes that she had eagerly tossed to the floor. Shelly's timing had been perfect, for Steve and Lara had just finished their lovemaking. Was it a coincidence, or had Shelly been at the other side of the door listening and waiting? Probably the latter, Lara decided disgustedly.

When Steve, clad only in trousers, opened the door, Lara had finished dressing and was standing behind him. Shelly gave her a quick, impassive glance then focused her attention on her brother. "We have to talk, Stevie," she said.

"About what?" Steve asked.

"About matters concerning this house."

"Oh," Steve replied morosely, as though he'd been expecting and dreading it. He opened the door wider and stepped aside, mutely inviting her to come into the room, but she remained in the hallway.

"I prefer to discuss this elsewhere," she said.

"But I'm not done dressing."

"I'll wait."

Steve frowned at her, then shrugged as he put on a

shirt. "Where do you want to talk?"

"Anywhere . . . alone."

The last word was sharp and cold, piercing Lara. She bit her lip, fighting to control an anger that was rapidly building inside her.

Tucking his shirt inside his pants, Steve glanced at Lara to see her reaction, but she was looking at Shelly, who in turn was carefully avoiding her.

"All right," he acquiesced, hearing no objection. He began to follow his sister.

Lara watched them leave, her hand on the door, ready to close it. The anger that was stirring inside her grew restless, like an animal locked in a cage causing it to fling itself against the bars and demand release.

How dare Shelly treat me as if I were invisible! Who the hell did she think she was, anyway?

The anger snapped the bars and broke free.

"This is a family matter," Shelly said coldly when Lara found them in the library.

"I *am* family," Lara reminded her, her tone equally frosty.

Shelly let out an exasperated sigh, as though she were dealing with a pesty child. She turned to her brother, who was standing by the fireplace. "Would you please do something about this, Stevie."

Lara glared at her husband, tacitly warning him not to dare send her away.

"She is right, you know," he finally told his sister. "She's family now."

"Oh, for heaven's sake!" Shelly exploded, reaching for a gilded case on the mantel and extracting a cigarette. "She's not of Ludden flesh and blood. What we have to discuss here is no concern of hers. Now please, let's not be foolishly proud and childishly stubborn." She lit her cigarette with a crystal lighter, blew out a thin stream, then fully faced Lara. "It's nothing personal, I assure you, my dear, but I insist that you leave my brother and me alone."

"And I insist that I stay."

The boldness seemed to surprise then enrage Shelly. "Damnit, do something, Steve!"

"Come now, Shelly," he said, "you have no reason to exclude Lara like this."

Shelly gawked at him, as though he had cruelly betrayed her. Then she threw her hands up in furious surrender. "Very well! Have it your way!" She drew on her cigarette, then indignantly released smoke, reminding Lara of Bette Davis in countless movies. Overreacting again?

Shelly paced briskly across the book-lined room, stabbed her cigarette out in an ashtray along the way, then returned to Steve and Lara who were waiting expectantly for her to begin.

"Momma left this house to both of us," she said needlessly, again deliberately focusing her attention solely on Steve and excluding Lara. "But since I'm aware that you're not fond of this house, I would like to buy your half of it. You see, I don't want to sell our home to any stranger. I wish to keep it. I love this house, Steve."

Steve's shoulders began to lift in a no-problem shrug, but Lara clutched his arm, surprising and stilling him. He looked questioningly at her.

"Don't do anything hasty," she said.

Shelly's eyes flashed hotly at her, then cooled with forced control and returned to Steve. "You hate this house," she reminded him.

"But I find it charming," Lara said.

"You've no say in this matter," Shelly said without looking at her. Her eyes demanded some kind of agreement from her brother, but Steve was speechless, glancing at both women.

Realizing she was getting nowhere with him, Shelly then flared at Lara. "This house couldn't possibly mean anything to you. How many times have you been here? Twice? Or was it as much as three times? Certainly you've no sentimental attachment to it, dear!"

"It's a charming house," Lara repeated stubbornly.

"Yes, but it's more than that to me. I was raised here.

It's my home, a part of me. Now, if Stevie shared the same sentiment, then we'd both have to share or sell the house, but since he obviously does not, I fail to see why he shouldn't sell his half to me."

"He shouldn't because I might not want to sell—"

"But you're not—"

"I *am* family, Shelly."

"Momma left the house to me and Stevie." Shelly lifted her hair from the back of her neck, then, shaking her head, let it fall. "Oh, I knew you would complicate things. That's why I wanted to discuss this alone with my brother." Turning to Steve, she added, "Why won't you say something, for God's sake? Put an end to this silly dispute. Tell her how much this house has always meant to me."

Steve's head again swung back and forth to each woman, as though trying to determine which one was the more irrational, which one needed appeasing first. The look on his face evidently showed that he felt trapped, and Lara felt a rush of guilt.

"I didn't know you wanted this house, hon," he said to her.

"I just want you to think about it first, that's all. Discuss it with me."

"That's fair." This was directed at his sister.

"I don't think it's fair at all." Shelly shot back. "I'm the only one who sincerely appreciates this house. You couldn't wait to get out of this place. I distinctly remember you calling it a dungeon, a gloomy old house that deserves to be burned to the ground and its ashes buried six feet under. You loathe this house, Steve Ludden, and you never hid that fact. So why—" her voice rose to a theatrical whine "—*why* won't you sell it to me? You'd be rid of it forever this way."

"I'm just asking you to let me think about it."

"But there's nothing to think about, and you very well know it."

"That's not true."

Shelly, in frustration and controlled rage, lit another

cigarette. She let the smoke calm her to a degree, then she said in a slow, resentful tone, "You were never one to be easily influenced, Stevie. I always admired you as being one who knew and did what he wanted. In other words, dear brother, I thought you were strong."

"Don't use psychology—"

"I'm speaking the truth. You disappoint me greatly, Stevie. Greatly. Never, *never,* had I dreamed a woman would manipulate you like this, would . . . would control you."

"C'mon, Shelly, knock it off."

"I'm serious!" She shot a baleful glance at Lara, which was tantamount to a child sticking a tongue out at someone she despised. "You are letting . . . letting . . ." Her voice broke, rage overcoming her.

"Shelly," Steve said, endeavoring to placate her, "I'm just asking for a little time."

"You're going to let her influence you. I just know you are. And I'm so ashamed of you. If Momma could see you now. Oh, if she just could see you!"

Lara couldn't believe what she was hearing. Overreacting would be putting it mildly. Shelly was beside herself with fury; she was hysterical.

"Calm down," Steve urged, using his most soothing voice to no avail. "We're not going to accomplish anything if you don't calm down, Shelly."

"It's not fair." She was now wailing. "I've been here so much longer than she. I've spent my childhood here."

Lara rolled her eyes upward. How long was this going to go on? Then she saw Molly in the doorway and quickly tried to get Steve's attention, to make him stop this crazy argument. She didn't want her daughter to see how badly everyone was getting along. Here, she thought, was a child witnessing a group of adults behaving like children. What a horrible example! But when she looked back at the doorway, Molly was no longer there.

Shelly continued to rail on and on.

"It's still not fair!" she cried for the umpteenth time. "This house already belongs more to me than either one of you. I've furnished some of the rooms myself, helped restore many of them. Not you, Stevie. You were too busy elsewhere. You disappeared as soon as you left high school.''

"You went away to college, too," Steve reminded her.

"But I didn't stay away," Shelly countered. "I came back during vacations and long weekends. You didn't come back even during the summer, dear brother. Only at Christmas. Why was Christmas so special, anyway? Was that when the guilt became too unbearable?''

"C'mon Shelly, let's not go through this again. Mom understood, and that's all that matters.''

Shelly glowered at her brother, at Lara, then back at her brother. She seemed to be fighting for control, and when she finally had it, she said in an even voice, "I want this house, Steve, and I think you should sell your half to me.''

After a long silence, Steve said, "I said I'll think about it.''

Another silence ensued, this one longer and more tense. At length, Shelly crushed out her cigarette, so furiously that one of her long fingernails broke against the glass rim of the ashtray. "Damn!" she cursed, then hissed at her brother, "I've work to do, a deadline to meet on my book." In passing Lara on her way to the door, she added, "I work to support myself.''

Lara gaped at her as she briskly made her exit. She felt her blood boiling with slow and steady anger. Exactly what was the woman implying? That she was a parasite? That she was lazy?

"I bet I've struggled harder than she could ever dream of!" Lara blurted at the now empty doorway. "I bet I've worked more in my life than—''

Steve's warm, strong arms slid around her from behind, abruptly silencing her. He said something she didn't catch.

"What?''

"I said, she always acts like this when she can't have her way. Mom used to give in to her, even pamper her. I guess you can say Shelly's . . . well, spoiled."

"She does behave like a spoiled child," Lara agreed. "Oh, Steve, maybe you should sell her your share. I don't know why this house means so much to me anyway. She's right, you know. She's known this house so much longer and has more reasons to be attached to it."

Steve gently turned her around until she was facing him, then he kissed her. "The house is half mine," he said, "and I'm at liberty to do whatever I want with it. And you're my wife, and I love you very much, and I want whatever you want."

"Oh, Steve," she sighed, resting her head against his chest.

"If you want to keep this house, you can," he told her, his voice deep and soft above her head.

"But you don't like it here, darling."

"I've been giving it a lot of serious thought. I've come to realize that my feelings about this place are actually childish. It's time I outgrow them."

"But why now, after all these years?"

"I can see how much you've grown to like this house."

"I do like this house so very much, but Shelly loves—"

"Never mind Shelly. Just think about what you want."

What *did* she want? she asked herself as her eyes peered past his shoulder and absorbed the magnificent richness of the library. The panel fireplace, the leather-bound books lining the walls and the wing chair brought cozy images to her mind. She and Molly would be comfortable and secure here. At last she would be able to give Molly something more than a cramped apartment.

"But, of course, it would mean living with Shelly," Steve reminded her.

"I don't know," she sighed again. "I don't know."

Steve cupped her chin in his hand and lifted her face to meet his. He kissed her, this time with lingering passion. "I want whatever you want."

But she wasn't sure what she wanted. She wasn't sure if this house would be worth sharing with Shelly.

"I'm going to have to give it a lot of thought," she murmured, then returned his kiss.

In the distance came the sound of the typewriter. This time the clacking of keys wasn't intermittent and hesitant; it was steady and furious.

Shelly's tantrum had surprised Lara, even stunned her. Now that there was silence and she was by herself in her bedroom (Steve had stayed in the library to phone and reassure himself that his restaurant was running smoothly), she could think clearly about what had happened.

Shelly had literally thrown a fit because she couldn't get her way. She had turned nasty and vicious.

And to think I almost gave in and urged Steve to sell his share of the house, Lara thought with disgust. She had been certain that desperation and panic were the reasons for Shelly's embarrassing behavior. She had even felt a stab of pity for the woman.

But now she realized that this wasn't exactly the case. Steve had opened her eyes, and the silence and solitude had opened them even wider. Shelly was a spoiled bitch, pure and simple. When she saw that she wasn't getting her way, Shelly threw a childish temper tantrum. Lara was now surprised that Shelly hadn't thrown herself onto the floor, kicking and thrashing about, or held her breath until her face was purple.

I almost fell for it, Lara thought again, shaking her head in disbelief.

If Shelly had behaved in a mature manner and had calmly explained how much the house meant to her, Lara would have understood. An agreement to sell would have been quickly made. But instead, as soon as Lara had mentioned that she too had grown to love the house, Shelly exploded.

And what's more, that parting remark had been totally uncalled for. Shelly had cruelly insinuated that Lara was after Steve's inheritance.

Well, if Shelly could be nasty, then so could she, Lara

resolved. She'd take her sweet time to make up her mind.

To sell or not to sell? she poetically asked herself. The house was lovely, and she really had fallen in love with it. She loved the luxury of having so many rooms. She loved how big and spacious it was, but was it big enough to share with Shelly?

Yes, she would give this house a lot of thought. Perhaps Molly could help her come to a decision. She would ask questions and feel out her daughter about living here. She'd even write a list of pros and cons and discuss it some more with Steve.

But one thing was certain. Shelly's terrible tantrum was not going to affect her decision in the least.

Lara could not stop thinking about the house but simply could not come to a decision.

She had wanted a long talk with Steve, but something came up at the restaurant and his presence was needed. Since the restaurant was a two-hour drive each way, Steve would not be back until late tonight. The distance between his work and the house, she knew, was a definite minus, but on the plus side was the new competent manager who could share the day-to-day responsibilities.

Well, when he comes back we'll have that long chat and come to a definite decision.

But right now she would talk with Molly. She really didn't know how her daughter felt about this house. If she disliked it, then the matter would be settled immediately; they would sell. After all, her daughter's happiness came before anything. This was a vow she had made a long time ago, even before she had met Steve, and she was determined never to break it.

She found Molly outside on the south lawn, lying on the grass and staring up at the sky. It was a warm, clear afternoon with a cool breeze blowing in from the ocean. The smell of salt was sharper than usual in the air. Lara sat down beside her daughter.

"What are you doing, sweetheart?" She smiled.

"Watching the clouds."

"Seeing faces in them?" It never ceased to amaze Lara how her daughter could amuse herself so well.

"I jus' saw a whole army of knigh's, Mom," she said.

"Knights, you mean?" Lara clearly pronounced the "t."

"Yeah." Then Molly repeated, concentrating, "Knights . . . I saw King Arthur . . . too."

Lara looked up at the sky, pretending to join her daughter in the game, but it was the house that was on her mind. How to bring up the subject? Should she be direct, or send out feelers? When she looked back at her daughter, she saw that Molly was watching her, already aware that something other than the shapes of clouds was on her mind. She sighed. She should know by now that Molly was a very perceptive child, and that the direct approach was the only approach with her.

"Do you like this house, sweetheart?" she finally asked.

"Oh yes, Mom!" The girl's face brightened. "I wish we could stay here always."

The enthusiasm surprised her. "You really mean that?"

"Yeah. Bud I don'd like the cellar, though."

"The cellar? What were you doing down there?"

"Explorin'," the girl answered in an uncertain voice. When she realized she hadn't done anything seriously wrong and that her mother wasn't going to scold her, she added, "But I love the house, Mom. Love my room. Preddy. I mean, pre*t*-*t*y. And all the rooms . . . and the big yards. Can we stay here all summer, Mom?" Her voice rose with hope.

"Wouldn't you get lonely?" Lara asked.

Molly shook her head. "I've a new friend. Dinah." She looked around her. "Dinah? Dinah? C'mon, Dinah . . ."

"Actually, sweetheart, I'm talking more than just a summer."

Molly's eyes widened, staring at her lips to comprehend more thoroughly.

Lara swallowed, then continued, "Would you like to stay here . . . permanently?"

The girl didn't even have to think about it. She nodded enthusiastically.

"It would mean enrolling in a new school in the fall," Lara reminded her.

"Thad's okay."

Lara hadn't expected it to be this easy. "You fell in love with this place just like I did, didn't you?" she whispered, somewhat amazed.

The girl didn't answer, only watched her mother relax with relief.

"Of course Shelly isn't going to be pleased," Lara said, mostly to herself, then smiled and kissed her daughter's forehead and cheek. "But we're going to be very happy." She rose to her feet. "Well, I'll leave you to King Arthur and his knights."

"Mom?"

"Yes, sweetheart?"

"Can I plant a garden?" Molly asked, making an effort to speak slowly and clearly. "Two gardens?"

The request surprised Lara, for she never knew her daughter had any interest in gardening. "I really can't see why not." She shrugged after a slight pause. "You can plant a hundred gardens, if you want."

Then, smiling, she went into the house—*her* house.

7

The thought of living here excited Molly. The only things that bothered her were going to a new school in the fall and living above a creepy cellar. But going to the school, she told herself, was a long way off yet; she still had a whole summer ahead of her. As far as the cellar went, well, she just wouldn't go down there again, that's all. She'd pretend that the dark, gloomy place didn't exist.

The metal box she had taken from the cellar was now in a drawer in her room, hidden under her jeans. After her mother had left her alone on the lawn she watched a few clouds scud across the sky, then jumped up and ran to a garden shed, which was a miniature replica of the big house. There was a padlock on the door, but it was unfastened. Shelly or Margaret had never bothered to use this lock, claiming there was nothing worthwhile to steal anyway, and since Shelly did most of the yard work (a teenage boy came in once a week to mow the grass, but nothing else), she had grown tired of searching for a key that she had a habit of misplacing. So now Molly had no problem entering the shed and finding everything she needed—shovel, hand rake, watering can, and a wheel-barrow. There were tools also in the cellar of the house, but she suspected nobody used those. They had long been forgotten and were probably too rusty anyway.

Starting first with the south side, at the border of the property where a small grove of flowering crabapples and dogwood trees began, she turned over the grass. With shovel and rake, she labored until she had soft, rock-free soil. The dirt was dark and, she hoped, perfect for a garden. The plot was small, only four feet in both length and width. But she reminded herself she had only a small bag of seeds to plant here, and she was afraid someone would be angry and object if the garden was too big. Besides, she had decided to make a separate garden for each bag of seeds, and since there were four yards surrounding the house, she decided to have a garden in each one.

After she was done with the south side, save for the actual planting, she proceeded to the north. Here she dug up a four-by-four patch not far from a bed of marigolds that had just begun to germinate. By the time she had completed this, the sun was sinking behind the trees that bordered the property.

That night Molly slept soundly, but the next morning her body ached from the previous day's digging. Yet she refused to let this deter her from completing her task. After a quick breakfast of cold cereal, she started on the third garden, the east, which faced the ocean. She enjoyed this side, for as she labored, the sea breeze incessantly caressed her, never allowing her to be sticky with sweat. But on the west side, facing the street (which was below the hill and hidden from view by a large iron gate and trees) the sun cruelly broiled her. By the time it reached its zenith, Molly was done. Hot and famished, she washed her face with cold water, then ate the lunch that her mother prepared for her.

"Busy little girl, aren't you?" Lara smiled, eating a chicken salad sandwich with her in a cozy nook in the kitchen. Steve was still away at his restaurant, and Shelly was somewhere in another part of the house. Lara didn't know where, and didn't care. "I never knew you had an interest in gardening," she added.

Molly hadn't known either. It wasn't until she'd found

the seeds that she'd become interested—or maybe curious
was a better word, for she was eager to see what the seeds
would become. She hoped they'd be big, pretty flowers
since she didn't much care for vegetables, especially peas,
carrots, and green beans.

"Think Shelly will be mad?" Molly was suddenly
worried. "I didn'd make doo much of a mess with the
yards, did I?"

"Don't worry, sweetheart. If she does get mad I'll just
remind her that the yards are just as much ours as hers.
No," she reassured her, "don't worry and just have fun.
I'm sure you'll find gardening a wonderful learning
experience."

Relieved that Shelly wasn't going to yell at her, Molly
quickly finished her lunch, got the metal box of seeds
from her room, and planted her four gardens. After some
deliberation she sowed the sole acornlike seed on the
north side. On the four-by-four plot of loose earth it will
have more than plenty of room to grow, she thought.
Then with the watering can, which she repeatedly refilled
from an outdoor faucet, she drenched the gardens. When
this was done, she experienced a delightful glow of
satisfaction. She had done something grownup all by
herself! Now all she'd have to do was water the gardens
every day and watch them grow.

She couldn't wait to see what would come up.

Every day, almost every hour, Molly checked the
gardens. A week went by and nothing germinated. Soon
Molly was discouraged. Maybe she'd done something
wrong. Maybe she had planted the seeds too deep, or
maybe not deep enough. Maybe she hadn't watered the
gardens enough, or maybe too much. She was about to
give up when at last she saw a change in the south garden.

The soil had little cracks, where seedlings beneath were
pushing their way through. Molly beamed proudly, as
though she herself had created the little plants. When her
cat appeared and rubbed its body against her legs, she
scooped it up into her arms and exclaimed, "See, Dinah?

I did id all by myself!''

The animal must have felt Molly's joy, for it soon began to purr and rub its face against the girl's.

When Steve finally came home, Molly was sitting on one of the steps of the grand staircase in the front hallway. On her lap was Dinah, purring softly, ready to fall into one of its countless naps. Through the mahogany railings, the girl watched the happy scene below her. Her mother, who had met Steve at the front door, was now hugging her husband. Molly smiled vicariously, absently stroking her cat's orange fur. Then the smile widened as her stepfather's lips covered her mother's. Will I ever find romance like that? she wondered dreamily.

When her mother disengaged herself, Molly was able to read her lips. "You were gone long enough, Steve," Lara said, her expression accusatory.

"I've been looking around," Steve's lips replied.

"For what?"

"I've found this house, hon, that I know you're gonna love. It's a cape, brand new, and it's only a ten minute drive to The Four Winds."

Lara shrank away from him. "But . . . we have a house."

He pulled her back into her arms. She didn't resist, but she was tense. "This place here is too far away from work."

"You said if I wanted to stay, I could. You said it was up to me," she reminded him.

"Yes, I know. But when I saw this new—"

"You admitted that your bad feelings for this house were silly . . . groundless."

"Yes, I know, but when I saw this cape in the paper, well, I decided to have a look. It's a real nice house, Lara. Reasonable price, too. And everything's brand new, not old like this . . . this . . ." He didn't bother to finish. "You should see the kitchen. Built-in dishwasher, garbage compactor. You'll love it. I just know it."

"You don't understand. I like old things. There's

something—oh, I don't know—graceful, I guess, about them. They're real, solid and original. Do you understand what I mean?''

Steve sighed, betraying frustration and disappointment. "You should at least see this place."

"Oh, all right, I'll see it," she promised half-heartedly.

"But with every intention of not buying it, I suppose."

"I said I'll see it, didn't I?" Her countenance was suddenly hard, her eyes flashing annoyance.

"Forget it." Steve abruptly released her from his embrace. He started toward the stairs, mumbling something that Molly couldn't catch.

"But I already told you I like *this* house, Steve!" Lara cried.

He stopped and returned to her. "You told me that you'd think about it," he clarified.

"And I did. A lot. I even discussed it with Molly."

The girl's hand stopped stroking the cat.

"And?" Steve prompted.

"She loves this house, too."

He sighed again.

"And I don't see why we should do anything hasty. You need time away from the restaurant, so why can't we stay here for a while? We could always look at this as a badly needed vacation."

Steve seemed to be frantically searching for something to say. "You and Shelly don't get along," he reminded her.

"I don't even see her most of the time. She's usually too busy with her book—or whatever it is she's writing."

"It's a personal thing with you, isn't it?" he said after a long pause.

Lara looked surprised—surprised that Steve had seen clearly through her? She quickly affected innocent confusion. "What are you talking about, Steve?"

"It's simply pride." He nodded confidently. "You don't want Shelly to get her way because you're determined not to let her push you around."

"Well, the house is just as much ours as it's hers!" she

said, flaring.

"Yes, I know—"

"Then why doesn't she sell her half?"

"You know why. She loves—"

"Molly and I love this house, too."

Molly flinched on the staircase. She didn't like seeing her name on angry lips; it left a heavy feeling in her stomach. It was almost as if her mother were pulling her into their fight, as if it were half her fault. Why couldn't they still be kissing, like when Steve had first come in? That had been nice, like maybe something out of a Harlequin novel that she'd never read but someday would.

Deciding she'd had enough of playing Secret Spy, she lifted Dinah into her arms and quietly retreated to her bedroom. Downstairs, in the foyer, the quarrel continued.

All the gardens, except one, were growing fast. It was almost as though they'd been waiting for a green light, and now that they had it, there was no stopping them. The west garden, which faced the street, seemed to be growing the quickest. There were three perfect rows of green plants, all standing straight like diminutive soldiers, and all were exactly the same height, which Molly found fascinating and a little eerie. They had broken ground simultaneously and sprouted new leaves every other day. Presently each had ten leaves and stood three inches tall. Molly wondered if these plants had flowers, would the flowers all be the same?

The south garden, however, wasn't as speedy—or as orderly. Every plant, it seemed, was different here. Some shot up with rigid stems, some sprawled vinelike along the ground, and others sat like plump, miniature bushes. Each grew at a different rate. Whenever Molly watered this garden, she'd find herself spending a lot of time studying each plant (24 in all), for each was unique. Here, too, she was eager to see if flowers would bloom.

The north garden was what Molly christened The

Lonely Garden. Only one seedling occupied the four-by-four patch of dark earth, and so far it was ugly, reminding the girl of a small, brown artichoke growing all by itself. It was scaly and woody. She couldn't imagine it ever producing a flower, but she watered it faithfully anyway, for it was definitely alive and growing. Already, within a week, it had doubled in size.

Then there was the east garden, the most disappointing of all four. It was still bare earth. This one was on the ocean side, prompting Molly to think that maybe this had something to do with its inability to grow. Or maybe the seeds had been no good to begin with. Or maybe it was just simply slow. Just in case it was merely the latter, Molly watered the bare soil as frequently as the others.

Who knows? The garden might surprise her.

"Mom, if Steve doesn'd like the house, I won'd mind if we don'd s'ay."

The statement was abrupt and unexpected, rendering Lara speechless. It was lunchtime, and she was fixing Molly a tuna sandwich in the kitchen. Steve had gone into town for the newspaper and some groceries, and Shelly was in her study, either sleeping or staring at blank paper, for no sounds from the typewriter had been heard for some time now.

At length Lara found her voice. "What gave you the idea that Steve doesn't like this house, sweetheart?" Her daughter was at the table, waiting for an answer.

The girl looked away for a moment, and her cheeks colored. "I . . . I was playing Secret Spy," she admitted sheepishly.

"Ah." Lara nodded, understanding now. Secret Spy, she knew, was a game that Molly sometimes played. It was like eavesdropping with the eyes. As long as the girl could see a conversation in progress, she could "hear" it.

"You know I don't approve of you playing that game," she said needlessly. "But anyway, we're staying here—at least for a little while."

"But, Mom, if Steve doesn'd—"

Lara, sitting opposite her daughter, reached out and sandwiched the girl's hand in hers. "Aren't you tired of living in small apartments without yards?" she interrupted gently. "I already can see that you love having a yard to play in, Molly."

"I do, Mom, bud . . ."

"Bu*t*, Molly, bu*t*," Lara corrected patiently.

The girl nodded, but she didn't repeat the word. "Steve doesn't like the house," she said again, this time concentrating on her words.

"That's for me and Steve to worry about, sweetheart, not you."

This didn't seem to satisfy Molly, who stared gloomily at her hand, which was still covered by Lara's. Lara shook the hand gently to get her attention again.

"I said it's not for you to worry about," Lara repeated. "You understand?"

"You could ded—I mean, *get*—another house with another yard."

Lara sighed, realizing it was not going to be easy to make her understand. How could she tell her that the reason she was not leaving this house was that Shelly wanted her to do exactly that? This child was too young to understand such determination, wasn't she?

"I want *this* house," she said slowly. "Sweetheart, I've been used many times in the past, and I'm not going to be used anymore. You and I are not going to go without again. You understand now? We both deserve the best. And nobody—" especially Shelly, she mentally added "—is going to stop us."

Molly stared at her, trying very hard to understand. She squeezed her daughter's hand, then released it, giving her what she hoped was a big, reassuring smile.

"I don't want you to worry about anything," she reiterated, "except, of course, your speech. Have you been practicing your t's and g's?"

Molly nodded, then as guilt took hold, shook her head. The Hearing and Speech Center had given her a list of words that she was to read while placing a hand against her throat or over her mouth. The *g,* if pronounced properly, would vibrate the hand against the throat, and the *t* would fan air into an open palm. The school, which was closed for the summer, urged her to practice at least an hour each day. Molly had done so faithfully at first, but now had grown bored with the exercises.

"I want you to practice, Molly," Lara said firmly.

"I will, Mom," she promised as she finished her sandwich.

Then she excused herself and headed not in the direction of her room but toward the outside door.

"Young lady!" Lara clapped her hands loudly so that Molly would hear.

"Yes, Mom?"

"I presume the list of words is upstairs in your room."

"I'll practice later, Mom. First I dod—*got*—to do something else."

"Such as?"

She looked at the door as though something were calling and compelling her, then back at her mother. "Water the gardens," she said carefully, then was gone.

8

Steve knocked on the door to his sister's study. The typewriter stopped, and Shelly answered in a petulant voice, "Who is it?"

"Steve."

There was a rush of final typing, then the door swung open. "You know I don't like to be disturbed when I'm writing." She was dressed in a long silky nightgown and her dark, walnut-colored hair cascaded loosely to her shoulders. She reminded Steve of a heroine on the cover of a gothic romance novel. A candle in one hand and a gloomy castle in the background would complete the picture.

Although it was midafternoon, he was not surprised to see his sister dressed this way. He knew she often wrote in sleeping apparels, claiming it helped her writing to be casual and fluent.

"Well, what do you want?" she demanded.

"Let me in," Steve said, his own voice equally demanding. "I want to talk to you."

"Now? I'm on a roll."

"It's about the house." Deciding not to wait for her permission, he entered the room and walked directly to the Queen Anne desk, which was littered with typewriter, papers and reference books. He cleared a spot and sat on the edge. Then crossing his arms over his chest, he waited for his sister's cooperation.

She sighed and closed the door. "Damn you," she muttered under her breath.

"Love you, too."

Shelly ignored the remark. "What about the house?"

Steve didn't answer, too busy absorbing the room. Mahogany surrounded him, so much so that he could almost smell the wood. It was in the furniture, around the long, multi-panel windows, door, and fireplace. Even the stand supporting a large, 12-pound dictionary was of mahogany. The sunlight splashing through the windows made everything gleam reddish, like the highlights in his sister's hair. Yes, he could see why his sister and wife were attracted to this home. He, too, would want to stay here . . . if it weren't for the cellar.

He had told Lara that he knew his uneasy feelings toward this house were silly and childish, but what he didn't tell her was that he nevertheless still had them. He was determined to ignore these feelings, but they were as stubborn as he was. Perhaps if he did stay here for a while, instead of running away, he'd gradually lose that churning coldness in his guts.

"Look, if you must daydream, please do it elsewhere." Shelly's crisp voice pulled him out of his revery.

He looked at her, then suddenly asked, "Have you ever gone into the cellar?"

The question seemed to surprise her. "Once. Twice. Why?"

"Not even to check the furnace or the fuse box?" he replied, ignoring her question.

"That's a plumber's job or an electrician's. Why?" she asked again.

"When you did go down there, didn't you find something . . . I don't know, strange, I guess?"

"No. I found it creepy, though. I remember that I couldn't find any light down there."

"The bulb burned out when I was a kid, and I don't think anybody ever replaced it. Why is that, I wonder?"

"Why these questions, I wonder?" Shelly's voice grew

sharper with impatience.

"Why didn't you, or anyone else, ever change the light bulb?"

"Why didn't *you*?"

"I asked you first. C'mon, Shelly, tell me the truth. Did you not change the bulb because you didn't want to go down there?"

"I already admitted that I find the cellar creepy, and since there's no reason for me to go down there, I don't. Therefore, why bother to change a light bulb, especially when I don't even know where the light switch is."

"There isn't any. It's a pull chain, and the ceiling is awfully high—at least that's what I thought when I was a kid."

"Steve, did you interrupt my work just to talk about the cellar?"

"No. I was just wondering how familiar you are with this house—the house which you love so dearly."

"I'm not familiar with the cellar. So what?"

"You have to admit, especially with Mom gone, this place is much too big for you."

"Steve, will you please get to the point." She reached for a cigarette from a delicate porcelain case on the desk.

"The point is, what's so goddamn special about this house?"

She looked at him for a lingering moment as she lit her cigarette. After she exhaled a long white stream of smoke, she said, "I saw you admiring this room a second ago, dear brother."

"It has admirable qualities," he agreed, "but not enough to be so hostile to my wife about it."

Shelly arched a pencil-thin eyebrow. "Hostile? Whatever on earth are you talking about?"

"You know damn well what I'm talking about."

Shelly sat in the wing chair behind the desk, thoughtfully drew on her cigarette, then tilting her head back, blew the smoke toward the ceiling. "Lara," she began scornfully, "thinks you are wealthy. When you introduced her to Momma and me, her eyes were as big as

Little Orphan Annie's, gawking at everything in this house. She was positively drooling, and I could see that she was blinded by the glitter. She must have been quite shocked when she learned that Momma died broke, that only this house was all she had left—a house that she gave to both of us. Tell me, how did she handle the disappointment?''

"She was not disappointed."

"No? Are you saying that she doesn't want this house?"

"It's more of a personal thing. Something that your childish tantrum has created."

Shelly smiled coldly. "That's what I always liked about our relationship. We're so frank with each other." The smile faded. "I still say you married a gold digger who's made the horrible discovery that most of the gold is yellow paint. Dear brother, you cannot convince me that she wouldn't use her claws to get my half of the house. I despise such desperation."

"If she uses her claws it'll be because you're using yours. Jesus, Shelly, what is it with you two? You can't get along with each other, and you both own the same house—"

"*You* own it," she interrupted hotly. "Not she!"

"Same difference. She has as much say about it."

"That's positively disgusting."

Steve felt something twist, then tighten inside him. Damn her! he thought. Just because she didn't believe in sharing things with anyone, she shouldn't condemn anyone who did. He could remember an incident when her editor suggested collaborating on a book with another romance writer. Shelly had adamantly refused, had even thrown one of her sickening tantrums. He didn't think she had ever shared anything with anybody in her entire life, not even a candy bar or a toy. And this house would be a first for her.

"Are you finished?" he heard her say, again breaking into his thoughts.

He sighed hopelessly, forcing his insides to relax. "I

suppose there's no chance of you selling your half to me."

"You suppose right."

"But Mom's gone. The house is too big. There's so much to clean—"

"I've professionals who come once a week, and a kid who mows the lawns."

"Why can't you buy another house? Move to New York, closer to your publisher?"

"Why can't you move closer to your little restaurant?"

Steve stared at her, and she stared back.

"Sure you won't change your mind?" he said at length, already knowing the answer.

"Not a chance."

"You're doing this to be spiteful to Lara," he told her quietly.

"And she's doing this to spite me."

Their eyes continued to hold, this time glaring in resentment. It was Shelly who finally broke the contact. Taking a last drag, she crushed her cigarette out in an ashtray and pulled her chair closer to the typewriter in front of her.

"Got a deadline to meet, dear brother," she said, then hit the first key, dismissing him.

Steve got up from the desk and left the room, thinking it was utterly hopeless. Shelly and Lara were equally obstinate. He felt like a referee to whom no one paid any heed. This house, even with its 27 rooms, was definitely not big enough for these two females.

Molly could sense a change. It was as if a cloud had passed, darkening and chilling the big house. Although her mother had told her stepfather that he badly needed a vacation, he spent long hours at the restaurant. Molly suspected he did this to get away from the house and still felt uneasy about it.

It was the cellar that kept him away, of that she was somehow certain. The cellar made her uneasy too, but whenever she thought about it, she'd push it out of her mind. It was rather simple to do. She didn't even let herself think about where the plants in her gardens originally came from. Proud of her gardens, she was determined not to let anything spoil her accomplishments.

Now if only that dark and cold cloud would pass. It was making her mother very unhappy, and it was making Molly sad. She so much wanted her mother and stepfather to be the perfect couple.

"When Steve comes back," she had told her cat once as she held it in her arms, "I'll tell him nod do think 'boud the cellar. I'll tell him do do whad I do—pretend id isn'd even there."

But whenever Steve came back to the house his face would be hard and stern, and the cloud would be darker and colder. Molly never found a good time to give him her advice.

Something was wrong with the east garden. It was still an empty patch of dirt, where not even a weed grew. The other gardens were doing so well. The plants on the west side were six inches tall now and were still all alike. And on the south side the garden was too small, for the plants were beginning to sprawl out onto the lawn. And the Lonely Garden's artichoke-like plant had grown to the size of a cantaloupe.

But the east—nothing, and it was beginning to bother Molly. Somehow she felt that if she didn't succeed with this garden her sense of accomplishment would not be complete. So one morning, when the sun was strong and the clouds were few and thin, the girl rummaged through the shed, hoping to find a garden hose and a sprinkler. Maybe a good soaking would get the seeds started. The past few days had been hot and dry, and maybe the watering can hadn't been enough.

After a lengthy search, she finally found a green vinyl hose buried under a small pile of lumber in a corner. Molly found one end of the hose and pulled it out, inch by inch, until a tangle resisted her. She gave it a violent yank, and the hose broke free from its hiding place, knocking boards aside. There was a nozzle attached to the hose, but no sprinkler. She searched some more and even considered looking in the cellar, but quickly killed the idea.

The cellar did not exist, did not exist . . .

Deciding that the nozzle would have to do, Molly then went back outside, attached one end of the hose to an outdoor faucet, and stood before the east garden. She twisted the nozzle and a forceful stream of water jetted out, coughed violently with air, then spat out more water. As Molly turned the nozzle some more, the stream widened until it was spraying mist. Sunlight caught the fine drops, causing a faint rainbow between her and the garden.

"Look, Dinah!" she exclaimed, for her cat had suddenly appeared at her ankles.

Molly made rippling motions with the mist, swinging the hose to the left, then to the right. Incomplete rainbows appeared and vanished at random. "Nead, huh?" She smiled at the cat.

Then she noticed that something else seemed to be rippling.

She held the hose stationary for a moment, letting the water shoot high into the air and fall steadily to the ground like drizzling rain. The soil, which had darkened with dampness, was riddled with pockets of water. She stared at this, wondering if she had imagined the rippling motion. What she had seen—or thought she had seen—was something like a wave. It had taken a second for her to realize that it was the ground she'd been looking at, not the water. Had she just experienced an earthquake?

It rippled again.

A wind caught and moved the spray of water in the air and dumped it on Molly. It was ice cold, and she gasped but did not jump away. Instead, she gawked, transfixed. The ripple was gone again, prompting her to wonder if it had occurred at all. One thing was for certain now; it was no earthquake, for she hadn't felt a rumble below her feet.

Yes, she must have imagined the rippling motions.

But the basic question still remained. Why was nothing growing here? Were the seeds no good?

Molly contemplated digging up one of the seeds to see if anything had happened.

The cat, curious, moved along with her as she crawled alongside the garden.

"Godda see somethin'," she told it.

She leaned forward and rested a palm on the dirt. It was surprisingly warm and dry, such a contrast to the cool and damp grass on her knees, but giving this no further thought, she began to dig.

It rippled again! This time not only did she see it, she felt it. There was a definite undulating motion under her hand, then to her surprise and horror the soil began to split where her hand rested.

She scrambled back in the safety of green grass, but not before noticing what was in the new, small fissures. There was a swarm of something beneath the surface, a mass of something, a squirming mass.

The cat sniffed at one of the cracks to investigate.

"No, Dinah, no!" Molly reached out for the animal but was too late.

The cat hissed and would have fled if the mass hadn't already spread toward it, first covering the front paw, then the limb and neck. Molly gaped, paralyzed with disbelief and horror. The tiny things that were spreading and rapidly covering her cat were like greenish-black maggots with wings that fluttered with blurred rapidity but did not fly. There were so many of them—hundreds, maybe thousands—and they moved in one rippling mass.

"Dinah!" Molly screamed, once the paralysis broke. The cat seemed to be looking at her, its golden eyes bulging in terror. Its body was now a dark, moving coat, shimmering greenish in the sunlight.

Molly reached for the cat, but, even in her desperation,

could only bring herself to grab the head. She pulled, like one would try to free a victim in quicksand, but there must have been more of these insects—or whatever they were—under the ground, for she could feel the cat resist her. It was going under.

"No, Dinah! Please, no!" She tugged at the head with all her strength, but it was now like trying to release something embedded in concrete. Yet she pulled and pulled.

She felt the warm mass crawling on her hand and spreading up her arm. She shivered with repulsion, but firmly willed herself to hold on. The mass was coating her like sticky paint. It felt thick and slippery on her skin, and she found herself filled with a sudden urge to find a body of water to jump into and cleanse herself of the crawling slime.

Then she became aware of the ground splitting under her. Until now, she hadn't realized her knees were on the soil. Gasping, she looked at the winged maggots on her hand and arm, then looked down at her knees. More of these creatures were surfacing, flowing thickly along her lower legs, covering her calfs, and sliding into her Nikes. Again she shivered. She could feel the insects wedging themselves between her toes, sticking them together with their glutinous bodies.

Molly opened her mouth to scream, but was too horrified to utter a sound. Eyes and mouth wide open, she still clung to Dinah's head. She didn't want to let go. She loved the cat! Please, let her go!

She saw that the head now was just like the rest—greenish-black, shimmering and swarming. There was a glimpse of eyes, then these too disappeared. At last, with a gurgled cry, the only sound her throat could expel, she released her grip. The cat sank into the soil and into that horrible lake of insects. She could not hear the cat, but in her mind it shrieked and shrieked.

Then she remembered her own predicament. Horror rushed back, knocking aside the grief. Her legs and now both arms were covered. She jumped up and slapped her legs frantically, as though putting out fire. Then she slapped her arms, then her legs again, not knowing which extremity to concentrate on the most. Panic exploded inside her, and she ran, slapping, slapping, toward the house.

"Mom! Mom!" Not sure if she was loud enough, she screamed until she could feel the veins in her neck bulge. "MOM!"

Her mother flung open the kitchen door and ran out toward her. Molly, seeing her, stretched out her arms, legs still pumping frantically. Never was she so petrified. She felt like a five-year-old, wanting her mother so badly. "Mommmieeee!"

"Oh, my God! Wha—" Lara began slapping away at the girl's arms and legs.

"Ded 'em off! Ded 'em off! Ded 'em—"

Slap-slap-slap-slap . . .

Molly clenched her eyes shut and bawled. "Mommie . . ." It seemed certain she'd die, she was praying her mother would save her, would do better than she had done, wouldn't let her go to them, as Dinah had done to—

Slap-slap-slap . . . *slap-slap* . . . *slap* . . .

The slaps, she suddenly noticed, were not as frantic and rapid anymore. She opened her eyes and looked down at herself. Hiccuping and swallowing sobs, she saw that most of the wiggling mass was off her and on the ground. She helped finish slapping and brushing the rest from her arms, then with her mother began stomping and mashing the insects that, now sluggish, carpeted the grass. When they had finally ceased moving and lay like a greenish-black oil spill on the lawn, Lara staggered back, gasping, her hand at her throat.

"What on earth—" She had reacted instinctively, and now was gawking incredulously at the swarm of dead insects. She couldn't seem to believe how many there were. "Where did they come—" She didn't finish, for Molly was looking at the garden, terror evident on her pale face.

Both of Lara's hands shot to her mouth. "Oh, my God!" She had thought it was dark earth she was seeing, tinted greenish from the lawn surrounding it. Then she realized the soil was moving, rippling.

"Mom . . . I—I didn'd . . . know . . . " Molly began between hysterical sobs. She didn't know what to do, except sob and look frantically at her mother.

But her mother thought of something. She spotted the garden hose, ran to it, and bombarded the dark patch with water. The force of the spray pushed aside a small clump covered by the insects. Molly stared at it, then dropped to her knees and retched into the grass as she realized what it was.

"Dinah!" she wailed. It was her cat. They were . . . they were *eating* it!

She wailed again, this time unintelligibly.

Lara frantically sprayed the entire plot but wasn't succeeding. If anything, the water seemed to be strengthening the mass, for it was beginning to spread and spill out onto the lawn. In frustration and panic, she threw the hose aside and looked around for something else. She saw that the shed was open and bolted toward it. Molly, wanting to help her mother and not wanting to be left alone, ran behind her.

They each found a shovel and rushed back out. Molly wasn't sure what her mother's plan was until she saw her slam the back of the shovel violently and repeatedly against the soil and the insects, then she did the same.

"Harder! Harder!" Lara screamed at her as she, herself, brought the shovel down with as much force as she could muster. Molly strained to be as forceful. Together, the two slammed the earth with powerful blows, over and over, raising plumes of dirt and slicking the ground with the insects' lime-colored innards. Molly gagged, turning her head aside as a stench assailed her nostrils. It was a stench that reminded her of human excrement, and it grew stronger with each whack. As her dry heaves continued, her hands repeatedly raised the shovel and slammed it down.

Once, she glanced over at her mother.

"Harder! Harder!" The woman was like a machine, her mouth tight with resolution while the shovel violently attacked the ground.

Molly then turned herself into a machine. She blocked everything out, especially the horrible smell. She concentrated on the heavy shovel which she clutched and swung with both hands.

Then, after what felt like hours, her mother threw the shovel aside, grabbed Molly's shoulders, and pulled her away toward the house. When they reached the door, they collapsed on the stoop, hugging each other.

"Mom, I—I'm sorry . . ." Molly gushed. Lara pushed her face closer against her breasts, muffling the girl's words.

"It's okay, sweetheart. Okay. We got 'em all."

But Molly began sobbing again. And the more she sobbed, the more her mother rocked her in her arms.

"It's my fauld," the girl went on. She peeked out behind her and through the film of tears saw the stains on the ground, stains that were yellowish-green from the insects' mashed bodies. They were so ugly, so . . . evil. Shivering, she quickly buried her face again. What had she done? What had she started?

Then an image of Dinah filled her mind, and her body convulsed more violently with sobs.

"M-my fauld!" she wailed again. "I—I planded the darden, and I killed D-Dinah!"

"It's all right, sweetheart. All right." Her mother soothed her, stroking her flaxen hair, holding her tighter. "We got 'em all. Everything's going to be all right."

It took Lara at least a half hour to calm her daughter.

Part II: The West Garden

9

It rained, on and off, for three days. Sometimes it poured, sometimes it sprinkled, and sometimes it did nothing except hide the sun. The ocean was darker than usual, the waves foaming and crashing angrily against the rocks below the east wall. Up until now the weather had been calm and pleasant. Molly felt responsible, certain that she had unleashed something stormy and furious when she had unearthed those horrible insects.

She stayed in bed during those three days and thought of her cat constantly, no matter how hard she tried to push the image out of her mind. She told herself that she had only known the animal for a short time and had no reason to feel so attached to it, but she did. She loved Dinah, and worst of all, she had killed her. She would never forgive herself.

When she wasn't thinking about the cat, she was reliving the horror of winged maggots blanketing her. They had felt wet and warm on her legs and arms, a warmth that pulsated with life. And they had squirmed all over her. Somehow that was the worst part. It had felt as if her skin literally had been crawling.

Every time she thought about this she'd force her mind to think about something else, and invariably it would shift to Dinah. Again she'd plead with her mind to change to something else, and it would—back to the crawling maggots. Back and forth. Back and forth.

Even in her dreams it was the same—the cat and the maggots.

One night, when she couldn't tolerate it anymore, she screamed. The door to her bedroom flew open, and in the darkness she saw someone rush toward her. She sobbed with relief, certain it was her mother coming to comfort her, but when she felt thick, hard arms around her and caught a faint whiff of stale whiskey, she knew it was her stepfather.

Then the lamp on the nightstand went on, gently illuminating the room. Steve, on the bed with her, looked down with worry and concern. In the doorway Lara appeared, tying her robe tighter around her.

"You all right, hon?" Steve asked. Molly, squinting from the sudden light, strained to read his lips.

"Hearin' aid," she muttered, reaching for the device next to the lamp. "Nigh'mare," she explained as she put it on.

"About the insects?" he said.

She nodded. She wanted to rest her head against his shoulder, but he was wearing only a pajama bottom. His naked torso made her feel shy and awkward. "I'm all righ' now," she said.

"You sure?"

She nodded again.

"What happened was probably normal, you know."

This surprised her. "Id—I mean, it was?"

"Sure. You probably hit a nest or something."

"What were they?" she asked slowly, trying to pronounce the consonants correctly.

"Well, when I went to see what it was, there was nothing left. Looked like the rain had washed everything away. But from what your mother told me, I'd say you had disturbed some kind of flies, or ants maybe. Nothing worth having nightmares about, hon."

But flies and ants don't eat cats, do they? she was tempted to ask. She hadn't told her mother or Steve about Dinah. They just thought the cat was missing.

Molly would have told them, but each time she tried, her chin would tremble, her throat constrict, and her eyes burn with water.

Steve smiled to reassure her that there was nothing to be afraid of, and when she tentatively returned the smile, he turned to Lara in the doorway and nodded at her, tacitly telling her that everything was under control. Lara studied Molly to be sure, then retreated to her own room.

Molly, now alone with Steve, found herself even more uncomfortable, for she still wasn't as ease with her stepfather. Until now there had been no males in the family.

"Don't be shy," he said. There was a hint of a smile that betrayed amusement. He seemed to think that her bashfulness was rather sweet.

"I'm not," she denied, again concentrating on her speech.

There was an awkward silence as Steve widened his smile. He tried to think of something to say that would put the girl at ease, but couldn't. At length he patted her leg under the blanket, kissed her forehead, and stood up. "Good night, hon," he said, maintaining the smile. Then he headed for the door.

There were so many things she wanted to ask and knew this would be the perfect time, but her shyness kept her silent—until he closed the door. "Steve!" she blurted out.

The door reopened. "Yes, hon?"

"What . . . what did you find in the cellar?"

The question surprised him. He lingered in the doorway, speechless. Then frowning, he slowly returned to her bed. This time he did not sit down, but hovered above her. The lamp on the table below him made eerie shadows around his eyes and mouth, almost like what Molly used to make with a flashlight under her chin as she stood before a mirror. Her own reflection used to scare her, as her stepfather was doing right now.

"What are you talking about?"

"Didn't you ever go down there?" she asked, not

wanting to admit she had played Secret Spy, had found out about his dislike of the house and had guessed the cellar was the cause.

"No," Steve said, too quickly.

Molly suspected he was lying. "Never?"

He looked at her, then sat on the bed. To the girl's relief, the shadows slid off his face, and he was once more the friendly, handsome prince.

"Well, a few times," he slowly admitted. "I was about your age, maybe younger."

"Did you find anything?"

"Sure." He shrugged, fell silent, then added. "Old things."

He wasn't being honest with her; somehow she could tell. He was trying too hard to be nonchalant.

"What kind of old things?" she asked. *Something like a box of seeds?*

He shrugged again. "Oh, like . . . like flowerpots, tools, junk. Why do you want to know?" he suddenly demanded.

"Wondering," she answered simply.

Their eyes locked. Steve tried to probe deeper to find the reason for these sudden questions, but Molly at length averted her head.

"Why do you hate this house?" she asked when she looked back. As usual, curiosity was the dominating force.

"You sure have a lot of questions, young lady."

Molly felt her face burn and color. "I-I'm sorry . . ."

"No, no," he sighed. "You've every right to ask . . . and I should start acting like a man instead of a frightened kid. You're right, I don't like this house. I find it, well, too old for my taste."

"Do you think it's haunted?"

"No, of course not."

"Then what's wrong with it?"

He searched her face, again trying to learn why she was asking these questions. "Look," he finally said, patting her leg and rising for the second time, "I've got a lot of paperwork to do in the morning. Gotta get some shut-eye. Okay?''

Disappointed, Molly nodded.

"Sweet dreams for a change, all right?''

She nodded again.

Looking down at her, he smiled, but she could tell this smile was masking something. She was certain she had hit a nerve. He gave her an affectionate wink, then turned toward the door. Halfway he stopped, kept his back to her for a moment, then looked over his shoulder. Another moment passed before he spoke.

"Did *you* find anything in the cellar?''

Molly considered telling him about the strange feeling she had experienced in the dark cellar, about the weird mist that grew stronger and stronger, especially in that section where the floor was bare earth and where a stone had fallen and revealed a metal box. She wanted to tell him about the red light that had escaped from this box and the aura of magic that had surrounded her. She wanted to tell him all this, but she knew he was holding something back, and she didn't believe it would be fair if she told everything and he nothing. So pride kept her silent.

"What did you find?'' he pressed, now certain that she was withholding something from him.

"N-nothing,'' she lied.

He didn't believe her—it was evident on his face—but he said nothing. He nodded tiredly, mentally saying good night to her again, then quietly closed the door after him.

Molly stared at the door for a long while, then she reluctantly took off her hearing aid and turned off the lamp.

She fell asleep, dreaming of greenish-black maggots and Dinah. She tossed and turned, but this time did not wake up screaming.

The next morning, which promised to be another wet, gray day, Lara tried to persuade Steve into staying home, but he told her there was a mountain of paperwork waiting for him at the restaurant. He knew she didn't believe him, and he felt guilty, for it wasn't the truth. He had paperwork, sure, but it was no mountain, and what's more, it wasn't anything that couldn't wait. What he didn't, or couldn't, tell her was that he felt claustrophobic in this house despite its size and needed to get the hell away from it—again.

He told her he'd be back sometime in the afternoon, but after he spent a few hours at The Four Winds, he stopped at a pub on the way back, which was a mistake, for the Scotch surprisingly sharpened his mind rather than dulled it. The drink aroused the house's cellar, which until now he had managed to keep buried in a deep, out-of-the-way corner of his brain.

The cellar. Inwardly he shuddered and began using the Scotch to warm his insides, since it already had failed to numb his mind.

The cellar.

He remembered the awful darkness. Outer space couldn't even be this dark, he thought. He had been so scared—he remembered that as though it were yesterday —but he was seven then, probably the age when the imagination was the most creative and active. Yet he was certain it had been more than a child's imagination.

He remembered groping through the cellar. The flashlight had penetrated the dark in the same feeble way that it would penetrate a heavy fog. The dark simply ate the light. And he remembered the "bad feeling" in the air. Something stirred. That was the only way he knew how to describe it. The air stirred like water as he walked through it. It was that thick.

Then he had found that room at the other end of the house. Here, the air was the thickest. He had felt something unnatural all around him, and it hadn't been his imagination.

Steve ordered another drink. Dimly he heard laughter and chatter all around him, yet most of his mind was still in that silent cellar, where only his heart, beating too loud and too fast, could be heard. When his second drink arrived, he lifted his glass and caught his reflection on a small framed mirror advertising Budweiser beer. It was a cheap mirror, like one you'd win at a carnival for throwing darts or toppling a pyramid of leaded milk bottles.

It wasn't like the mirror he had found in that cellar—the cellar where black magic had been performed long, long ago. He had heard the talk among the townsfolk. Friar Roger Bacon's "Art" had made its way across the waters to this country, and then Dolly used it, they had said. She had summoned a devil, and the devil had burned part of the big house and the family inside it. Steve hadn't believed them, but when he found the mirror and saw what it did, he went to the library and did some research. Friar Roger Bacon had owned such a mirror.

In that room at the end of the cellar, Steve had found things half buried in the earth floor—a ring, a coin, and a shard of glass which, when he brought it upstairs to daylight, shined silver. It was part of a mirror.

Steve now took a large swallow of his drink, not wanting to remember anything else, but his mind seemed determined to push the past into the present. There was no choice but to brace himself and surrender to the memory.

Seven-year-old Steve Ludden had almost dropped the triangular shard when he looked into it. Instead of seeing his own reflection he saw his father staring back, his eyes and mouth round with what looked like sudden horror. Then the man's hands flew up in front of his face, as though to protect it from something that was coming and would inevitably destroy it. Steve could almost hear his father scream a trailing "Noooooo!" Then there was confusion as something slammed into the man. There was what looked like a shattering of glass, then his father's head was sliced free from the neck, the mouth still soundlessly shouting the negative word. And at that moment, Steve's hand shook and the image in the mirror gave way to an image of himself.

Steve gawked at himself and for an instant thought of tilting the shard forward or backward to bring back his father's image, but revulsion overcame curiosity and he let go of the glass, as though it had stung him.

Three weeks later his father died in a car accident. His Mercedes slamming into the back of a trailer truck, and sliding under it, he was decapitated.

Laughter and a voice jolted Steve into the present.

"A refill, buddy?" a young, mustachioed bartender repeated, glancing at his glass which, save for the melting ice, was empty.

Steve found himself cold and sweaty and tense. Wiping his forehead with the back of his hand, he nodded. "Yeah, give me another."

Wordlessly, the bartender made him a fresh drink, slid it toward him, at the same time clearing his old glass, then went away to busy himself with another customer. Steve watched him dully, taking a large sip of his drink. Then he slipped into the past again.

Before his father died, he had picked up the dropped mirror piece, stuffed it into his pocket, and later put it in a cigar box where he kept his jackknife, baseball cards, and other treasures. It wasn't until several months later that he looked into the glass again. He knew what he had seen before was his father's death. This time he saw his mother. At first he didn't recognize her, for the woman staring back at him was old, emaciated and moaning in agony.

Gradually he did recognize her, and knew she would die painfully in bed, at an old age. Then, not wanting to see anything else, he broke the mirror.

No, he didn't break it then, Steve suddenly realized. No, it was later. Later after . . . after . . .

Now his mind was fuzzy, the sounds in the pub washing over him like waves lapping a shore.

After . . . after . . . after *what?*

He didn't want to remember what else he'd seen in that damn mirror. He could sense the memory surfacing, and he fought it back down into the deep subconscious where it belonged.

But I destroyed that glass, he thought, so it wasn't possible for Molly to have gotten ahold of it—unless she found another piece. Or maybe she had found something else in that miserable cellar.

He had found something else eerie. It was a ring and it . . .

Don't want to think about it!

He swallowed a large mouthful of Scotch, which burned and made him cough.

I won't think about it!

"Buddy, you all right?"

"Huh?" He was momentarily surprised to hear the bartender's voice, again having forgotten where he was. "Yeah," he managed, wiping his mouth that the violent cough had dampened with spittle. He was now even colder and sweatier. Christ, these little trips down memory lane were doing a fucking number on him!

"You sure?" the bartender asked.

"Yeah." Steve nodded more firmly, then downed the rest of his drink. "Give me another," he said. And this time he'd enjoy it, he vowed. He'd stay in the present.

Lara watched the rain streak the window and the gloomy clouds darken until the night made them black and then invisible. She watched her reflection in the window for a while, sadly saw part of the candlelit dining room behind her on the glass, then walked away. She blew out the candles on the long table, gathered the good china plates and crystal goblets, and carried them into the kitchen. Then she shut off the oven, where a roast was shrinking and turning black. After Molly had had a slice when it was juicy, Lara had put the roast back in the oven to keep it warm for Steve. But that was hours ago, and Steve was still not home.

Damn him! she swore under her breath. It was better to curse than give in to the tears that were burning behind her eyes. He'd been late a lot recently. Why? Did he really hate this house *that* much? He said he had outgrown his silly bad feelings about it, didn't he?

The sound of Shelly's typewriter floated down from upstairs, and from outside came the whistling of wind. Lonely sounds, Lara thought, then pushed it from her mind. There was no need for self-pity, she told herself. She had a lot to be thankful for. Steve was busy, that's all. As his mother had done, she really should admire his ambition and his determination to be successful.

Glancing at a nineteenth century banjo clock, she saw that it was almost midnight. No longer very hungry, she made herself a light meal of tea and toast, then went into the library in search of a book to read. The last time she was in here she had read a book about insects. After that horrible incident with the swarm, she found herself curious about the creatures she had killed. Never in her life had she seen any bugs like those; thinking of them now made her shudder. But the book hadn't helped her. Since there were about 800,000 different species, one book could not possibly list, never mind illustrate, every one of them.

Best thing to do was forget the incident ever happened. She had urged Molly to do the same, but the girl couldn't. The poor dear had woken up screaming. Well, she was sure it would fade in time.

Lara selected an Agatha Christie novel, then went upstairs toward their bedroom. En route, she stopped at Molly's door, listened a moment, then opened it to peek in. From the soft light in the hallway she could faintly make out her daughter's form on the bed. Confident that Molly was sleeping peacefully, Lara then entered the room and kissed her forehead.

"I love you, sweetheart," she whispered, experiencing a rush of warm emotion as she said the words. The girl stirred but didn't awaken. Lara kissed her again, this time on the cheek, then quietly left the room.

In her own room she changed into her nightgown, then

went into the adjoining bathroom and washed her face and brushed her teeth and hair. When she finally slipped under the covers and opened her book to the first chapter, she heard a car approaching the driveway. She closed the book and listened. The motor stopped and the car door slammed shut, a sharp yet muted sound.

Lara glanced over at the lamp on the nightstand, wondering if she should turn it off and pretend she was asleep. This way she'd avoid any argument. She could wait until morning to ask Steve why he'd come home so late, for she was certain it was his car she'd just heard.

When she heard the front door close, she reached over and turned off the lamp, at the same time placing the book on the table. Then, lying back against the pillow, she listened in the dark to the sound of footsteps ascending the stairs.

Maybe she should confront him now, she thought, but then, she knew she was too hurt and angry to talk sensibly with him. She would probably be too unreasonable, too much of a nag and a bitch. Yes, it'd be better if she cooled off first. Wait until morning.

She closed her eyes to narrow slits, pretending she was in a deep sleep. The door opened, and Steve's dark frame stumbled into the room. Preceding him was an overpowering stench of stale whiskey.

Damn him! Lara cursed silently, biting on her lower lip. She still kept her eyes closed to small slits and her body immobile. She'd wait until morning, she vowed. Things would be different then, clearer in the light.

"Heeey, sweetheart . . ." Steve leaned close to her face, fanning her with his hot, whiskey breath. He almost lost his balance, lurching forward, but he caught himself in time. "You asleep?"

He was loud enough to wake even Molly, Lara thought.

"Awww, sweetheart, don't be asleep. I'm horny. Horny as hell. C'mon, don't be asleep."

He leaned closer, as though endeavoring to see her face

in the dark. This time he lost his balance and fell onto her.

Damn! She rolled away from him, bolted upright and snapped on the light.

He clumsily pulled himself up and blinked stupidly at her with bloodshot eyes. He grinned at her. "You're awake!" he exclaimed.

"And you're drunk!" she hissed.

"And horny," he added, raising a reminding finger. "Christ, am I ever!" He started fumbling at his shirt buttons.

"No way."

"Huh?" He was still struggling. Finally in frustration he pulled the shirt apart, popping the buttons. Wiggling out of the shirt and swaying slightly, he began to undo the buckle of his belt.

Lara watched as tears filled her eyes. She was disgusted with him, but mostly disappointed. She had thought everything would be so perfect when they came to this house. She'd been so certain that he'd take time off from his restaurant and spend most of it with her and Molly. She never thought he'd turn into an inconsiderate, drunken jerk. This was not the man she had married!

Reaching over, she turned the lamp off.

"Hey!"

There was a sudden crash as he fell with one leg still in his trousers. To some it would have been a funny, even hilarious moment, but Lara was angry to the point of tears. In the morning, she reminded herself for the ump-teenth time. She would talk with him in the morning.

Steve freed his leg from his pants, then scrambled onto the bed. Lara tensed, dreading the inevitable. He wrapped his arms around her and awkwardly pulled her toward him. She planted her hand against his chest, firmly stopping him from getting closer.

"No, I said!"

"Awww, why not? Y'wouldn't believe how horny I—"

"Not in this condition, Steve. No." If he made another attempt, she would leave the room. There were plenty of other beds in the house.

But he relented. Cursing, he turned over until he had his back to her and much to her surprise, was soon snoring. But before this, she heard him mutter under his breath, "Everythin' was great until I came back to this fuckin' house."

So it was still the house.

Well, she'd have a long talk with him in the morning. Everything would seem different then, and they'd communicate and bring everything out in the open. She was determined not to let anything hurt her marriage.

But when morning came Steve was already gone.

When the sun penetrated the rain clouds Molly found herself gradually feeling better. She still felt pangs of remorse and sorrow whenever she thought of her cat, but they weren't as sharp as before. It was like a knife that was, after repeated use, growing blunt. If anything, she was numb. She could now function and was no longer confined to her bed.

She practiced her t's and g's, repeatedly going over the list of 50 words that the Hearing and Speech Center had given her. She read aloud each word five times, then later in the day went through the list again. Then she started a new jigsaw puzzle. This one was of the Neuschwanstein Castle built by Mad King Ludwig. As Molly searched for pieces, she found herself beginning to relax, daydreaming about all kinds of things. At last, she had control of her mind. Whenever the cat entered it, she'd swiftly push it out.

Yes, she was springing back, slowly but surely. By the time she finished this 500-piece puzzle she was able to think about the cat and the horrible incident in her garden with some detachment, almost as if it were something in the newspaper or on TV.

She started watering her gardens again, with the exception of the one on the east side. Earlier she had believed the swarm of maggotlike creatures had come from the seeds she had planted, but now she was pretty sure that this wasn't what happened at all. Maybe these creatures had gathered to eat the seeds she had planted, and that was why these seeds never grew in the first place. It was rather simple. And what they had done to Dinah was one of those freaky things. You just had to learn to block it out of your mind. After all, the world was full of freaky, scary things, wasn't it?

Now she found the west garden was growing at an astounding rate. She was an even five feet tall, and the plants were now taller than she. The last time she had visited this garden these plants had been somewhere near her waist. Had the three days of rain made them spurt up? They were still identical, though, every plant the same height with the same amount of leaves and—Molly examined closer—buds.

They would be beautiful, for the plants themselves were pretty with their glossy, green leaves, so glossy that they looked like they'd been polished or waxed, she thought.

Molly watered each plant, giving them all an equal drink. Soon, they would flower, and in keeping with their character, they would all bloom at precisely the same time.

She couldn't wait.

10

Lara found herself spending most of her time either in the library or in her bedroom, reading mystery novels. She had read more in these last two weeks than she'd read in two years. There was nothing else to do. There was no sense in cleaning the house, since a married middle-aged couple came in every Wednesday to vacuum and dust most of the rooms. There was no sense in cooking big meals, since Steve hardly came home for them, and Shelly did her own cooking, which was usually in the middle of the afternoon and in the middle of the night.

No, there was nothing for Lara to do except read and read. She was in the middle of a Lawrence Sanders novel when Shelly breezed into the library, holding aloft a bottle of champagne and a half-filled glass.

"Congratulate me, Lara, dear," she sang, sipping on the glass. It was clear she had no intention of offering Lara a drink.

"On what?" Lara asked, curious.

"At last I've finished the book I was working on."

"Congratulations," Lara said half-heartedly.

"Honestly, you could show more enthusiasm."

"I'm sorry." This time Lara meant it. She closed the book on her lap and gave her sister-in-law full attention. "I hope it's another best-seller for you."

"Oh, it will be, it will be. I've no doubt about it."

Shelly was radiant, beaming with what was probably pride. Lara just realized the woman was wearing makeup, something she hadn't done for several weeks, probably not since she had started work on the book. Also, instead of wearing a flowing nightgown, she was clad in an airy, white sundress. She looked stunning, and Lara felt a twinge of envy.

"I can't wait to read it. What is it about?" Lara asked.

"Romance, of course," Shelly said, as though answering a ridiculous and needless question. "It was definitely my most difficult—and rewarding. Yes, I'm sure it'll also be my most successful."

So much for modesty, Lara thought.

"Oh!" Shelly exclaimed, suddenly aware of something. "Lara, dear, if you want some champagne, do get a glass and I'll pour you some."

"No, that's all right."

"You sure, dear?"

Lara nodded. Her sister-in-law's sugary voice was beginning to sicken her.

"Well, if you insist." Shelly smiled, finishing her glass and refilling it. "I feel so wonderful today. I always feel like this after I finish a book, and . . . I always throw a party."

The way the last sentence was separated from the rest, Lara knew it was something deliberately tossed at her, something that she was supposed to catch. Shelly was watching her over the rim of her glass, obviously waiting for a reaction.

But all Lara could think of to say was, "Oh?"

"You wouldn't mind, would you?"

"No, of course not. Why would I?"

"A party here," Shelly emphasized.

"You always have them here?"

"No. The parties were usually at my friends' in New York, but this time, since the house is finally mine—oh, please forgive me, *half* mine—I feel it's time I have my own party at my own place."

"What kind of party?" Lara asked, not certain if she wanted to know.

"Of course you're invited." Shelly smiled sweetly, eluding the question. "But I'm not sure if you'd feel comfortable with my friends."

"What kind of party?" Lara demanded.

"A good party!" The smile fleetingly turned to a snarl, then back to a pseudo-smile. "I'm afraid some of my friends are what you'd probably refer to as positively wild."

"What do you mean?"

"Oh . . ." Shelly shrugged and took a seat by the cold fireplace. She leaned back, crossed her shapely legs and airily took a sip of champagne. "They might be a bad influence on your daughter. You may have to keep her away."

"Shelly, what kind of party do you intend to have?" She wished the woman would be frank. "What would your friends be doing?"

"Oh, you know, the usual, dear." She shrugged again. "Drugs, sex, and rock and roll."

Lara stared at her, then said firmly, "No."

"No? No what, dear? Are you telling me what I can or cannot do?"

Fighting for control, Lara replied in an even voice, "All right, I'm not telling you; I'm asking you. Please don't have a party like that here."

Shelly let out a short laugh, then took another sip of her drink before answering. "I already reminded you that this house is half mine, and I see no reason why I should not have a party here. If you fear that my friends and I may corrupt your sweet, little daughter, then I suggest that you take her away from here for perhaps a few days."

"A few days?" Lara couldn't believe her ears.

"Yes. My parties sometimes do last a while," she said, somewhat proudly.

"This . . . this is ridiculous."

"Oh?"

"This house is half mine now, and I should have some say about this. I shouldn't have to leave for a—few days!"

"And the other half of this house is mine. If I wish to have a party, there isn't a damn thing you can do about it, dear."

Lara stared at her, seething. She was sure Shelly was doing this deliberately, so she'd sell and move out. Well, she wasn't going to fall for it. Let her have her silly party, but she wasn't going to budge from this house.

"I'm not leaving," she declared firmly.

Shelly's thin brow arched in amusement. "My, my, you are a feisty one—and stubborn, I may add. They say *I* overreact?"

"I'm not overreacting. I just simply refuse to—"

"How is Stevie, incidentally?" Shelly cut in, deliberately to steer the conversation in another direction. "Come to think of it, I haven't seen much of him recently."

"He's fine," Lara answered curtly, wary of the abrupt change of subject.

"You don't see much of him either, do you, dear?"

Lara didn't answer, for it was none of this woman's business.

"Are you two having marital problems?" Shelly asked, a cruel snicker in her voice.

Lara forced herself to appear unabashed. This woman was only assuming, she told herself. Shelly was not really aware of the trouble that was going on between her and Steve. She successfully had masked it from her daughter, from everyone. It simply was not that obvious.

But this belief was quickly shattered when Shelly added, "You are a foolish woman to allow an inanimate house destroy a precious relationship. Actually, I've written something like this once. It was my second book, I believe, or perhaps my third. Anyway, I'd written about this darling couple who had let a beach house come between them. He, the hero, wanted a cozy cabin near a lake in the mountains, but the heroine coveted the luxury and glamour that came with a beach house in Malibu. Do you know what happened to them in the end, dear?''

"No, I don't. Nor do I want to," Lara said flatly, clutching the book on her lap, then rising to her feet.

"They got a divorce," Shelly said anyway, "but it was still a happy ending—for the hero, that is. He went on to meet a lovely woman who didn't care about a fancy house but just cared about him.''

Lara tried to block out the words, but it was too late. The sweet voice dripped like thick syrup in the air and clung to her. She started for the door. "It's none of your concern," she said, struggling to keep her voice steady and her head up. When she left the room she could hear Shelly laughing softly between sips of champagne. Or was this just her imagination?

Holding the book against her breast, Lara hurried up the stairs to her room. Forget everything that was said, she told herself. Block it out!

But she couldn't. Shelly's words clung to her mind. The woman had spoken the truth.

When she had rushed to her room, Lara had intended to finish reading her book there, but when she reached the room and closed the door after her, she threw the book onto the bed and stared pensively out the window, which faced the western front of the house. She leaned against the glass and let her eyes freely spill tears.

Yes, Shelly had spoken the truth. Lara was allowing this house to ruin her marriage. Until now she had refused to accept this, repeatedly assuring herself that Steve would adjust to the house. When the time was ripe, they would have a long talk. She would manage to convince him how silly his behavior was. She had been so certain he would come around eventually. She just needed to be patient, that's all.

But she wasn't certain of this anymore. Time, it seemed, was doing more harm than good, widening the gulf between them. When, she wondered, was the last time they had spent an evening together? A week ago?

Two weeks ago?

Yes, there was no doubt about it. Her marriage was faltering, and something needed to be done very soon or it would be too late. And what's more, she suddenly realized, crying was not going to do a damn thing. She moved away from the window for a Kleenex and began dabbing her eyes. She would have to stop feeling sorry for herself and do something.

Sniffing back the rest of her tears, she returned to the window and thought about their small apartment in Massachusetts. They were to pay one more month's rent on it and then move the furniture, little that they had, into this house. Perhaps it'd be best to wait awhile. Perhaps they should go back to the apartment and discuss everything fully. Maybe when he remembers how small and claustrophobic the place is, he'll want to come back here.

This, she knew, was hope talking, and she swiftly tossed it out of her mind. She needed to be objective about this. The house, she admitted to herself, meant a lot to her, but Steve meant more. And, to be truthful, Molly meant even more. Molly was a part of her, and she'd do anything in her power to keep her happy.

As she thought of this, she spotted her daughter in the garden below. The girl was on her hands and knees, weeding the plants. I'll talk to her, Lara suddenly decided. If she doesn't mind going back to the apartment, then it'll be all set.

The moment Lara stepped outside, Molly looked up and watched her mother approach her.

"Lovely garden." Lara smiled as she took in the healthy, green plants. They looked almost artificial, for they were all identical. "You certainly have a green thumb, sweetheart."

Molly beamed with pride, then said carefully, "They all got buds, Mom. They're all going to bloom at once."

"So I see." There must have been hundreds of buds for such a small garden. "What kind of flowers?" she asked.

Molly shrugged. "I don't know. That's why I can't wait to see."

"I'm glad to see you've found a little hobby." Lara smiled.

The girl returned the smile, nodding that she, too, was glad. Then there was an awkward silence as Lara searched for the best way to word her question.

At length, she said, "Would it disappoint you terribly if we go back to the apartment, sweetheart?"

The question seemed to surprise Molly, for she frowned and studied her mother's face a moment. "You don't like it here no more, Mom?"

"Oh, it's not that. It's just . . . well, it's . . ." Her face reddened as she tried to avoid telling the truth.

But Molly seemed to know anyway. "It's because of Steve, huh?"

Lara's first instinct was to deny this, for she wanted Molly to believe that she and Steve had a wonderful, flawless marriage. Then she sighed sadly and nodded.

"He still doesn't like the house," Molly said.

Lara nodded again.

"There are some parts I don't like 'bout the house, too," the girl admitted, "but I just don't think about them. I pretend they're not there."

"What parts?"

"Well, the cellar mostly. Especially one end of it. I just don't think about it. That's what Steve should do, Mom—pretend it's not there."

Lara stared at her, then gave her a wan smile. "I'm afraid he's not good at pretending, sweetheart. Anyway, you still haven't answered my question. Would you mind if we moved back to the apartment? Maybe later we'll buy a new house with a big yard."

"If it'll make you and Steve happy, I won't mind, Mom."

The words, uttered slowly and carefully to pronounce the consonants correctly, touched Lara, bringing tears to her eyes. She blinked them back and widened her smile. "You sure?"

"Sure I'm sure." Molly grinned, matching her smile.

"Oh, sweetheart!" Lara hugged her daughter. "I love you so much. I'm going to make this up to you. I promise."

"Huh?"

Lara had forgotten herself for a moment and buried her face in the girl's soft hair, where her lips couldn't be seen. She pulled back, wiping a tear that had managed to escape. "I said, I'm going to make this up to you."

"You don't have to."

"Oh, sweetheart." Lara hugged her again, then said, "Well, I'll leave you with your garden. Later I'm going to have a nice, long talk with Steve." She turned toward the house.

"Mom?" she heard when she reached the door.

"Yes?" she replied loudly.

"Can we not move until after these flowers open?"

Lara could see the buds on the plants were swollen and would bloom very soon, probably during the night. "Sure," she said. "I don't think we'll be leaving that quickly."

Satisfied with the answer, Molly dropped to her knees and resumed weeding.

11

Lara sat at the kitchen table, a cup of tea in front of her. No sounds came from Shelly's typewriter, and the silence, she found to her surprise, was actually distracting. So she turned on a radio and let soft rock fill the air. She was deep in thought while Neil Diamond and Dionne Warwick sang their songs.

First thing, she knew, would be to have a talk with Steve. She would have to try to get him to open up again about why this house bothered him. The last time he had talked about it he mentioned Friar Bacon and the legends that surrounded him. They were stories about medieval sorcery, demons and a weird mirror. There was more, but he had suddenly declined to talk about it. Instead, he had become horny, Lara remembered, smiling somewhat sadly. That was probably the last time he'd been romantic—while sober.

How had she succeeded in making him talk that time? Then the answer came to her—romance, or probably in his words, sex. He had talked effusively when contented and relaxed, she remembered now. She'd get him into a romantic, relaxing mood again, and what better way to start than with a romantic, relaxing dinner?

A romantic dinner would be wonderful! She would have it in the big dining room under the crystal chandelier, and she would have his favorite, lobster casserole and champagne. Later, in their room, they would make love, talk and make love again.

Their marriage would be strong once more.

But when the doorbell rang, her plan was shattered. It was Newport Liquors delivering a case of champagne, among other alcoholic beverages. "Miss Shelly Ludden?" a paunchy, bald-headed man demanded, extending a small clipboard at Lara.

"No, I'm—"

Before Lara could finish, Shelly appeared and took the clipboard from the delivery man. After the receipt was signed and the door closed, Shelly turned to Lara and smiled sweetly. "For the party tonight."

"Tonight?" Lara echoed disbelievingly.

"Yes. Are you objecting?"

"Isn't this rather sudden?"

"It's a spontaneous party," Shelly explained airily. "Those kind are usually the most exciting."

Lara, momentarily speechless, stared at the cartons on the foyer floor—brandy, gin, vodka, Scotch and, of course, champagne. Apparently Shelly was expecting a sizable crowd.

"How many are coming?" Lara asked at length.

"Twenty. Thirty. Just a few of my close friends from the city."

"But I had plans," Lara said, tearing her gaze away from the cartons and looking at her.

"Well, I did tell you about this, dear."

"Yes, I know, but I didn't think it'd be tonight."

Shelly gave her a that's-your-problem shrug and pivoted toward the stairs. "Ciao," she said, then hurried up the steps.

Lara felt a heavy, cold feeling in her stomach, disappointed and at the same time angry at her sister-in-law. That woman was probably having this party deliberately to make Lara uncomfortable in this house, and Lara would have played at her own game—but there was Steve to think about first.

Lara sighed, swallowing her anger and pride. Now

she'd have to change her plan, for a romantic dinner was definitely out. Then she thought of dining at a restaurant. Yes, that would be equally wonderful. She and Steven could go to a quiet, elegant place—but, of course, not to The Four Winds.

But then, Molly would have to come with them, and that wouldn't be romantic. And after the restaurant, what then? Come back here and party?

Lara felt that cold anger rushing back, stronger than ever. Maybe she should just tell Steve that she was willing to sell their share in the damn house. It'd be better all around, and she wouldn't have to put up with Shelly anymore.

Lara went outside in search of Molly, but after looking everywhere, she returned indoors and finally found her in the attic.

"Never expected to find you here."

Molly had several boxes of old jigsaw puzzles in her arms. Each of these boxes was limp, almost shapeless, and tied shut with frayed twine. "Hope all the pieces are here," she said.

While helping her carry some of the puzzles to her room, Lara explained her plan.

"But I'd make a threesome," Molly protested.

"That'll be all right, sweetheart."

"No." Molly shook her head firmly. "You and Steve godda be alone. I'll be all righ'. I'll jus' stay in my room and do these puzzles."

"I'm not sure if that'll be a good idea. You see, there's going to be a party here and—"

"I know."

Lara blinked, surprised. "You do?"

Molly nodded, and her face began to color.

"Oh, you played Secret Spy again, didn't you?"

"Yeah."

"Honestly, I don't know what I'm going to do with you."

"I'm sorry, Mom. I saw you and Shelly talkin' and—"

"Never mind, it doesn't matter. So now you know why

I don't want you to stay here alone tonight."

"Bud—I mean, bu*t* I'll be all right, Mom. I won't go near the party. I'll stay here in my room."

"Well . . ." Lara hesitated.

"Please, Mom, please."

"Why don't you want to come with us?"

"Because I know you want to be alone with Steve. You . . . you want to make everything right again with him."

Lara stared at her daughter, stunned at such perception. It never ceased to amaze her how much Molly was aware of things. Her hearing loss seemed to make her more observant than most people.

"Yes, you're right, I suppose," she said when she found her voice. "I need to be alone with him. But are you sure—"

"I'm sure, Mom." Molly smiled, knowing that she was winning. "I'd jus' do my puzzles tonight. I'll even lock my door, if you want me to."

"Yes, that would be a good idea."

"Then I can stay here tonight?"

Lara thought about it for a moment, then, taking a deep breath, nodded.

Molly threw her arms around her and almost knocked her over. One would think that Lara had just announced that they were going to Disneyworld.

When Steve came home three hours later, Lara was relieved that he hadn't picked today to be late and drunk, but noticing his clothes looked limp and his eyes were tired, she felt a pang of guilt. These long trips back and forth from work were doing a number on him. If he— *they*—lived closer to his restaurant, he wouldn't have to spend so many tedious hours on the road.

"Oh, Steve, do you still love me?" She wrapped her arms around his waist and turned her face upward for a kiss, which he willingly gave her. They were in the foyer, and the front door was still partly open.

"Of course I do, hon," Steve said. "Never stopped."

Lara buried her face against his shoulder. "How does a lovely dinner out sound? Just the two of us?"

"Gee, I don't know. I'm beat. I—"

"Please, Steve. We need an outing together. We need . . . well, to talk."

Steve groaned. "I'm not in the mood to—"

"Please."

"Why can't we talk here, then?"

Lara told him about Shelly's party, finishing with, "And I want us to be alone tonight, not with a bunch of people."

"And then, maybe, we could stay over at a nice hotel," he suggested.

"Hotel?"

"Sure. To talk some more and do whatever comes naturally."

"Well, I don't know if a hotel would be such a good—"

"Never mind, it was just a thought."

He started to disengage himself from her, but she tightened her arms around him, suddenly filled with a horrible fear of losing him. This was no time to reject any of his suggestions. Her marriage was fragile, and it wouldn't take much to shatter it.

"A hotel sounds like a wonderful idea," she said.

"Great." He kissed the top of her head. "But let me take a shower first. I *am* beat. That trip back and forth—"

"I know, darling. That's partly what I want us to talk about."

He looked at her, as though finally understanding. "Yeah, we do need to talk," he agreed. He gave her another kiss, then gently freed himself from her embrace and went upstairs to shower.

Lara knocked on Molly's door. After the fifth or sixth rap, the girl opened it. "Steve and I may be staying overnight at a hotel," Lara told her, "So maybe you should come with us, after all. You could stay in another room."

"But I'll still be a threesome, Mom."

"Don't be silly. Besides, I'll be worrying all night if

you're here alone with . . ." She let the sentence go unfinished.

"Oh, Mom, I'm nod a baby. I'll be all righ'."

"Your t's," Lara reminded automatically, and before the girl could respond, added, "You sure, sweetheart? We might not be back until sometime tomorrow, you know."

"That's okay. I'm sure."

"No, you're not a baby, and I suppose it's time I stop treating you like one, isn't it?"

Molly nodded, giving her a small but warm smile.

Lara fondly touched her daughter's cheek, held her fingers there for a lingering moment, and whispered, "Thank you. I love you." Then she hurried to her own room.

As she packed clothes for the evening, her mind repeated the same question over and over. Am I doing the right thing?

Molly couldn't believe her eyes when she went outside to her west garden. Only about four hours had passed since she was last there, weeding the plants, and already there was an incredible change. She had seen it the instant she opened the front door, although the garden was over a 100 feet away, near the iron gate by the road. She had spotted a rainbow of colors.

The garden, at last, had bloomed!

As she ran toward it, she could smell the sweet fragrance. It was a cross between a lilac and maybe a rose. It was the sweetest scent she had ever smelled, sweeter than any perfume, sweeter than candy, sweeter than . . .

"Wow!" she exclaimed when she reached the garden. The flowers were huge. Now that these plants were directly in front of her, the scent was overpowering, causing her to gasp and take a backward step.

After a moment or two, her nose seemed to adjust, for the smell didn't seem as strong anymore. She moved closer and studied the flowers. They were all the same in size and form, only the colors were different. They each had the protruding horn-shaped center, resembling a daffodil, but the base supporting it was fat and round, like a carnation. And these flowers were huge, about a foot in diameter. And the scent!

What kind of flowers are these? Molly continued to study them, trying to find something different, besides the colors, with each one. Maybe a book in the library would help her identify them.

She cupped a flower with both hands, hesitated a moment, then lowered her head and breathed in the scent.

Then she staggered back, covering her nostrils with her hands. Jeez! Never had she smelled anything so strong! It actually snatched her breath away!

Then the choking fragrance subsided, and she dropped her hand from her face. Now she felt a little light-headed and made a vow never to smell these flowers at a close range again. From a slight distance the scent was kind of nice, and she was beginning to really like it. It made her smile and feel dreamy.

Yes, the flowers smelled nice, just as long as she didn't put her face into them.

What about putting them in vases throughout the house? It would make all the rooms smell pretty. She'd be sure not to put too many flowers in one room, that's all.

As if in agreement, a breeze swept through the garden and gently stirred the plants, making their horned faces nod at her. Then Molly noted that the sun had set behind the trees and shadows were darkening the flowers. Soon it would be too late to see anything.

Pressed into a quick decision, Molly ran back to the house to find a pair of scissors. As she reached the door, Lara and Steve stepped out. They were both dressed in their best outfits, her mother in a pretty blue dress and Steve in a dark suit. In Steve's hand was an overnight case.

"So there you are," her mother cried in relief. "We've

been looking all over for you."

"The flowers opened up, Mom!" Molly enthusiasticlly pointed to the garden.

"Why, so they did," Lara said, glancing at the flowers in the distance. Surprise registered on her face, then concern about her marriage and her daughter pushed it away. "You sure you'll be all right, sweetheart?"

"I already told ya a hun'red times, Mom. I'm gonna be okay."

Lara hesitated. "I've made some sandwiches for you. They're in your room. Now remember, stay in your room and watch TV or something. And stay away from Shelly and her friends."

Molly nodded, a little impatiently. "I will, Mom. I will."

"Well . . ." She glanced at Steve, then back at Molly, as though wondering again if she was making a mistake leaving like this.

"You're not going to China or to another planet, Mom," Molly said.

"Right." Lara laughed, not at the remark but at herself. She kissed her daughter's cheek. "Take care. I'll see you tomorrow."

Steve, also, gave Molly a quick kiss on the cheek. "I'm not worried." He winked at her. "I know you're a big girl now. So, I'll see you tomorrow."

Beaming, Molly nodded. She liked how her stepfather could make her feel like a grownup sometimes, make her feel . . . well, normal. She really hoped everything worked out swell between him and her mother.

She watched them get into the Cutlass. When they left the driveway and pulled out onto the road, she waved. Her mother poked her head out the window and shouted something, but Molly only heard the word "party" and assumed she was telling her to stay away from it again. When the car disappeared down the street, Molly dropped her hand and ran into the house.

In the kitchen, rummaging through a cabinet drawer that was filled with pens, pencils, batteries and other

junk, she found a pair of scissors. Then she searched for
a basket. When she couldn't find any, she grabbed a large
stainless steel bowl and hurried back outside.

It was amazing how once the sun set, darkness
thickened with incredible rapidity. Even the temperature
was dropping fast. A moment ago the wind had been soft
and balmy, but now it was chilly. Setting the bowl on the
ground and clutching the scissors with her right hand,
Molly began to cut the flowers.

The wind, blowing in from the ocean and skirting the
house, grew stronger, rippling through the garden. The
flowers' heads were nodding vigorously now, as though
encouraging and urging the girl onward, to work faster.
There was no strong scent this time, for the wind had
whipped it away. A good thing, Molly thought, otherwise,
the heady fragrance eventually would have been too
much and forced her to stop cutting. This way she was
able to fill the big bowl.

When she was done she ran back into the house. The
moment she was inside, the scent hit her, causing her to
drop the bowl onto the floor.

She jumped back, covering her nose with both hands.
Too strong! It was like dropping a whole bottle of
perfume.

Still cupping her nostrils, but now with only one hand,
she returned to the fallen flowers and gathered a small
bunch. She went into the dining room, found a crystal
vase, filled it with water from the kitchen, then slid the
flowers into it. She put the now full vase on the long table
in the dining room, then went into the living room, found
another vase and filled it.

She put vases of flowers in seven rooms, saving the last
bunch for her own room.

In no time the house took on a new odor, as though she
had run into all the rooms and sprayed them with air
freshener. It was a nice smell, Molly thought, a sweet
smell.

An hour later the people began to dribble in for the
party, and Molly thought some of them were weird.

There was a woman who was tall and skeletal with a crew cut; she looked like a boy. And there was a young man who looked like a girl and wore a flowing cape, shiny knee-high boots and inch-thick makeup.

Molly watched the people below through the second floor banister, then when she grew bored with this, she retreated to her room. When she closed the door the floral scent hit her. Strong but pretty, she reflected again. It will go away; scents always do, in time.

She sat at a card table and tried to concentrate on a puzzle that she had taken down from the attic, but it was hard to keep her mind on it.

She kept looking over at the vase of flowers she had put on the window sill. She couldn't stop admiring them. They looked and smelled so pretty.

So sweet.

12

The restaurant Lara had selected was perfect for a romantic dinner. It had everything—a private table, candles, a fresh rose. Perhaps the only missing ingredient was a wandering violinist, but the soft piped-in music was just fine, succeeding in lulling Lara and Steve into a tranquil, dreamy mood.

Steve ordered wine. After they drained their first glass and began their second, they were ready to talk, but first Steve reached for Lara's hand across the table and kissed it. This surprised her, for he had never done this before.

Quietly, he said, "I love you."

The words thrilled her. It was amazing how they had such power to make her happy, to make her feel as though she were floating. Almost like magic words, she reflected, more potent than abracadabra.

"I love you, too," she whispered back.

She took another sip of her wine though she was already giddy. The drinks, the restaurant, and the beautiful words were turning her insides to mush. If this kept up, she feared Steve would have to sweep her off her feet and carry her . . . to her room? Just as Rhett Butler had done to Scarlett O'Hara?

"You seem to be a million miles away," she heard Steve say.

"I am." Lara smiled, then, not wanting to explain,

said "It's been so long since we've been romantic like this."

Steve nodded, agreeing.

"I'm sorry about the other night, the way I had tried to . . . well, force myself on you. I was drunk."

"It's okay," Lara replied softly.

"I'm afraid I've been drunk a lot lately."

"And I think I understand why."

"You do?"

Lara nodded. "The house still bothers you."

The silence that followed convinced her she was right. They listened to the faint instrumental music for a few long seconds, then Steve said, "I can't help it, hon. I know how childish I must seem to you, but I just don't like that house."

"And I don't think I like sharing it with Shelly anymore."

The admission surprised him. "I thought you loved the place."

"Oh, I do, but there are things that I don't like about it now. There is too much hostility between Shelly and me, and I don't think it would be very healthy, especially for Molly, to live in such an atmosphere. Most of all, I don't like what it's doing to our marriage, Steve. The house seems to be pushing you away from me."

"So what are you saying?" His frown deepened with puzzlement.

Lara drew in a deep breath then expelled it slowly.

"I think you should sell your half of the house," she said at length.

He stared at her, as though unable to believe what he had heard. "Are you . . . serious?"

"Yes," Lara replied, thinking that her love for the big house and the desire to keep Shelly from getting her way were small sacrifices for saving her marriage. She gave him a smile to show that she, indeed, was very serious.

"Hey, that's great news. You're sure now, aren't you?" he insisted.

Lara nodded, forcing herself to maintain the smile.

"It's only an old house," she said, as though to convince herself.

"Great!" he exclaimed again, then leaned over the table and kissed her. His lips on hers felt warm and wonderful.

Yes, letting go of the house would be a small sacrifice, she told herself again.

Shelly was delighted that all, except two, of her friends arrived for her completion-of-a-novel celebration. Everyone, she could tell, was having a marvelous time. The booze was flowing freely and the joints were burning ceaselessly. As for the food, well, it didn't matter that no one was hungry yet, although she had spent most of the afternoon preparing ham and turkey salad sandwiches, as well as macaroni and potato salads. There was still plenty of time to eat, she told herself. Right now her friends were concentrating on having a good time.

The stereo blared heavy metal in the living room; in the main study a radio blasted country music; from the dining room came rock of the fifties and sixties; and from the library, Mozart. It was a discordant blend, a vicious competition that was no longer music but noise. Not that it mattered, for no one was really listening.

And it was deafening, vibrating the walls of the house. Again it didn't matter. The nearest neighbor was a good acre away, and Molly, upstairs, certainly wouldn't mind. She could always turn off her hearing aid.

Yes, it was a great party, probably her best. Maybe this was a sign that the novel she had just completed also would be her best. Shelly sure hoped so.

Someone passed her a joint, and she gratefully drew on it, then gave it back. A sweet scent filled her nostrils. Sweeter than usual, she thought. Her eyes penetrated the smoky haze that filled the big living room and spotted a vase of flowers on the fireplace mantel. Who had put those there? Lara? The flowers were certainly lovely, but she had never seen anything like them before. Perhaps they came from those silly gardens of Molly's. Shelly hadn't bothered to look at them, having been so busy with her novel and all, but if this was a sample of what those gardens were producing, she should definitely have a look at them one of these days. These flowers were so pretty. Their vivid colors of red, yellow, and purple seemed to cut through the haze in the room, almost as brilliant as neon lights in a fog.

She started toward them. Halfway across the room she noticed the sweet scent was stronger. At first she had attributed the smell to the many joints burning in the room, but now she believed it was actually from these flowers sitting on the mantel.

Strange—lovely, but strange!

She adored flowers and had grown many herself, but never had she come across anything with such a distinct fragrance. Even her lilac trees weren't as strong as this.

A young man intercepted her, wrapping muscular arms around her back and pulling her tightly against him. She tore her gaze away from the vase of flowers and saw that it was Jake Wheeler holding her. He was a handsome actor who was doing more modeling than acting.

"Dance, beautiful author?" He flashed big, capped teeth.

Shelly laughed, then shrugged.

"What's so funny?" he asked, pulling her even tighter against him. She could feel his hard chest and thighs.

"To what music are we to dance?" she asked, forgetting about the flowers. "Kenny Rogers, Van Halen, Elvis, or Mozart?"

"Why not to all of them?"

Shelly laughed again. "Why not?"

Jake laughed with her, widening that dazzling smile of his. Then he swirled her around, creating his own rhythm. When he pulled her back into his arms, he crushed her breasts against his chest, then pushed his pelvis against hers. He developed another rhythm as he pushed, then rotated his hips. Soon Shelly followed his beat and did likewise with her own hips. She could feel him hardening against her and laughed for the third time.

"Now what's funny, my lovely novelist?" he asked, although he too was laughing.

"No reason. Just happy."

"Wanna be happier?"

"Sure?"

He kissed her, and in response she pushed her tongue into his mouth. Then she felt his hands on one of her breasts. She moaned with approval, arching her back toward him. Just as she was ready to suggest that they use a bedroom, another young man joined them. It was Tony, but she couldn't remember his last name, only that he was a photographer who'd done several covers for national magazines. He was a friend of a friend and he was damn attractive, almost as attractive as Jake.

He said, "May I cut in?"

"Fuck off." Jake jerked his head toward the part of the room behind him.

But Shelly disengaged herself from Jake and slipped into the other man's arms. "Hello, handsome," she purred.

Jake grumbled, shook his head, but didn't protest. He went in search of another drink.

"Hello, beautiful," Tony what's-his-name replied, after watching the young actor disappear into the crowd. "What's your new novel about?"

"Never mind about that. Just make me happy."

"And how do you want me to—"

Before he could finish, her mouth was on his, her body pressing and rotating against him. When she knew she had aroused him, she threw her head back and looked squarely at him.

"In love?" She grinned.

"Very much," he replied, returning the grin.

She giggled, pulled on a joint that was passing by, then glanced around the room. It was a mess, but who cares? She knew the room would be cleaned up later, and nothing valuable would be destroyed since she had moved many of the precious breakables into a locked spare bedroom.

Lara would simply die if she saw the house now!

This thought brought a fresh flood of giggles and laughter that didn't seem to stop until she noticed that Tony had something in his hand and was offering it to her. He had reached for it on the fireplace mantel.

It was one of those pretty flowers. A red one.

"A token of my love," he said.

"How trite and insincere—and sweet." She took the flower from him and brought it to her nostrils.

"Oh, my God!" she suddenly gasped. "This flower is horribly strong!" She let go of the plant, as though it had stung her. Then holding her nostrils, she waited for the scent to fade. "My . . . God," she said again.

"Does this mean you reject my love?" Tony grabbed his chest, feigning grief.

The odor now almost gone, Shelly dropped her hand and reached for his. "I'll show you love," she said, then led him toward a bedroom upstairs.

The flower she had dropped was quickly forgotten, and no one noticed it on the floor. People unknowingly trampled it until its petals were shredded and pulverized, until it was reduced to what looked like red dust.

And like dust, it puffed upward and floated in the air.

In her room, Molly found a piece of the jigsaw puzzle and snapped it into place. She felt a fleeting surge of triumph, but it wasn't as strong as usual. She began to look for another piece, at the same time watching a rerun of *Gimme a Break* on the portable TV that she had brought up from the recreation room. Nell Harper was yelling and shaking her fist at her friend Abby, who was crouching and pouting.

But neither the puzzle nor the TV held Molly's attention for long. It was the flowers on the window sill that she stared at the most. The scent now was thick, and she wasn't sure anymore if it was a good smell or a bad one. It was still sweet, but it was on the borderline of another kind of odor. She couldn't decide exactly what kind, though.

As she stared, her vision blurred and the vivid colors of the flowers smeared and ran into each other. She blinked. Her vision cleared and the flowers resumed their shapes. She rubbed her eyes, thinking maybe she was tired, or maybe she had caught some kind of bug, for her head was spinning a little and she was experiencing a faint floating sensation. Like the smell, she wasn't sure if it was a feeling she liked.

At length she gave up on the puzzle and lay down on the bed to watch Nell and Addy, the former was still yelling and the latter still pouting.

Then the girl looked over at the window again. It was nighttime, and the panes of glass were black, a sharp contrast to the colorful flowers. So pretty, she thought.

She couldn't stop admiring them.

After dinner, Steve and Lara took off their shoes, held them in their hands, and strolled along the beach near the restaurant. It was a perfect night for this, warm and calm. They sky was freckled with countless stars, and the moon, almost full, cast a platinum, ragged path across the ocean. The faint aroma of salt, tinged with seaweed, intermittently blew in from the water, and the cool surf lapped and tugged at the couple's naked feet, as though determined to sweep them into the ocean along with whatever else it could find on shore.

Lara loved the pulling sensation the water made, especially between her toes. "Beautiful night," she murmured dreamily.

And to her delight Steve stopped, pulled her into his arms and kissed her, gently at first, then hard and hungrily. "God, I love you," he moaned.

"Oh darling, I love you, too," she whispered, returning the kiss. "Everything's going to be all right now."

He pulled his head back to look at her. The moon made the whites of his eyes gleam, but the rest of his face was in darkness. "You sure you have no second thoughts?" His voice was gentle, full of concern and compassion.

"You mean about the house?"

He nodded. Reaching for her hand, he began strolling along the edge of the water again.

"You mean more to me than any stupid house," Lara said, walking beside him. A wave, larger than usual, slapped her knees, surprising and stunning her with its coldness.

"Why do you love that house so much?" Steve asked curiously, after a thoughtful moment.

Lara weighed the question in her mind. Why *did* she love that house, especially in such a way that it was almost an obsession with her to keep it?

At length she said, "I'm not very sure, darling. That house is beautiful and charming with all its antiques. It seems so . . . so established. Yes, I guess that's what it is. When I first saw the house I saw a chance to finally have roots, a sense of establishment. I guess, deep down, I've always wanted a big house, a house with class and style, but all I could ever afford were apartments. So when I saw this house, well, I fell in love with it. And when I found out that Shelly was determined to have it, I wanted it all the more. I'm afraid my behavior was very immature and selfish. I acted like a kid wanting a toy that another kid had."

"We'll buy a house, hon," Steve promised. "The restaurant's doing well this year, and with the money we'll get for selling our half of the old house—"

"It's all right, darling," she interrupted gently. "I've learned my lesson. I almost lost you, and I don't want that to happen again. I've already told you, our marriage is more precious than any house."

"But you still love that place," Steve insisted, his voice betraying guilt. "And so does Molly."

"I just want Molly to have a home with a yard, and when I saw four yards, well . . ." This time it was she who stopped for a kiss. "I don't want to talk about the house anymore. It just makes me think about Shelly, and that's the last thing in the world I want to think about right now." She wrapped her arms around his neck and pulled his face toward hers. "We can talk later, but right now I want . . ." She kissed him.

Soon they were lying on the sand, their feet still in the water. The waves gently lapped at their ankles, then rose to their calfs, then their knees. The ocean was like a child tugging impatiently for their attention, but no matter how demanding or determined, it couldn't seem to interrupt their lovemaking.

Leading the handsome photographer by the hand, Shelly waltzed out of her bedroom and back out to the party. Tony the photographer had been good in bed, but she'd had better—Jake, for one—and thinking of Jake, she let go of Tony's hand and went in search of him. Threading her way through the people, pausing to take a sip of someone's daiquiri and a drag of someone else's cigarette, she finally found Jake shooting pool in the recreation room. That was when she noticed a change in everyone around her.

She saw a disconcerting grimness in Jake's face as he shot a billiard ball across the table. Then she looked around and found similar expressions everywhere.

What in God's name was going on?

Jake, who had been leaning over with a cue in his hand, straightened up and looked at Shelly. His eyes held a gleam that she'd never seen before. She found herself tensing, actually taking a backward step.

"Jake?"

He smiled, lowering the cue onto the table, his gaze never leaving her. The smile, instead of warming her, chilled her.

She looked around the room. Nobody was watching her, but they all still had that dark, stern expression. Seeing this, she noticed there was no laughter in the room or anywhere in the house, only the loud, raucous blend of music.

Jake reached for both of her hands and drew her toward him. "My beautiful author is back," he said in a husky voice, maintaining the horrible, cold grin.

Shelly fought the impulse to wrench herself free but did not want to make a scene.

"Jake," she repeated, "what is wrong?"

"Wrong? Why do you ask that, my love?"

Was she overreacting, as usual? Maybe she had drunk a hallucinogenic drug that someone had slipped into a drink. She studied the young actor's face for a lingering moment, squinting her eyes. Was it her imagination? Was the grin actually cold and hostile, or was it warm and friendly? And was the gleam in the eyes hinting . . . madness?

Was she seeing something that wasn't there?

"Stop staring at me like that," Jake said, his tone surprisingly harsh.

No, it wasn't her imagination. Something was very wrong, and by staring at Jake she had made it worse. His face was reddening while the grin and the eyes widened.

"I said stop staring at me like that!"

"You . . . you've changed, Jake."

"Changed? How?" he demanded. The smile dissolved and became a snarl.

Gracefully, Shelly tried to extricate herself from him, but his hands gripped her arms tighter, hurting her.

"L-let me go!" Her voice was weak and timid, not firm as she had intended it to be.

"How have I changed?" he demanded again.

"I don't know. Maybe I'm not feeling well; maybe it's something I drank. Just . . . just let me go . . . please."

He glared at her, but kept hold of her. "I don't like you Shelly Ludden," he said slowly, menacingly. "Do you know that?"

"Jake, for the last time, let . . . me . . . go!"

"Do you want to know why I don't like you?"

"No, I don't. I don't care—"

" 'Cause you're a slut, Shelly, and you rejected me for an asshole. And no slut, Shelly, rejects *me* for an asshole."

Shelly felt panic rising inside her. What on earth was

wrong with Jake? He was crazy. Maybe *he* had drunk acid or something. "Jake!" she cried, now twisting desperately to free herself. "Get your hands off me—*now*!"

"I'm going to make you pay for what you did to me, bitch."

Then panic erupted, nearly suffocating her. His grip on her was too strong. Unless she kneed him in the groin she would not escape from it. Frantically, she glanced at the people around her. Most of them solemnly were watching her, but none were intense with hatred as Jake was. "Get him away from me!" she pleaded.

To her relief, a brawny young man came over. "Get your fuckin' hands off 'er, fella," he snarled, his face inches away from Jake's.

But Jake, although he was at least three inches shorter and 20 pounds lighter, lifted his chin in defiance. "Fuck off . . . *fella*."

The brawny man's temper flared. His eyes blazed and a nerve jumped furiously in his jaw. With his huge hand he seized Jake's throat and threatened to lift him off the floor.

Shelly broke away, then from a safe distance shouted, "Don't hurt him, for God's sake! Just get him out of here!"

The young man considered this, keeping Jake in his grip. He reminded Shelly of Frankenstein's monster dumbly debating whether or not to kill his prev.

"Get him out of here!" Shelly reiterated.

This time he listened. Releasing his hand from Jake's throat, he twisted the young actor's right arm until it was pinned against his back, then shoved him out of the room. Jake's eyes, Shelly noted, still had the wild, maniacal gleam. He struggled, determined to overpower the bigger guy as he was pushed through four rooms and out of the house.

Shelly watched, stunned, as the muscular man slapped his hands clean, like a barroom bouncer in a slapstick comedy. Leaving the door open, he walked back into the foyer, then disappeared into the crowd. Shelly looked out into the night and saw Jake pick himself up from the walk, stagger, then start back toward the house.

"Go away," she hissed, then closed the door, locking it. As she expected, Jake soon began to pound at the door, determined to get back in. Shelly quickly moved away, not wanting to hear such desperation. She shivered, for she was suddenly reminded of an old horror movie she'd seen, something about the living dead. Corpses had risen from their graves and tried to force their way into a house, pounding doggedly to get at the people inside, just as Jake was doing now.

What was wrong with Jake?

Too much booze? Too much drugs?

Hugging herself, for the shivering would not cease, Shelly tried to lose herself in the party. She liked Jake, but she also liked everyone else here. She really shouldn't concern herself with one person and let him spoil the party for everyone else.

A woman looked at her strangely, and Shelly, not certain why she was being stared at like this, forced a smile. But the woman only snorted and looked away.

What was going on?

Why was everyone acting so . . . so weird?

She threaded her way through the living room, noticing not one person was laughing or smiling, no matter how friendly she tried to be, but in the dining room it was a little different. Some of her friends seemed to be in a sour mood, some depressed, but at least there were some smiles and amicable chatter. The atmosphere in the main study and library were much better, almost jovial, but in the recreation room, where Jake had played pool, hostility was unmistakable in the smoke-filled air.

"What is going on?" She uttered the thought out loud this time. People glared at her, eyes hard with . . . hate? But why? She had done nothing to harm or offend anyone. Or had she? She tried to think back, but could come up with nothing.

When she had left with Tony for the bedroom everybody was having a wonderful time, but when she came back out, everything was different.

Something had happened while she and Tony made love.

But what?

Maybe Tony would have some ideas, she suddenly thought. She looked around for him, but before she found him her eyes caught the mess on the floor near the pool table. One of her favorite porcelain vases had fallen from a table and been smashed to pieces. Groaning, Shelly kneeled to pick up the broken shards, then gave up and dropped them back onto the floor. Someone, probably Jake, had crushed and ground most of the pieces with his heel while playing pool. Also, Shelly noted that flowers had been stepped on, almost beyond recognition. Absently she picked up a few petals, then let them fall through her splayed fingers.

Who had put these flowers here? Where had they come from?

She stood up and brushed off her hands, for yellowish, pollenlike dust was stuck to them from the petals. As she rubbed her palms together, a sweet but choking odor assailed her.

"Whew!" She turned her head aside and held her hands farther away. Then she threaded her way toward Tony and had him smell her hands. He, too, pulled his head back, wrinkling his face as though he had just taken a whiff of smelling salts.

Then Shelly asked him what he thought was happening to her party.

Molly shut off the TV, her hearing aid, then the lights. She tried to let the silence and darkness tranquilize her, allowing her imagination to wander. She pretended she was a beautiful movie star lying on her bed in her dressing room. There were fans outside her door, pleading for her autograph, but she needed her beauty sleep. There were flowers all around her, all from her fans, of course.

But they—the flowers—were keeping her up.

The smell was too strong.

Molly told herself that it wasn't so; they were lovely. They made the room smell the way a movie star's dressing room was supposed to smell.

But she couldn't convince herself. She was not a movie star, and this was not her dressing room. There were no loyal fans banging at her door. The noise that she heard now and then came from the party downstairs, and the flowers no longer smelled lovely. She now knew that the odor was so sweet that it was rotten, like meat that had gone bad.

It was now the smell of decay.

Molly considered opening a window, then rejected the idea. The outside air would probably only make it worse. So she turned the lamp back on, climbed out of bed and took the flowers into the bathroom down the hall. Here, she flushed them down the toilet.

She felt a tinge of sadness, hating to see something she had grown be destroyed, but the smell . . . Her room was too small for such a strong fragrance.

After the flowers had spiraled out of sight, she closed the lid of the toilet, then went back into her room. Without her hearing aid, the noise from the party below bounced off her ear, vibrating with loudness

It made her uneasy. She wanted to peek at the party, yet she didn't.

She closed the door to her room, hurried back into her bed, and snapped off the light. The silence and darkness returned, and this time she managed to let her imagination carry her away.

She was on a barge and was a queen, not Cleopatra but someone younger and yes, even lovelier. She drifted and drifted while servants fanned her with big ostrich feathers.

On the banks of the river handsome boys waved and blew kisses at her. She lazily returned the gestures while she continued to drift . . .

And drift.

And beyond the banks there was a party. A loud party. It was a party beyond control.

13

The young actor eventually became exhausted. He had pounded fiercely at the thick oak door, but the sound, he knew, was lost amidst the cacophony of music inside. He resorted to kicking at the door and tugging at the large brass handle, but it was useless. That bitch Shelly had locked him out, and locked him out damn good!

Jake had cursed her, calling her everything from a spoiled snob to a flabby cunt. Then, when he was leaning against the hard wood of the door, breathing laboriously and sweating profusely, he began to forget why he was so damn furious. A whiff of cool salt air cleared his head somewhat, yet made his memory even fuzzier.

What had happened?

Why was the damn door locked anyway? He could hear that a party was in progress, and he could remember actually being at this party. So why the hell was he standing on this side of the door?

He rubbed his drenched forehead. He didn't feel too well all of a sudden. He felt like he used to feel when he was a teenager and had drunk too much beer too fast. Everything around him was spinning, and his lungs were heavy and tight, as though squeezed together with twine or something. His skin was cold and clammy, and he knew that any minute now he was going to throw up.

He pushed himself away from the door, stumbled over to the side of the circular driveway, and did exactly that.

Then he lost consciousness.

And while he was under, the salt air continuously caressed him, filling his lungs and his head, filling him until his memory of the party was no more.

Tony told her he was just as puzzled as she, but he didn't want to talk anymore about it. He wanted a drink, so he abruptly left her and headed for the kitchen where, on the central island, the numerous bottles were standing. This incensed Shelly. She wasn't certain why, but it did.

Her emotions, it seemed, were like a group of wild animals. Usually each was on a leash confined to a cage, but now they were all loose, wild and out of control.

She had no reason to be angry with Tony. So what if he left her—rudely at that—for a drink? And come to think of it, she needed a drink, too.

When she reached the kitchen, Tony was just emerging. He gave her a curt nod, and she experienced a fresh stab of anger. He thinks I'm a slut, she thought. That's what he thinks!

She forced down a caustic remark and entered the kitchen. As she poured herself a glass of champagne she became aware of someone watching her. Looking up from the glass, she met a woman's gaze. It was Maggie Tracy, another romance writer.

"Hello, Maggie," Shelly said, greeting her, but the woman said nothing in return, only continued to stare.

Shelly never liked Maggie but had invited her here because she didn't want anyone to suspect she was envious of the woman's literary talent. She and Maggie were both successful, but the critics always favored Maggie over her, and this bothered her—especially now.

Shelly found herself glaring back at the other woman with only the central island separating them.

"What the hell are you looking at?" Shelly demanded.

But the woman continued to glare.

"Stop staring at me," Shelly demanded, then realized with some surprise that these same words had been uttered by Jake. What did this mean?

What the hell was happening? she asked herself for the hundredth time.

She was about to take her glass and leave the kitchen when Maggie said, "I read your novel, the one you've just completed."

"But, dear, it's not even published yet." Shelly gave her a short laugh.

"I've read the manuscript."

"You wha—"

"In your study." Maggie shrugged her shoulders. "I helped myself."

An acrid feeling began to scorch her insides. "Why, you had no right to snoop—"

"The work is rather good, but as usual, it is inferior to any of mine."

Shelly's hand fought a sudden impulse to toss the champagne into the other woman's face, but the glare was confusing her. Shouldn't Maggie be smiling complacently at her? Why in God's heaven was she angry, then?

"You've stolen not only the overall theme from one of my earlier novels, but some of my characters as well," Maggie said accusingly, as though reading her thoughts. Her words dripped with contempt and indignation. She skirted the central island, moving closer.

"Don't be silly, dear." Shelly took a step back, then another, clutching her glass of champagne. It was true; she had taken two characters from Maggie's earlier novel, dressed them up a little differently and put them in her new work. As for the themes and ideas—well, they were a dime a dozen. "Don't be silly," she said again.

"You are . . . disgusting," Maggie hissed, and for an instant it looked as if she would actually slap Shelly. The woman's hand was raised, long fingers splayed, but it then closed into a fist, hesitated a beat, then dropped. "Yes, disgusting!"

Then she sneered at Shelly, passed her, and was gone.

Shelly watched the kitchen door swing back and forth for a lingering moment. In all the years she'd known

Maggie, and they were many, she'd never seen the
woman lose her composure like this. Maggie had always
been one to mask her feelings. Nothing flustered or
rankled her. Only her novels were passionate and
emotional.

This was a side of Maggie she'd never seen before.

Then Shelly remembered that she, herself, had a reason
to be furious. Maggie had snooped in her study and read
her manuscript. The nerve of that bitch! Even Momma
hadn't been allowed to read any of her work before it was
published, and no one was closer to her than Momma
had been.

Draining the glass and then refilling it, Shelly went
back out to the party. She struggled to push Maggie out
of her mind, determined not to let the woman spoil her
celebration. She took another sizable swallow of
champagne, but instead of extinguishing the bitter fire
inside her, it seemed to make it flare and spread. Like
trying to douse a kitchen pan fire, she reflected, liquid
only made it worse.

God, she despised that woman now, more than she'd
ever despised anyone.

Looking around the living room, she then spotted
Tony. The inner fire flared again. She despised him, too,
almost as much as the writer. No, she decided on second
thought. She despised them both equally.

She took yet another large sip, no longer caring that
she was fueling her ill will. Over the rim of her glass she
watched the young photographer.

He was deep in conversation with a small group of men
—and he was talking about her. She was certain of it! She
could almost hear him recount their upstairs sexual
encounter that had taken place less than 15 minutes ago.
He was telling them what a slut she was. Telling them that
she was dirt.

Damn him!
Damn Maggie!
Damn—

With her free hand she touched her forehead. God, was she dizzy! She felt as though she had drunk a case of champagne rather than a few glasses. The room was spinning, and the people's faces were blurring. She closed her eyes, drew in a breath, then reopened her eyes. The room stopped spinning, but the faces were still a little fuzzy—recognizable, but still fuzzy.

She waited a few minutes, until she felt steady and strong enough, then she moved through the crowd. Nobody's laughing, she thought again. Everybody is so damn sober and grim, and yet, everybody seems to be drinking.

"What's the matter, damnit!" she snapped aloud at everyone in general, but only a few gave her a glance. Everyone was in a sour mood.

Just like her.

Fuck 'em all! She went into the next room, and then the next. She found herself staggering and stumbling. Maybe she had drunk more than just a few glasses of champagne. She leaned against a fireplace, touched her forehead again and waited for the dizziness to subside.

Then she saw a commotion on the camel back sofa. She had to blink to clear her vision. It was like peering into an aquarium; the air seemed watery, making everything waver. She saw two men and a woman. The faces were familiar, but her mind was too hazy to remember. It wasn't their faces, anyway, that arrested her attention; it was their naked bodies. They were engaged in sexual intercourse.

Shelly's brain told her she should be shocked and furious, for the threesome should at least have had the decency to go into one of the bedrooms, but instead, she felt a strange detachment. Everyone else, it seemed, felt the same way, looking away, as though bored.

Shelly watched for a minute, then she, too, grew bored. She was ready to leave for another room when she heard the woman on the sofa scream. It wasn't a piercing scream but sounded as though a wall of glass had muted it. It was almost dreamlike, and what she saw was almost dreamlike, too.

The woman was on her hands and knees with one man in front of her and the other behind her, but it was at the latter that Shelly found herself staring. This man held something in his right hand. At first she could not make it out, because it blurred in her wavery vision. Then she saw a silvery gleam as it caught the light on an upward swing. It rose in a wide arc, high above the man's head, then it fell back down in slow motion. Then it plunged into the woman's naked back. When it rose again, it dripped bright red liquid, then it sprayed the liquid as it swung upward again. It was a knife—a carving knife from the kitchen.

Shelly thought of screaming herself as the knife kept plunging into the woman's back, shredding it into a crimson, pulpy sea, but instead, she was mesmerized, fascinated with the repeated motion of the knife. As though hypnotized, she watched the blade, once silver, turn redder and redder. The woman was still screaming, twisting and thrashing to get away, but the man in front of her held firm. This, too, seemed to fascinate Shelly.

When the woman stopped and slumped forward, Shelly backed away, still thinking she should react differently. She knew she had just witnessed a horror, but why wasn't she feeling any of this horror? Why was she feeling so . . . detached?

Still woozy, she staggered toward another part of the room. Nobody, she noted, was concerned about the woman on the sofa, so why should she be? Sipping on her drink, she allowed herself to forget about the killing. She found a man crumpled in a corner on the floor. Unconscious from too much booze? She tried to remember the face—after all she did know everybody she had invited—but no name came to mind.

Then she spotted a dark stain on the man's ample belly. She had to move closer to be sure, her eyes still blurry. Then when she knew what she was looking at, she stopped. She should have let out a gasp, at least, but she didn't. She was too fascinated.

The dark stain on the man's paunch was blood, and it was still wet and spreading. In the center of it was a knife. Somebody's robbing my kitchen, Shelly thought dimly. Then she saw that the blood was dripping onto the floor. And somebody is ruining my carpet!

Shelly felt fury erupt inside her again. Didn't anyone know how dear this house and its furnishings were to her? Didn't anyone care about her feelings at all? She loved this house, loved it more than anyone in it. The house was part of her. It was her friend, was always there, warm whenever the city was too cold.

Damn anyone who'd try to hurt her friend!

When she saw Tony, her fury exploded. He was making love to Maggie on the carpet in the middle of the room, and everyone was stepping around or over them, scarcely giving them a glance.

Shelly lunged after the couple. "Damn you!" she shrieked, raking her nails across Tony's bare back. Both he and Maggie turned and glared at her, but their eyes were no longer normal. They had taken on a reddish shine. Then something began to drip from them like thick raindrops, except the color was bright red. Blood? Shelly frowned, more confused than horrified. As before, she stared in speechless fascination as the bloody tears trickled in huge droplets down their faces, streaking and smearing the cheeks red in their wake.

Shelly suddenly wanted another sip of champagne, but the glass had been discarded somewhere along the way. So she stared stupidly, mouth agape, at the couple.

Tony grinned at her, the same way Jake had done before she had him thrown out, but this grin didn't chill her as the other had. It surprised her then, remembering that he had probably told everyone she was a slut, infuriated her. She reached out and dug her long nails into his cheek.

Maggie howled in protest but did nothing to avenge her

temporary mate, and Tony only continued to glare and grin. He hissed at her, and Shelly hissed back, sounds that were strange and distant to her ears. Then Tony's mouth parted and watery blood trickled out, staining the teeth and reddening the gums. The blood, partly turning to pink froth, drooled down his chin and wormed its way down his chest. Shelly watched as it coursed its way down his torso and finally puddled on the carpet beneath him.

"Damn you!" she cried. "I love that carpet!"

Tony did nothing, just glared and kept his mouth parted so that the blood could stream continuously, like water from a hose.

"Stop it!" she screamed. "Stop it, stop it!"

She raked his cheek again, wishing he'd do something besides glare at her like that; even cold laughter would have been better. The stare was making her more furious, and she found herself matching that glare, throwing back the hate that he was giving her.

"You're ruining my carpet, you bastard!"

But he didn't care. Nobody here cared!

"Damn you! I'll make you pay. I'll make you . . ." Her threat died in her throat as she glanced at a wall. Something was rippling beneath the silk, floral wallpaper. Shelly gawked at it until her fuzzy vision cleared a little, as though by sheer will and determination. Then she saw what was on the wall. Termites!

Termites were eating her house!

"Oh . . . my . . . God." She didn't know whether to scream with rage or weep. "My . . . house . . ." She looked over at the wall with the fireplace. More bugs were crawling over the paneling, chomping and chomping.

She looked frantically at Tony, who stared evenly back.

"My house!" she yelled at him. "They're eating my house!"

He still said nothing. Next to him Maggie hissed at her, like a snake, readying to attack.

"Damn you! Damn you all!" Shelly knew she was

overreacting, but then, she always did. She lifted her hair
from the back of her neck and glanced around her. What
to do? Her eyes locked on the fireplace poker. She'd
show that bastard Tony a thing or two. She'd teach him
not to treat her and her house with disrespect!

Seizing the poker, she swung it toward the
photographer, but his agility surprised her. Before she
could slam the heavy instrument against the side of his
skull, he grabbed it and yanked it away from her.

She gasped, then staggered back, still light-headed
from . . . champagne?

Then, he slowly rose to his feet, looking like some kind
of naked god holding aloft a spear, his horrible glare
never wavering. It bore into her, burning with hatred.
Shelly should have cowered in a corner under that gaze,
but she stood up to him, locking her eyes with his. She
hated him. God, how she hated him. And, she knew he
hated her. In fact, everybody in this room, in this house,
hated everybody else. The air was electrically charged
with the black emotion.

Tony raised the poker high over his head, then with all
the strength he could muster, let it crash down onto an
antique tavern table.

"Noooo!" Shelly cried belatedly. The poker had
snapped the piece in two. "That's Poppa's," she wailed.
"I was with him when he bought it. He loved that table
. . . and so did I!"

Tony coldly watched her. The only change in his hard
countenance was a faint, complacent smile.

Shelly lunged for the poker, but Tony, being so much
taller, lifted it high over his head and out of her reach.

"It's only a table, Shelly." He spoke at last, his voice
emotionless and flat like a robot's.

"It's more than a table," Shelly retorted. "Everything
in this house was important to Poppa. It showed that
he'd made it, that he was a success."

"And that's why you love this house? Because your
daddy did?"

"It's no concern of yours. Just give me that—"

"Like daddy, like daughter. You both became successful. There was a lot of love in this house, eh?"

Shelly didn't answer.

The faint smirk on Tony's face grew more evident. He looked over at Maggie, still beside him. "What do you think of all that love in this house?"

Maggie hissed again, snakelike, catlike.

The photographer's grin vanished altogether. With the hard, grim countenance back, he aimed and slammed the poker into the chandelier above him. Crystal exploded with a sharp crack and tinkle, then colorless shards sprinkled down on them.

"You fucking bastard!"

Tony and Maggie ignored her and turned to each other. They kissed, then dropped to the floor to continue their lovemaking. In his hand, Tony still clutched the brass poker.

Rage shook Shelly. Certain that she'd never find the strength to pry the instrument from Tony's grip, she searched for something else. In the next room, the main study, she grabbed a silver letter opener from off the desk. The instrument felt heavy in her hand, the ornate handle etching its carving of a twisted serpent into her palm, giving her a sense of power and a surge of confidence. She ran back into the other room, back to Tony.

Never had she experienced such determination to kill. Her body trembled with the urge, her blood pounding in her head, nearly blinding and deafening her. Nothing was going to stop her.

But when she reached Tony, she found that someone else had beat her. Tony and Maggie lay immobile in each other's arms, their skulls smashed, reminding her of crushed eggshells, but instead of yolks and whites seeping through the shattered crowns, it was blood and clumps of gray brain matter she saw. Standing over them was a man holding a gilded candlestick that had been on the fireplace mantle. He turned to Shelly, glared at her, then went away.

Shelly watched him leave, stunned. Then she dropped to her knees and plunged the letter opener into Tony's chest. She did this over and over, because the more she did this, the better she felt.

"Bastard! Bastard!" she screamed.

She still could hear the termites in the walls, chomping, so she screamed louder to drown out the sound.

"Bastard! . . . Bastard! . . ."

Certain sounds or tones, if loud enough, would penetrate Molly's silent world. Usually these sounds would be felt rather than heard, or sometimes it would be just a hint of a sound. But when these reached her, she would know there was noise around her—a lot of it.

And when it managed to wake her up, then there was cause for alarm.

In the dark Molly sat up in her bed and reached for her hearing aid. When she snapped on the plastic device she was able to hear more noise, but because she had nerve deafness, it was difficult to differentiate the sounds. Her hearing was something like the keys on a piano, with most of the keys broken. Some notes could be heard, but with so many of them missing, it was nearly impossible to make out a tune.

Molly climbed out of bed and pressed her head against the door. She heard some more but still couldn't make it out. Then she opened the door and timidly stepped out into the hallway. Her heart thundering, certain that something was wrong, she moved toward the stairs and looked down over the railing.

Now that she could see the people's mouths, she knew what she was hearing. Screams. Everybody, it seemed, was screaming, and everybody seemed to be going crazy.

Molly gaped, fear paralyzing her. She remained frozen for a long moment, trying to understand why everyone was screaming the way they were, and why some of them had such mean, hideous expressions on their faces. Then the paralysis broke and she bolted for her room.

When she reached it she locked the door, then put a chair under the knob for good measure.

14

The hotel room overlooked the ocean, but the water was black under the night sky. Only the whitecaps of the waves and the spectral reflection of the moon could be seen, but Lara still found it romantic. As she stood on the third-story terrace, she smiled in remembrance of their lovemaking on the beach less than 30 minutes before. It had been wonderful with the sand under them, the waves lapping their legs and the salty breeze fanning their bodies.

Steve stepped out onto the terrace and, from behind, slipped his arms around her. He kissed her neck, then a spot behind her ear, making her shiver with delight. "I love you." His voice was husky and muffled against her skin.

Lara, still smiling, moaned softly, savoring the delicious sensation his warm lips made on her ear and neck. The night had only just begun.

Then she thought of Molly. Was she all right? The question had appeared out of nowhere, as though her motherly instincts had been in the wings all night, waiting for a moment, no matter how brief, to rush to the center of the stage.

Had she been wrong to leave her daughter behind? Wrong to leave her alone with—

"Hon?" Steve whispered, gently turning her around to face him.

"What?"

"You're tense all of a sudden. What's wrong?"

"I'm sorry, darling."

Lara sighed, burying her face in Steve's chest. She couldn't stop worrying. Why did she have to start thinking about Molly? The night had been so perfect until now.

"Hon." Steve gripped her shoulders, urging her to look at him. "What's the matter?"

She sighed, realizing it was useless. Once the worrying started, it could not be stopped. "I'm worried about Molly."

"Why?"

"I'm not sure if I did the right thing leaving her alone with Shelly and her friends. Steve, what kind of people are her friends, do you know?"

"I've never met any of them."

"Do you think Molly will be safe with them?"

"Sure. Why, what kind of people do you fear they might be? Murderers? Child molesters?" There was a faint smile on his face, as though he found her apprehension amusing.

"You think I'm worrying needlessly, but I can't help it. I *am* worried."

"Oh, hon, she'll be all right. I'm sure my sister doesn't have any psychos for friends."

"But I bet she has weirdos, potheads and—"

"Nobody's going to hurt Molly," Steve assured her, his voice suddenly gentle. He kissed her forehead, which was level with his lips. He was endeavoring to soothe her, but she couldn't push Molly out of her mind.

"She's so vulnerable, Steve. People could take advantage of her because of . . ."

"Her handicap?"

She nodded.

"Hon, she's a brilliant kid. She can take care of herself, and it's time you start letting her. You're overprotecting her."

"That's not true."

He didn't answer, didn't have to. Lara knew he had spoken the truth. "Oh Steve, I just . . . I just can't help it. I don't want anyone to hurt her. She's been hurt so much. The kids at school take advantage of her, call her names right in front of her. They think she won't hear them, but she can always tell what they're doing. She can tell whenever she's the butt of a joke. And they make fun of the way she talks, Steve. She came home crying one day because a kid wanted to know why she still talks baby talk. Now she's too shy to talk to people, afraid someone will mock her or laugh at her."

"But overprotecting her isn't going to solve anything."

"Oh, I know that. I just can't help it."

Steve searched her face, and his eyes gleamed with admiration. "A genuine mother, if ever I saw one." Then he covered her lips with his. The kiss was long and gentle, appeasing her to a degree. When he pulled his head back, he said, "Maybe you should give her a call."

"She wouldn't hear the phone ring, and besides, she has a difficult time talking into it."

"Talk to Shelly. Have her put Molly on. Maybe you'll feel better if you hear her voice."

Lara mulled over this. Perhaps it was a good idea. She could just ask her daughter if everything was all right; that shouldn't be too hard to do. She'd repeat the question until Molly understood it.

"Yes," she decided at length, "I'll do just that." She gave Steve a quick kiss, as though thanking him for the suggestion, then she reached for the phone.

Molly strained to hear everything that was happening beyond her locked door. She caught screeches which were within her limited hearing range. Certain high-pitched sounds she could hear, but mostly there was only frustrating silence—a silence that was frightening her. She wished she could hear what was happening; she hated knowing something terrible was going on, but not knowing exactly what it was.

She wished her mother were home.

She tried to lose herself in the jigsaw puzzle but couldn't keep her eyes away from the door, as though expecting it to burst open at any moment. She turned the TV back on, but that didn't hold her attention either. There was nothing she could do except wait. But wait for what? For the party to be over? For her mother to return in the morning? Which would be first? She remembered her mother mentioning that the party might last all night—and morning.

Another scream reached her ears. Cold goosebumps popped out on her arms. She rubbed them, endeavoring to warm and smooth her skin. Was that a cry for help she had heard? Why was someone screaming? Was someone being . . . murdered?

Mom, don't go to that hotel. Please change your mind and come back home!

Another scream touched the edge of her hearing, then was snuffed out by silence. Molly could feel, almost hear, blood pounding in her ears.

Maybe she should call the police.

But you hate to talk on the phone. You can hardly hear yourself talk into it, never mind hear the person on the other end.

But she had to do something. She had to get help. People were screaming downstairs.

Molly kept rubbing her arms, but the goosebumps and the chill wouldn't go away. Suddenly she experienced an overwhelming urge to cry, I'm not a baby, she told herself. I'm brave like Nancy Drew.

Yes, she would have to be calm and call the police.

Decision made, she mustered up courage and unlocked her bedroom door. The nearest phone, she knew, was in her mother and Steve's bedroom, which was two doors away—and closer to the stairs.

As she stepped out into the hallway, she heard a series of screams. It occurred to her to turn off her hearing aid, for maybe complete silence would be better than semi-silence, but she couldn't bring herself to do this. She already felt too vulnerable.

Commanding herself not to look over the banister to the foyer below, she hurried toward her destination, but before reaching it, her eyes disobeyed and glanced below. A mistake! A man caught her glance, and the horrible expression on his face made her freeze. Never had she seen such rage in someone's face. Lips were curled back exposing too many teeth, nostrils flared rhythmically like a furious pulse, and the eyes—oh, the eyes—sparked violent fire. A rabid dog, she thought, couldn't even look this mean. This was a face of a murderer. She was sure of it.

The man began to climb the stairs toward her.

No, nooo! her mind screamed. Then she remembered she was standing stock-still. She broke into a run, at last reached her destination, and slammed and locked the door after her. Then for a horrible moment she wondered if maybe she'd been wrong in believing there was a phone in here. She almost cried out in relief when she spotted it on the fancy antique desk.

But when she picked up the receiver it dawned on her that she didn't know the police department's number.

Call the operator, stupid!

With a trembling finger, she dialed "O". After what seemed like forever, a faint voice came on. She could hear a continuous mumble but could not make out any words.

"What? What?" she repeated, pleading for clarity.

But only more indistinct mumbling answered her.

"Ded me the police," Molly demanded into the phone, praying that she had replied correctly.

But the frustrating mumbling was back, louder and markedly edged with impatience. Molly fought back the panic that usually came whenever she knew communication would not be possible.

"I need the police!" she cried into the receiver. "The police!" Abruptly, Molly realized the operator had no way of knowing where this call was coming from, and to add to the frustration, she didn't even know the address of this house, only its name. "Ludden House," she blurted desperately. "I'm ad Ludden House." She let the tears that were burning her eyes spill down her face. "Please! Ded the police!"

The faint, mumbling ran on again, then nothing. With a sinking, horrible feeling she knew the operator had hung up on her.

She started to dial the operator again, then saw the knob on the door twist to the left, then to the right. It moved slowly, then furiously. In her mind she could hear it rattle.

She gawked at the door, then remembered the windows and ran to one of them. Under the weak moonlight she could see the ground far below. If she jumped from the window she'd land on hard earth and hurt herself, maybe even . . .

Refusing to think of the horrible possibility, she looked back at the door. The knob was still turning side to side, and now the door was shaking. Whoever was behind it was trying to break it down!

No, nooooo!

Lara let the phone ring 15 times, and even then she hesitated to hang up. Troubled and fighting the alarm that was stirring inside her, she stared numbly at the phone. Why wouldn't anyone answer? There are at least a half dozen phones in that house. Somebody should have answered, especially if there's a party.

Finally, Lara hung up. She still wanted to stay at the hotel, but she knew she would not enjoy herself until she was certain that Molly was okay.

"No one answers," she said, sitting down on the edge of the bed. Steve moved toward her and gently massaged her back.

"Don't be such a worrywart," he whispered.

But she scarcely heard him or felt his touch. "Why didn't anyone answer?"

"Loud music, probably."

She mulled this over and even tried to convince herself that Steve was right. Loud music would drown out the ringing of a phone, but again she remembered how many phones were in that house. Certainly someone would happen to be near one, and the shrill ring from a nearby phone would be heard over the music, wouldn't it?

Somehow, perhaps due to motherly instincts, she was certain something was wrong.

She drew in a deep breath, and when she released it in a long sigh, she came to a decision. "Steve, I want to go home."

Steve's fingers massaging her neck and shoulders stopped, then fell away. She could feel him stare at her back. After a long moment, he said, "You sure?" Disappointment was evident in his voice.

"Yes." She turned around to face him. "Darling, I'm so sorry for ruining everything, but . . ."

"But you can't stop worrying," he said.

She nodded, not certain if she had detected a hard edge in his voice. "I'll make it up to you," she promised.

"It's okay." He gave her a smile, but she couldn't tell if the smile was genuine. "Well, might as well start packing—for the second time today."

"I'm sorry," she said again and kissed him to prove it.

"I understand."

But she didn't believe him. This was something only a mother would understand.

Molly huddled against the window frame, shivering with fright. Her eyes never left the door that was still rattling violently. She saw light under the door, and a shadow appearing and disappearing like a wave as someone retreated, then slammed against the wood.

No, nooooo. Please, God! Make him, her—it—go away!

And for a moment there was actually stillness.

Molly sobbed with relief, then cried out in horror as the person on the other side slammed against the door with stronger force. Shoving a fist into her mouth, a reaction that she thought only occurred in dramatic movies, she pressed harder against the window. She squeezed her eyes shut, hoping that when she reopened them she'd find herself awakening from a dream and see no knob twisting, no door rattling.

Opening her eyes, she looked out the window, now seriously considering jumping out of it. She struggled to push up the sash, and for a horrible instant thought it was nailed shut. But after straining and using all her strength, it gave, skidding to a halt after a few inches. With determination she persevered until it gave again and rose three more inches. Now it was wide enough to squeeze through.

Then her head shot back toward the door. It was still locked. She didn't have to jump out yet. She'd wait until the last minute, until there was no choice.

She heard shouting, and realized with numbing dread that there were at least two persons behind the door, for there were two difference voices. She couldn't, of course, make out the words which were only dull stabs of sound punctuating the pounding of blood in her ears.

"Go away!" she cried. "Please! Please!"

Why were they after her? What had she done?

She started to crawl through the window, telling herself she'd only break a leg or arm. She wouldn't die.

Then her ears picked up another sound—long and wailing—but since she could not tell from which direction the sound came, she assumed it was from behind the door. She could not imagine what the sound could be, and not knowing intensified her frustration and panic.

At that moment the door burst open. A young man and a lady with orange hair spilled into the room from the door's sudden release. They fell onto the floor, and Molly, seeing that they were struggling to their feet as though intoxicated, seized the moment to make her escape. She pushed herself away from the window, leaped over them, and bolted out of the room.

When she reached the hallway she fleetingly saw more people coming up the stairs. Everyone had that horrible look of fury on their faces. Angry enough to kill, she thought. For a quick instant she stood indecisively, trying to think of a place to hide. Then she broke into a run back toward her own room where she locked the door and once again jammed a chair under its knob.

Also once again, the pounding soon began.

Molly pressed her back against a corner and slid to the floor. She began to cry, for she didn't know what else to do. It was either this or scream, and she was suddenly too weak to scream. She buried her face in her hands and sobbed convulsively.

Again she heard that confusing wailing sound. Then through her blurry tears she saw lights flickering at the window—red, blue, red again.

She jumped up and ran to the window. Then her tears were those of relief.

The police were here.

15

When they reached the driveway of the big house Lara's hands gripped the dashboard, as though to restrain herself from moving ahead faster than the car, and when the car stopped she flung open the door and bolted past the police cruisers and vans. Blinding red and blue lights swept across her.

My baby! My baby! she cried inwardly. A police officer intercepted her, and the cry reached her lips. "My baby! My baby's in there!"

Behind her, Steve said something, and the officer glanced at another officer. There was a nod of approval, then the first officer stepped aside and Lara dashed toward the front door. Steve and the officers followed.

Before she reached the door, it sprung open and two policemen emerged ushering a small group of people to the van in the driveway. These people's eyes, she fleetingly noted, were cold, shiny, and detached, unaware that policemen were leading them to a vehicle. They even seemed unaware that they were walking. Also, she caught the chilling contempt on their faces. Something embittered them, but it wasn't the police or their surroundings. The fury seemed to be focused at something inside them, perhaps at something that existed only in their minds.

"What the hell happened?" she heard Steve demand.

"We're not sure yet, sir," the officer replied.

But Lara's main concern was about Molly. Where was she? Was she safe? Without looking around her, Lara rushed for the stairs, thinking and hoping the girl would still be in her room. When she reached the room, cold panic gripped and twisted her stomach muscles. Molly was not in here.

Then, just as she was ready to run out of the room to search elsewhere, her eyes spotted the closet door. She had forgotten about the closet in here, and she opened the door, peering into the darkness. She pushed clothes aside and found a black form on the floor, hugging the wall.

"Molly?" She dropped to her knees and reached for the form. At the touch it scrambled deeper into the closet. "Molly," she spoke louder and clearer, "it's me, Mom. Baby, are you all right?"

Molly must have heard and recognized her voice, for she then scrambled forward and threw her arms around her mother. She was sobbing hysterically.

"It's okay, baby. It's okay." Lara stroked the girl's hair, holding her tightly against her. "I'm here now. Everything's going to be okay."

They held each other for a long while in the silent and dark closet. Lara did not loosen her hold on her daughter until she was certain there were no more sobs and that the girl was spent and limp. Then she kissed her daughter's wet cheek and led her out into the light.

An officer and a paramedic met them. "She's all right," Lara informed them, keeping an arm around the girl's shoulders.

The paramedic appraised Molly from a slight distance, then satisfied that she indeed was fine, retreated into the hallway. The officer tarried.

"You sure?" he said.

"Yes. Please, if you have a lot of questions, ask them later. Right now, I'm not thinking right. I . . ."

"Sure, ma'am, I understand. Your husband already

filled me in a bit. I just want to be sure your daughter here is okay."

"Yes, I think she is." Lara looked at Molly resting her head against her shoulder. The girl was pale and seemed exhausted—but safe. Thank God for that!

"Well, I'll be seeing you later." The officer nodded, then turned and left the room.

Lara was surprised to find her own cheeks wet with tears. The fright and relief had made her cry without realizing it. She wiped her eyes, then she turned Molly toward her.

"Sweetheart, what happened?"

Molly told her about the screams she'd heard, the crazed look on the people's faces she'd seen in the foyer and stairs, and about the couple who had broken into the room. "I-I called the police," she finished.

"But nobody touched you. Nobody hurt you, did they?" Lara wanted to be certain.

Molly shook her head. Her eyes began to well up with tears again, but she succeeded in sniffing them back. "No," she said, shaking her head for the second time. "Mom, what happened?"

"I don't know, sweetheart."

"They all looked crazy. They looked—" she paused to search for the right word "—mean. I thought they were gonna kill me, Mom."

"Everything's under control now. The police are here."

"But what happened?"

"Maybe they took drugs. I don't know. I just came back. But I promise you I'll never leave you alone like this again."

"I am a big baby, after all, huh?" Molly said miserably.

"No, you're not a big baby. You're just . . ." She let her voice trail off as she swallowed the word "vulnerable."

"I love you so much," she told her when she spoke again, "and I don't know what I'd do if I lost you."

"I'm sorry, Mom."

"Sorry?" The contrition surprised her.

"I scared you an' I spoiled your night with Steve."

"Oh, sweetheart, that's not what's important right now." What's important, she thought, is that Shelly pays for this! She did this deliberately! She scared the poor girl just to get even with me.

But when she looked down from the stair railing, she found herself not so certain anymore. Paramedics and officers were still shepherding people out of the house, as though they were mindless zombies. Some were slapping at the air, as though something or someone were in front of them, and some were shouting obscenities, and some were screaming in what sounded like excruciating agony.

As Molly had said, some had horribly mean visages.

Madness, the word rushed to her mind. Everyone at the party had gone mad. But why? What happened?

Then Lara noticed the destruction. A beautiful seventeenth century Pilgrim tavern table had been broken in half. An ancient tapestry had been torn from the wall. The chandelier had been smashed. A slat-back chair was upturned with a missing leg, as though it had been hurled against the wall, where there was an ugly gash.

Lara's hand rose to her mouth in disbelief. She knew Shelly would have never allowed this, so this could not have been her doing; the woman loved this house and its furnishings. No, it was something beyond her control.

But what? What on earth happened here?

Holding Molly close to her, they both descended the stairs. Lara's eyes searched for Shelly, but could not find her anywhere. Then they spotted Steve, who had just emerged from the dining room, an officer at his side. The house had been almost emptied of people.

"Where's Shelly?" Lara managed to keep her voice low, but still the indignation she felt was evident.

But Steve signaled her with a faint nod to wait a moment. He walked the officer to the front door, said something to him, then closed the door. For a lingering moment he stood there with his back to Lara and Molly, then he turned to face them. There was grief on his face, and his blue eyes were wet, although he repeatedly blinked to keep them dry.

"Where's Shelly?" Lara demanded again.

Steve glanced at Molly, as though debating whether or not to ask her to leave the room. Then, apparently deciding against it, he cleared his throat and said, "Shelly's on her way to the hospital. They all are."

"Why? My God, what happened, Steve? Molly told me two of them broke open a door trying to get in after her."

"Nobody's sure what happened. The hospital will run some tests and maybe find some answers. Right now they think maybe it has something to do with hallucinogenic drugs or something like that. Everybody just freaked out, I guess."

"Did anybody get hurt?"

"Some suffered nasty bruises and cuts. There were some fights here. From what some of them were saying, it seemed most of them were paranoid. A lot of them believed people wanted to kill them, therefore were reacting in self-defense."

"Did anybody . . ." Lara had to swallow before she could finish ". . . get killed?"

Steve's chest rose then fell in a sigh. "No, thank God."

Lara, too, found herself sighing with relief.

Then Steve added, "But according to Officer Sanderson, Shelly claims to have killed two people."

"Then?" Lara's right brow arched in confusion, expecting him to elaborate.

"She hallucinated the killings."

The next morning Lara began to clean the house. Molly, insisting that she help, washed the kitchen table, counter and floor, for there were spills everywhere. Steve went to the hospital to see Shelly.

Lara found the task of rearranging and uprighting furniture and gathering broken pieces heartbreaking. So many things in here had survived for hundreds of years, she reflected, and in one night they were destroyed needlessly and irreverently. In the study a Tiffany lamp had fallen over the desk and smashed its glass shade on the floor. In the recreation room the Turkish rug was permanently scarred with black cigarette burns. The pool table was ripped, and a Chippendale armchair lacked an arm. In the foyer the face of the grandfather's clock had been smashed, and the hour and minute hands were found in another room. It took Lara the entire morning and most of the afternoon to clean up. When she was done she had a long list of things that needed to be repaired. She would give the list to Steve and have him decide what should be salvaged or discarded.

When Steve finally came home it was late afternoon, the sun casting more shadows than beams. The rooms were dim, as they usually were at this time of day, but they were not as dreary as was Steve's countenance when he entered the house and headed wordlessly for the small portable bar in the library. Lara, watching him, waited until he sat down in the winged chair near the fireplace and took several sips of his Scotch, then she joined him, sitting in an opposite chair.

"How is she?" she asked softly.

Staring pensively at the amber liquid in his hand, he seemed surprised to hear her voice. He looked up slowly, as though awakening from a dream. "Not too good, I'm afraid." He took a long sip, savored it on his tongue, as though stalling for time, then swallowed. He didn't seem to want to talk about his sister but wanted to forget and enjoy his drink. But Lara was waiting, and he knew she had every right to know what he had learned at the hospital.

"Nobody is certain what's wrong with her," he said at length. "She is definitely hallucinating, along with the others who were here last night. They're running tests, but not all the results are in yet. So for the time being they're working in the dark."

"LSD?" Lara wondered out loud.

"They don't think so. The hallucinations are continuous, and there are no signs of them fading. The most puzzling part is that everyone seems to be having exactly the same reactions."

"What do you mean?" Lara moved forward to the edge of the seat.

"All are angry at someone in their minds. They all believe that someone wishes to harm them, even kill them."

"Paranoia?" She remembered this had been surmised last night.

"Yes. So far only one person seems to have overcome the drug, or whatever the hell it was. He came to the hospital when he heard that everybody at the party had been admitted. I don't remember his name, but he's an out-of-work actor and was here last night. He said he couldn't remember too much, only that he was at the party one minute and then lying on the ground near the driveway the next. The police and a doctor urged him to try to remember everything he'd taken at the party, but he claimed he'd only drunk whiskey and smoked one joint. Nothing else."

"Joint . . . whiskey?" Lara mused over the possibility.

"Not everybody was drinking whiskey, but all the booze was confiscated last night and they're testing, just to be sure. Same for all the marijuana and cocaine they found here and on the people, but so far nothing out of the ordinary was discovered."

"But this actor is all right now, isn't he?"

"They're testing him to be sure, but he seems okay, except for that blackout. He doesn't remember anything, and the hospital and police think maybe he hadn't been at the party long enough for this thing, whatever it is, to have a strong effect on him. If he had stayed longer, maybe he'd have been just like the rest of them."

"Do you think Shelly will be all right?" She realized no one at the hospital could possibly predict the outcome, but she wanted to know what Steve's gut feeling was.

"I don't know, hon. I really don't." He took another swallow, stared thoughtfully at the glass, then went on, "She's in the psychiatric ward—they all are. That place is pandemonium. It's as if everybody in there is having a horrible nightmare but can't wake up. It goes on and on."

"Oh, my God," Lara whispered.

"The screaming never stops," he continued, "and the air is thick with hate. Everybody resents everybody else. Nobody trusts anyone. It's real bad in there, Lara. I could only stay in that ward for about fifteen minutes at a time. All the screaming and bad vibes would get to me, and I'd leave for a while."

"Did you talk with Shelly?"

"Sure."

"Did she recognize you?"

"Yeah, she recognized me all right."

Lara expected him to continue, but instead he drained his glass and rose to prepare himself another drink. He took his time, and she suspected he was stalling again, reluctant to talk. So once more she waited patiently for him to return to his chair and indulge in several swallows of Scotch.

"And?" she prodded when she felt he was ready to speak.

"She knew who I was, but she was certain I wanted to kill her. She said she'd kill me first. She said she knew you and I wanted her house and would do anything to take it away from her. I tried to convince her that this wasn't true, that we had no intention of killing her, but she wouldn't believe me. And then . . ." He paused and gazed unseeingly past Lara. There was grief in his eyes, a deep sadness that infectiously squeezed her heart and pained it. "And then she made a show of reaching for something from under her pillow. From the way she did this, I thought she had pulled out a gun, but there was nothing in her hand. She pointed this imaginary gun and screamed, 'I got you first, bastard!' And then she made the motions of slipping this gun, or whatever, back under her pillow. Then she lay back and closed her eyes.

"I stared at her, wanting to talk some more. It was so frustrating not being able to reach her, to convince her that I had no intention of hurting her. I wanted to tell her that she was my sister and, although I had rarely seen her in the past few years, I still loved her. But I could see she had shut me out—had killed me, I realize now. Everybody in the rooms around me was screaming or crying hysterically, and my nerves couldn't take too much more, so I left the ward for a while and went to the hospital cafeteria for coffee.

"When I returned about a half hour later, Shelly was sitting up on her bed, but the moment she saw me she let out this horrible shriek and nearly clambered up the wall behind the bed. Never had I seen such terror on her face, or anyone else's for that matter. The sight of me had petrified her."

"But why? I wonder," Lara said, her voice barely audible. For a moment only the sound of ice in Steve's drink clinking against the glass was heard.

His gaze, which had been focused on the wall of books behind her, slid toward her face and lingered. "Ghost," he uttered simply. "She really believed she had killed me and now thought I had returned to avenge my death. I told her I had not returned from the dead, but she claimed she could see worms crawling out of my ears and nostrils. She said she could see a red gleam in my eyes, which proved that a soul from hell was manipulating my body. There was no appeasing her, Lara. Her screams were so loud and horrible that I actually had to cover my ears. I ran to get a doctor or a nurse, hoping someone could give her a sedative, but the nurses at the main desk told me Shelly already had a sedative and couldn't have another one too soon. I told them that the sedatives they had given her couldn't have been very good since she was hardly sedated. The nurses replied they were fully aware of that, and that was also why they weren't willing to chance another dose. The doctors weren't certain what they were up against."

"Oh, Steve, I hope she pulls out of this," Lara said. She was surprised at how terrible and sad she actually felt. She had always considered herself a sincere person, one who was never hypocritical. If a person she disliked was suddenly taken ill or had died, her feelings for that person would not be altered. Only hypocrites felt compassion for or mourned people they didn't like, but now she realized she was wrong, for she felt a heavy sadness and sympathy for her sister-in-law.

She knew now that she didn't really dislike Shelly; their personalities just weren't compatible. Perhaps this was because they were alike in too many ways, equally obstinate, even theatrical.

"Well, it looks like she won't be living here for a while," she heard her husband say.

"Maybe not," Lara said. "Maybe she'd recover quicker if she were back in her own house. You know how much she loves this house, Steve. Maybe it would actually help."

"You think she should come back here?" he said, as though not certain he had heard right.

"Yes. A hospital can be so . . . so cold. I really think she'd have a better chance of recovering—"

"But she could be dangerous," he reminded her.

"I know, but . . . well, we'll be careful. Very careful."

Steve stared at her, weighing her words. After a long pause he shook his head. "Bad idea. We're not qualified. We don't have the equipment, and we don't know what we're dealing with."

"But she's alone, and I know how much she loves this house. It might uplift her somehow if she's here, bring her to her senses . . ."

"No," Steve said firmly. "Too risky."

"But, I really think—"

"No." His tone was sharp and final. In a softer voice,

he added, "There is nothing we can do to help her. Nothing. And besides, the hospital may refuse to release her."

She knew this was probably true, but she hated this sense of helplessness. "Maybe we should leave the house," she said after a long silence.

"Is that what you want?"

"It wouldn't be right to stay here."

"Is that what you want?" he repeated, demanding an honest answer.

"I . . . I don't know." She was surprised to find hope fluttering inside her, like some kind of uncertain insect not knowing whether to remain hovering in a low, inconspicuous corner or soar openly. "I don't know," she said again. "What do you want?"

"We're not going to get anywhere if we keep answering a question with a question."

"I just want you to be happy, Steve."

Steve sighed and helped himself to another drink. "And I want *you* to be happy," he said, looking at her over the rim of his glass before taking a swallow.

"Well . . ." She still loved the house, and if he didn't mind anymore then she couldn't see why they shouldn't stay. "It *is* close to the hospital," she pointed out.

He shrugged, as though to say it did not matter one way or the other.

"We could stay until Shelly is better . . . is back home. You sure you wouldn't mind?"

He shook his head. It was a faint, almost imperceptible gesture, but she saw it, nevertheless. He wouldn't mind.

"Darling, maybe it's time you fight this fear of the house. If you could do that, we could be so happy together."

"Yeah, maybe you're right."

"We'll talk about it," she vowed, leaving her chair and kneeling on the rug at his feet. "We'll talk and talk, and we'll remove that fear from you. That's how you do it, darling. You talk it out of your system."

"Yeah, maybe you're right," he said again, muffling the words as he drowned them with his drink.

Lara rested her head on his lap. "But, of course, if it doesn't work and you're still having uneasy feelings about this house, then we'll leave." He made no reply, so she went on. "We're both going to be happy here now. I can feel it. Can you, darling? Can you?"

But all she could hear was another faint "Yeah" and the sound of ice clinking against glass as he upturned it and drained its contents.

Part III: The South Garden

16

Steve visited his sister daily and was discouraged to find no improvement. Shelly, he could see with apprehension, was wasting away. She refused to eat, thus had to be confined to her bed and fed intravenously. Whenever she saw him she'd scream, still certain he had returned from the dead. So most of the time was spent watching her from behind a one-way mirror or spent drinking coffee in the cafeteria.

Sometimes as he watched his sister from behind the mirror he would experience a disconcerting feeling that he had seen the terror in her eyes and her screaming mouth before. But where? When? No matter how hard he concentrated, the answer eluded him. Yet he was certain he had already been a witness to this.

Lara had joined him a few times, but whenever Shelly saw her she'd shriek in horror and call her a demon. Since Lara couldn't see any sense in watching the woman behind a mirror, she stayed home most of the time.

When Steve wasn't at the hospital, he was at his restaurant. The business was running smoothly, and in actuality he was not needed there, but he told himself that his occasional presence helped keep his employees on their toes. If he stayed away too long they would slack off. Deep inside, however, he knew this wasn't true. He had a damn good manager now at The Four Winds, and as long as he had him the food and service would remain flawless. As if confirming this, a local newspaper had recently rated the restaurant four stars.

Yes, he was really not needed there. Success, at last, had arrived, and soon it'd be time to expand and open up a second restaurant, Four Winds II. Now if only his personal life was as successful.

He was beginning to fear that his sister would never recover. The hospital laboratories were still puzzled and no closer to finding the cause than the day Shelly and her friends had been admitted.

And the house still made him uneasy. He found himself still staying away from it, but this time Lara didn't seem aware of his absences as much; she was too busy cleaning and rearranging furniture. The latter was something Shelly had forbidden her to do. Yes, Lara was happy, and Molly, he noticed, also was happy. She had had a horrible scare, but like most children, she was resilient. She frequently asked about Shelly.

"I think I wanda be a writer like her someday," she had said.

He told her he bet she'd make a darn good one, for he could see she was an imaginative kid. Many times he had seen her amuse herself while she was alone. She didn't seem to need anyone to entertain her, only her mind.

Come to think of it, he mused, maybe *his* imagination was the root of his problem. Maybe it was time he faced it head on. Maybe he should go down into the cellar, where the bad feelings had originated, and maybe he'd find it not as frightening as when he was a kid of seven. A child's eyes and mind were usually so different from an adult's. Perhaps now he would find nothing but an old, harmless cellar.

He was a man now, for Christ's sake! He shouldn't be afraid.

Before he began his little excursion into the cellar, a flashlight in his hand, he went into the library and found a half-emptied bottle of Cutty Sark.

He took a hearty swig of Scotch, then descended into

the cellar's darkness. He thought of going back up the stairs and looking for a light bulb, but changed his mind. The socket was in the ceiling somewhere, and a step-ladder would be needed to reach it. Someday, he resolved, he'd put in a new bulb, but for now a flashlight would do.

Aiming the conical light ahead of him, he walked on the concrete floor as though it were made of glass. As he expected, and remembered, the air down here was thick and damp, on the chilly side. Like on a rainy morning, he thought, one needed a sweater.

Steve swept the light across the stones on the wall, spotted a web, and suddenly remembered seeing a web down here when he was a kid. He remembered breaking it just for the hell of it, and he remembered how it had stuck to his fingers; he remembered thinking that the spider, who he had known was lurking somewhere and watching him, did this on purpose to get back at him. He had peeled at the webs on his fingers for a long time and, growing scared, had run back up into the kitchen, stumbling and nearly falling off the stairs.

He remembered this as though it had just happened yesterday, instead of decades ago.

The cellar was also jarring other memories. It was the smell and the feel of this place that was doing it. A door in his mind was opening, and now he wasn't sure if he wanted to keep it open or go back upstairs where it would slam shut.

He moved onward, the flashlight's yellow beam feebly illuminating the way. With each step, something in his mind grew more evident. It was as though there was something concealed in a fog, and he was approaching it. The fog thinned as he grew nearer, then at last he saw—remembered—what it was. A ring.

Now that he reached the object in the fog, he could see it clearly. It had been a gold ring with a big ruby. He remembered thinking it was a pirate's ring, for there was an etching of a skull on one side and a crow on the other, and he remembered his disappointment when he put it on his finger that it was too big. It was even loose on his thumb.

He had found the ring in that other section of the cellar, at the far end of the house, where he had found other things. He had loved that ring at first, and when he was back in his room he had tied yarn around it. This enabled him to wear the ring without losing it. For most of that day he pretended he was a pirate, the richest and meanest that ever lived.

Later that day, just before the evening meal he noticed that the ring was cutting into his finger. The gold band was like a double-edged razor; it had cut through the yarn and was shrinking. The ring was going to cut his finger off!

He screamed, "Mommy! Daddy! Get it off! Get it off!"

His father rushed to the bathroom, smeared soap on it, then tried to wrench it free, but the ring kept cutting in. The finger began to bleed.

"What the—" His father's face had turned red with panic and frustration. Then he turned the faucet on and soaked the bloody ring and finger. That was when the cutting stopped. Like a warm-blooded organism, the ring froze. Had it been the warmth from his body, from his finger, that had made it shrink? he wondered now. The ring had been like a living thing, wanting his blood.

Steve shivered, then quickly blamed it on the damp air.

What happened to that ring? With some concentration he was able to remember that his father had worked the ring loose with soap and cold water. Then, as if the ring were a contaminated creature, his father threw it into the toilet and flushed it out of the house. The incident had flabbergasted both of them, but they never talked about it afterwards. They both let it slip into their subconscious.

And now, like a dead fish, it popped to the surface.

What the hell kind of a ring was it?

Now that he could remember it so well, he could also recall that as his father had tried to pry the ring loose, the ruby had become redder and redder as though filling with blood.

But that had only been the imagination of a child. That ring had not been a living organism. The whole incident had been the result of a fanciful imagination.

Hadn't it?

The air grew thicker with each step. Exactly as I remember it, he thought. It was the same sensation, the sensation of walking through something as palpable as liquid. You had to push through the air.

Maybe he should go back up.

Now something else began to take shape in his mind. Another memory. He hesitated, then mentally moved forward to push aside the shrouding fog.

There had been talk about Dolly Collins, the wife of the first owner, talk that had eluded him until now. When Steve reached the other side of the cellar, where the broken wooden door led to the room with the dirt floor, he found himself almost able to hear the voices that he had heard when he was a child. He remembered sitting in a barber chair. Leo was the barber's name, and while he cut his hair he talked with Steve's father.

So you're the one who bought the Collin's house, eh?

That's right.

Say, maybe y'can clear up a few things I'd been wondering 'bout.

Shoot.

Is it true there's a room in the cellar, something like a lab?

Lab?

Yeah, y'know, with all kinds of weird stuff, like jars with stuff inside 'em.

What kind of stuff?

Oh, I dunno. Rumors say she had dead babies, lizards' hearts, bats' blood. Stuff like that.

And who, may I ask, is 'she'?

Why Dolly Collins, of course. She's the wife of the first owner of that house.

Why would this Dolly Collins have a lab with bottles of

strange things?

Well, uh, they say she did some magic. Y'know, the bad kind.

I'm sorry to disappoint you, Leo, but I haven't found a laboratory in my cellar.

Mebbe the fire got rid of it all.

Fire?

Yeah. It burned a good part of the house down, but the cellar was supposed to been untouched, though.

Maybe this Dolly Collins salvaged her laboratory and moved everything to wherever she went.

She died in that fire.

Oh.

Her family died, too. Folks think she caused the fire. They think she knew how to bring up the devil from hell. They said she used to brag 'bout it. Even threatened some folks with this devil bit. "I'm gonna git the devil after ya," she'd say. Everybody in those days were afraid of her, but then mebbe they're only stories. It was a long time ago. Over a hund'd years, I think.

Interesting. My house originally belonged to a witch.

Yeah, I guess. But according to the stories, she didn't like to be called that. No, she called herself the Dark Princess, and claimed her magic was ancient, founded by a famous friar from the thirteenth century. Friar Roger Bacon, I think. She claimed some of his stuff had been passed down to her and boasted of owning things that she herself didn't understand. Things that had puzzled and fascinated her. She had hid them, buried them . . . as though they were treasures.

The fire, Leo. Do you know how she started it? And why?

Magic out of control, they said. She got a devil mad, so he scorched her, her family, and most of the house. The story has it there was one part of the cellar, Dolly's private room, that the devil didn't want destroyed, so it was as though there was no fire there.

Maybe the next owners took everything when they rebuilt the house.

Yeah, mebbe. Yeah, I think that's what happened. So there's no lab down there, huh?

There's a room down there, but it's empty. Dirt floor, stone walls. Not much of anything, Leo.

Ah well, I just thought I'd ask. Been curious, and I ain't ever met anybody who lived there until now.

Later that day Steve had gone into the cellar, to see if there was a laboratory down there. Before this he had never explored the entire cellar, for the darkness had scared him, but the conversation between his dad and the barber had aroused his curiosity, and he fought back his fear of the dark. He found the wooden door and the room beyond. To his disappointment there was no sign of it ever being a witch's chamber or laboratory—except for the ring buried in the dirt floor . . . and the piece of glass.

The mirror.

Now something else was surfacing in Steve's mind. Suddenly he could remember when and where he'd seen his sister's expression of terror before. Stopping in the middle of the cellar, he took a hearty swig of Scotch. The whiskey warmed him, but only briefly. The cold knot he had felt in his belly returned, colder and harder.

He had seen a woman screaming in horror in that piece of glass. At seven he hadn't recognized the woman, but now, in retrospect, he realized it was his sister he'd seen— 26 years older. And also, about 26 years older, he had seen himself. He could remember the image in the glass vividly now. It had been a man with streaks of gray hair at the temples. It had been a man clawing at his throat, gasping for breath. It had been a man who was dying.

"Steve?" a voice called, startling him. He swung around toward a rectangular block of light, where he had left the kitchen door open. It seemed so far away and small. He saw his wife in the doorway, blocking and deflecting some of the light, looking like something out of a Steven Spielberg movie.

"Steve?" she called out again. She seemed afraid to venture into the darkness.

"Here," Steve shouted in reply, then started toward

her. When he reached the kitchen, she glanced at the bottle in his hand and frowned quizzically at him.

"Just wanted to see if the cellar was the same as when I was a kid," he said.

"I'm afraid I've terrible news, Steve."

He noted her face was bloodless, her chin quivering. Muscles tightened and something slammed shut in his mind, detaching and protecting him.

"What?" he whispered.

"The hospital called. Shelly, she's . . ." Lara stopped, her voice failing her. She drew in a breath, then finished, " . . . she's passed away."

Steve stared blankly. The protective shield in his mind was working well, keeping the words from penetrating. Then the shield began to fail him. Like a stone wall it crumbled, losing one stone at a time. "What?"

She didn't answer; she knew he had heard.

"How?"

"Heart attack."

He stared some more, then when the last stone fell he took a long swig from his bottle and wordlessly went into the library and shut the door.

Molly was astonished to find the west garden wilted. All the flowers were gone. Only the stems and leaves remained, looking like an army of headless soldiers slowly crumpling to the ground. As if a giant sword had decapitated them in a single swipe, Molly thought. But where had their heads rolled? There was no sign of them anywhere.

Had they withered, then blew away?

Molly was disappointed. Although she had grown sick of their fragrance, she still wished the flowers had lasted longer. They had been so pretty to look at.

But when she saw the garden on the south side, her disappointment vanished. It had been almost a week since she had last seen any of her gardens, and yet one would think she'd been away for at least a month, so much had changed. Not only had this garden grown a lot, but the plants were now sprawling out onto the lawn. And the leaves were so much greener and more luxuriant than the garden in the west had ever been.

Molly found herself tempted to walk through the dense foliage but held back, not wanting to trample any of the plants. The garden was thick and crowded, like a jungle, she thought. Some plants were taller than she, some were wide with stems as thick as her arm, and some were low vines worming their way through other plants.

Yes, just like a jungle, she thought again, an exotic jungle. Most of these plants, she noted, had buds on them. They were all different, so unlike the other garden where they had been all indentical.

And they all seemed about ready to bloom.

17

Shelly's funeral, so close after Margaret Ludden's, was difficult for Steve. Although he remained tearless and silent, Lara could see the grief and guilt in his eyes, and especially in his behavior. He was drinking incessantly now.

Lara considered demanding that he stop, but she reminded herself that he was in mourning. Not only had he lost his mother and sister in a short space of time, but he was filled with regret for not having had shown them more love. The drinking will stop, she told herself.

One morning, a week after the funeral, Lara woke up to the sound of hammering. As was usual recently, she found herself alone in bed. Steve spent most of the nights sleeping in the library, either in a chair or on the sofa. This, too, she resolved, will stop. He just needed time to heal, that's all. Slipping into a robe, she went downstairs to investigate the noise.

She found Steve in the kitchen, nailing a board across the door that led to the cellar.

"Steve, what on earth are you doing?"

He paused to glance over his shoulder at her. "Boarding up the door," he said around a mouthful of nails.

"I can see that. But why?"

He pounded a nail into the wood, then started on another nail before answering. "Don't want anybody in the cellar."

"Why not?"

Again he let a moment pass before answering. "Stairs are rotting. Too dangerous."

She wasn't sure if she believed him. "Is there something down there you don't want me to see?"

"There's nothing to see. It's empty—and dangerous," he repeated.

"Maybe you should call a carpenter and have new stairs put in."

"Yeah, I will, when I get the chance."

That was all he was willing to tell her. Like everything else, pulling words out of him was tantamount to pulling crooked nails out of a board. Until recently she had been certain she could change him and make him communicate freely with her, but she wasn't very confident about this anymore.

Another week passed without much change. Steve remained silent and, if not at work, inebriated most of the time. She found herself alone with Molly at every meal and completely alone every evening in bed. It'll pass, she told herself constantly. She'd have to be patient. Time healed everything, didn't it?

In the meantime she decided to call a carpenter herself, since Steve was still too grief-stricken, too busy and, of course, too drunk to do it. The carpenter, a middle-aged man who resembled Kenny Rogers with prematurely gray hair and beard, removed the boards across the cellar door. "To keep my daughter from going on the stairs," she had told him, but he didn't seem to care why the door was boarded up. With a powerful flashlight he located the light socket and burned-out bulb. He replaced it with a 100-watt bulb, which failed to do much good, for the ceiling was too high and the cellar too vast. He searched for another socket but found none. "Sure's creepy down here," he muttered when his flashlight did not succeed in penetrating the gloom at the other end of the cellar. Then he dismantled the old stairs and constructed new ones. By late afternoon the job was completed.

After he was gone, Lara went down into the cellar. The

smell of sawdust was pungent, incongruously fresh in the old and dank basement. She looked around her, staying under the weak light. The area near her was dingy and shadowy, but beyond this in a surrounding sphere the light gradually gave way to incredible darkness. She didn't like this darkness, nor the air. Both were too thick, eliciting unbidden images of spiders and rats. Steve's not hiding anything, she quickly decided and hurried back upstairs.

When Steve came home that night, eyes bloodshot and bleary, he saw that the boards were gone from the door, and he frowned, as though wondering if he had actually boarded the door or just dreamed he had.

Still frowning, he turned to Lara. Not certain what his reaction would be, she tensed and gave him a tentative smile. "I called the carpenter myself, dear. He put new stairs in for us."

The frown deepened, as though he were trying to decide how to react. He pitched slightly forward, then straightened.

"You seemed to have forgotten all about it," she added. "What if the furnace needed fixing, or a fuse blew out?"

He sighed, then to her surprise plopped down at the kitchen table, buried his face in his hands, and began to cry.

Lara stared at him, stunned at first. Then she gently rubbed his shoulders and back. This is good, she thought. At last he is releasing his grief.

She continued massaging him, not saying anything. When he was done and was wiping his eyes with the back of his hand, he said, "I'm all right." His voice was unusually deep and gruff, as though he was embarrassed and struggling to regain his masculinity.

"It's good to cry," she said softly. "You've every reason."

He thought about this as he let her fingers soothe his tense muscles. "I feel so damn guilty."

Lara waited, expecting him to say more. When he

didn't, she encouraged him. "It's also good to talk, darling. What do you feel guilty about?"

He didn't answer, and she felt his muscles begin to tighten again. She continued to work at them. "Do you feel guilty about Shelly?"

He seemed to be concentrating on the sensation of her fingers on his shoulders and back. A minute passed, then at last he admitted, "Yes, and about Mom, too. But it's not only guilt, Lara. Right now, I don't—" He stopped, as though abruptly deciding not to continue.

"You don't what, darling?" she prompted.

"I want a drink."

He started to get up, but she applied pressure to keep him in the chair. "Please, darling, no drinks. Let's talk first."

He didn't protest. The massage was keeping him reasonably tranquil.

"You don't what?" she reiterated.

"I don't like myself very much right now."

"Why not?"

Once more he was reluctant to answer.

"Why not, darling? Please tell me. It'll make you feel better if you do."

"What're you, a fucking psychiatrist?" he snapped.

Lara recoiled, as though he had slapped her. Then she reminded herself that maybe a reaction like this was to be expected. She went on with the massage, as though nothing had happened.

"Sorry, hon," he sighed. "I really didn't mean to yell at you like that."

"You're miserable, darling, and I'm determined to know why." She paused, then asked, "Why don't you like yourself?"

"I can't shake my goddamn fear of this house. Because of it, I've made my mother and sister unhappy, and I'm making you unhappy."

"Maybe you should talk more about this fear. I mean, *really* talk about it."

"Yeah, maybe." But he sounded reluctant.

"It'll make you feel better," she repeated.

"Yeah. Yeah, probably."

Leaning closer, she wrapped her arms around his shoulders and brought her face forward until her cheek was touching his. His skin felt warm against hers, and suddenly she felt a surge of love for him. "I love you," she whispered, "and I hate seeing you like this. You're drinking too much. You're destroying the man that I love. Please, Steve, don't do that."

"I . . . I can't help it."

"But you want to help it, don't you? You want to be rid of the fear, don't you?"

"Yes." The admission was low, barely audible.

"Then you'll have to talk about it, all of it." When he didn't answer, she added emphatically, "You *must.*"

"It's the cellar," he told her at length. "I boarded it up because I hate it. It actually scares me, Lara. I think bad things went on down there, evil things, and this house is sitting on top of it, and I . . . I just don't like it."

"What kind of evil things?"

"There's a room down there, and I think that's where rituals and witchcraft were performed. You can feel it in the air when you go down there."

"Feel what?"

He opened his mouth to answer, but no words came out.

"What?" she urged.

"Evil."

The reply stunned her into silence for a moment. "But darling, how can you feel evil?"

"If you've been down there, you'd know."

"I have been."

He seemed surprised. "Why did you go down there?"

"To test the new stairs."

"Oh. And you felt nothing?"

"Well, I found it creepy. There's not enough light."

"Did you go to the other end of the cellar?" He turned to look at her.

She took a seat next to him at the table. "No, I didn't."

"That's where the room is. There's nothing in it now, but you can feel . . . something . . . was there."

"Evil?"

"Yes."

Lara's forehead creased. She was confused, not knowing what to make of what he was telling her.

"You think I'm crazy, don't you?" he said.

"No, no," she quickly replied, not wanting him to become reticent now. "But I wish you'd elaborate on this feeling of evil."

Steve mulled over this, looking away from her and staring at his hands that were now folded on the table. "It's a feeling of a presence," he said at length, "or maybe there's more than one. Whenever I'm down there I feel I'm not alone. I feel I'm somewhere I don't belong. I keep thinking maybe Dolly, the one who the lab belonged to, had conjured up something foul in the cellar."

"From where?"

"From . . . from wherever evil dwells."

"Oh."

Steve shot her a look, then returned his gaze to his hands. "I can tell you don't believe me, but I can't help it. It's what I feel. That cellar has been in darkness for a long time. Maybe when you practice witchcraft, ancient magic, or whatever, and then keep the place where you had performed these things in perpetual darkness . . . evil becomes a presence."

Lara touched his folded hands, as though to still what seemed to be an imagination out of control, but she could see he didn't want to be restrained. He wouldn't talk to her and was still concentrating on the dark feelings. She withdrew her hand.

He went on. "I've always felt the dark is where evil lives and waits, and the longer a place is dark, the stronger evil becomes."

Lara stared at him, nonplussed. Aware of the silence, Steve looked over at her. She was startled to find resentment in his gaze. Was the resentment from having revealed so much and received only silent skepticism?

"But they're only feelings," she pointed out, hoping to dispel the harsh gaze.

To her relief he leaned back in his chair and looked away, up at the ceiling, at a calendar on the wall, and then out the window. "Yeah, stupid, childish feelings," he muttered.

"I never said they were stupid, darling."

"But you think they're something derived from my childhood."

"I never said that either."

"Well, I must have been a kid with one helluva imagination. I *imagined* having a piece of mirror that forecasted people's death. I *imagined* a ring that tried to cut my fucking finger off. And I probably *imagined* a whole lot of other stupid things that I can't even remember anymore!" His voice was rising with anger and hopeless frustration.

Now he turned away from the window and glared at her. "I saw Shelly die in that piece of glass, Lara."

The statement hung in the air.

"What do you mean?"

"I remember seeing a woman in that glass, who I didn't recognize, but now looking back I'm sure it was Shelly I'd seen as she looked just before she died. She was screaming in that piece of mirror, and that was how she died, Lara—screaming! Who knows what she'd seen at the moment of her death, but it must have been horrible and it must have brought on her heart attack. Terror was still on her face when I saw her after she'd died—and that face had been vaguely familiar. It wasn't until I went down in the cellar that I realized I'd seen it in the glass."

Maybe he only thought he'd seen it, Lara mused. Maybe the darkness of the cellar had frightened him so intensely when he was a child that everything he'd found in it was blown out of proportion in his mind. "You had found this mirror piece in the cellar, hadn't you?"

He nodded. "But Shelly wasn't all I had seen. I remember looking at a man. Now I know it was me. And do you know what he was doing?"

Lara found herself holding her breath. Maybe she'd made a mistake in prompting him to talk openly about his fear. Maybe this was too complex, maybe even damaging.

"You . . . you don't have to talk about this if you don't want," she said weakly.

"I saw myself dying in the mirror. I don't know how or what was killing me, but I was in agony. I know that much. I was gasping. I saw myself clutching my throat, and I saw myself banging on a door. I wanted to get out of somewhere, but I couldn't. I saw panic. And I—"

"Please, darling. You don't have—"

"I'm opening up to you, damnit!" he shouted. "You wanted this!"

"I know, I know," she said, uneasily twisting the fabric of her blouse at her stomach. "But I don't like how it's upsetting you. And seeing this is upsetting me."

He glowered at her, then the harshness from his eyes dimmed and she could tell that he regretted the outburst. He puffed out his cheeks, released air, then said, "Sorry, hon, didn't mean to yell."

Lara gave him an understanding nod. They both stared at the tabletop in front of them, both awkward and at a loss for words. A moment passed between them.

Then Lara, clearing her throat, said, "Maybe you should think about seeing a doctor."

"You mean a shrink?"

"Well . . ." She hated that word, but it was exactly what she meant. "Yes."

"So you think I'm crazy then."

"No. You're troubled is what. You're letting a childhood fear carry over into adulthood. I think it'd be best for all of us if you'd find out why."

"I think what you're really saying is that it'll be better for our marriage."

Lara said nothing.

"Well, is it?"

She nodded, then conceded out loud, "Yes."

Steve absently made imaginary patterns on the table-tops with his finger. His mind seemed far away. At length he stopped creating patterns and looked over at Lara. Never had she seen such sadness in one's eyes.

He said, "I'll make an appointment right away."

Molly sat at the window in her room and looked out at the south side. She was bored and there was not much to see, now that it was nighttime and the view offered only the lawn and a border of lilac and crab apple trees, both of which had long since lost their flowers. The moon was close to full, but clouds kept hazing it over along with most of the stars. She wished her cat, Dinah, were still alive, for she missed her terribly tonight.

She thought of the swarm of insects that had eaten her pet, then quickly stifled the thought.

Then she thought of the couple who had forced their way into the room after her, their faces dark with fury, and she stifled that also.

Maybe she didn't like it here anymore. Nasty things that she couldn't understand kept happening here, and she had already explored all the rooms. Worst of all, she didn't like what the house seemed to be doing to her step-father and her mother. It was pushing them apart. She could see it and feel it. They were not in love as before.

For the first time since she'd been here, she was exper-iencing deep loneliness. Suddenly the house seemed too big, and she too small. Up until now she had thought she was immune to the feeling of loneliness. She had managed to toughen herself at school where most of her classmates found it easier to ignore her than make a special effort to communicate with her. Everybody was friendly to her, gave her smiles and waves, and now and then someone would include her in a group. But it was difficult to follow a conversation if more than two persons were involved. It seemed that whenever she'd try to read someone's lips, another person would start talking and she'd miss too much of what was being said. Since she couldn't catch everything, she would not add to the conversation, in case she'd say something unrelated and stupid, so she found it easier to settle for the silent smiles and waves. She had grown to accept the loneliness.

But now, the big house seemed to magnify it.

Yes, she sure missed Dinah. Maybe she'd have to ask her mother if she could have another cat. She could name it Dinah Two. She would make sure the cat didn't go near that plot of dirt on the east side, though. Grass and weeds covered it now, but one couldn't be too sure if a nest of bugs was still underneath.

Once more she pushed the image of the winged insects out of her mind. The thought alone made her flesh crawl.

She stared at the moon for a while, watching in mild fascination as blue-gray clouds drifted across it. Maybe if she stared long enough she'd see a flying saucer go by, or a witch.

Not that she believed in witches, of course. But as for flying saucers, that was a little different. It was possible for them to exist. Nobody knew everything about space and the universe.

Nobody knew everything about magic and sorcery either.

Molly looked away from the moon and rested her gaze on the dark outlines of the lilac and crab apple trees. The latter had thin, spidery branches, at the moment reminding her of old, gnarled fingers, bent and splayed as they stretched for the sky. A mild breeze made each finger wriggle separately, casting squirming shadows on the lawn.

Mesmerized, the girl watched the shadows writhe and darken as the moon brightened during a break in the clouds. The light was bluish and ghostly, and the trees and their elongated shades were black and flat, looking like ink that had splashed onto the ground. Then Molly's eyes swept toward the garden.

She was stunned to find that some of the plants had flowered. Scattered here and there were huge white blossoms, made brighter and paler by the moonlight. They were facing the house and actually seemed to be looking up at her window.

Molly counted five flowers. All were the same shape and size, round and as big as her face. She stared at them, unable to pull her gaze away. There was something about them that she found alluring. She wanted to get closer to them, and if it weren't for the barrier of glass in front of her, she suspected the attraction would have been stronger and irresistible. She would have gone down to the garden, to touch and smell the flowers.

As she stared, the flowers opened wider for her. The big white petals seemed to glow spectrally, now and then forcing the girl to rub and refocus her eyes. It was almost like watching spheres of light. She remembered reading somewhere that some animals stop in midstride in the middle of roads to stare at approaching car headlights. Lights paralyze them with fascination, just as they were paralyzing her now. Of course, the light from these flowers was nowhere as bright as headlights, yet their brilliance eerily entranced her.

Also, like staring into light, the shape could not be sharply defined. She could tell the flowers were spherical, but the edges were hazy. Through the obscuring haze she could discern shadows on the surface at one moment, then nothing at the next. She continuously rubbed her eyes. More shadows returned, then disappeared. She made out dark specks and smears. Sometimes there was a pattern, and sometimes there wasn't.

And sometimes there was a face, and sometimes there wasn't.

Molly strained her eyes to see clearer. Had she really seen a face? It was like looking at a cloud, or at the moon, or at the rough bark on a tree trunk. You could see faces anywhere, if you tried hard enough. All you needed was a pair of dots for eyes and a smear for the mouth and a little imagination.

The faces, when they reappeared on the flowers, had strange expressions. They each seemed to have a cold grin, and it seemed to be directed at her.

Imagination, she reminded herself.

Faces can be found anywhere.

Like the spidery tree branches and their shadows, the glowing flowers swayed in the mild wind. Big heads on scrawny necks, she found herself thinking. Nodding and shaking, as though lacking muscle control.

Faces went away, reappeared, went away . . .

Molly thought of averting her gaze, but her eyes would not move. These faces were utterly fascinating. Some seemed to be dainty while others were crude, almost ugly, but all had the same grin, a grin that was only a dark smear yet detailed enough to chill and, at the same instant, captivate her.

She didn't know how long she stood at the window, but when she at last found herself able to move away from it she noticed that a large cloud was shrouding the moon, cutting off the light. She couldn't see the flowers anymore, only a dark patch where the garden was. She contemplated waiting for the moon to return, then decided against it. It was late, and she was tired.

She climbed into bed. Tomorrow she would go to her garden and examine the flowers at a closer range. She bet she wouldn't find any faces in them at all, only spots and speckles maybe. She couldn't wait to see them.

The moon broke through the clouds again, illuminating a section of the room with platinum wedge-shaped light. She thought of getting back up and looking out the window again. She really was tempted, but she was also too tired. She closed her eyes and felt the attraction lessen. Tomorrow she'd see the garden, she reminded herself. Tomorrow would come soon enough.

Then she drifted off to sleep.

18

The next morning Molly could not find any white flowers in the south garden. She found five large buds where she had seen the blossoms from her window the night before and assumed the flowers had closed up. Maybe these flowers only opened at night, she mused. The buds seemed too firm and fresh for the flowers to be completely finished. Disappointed, Molly ran a finger across a bud; it reminded her of a miniature cauliflower, bumpy and bunched. It was green, and when she examined it closely she could see a hint of white petals inside. She wanted to pry open the bud a little but fought the urge, afraid she might harm the plant.

Reluctantly she stepped away and looked around at the other plants. Many of the flowers were beginning to open. Hints of color surrounded her, and she knew in another day or two these flowers would be in full bloom. Already she could tell that this was going to be a beautiful garden, more beautiful than the one on the west side had been. Peeking through some of these buds were the richest colors she'd ever seen. One plant in particular revealed a glimpse of shiny red petals, red and glossy as nail polish, and another was a bright pink, almost fluorescent.

How many will flower only at night? She looked back at the plant she had recently touched, the one she suspected had bloomed in the moonlight. She felt a strange attraction toward it, and this time slipped the stem between two fingers and reverently cupped the bud in her hand. To her surprise she found it warm.

Instinctively she withdrew her hand, but only for an instant. She felt the attraction again and gave in to it. She cupped the furled flower once more, this time letting its warmth penetrate her. Soon she found herself somewhat dazed, staring at the plant between her fingers. The other plants around her ceased to exist, along with the expansive grounds and the big house. A strong gust of salty wind assailed her, blowing her shoulder-length hair back like a flapping cape, but this went unnoticed along with the rest of her surroundings. Only she and the plant in her hand existed.

She sensed a presence, not around her, but in the warmth that was filling her. As long as her palm and fingers touched the bud, the sensation, or whatever it was, grew progressively stronger. She thought of withdrawing her hand again, but she found herself too filled with curiosity to do this. She wanted to know more about this plant, wanted the presence to reveal much more of itself.

A part of her knew she should be scared, or wary at least, but her sense of wonder, as usual, dominated fear. What are you? she silently asked, then waited hopefully for a reply.

Another gust of wind whipped her hair, this time catching her attention. With her free hand she peeled strands off her face and held them back until the wind died down. Then, to her disappointment, she realized she had been momentarily distracted and might have missed the awaited answer. The flower bud, she noted, no longer felt warm to the touch.

Now she wasn't certain if she had felt anything at all. Had she imagined the warmth and the presence filling her? She looked around at the other plants, as though expecting to find a clue of some sort that would tell her something unusual had actually happened. She knew she had asked a plant what it was and had waited for an answer—and this was beginning to disturb her.

Only a little kid or a crazy person would ask a plant a question. Did this mean she was acting like a little kid or a crazy person?

Molly moved away from the garden, then stopped when she felt something fuzzy against her ankle. Looking down she saw it was a vine, which had extended onto the lawn. This snakelike plant intrigued her, for she'd never seen anything like it before. Something like hair, yellowish-green in color, covered it. There were dark green knobs throughout, and she guessed these were buds readying to flower, like all the other plants. As she stared, she thought she detected a slight movement, a tiny slither, but like the presence and the heat, she decided the movement was only her imagination.

She looked toward the house and spotted her mother in the dining room window. At first she thought she was being watched, then realized her mother was staring unseeingly, deep in thought. Even from this distance she could discern a troubled and unhappy expression. Wanting to cheer her up, Molly broke into a run toward the house.

In the dining room, her mother gave her a smile, but this didn't deceive her. Molly could still see the sadness in the brown eyes.

"Whad's the madder, Mom?"

"Remember your t's," she reminded dully.

Molly repeated the question, slowly and correctly this time.

"Why, nothing's wrong, sweetheart."

Molly could tell she was lying. "Is it 'cause of Steve?"

Lara looked at her for a silent moment, as though trying to decide how much grief to unload on the girl. "There are problems," she conceded, "but none that can't be worked out, I'm sure." She gave another smile, as though to confirm this.

Molly, wanting so much to cheer her, returned the smile. Then she grabbed her mother's hand and began pulling toward the door. "I wanna show you something."

"What?" Lara let the girl lead her out of the house.

"The garden," Molly said when they were outside, walking toward the south lawn. She wanted her mother to think of something else besides her problems, and she wanted her to identify some of the plants.

When they reached the garden Lara didn't seem too impressed. At least not until she realized there was such a wide variety and that most were ready to bloom.

"My, you certainly do have a green thumb," she remarked to Molly.

Molly beamed. "Wait till you see the flowers," she smiled. "Pretty."

"Some blossomed already?"

"Yup. Last night. I saw them from my room. There were five of them, and they were big and white, bright as the moon, almost." She paused, wondering if she should mention about the faces she'd seen in them. Would her mother accuse her of making up things? Like a little kid or a crazy person? Deciding against it, she said, "The flowers closed up today. Do you know what kind they could be?"

"Mmmmm, moon flowers, perhaps." It sounded uncertain, more like a question than an answer. "I really don't know much about plants, sweetheart."

"That's okay." Molly was just glad that she'd succeeded in getting her mother's mind on something else other than whatever was troubling her. "Maybe there's a book on this stuff in the library."

"Yes, I think there is." Now Lara seemed immensely fascinated as her eyes continued to absorb the garden. She moved closer, stopping at the edge. Her gaze paused on a tall slender plant with a large bud at the top. "Sunflower?" she mused aloud. She seemed to be battling an urge to walk through the dense foliage toward it.

"You think that's what it is?"

"What?" She pulled her gaze away from the tall plant and looked at Molly. She blinked, as though endeavoring to pull herself out of a foggy trance.

Molly frowned. "What's the matter, Mom?"

"Matter? Why do you ask?"

"You look, I don't know, dreamy, I guess."

Lara smiled, and this time her eyes shined. "You know," she said after a thoughtful silence, "that's exactly how I feel. Dreamy. Would you mind if I stepped into your garden? I'd like to see that plant up close."

"Sure. I mean no, I don't mind."

Her mother nodded appreciatively, maintaining the ghostly smile. Molly watched, wondering why she was suddenly acting strange, almost like a zombie. Her movements were slow and sluggish as she picked her way among the plants, but then, Molly began to feel as though she were in a daze herself. As she followed her mother, she experienced an eerie floating sensation.

Was it something she had eaten? Or was it the plants? Were they giving off something odorless and invisible?

Whatever it was, she soon found herself not caring.

She threaded her way through the thick plants, marveling at the rich growths. She felt a sense of pride and a strange feeling of attachment. I've grown these, she thought. I've grown them all by myself, and they are mine.

And I am theirs.

She stopped. Her thoughts disturbed and confused her. Why had her mind made such a strange statement? Before she could think of an answer, she forgot what it was that puzzled her. Her mind was fuzzy; thoughts appeared, then disappeared tracelessly. Nothing seemed to stick. Her brain was coated with baby oil. It was slippery. Thoughts didn't have a chance to hang around. They slipped away—*whoosh*—like someone stepping on a banana peel.

Molly began to giggle.

Smiling, Lara glanced back at her. "What's . . . so . . . funny, sweet . . . heart?" she asked, as though each word demanded utmost concentration.

Molly opened her mouth to tell her, but her mind drew

a blank. "I forgot."

Lara seemed to find this mildly amusing, for she emitted a soft giggle, then continued toward the tall plant.

Molly gulped air to compose herself. She willed away the laughter and followed her mother. She felt the hairy vining plant at her feet and immediately thought of Dinah. She halted, then descended to her knees and stroked the stringy vegetation. The hair felt warm and silky under her hand, like fur—like Dinah's fur. To her surprise she didn't find herself needing to cry; instead, she found herself experiencing a sweet inner glow. She was reminded not that she'd lost her pet but how much she loved it. As she stroked the plant she closed her eyes and smiled.

Nice cat. Pretty cat. I love you so much, so much . . .

She heard something, a sound that, as always, was muted and indistinct to her ears. She opened her eyes and found her mother calling her.

"What . . . are you . . . doing?" Lara repeated when she saw that she finally had her daughter's attention. She was standing beside the tall plant, which was as high as she, its large flower bud in line with her face.

Molly stared blankly, trying to remember why she was on her knees caressing the vine. The glow she had felt not more than a second ago was gone. It had slipped away, like a person on a banana peel.

She giggled again. "I forgod."

"Your t's, child," Lara, pretending she was a prissy teacher, spoke in a stern voice. "Remember your t's." Then she, too, began to giggle.

"What's so funny, Mom?"

Lara, unable to talk, shook her head and held up a finger, urging patience from the girl. She held a hand over her lips as though to hold back some of the laughter. Her eyes spilled tears as she strained for control. When the giggles finally stopped, she swept tears aside with a finger and looked blankly at Molly. "I . . . forgot," she said.

Now Molly found herself uncontrollably laughing. Tears filled her eyes and momentarily blinded her, and when she regained control she found her mother not staring at her but in rapt fascination at the tall plant.

"Mom?"

But her mother seemed faraway. Her eyes were glassy, and her mouth was locked in a dreamy smile. She seemed to be seeing something in the flower bud, something that was making her happy.

"Mom?"

Lara turned slightly in Molly's direction, as though to give her one ear and one ear only. But when Molly didn't speak again soon enough, she returned her attention to the plant, already forgetting that the girl had called her.

Molly pulled at her sleeve. Again she received half-hearted acknowledgment. "Mom, what do you see?"

"See?" She gave the question full concentration. Her body swayed slightly, as though a mellifluous music were humming in her mind. "Why, I see . . . nothing. It's what . . . I feel . . . sweetheart."

"What do you feel?" Molly studied the tall plant, hoping to catch whatever her mother had caught. She felt a little light-headed, and when she moved closer, the sensation increased.

"I feel . . . weightless . . ." her mother said, still concentrating. "I feel . . . wonderful. Yes, . . . wonder . . . ful."

Yeah, Molly thought as she leaned even closer. I feel that way, too. Wonderful.

She examined the flower bud, her nose almost touching it. She found a crack where she could glimpse the color of petals inside. Something moved.

She waited for the movement again, but saw only a yellow slit. It's gonna be a yellow flower, she thought, suddenly feeling herself on the verge of another laughing spell. It's gonna be a sunflower like Mom thought, and it's gonna be a wonderful flower.

She covered her mouth with her hand and giggled into it.

Something moved inside the yellow crack again.

"Mom?"

"Yes . . . sweet . . . heart?" Lara kept her gaze on the flower bud, along with Molly.

"Something's inside there."

"Inside . . . where?"

Molly didn't answer.

"Where?" her mother repeated.

Molly frowned. Where what? What had she asked? "I forgot."

"No matter," the other replied, no longer interested. After a long silence, she whispered, "Lovely feeling, isn't . . . it?"

Molly nodded slowly, keeping her eyes fixed on the plant. The slit seemed wider, more yellow, and the euphoria she felt seemed greater.

"Garden of happiness," she thought out loud.

"What?"

The thought slipped away, and she didn't bother to make an effort to recapture it.

Again something moved. It was a black vertical slit inside the yellow horizontal slit. It had swept across, then disappeared out of sight. It had reminded her of something, and for an instant the good feeling vanished as a chill rippled through her. But what was it?

Her mother had not noticed the movement. She was smiling blissfully, her eyes now closed as she threw her head back and exclaimed to the sky, "Wonderful . . . wonderful . . ."

She spun around, keeping her eyes closed while dancing to music that still hummed in her head, and as she twirled like a ballerina she laughed in merriment. At each full turn she repeated, "Wonderful!"

The laughter was infectious, and Molly quickly forgot about the cold tremor that had gone through her. She began to imitate her mother, and soon both were pirouetting in the garden, filling the air with mirthful giggles. Each spin was faster than the last, and Molly squealed with delight as the world blurred past her. She glimpsed the big house, the border of trees, the lawn, the tall plant, the big house again, the trees again, the lawn again . . .

The eye.

She kept spinning, but the chill was back. Now she knew what the vertical slit inside the yellow slit reminded her of. An eye. A cat's eye or a lizard's. The tall plant was watching her, watching both of them.

Molly stopped, but the world didn't. It continued to swirl until she found herself too dizzy to remain on her feet. She fell to the ground and waited for the spinning to stop. Her mother fell next to her, still uncontrollably laughing.

"Wonderful . . . won . . . der . . . ful . . ." She rolled over in the garden but the plants were supple and sprang back.

Molly looked over at the tall plant, at the flower, at the eye. She blinked, waited a minute more until the spinning had completely stopped, then rose to her feet and examined the bud closely. The slit she had seen before was now gone, as though the eye had closed.

Her imagination?

She looked down at her mother, saw the happy face and again forgot what it was that had alarmed her. The heady joyous feeling rushed back. It was the ecstatic thrill of a roller coaster ride, the delight of eating and smellling something sweet, the warm pleasure of cuddling someone or something you love. It was all these good things and more. It was as if a happy button in the brain had been jammed and remained stuck in the "on" position.

Lara pulled herself back up, teetered a moment as her world continued to spin, then began to dance again. Molly joined her. They were in each other's arms when Steve suddenly appeared, shouting their names.

Molly hadn't noticed him until her mother stopped and looked over in the direction of the house. "Why . . . hello . . . dear." Her voice was enthusiastic, although faint.

Steve stared incredulously at them, rocking on his heels from an afternoon of steady drinking. "What the hell are you two doing?"

His bafflement seemed to strike Lara funny, for it brought on a fresh wave of giggles. "Come . . . join us," she urged, once she had gained reasonable control of her voice.

But Steve was hesitant. He looked at Molly, at the garden, then back at his wife. "Are you drunk?"

"Yes . . . yes." She nodded enthusiastically. "I'm drunk with happiness. Come, dear." Her arms signaled in flowing motions. "See how lovely these plants are."

Molly also began to urge Steve to join them. When her gestures failed to encourage him, she threaded her way through the garden toward her stepfather, stumbling once in her daze as her body moved quicker than her feet. Her face fell into a soft, fuzzy bush which made her sneeze, then laugh. She rubbed her face, which tickled from the plant, then crawled the rest of the way. Never had she felt this good in her life. Joy was like a wave, continually hitting and flooding her.

At the edge of the garden she reached her stepfather and pulled herself up by clinging to his pants, nearly toppling him over in the process.

"The garden's . . . nice," she said, her words difficult to release. Steve's face blurred, then doubled. She closed her eyes a moment, then opened them. This time Steve's face was clearer. As usual, she found him striking and handsome, her mother's Prince Charming. Someday she would find someone like him.

"C'mon," she said, then reached for his hand and with feeble strength tugged him toward the garden. He resisted for a moment, his breath, warm with the smell of whiskey, fanning her face. "Whew!" She waved away the odor, then found this, along with everything else, funny. She giggled, then pulled harder at his hand. This time he relented.

He said something, but she had her back to him. "What?" she said, turning to read his lips.

"Did Shelly grow this garden?"

"No, *I* did," she said proudly. "All by myself."

"Nice," he muttered, blasting her again with the

stench of whiskey. Then without exchanging any more words, he let her lead him to Lara.

"Garden of love," Molly declared as her mother welcomed Steve into her arms. They reminded her of couples she'd seen on the covers of thick paperbacks in drugstores, the ones that usually had the words "love," "ecstasy" or "passion" in their titles. Exotic flowers and greenery were usually in the background, and the couple's faces often betrayed heavy-lidded adoration. "I want you, I want you," the hero always seemed to be thinking, while the heroine answered, "Take me, take me."

"Garden of love," Molly whispered again. Then to her delight, her mother and stepfather kissed. Sighing blissfully, she clapped her hands. The kiss lingered and the embrace tightened. Then, as though unable to absorb any more of the warm, swelling emotion without releasing some herself, she flung herself around the couple and hugged them, straining unsuccessfully to circle her arms completely around them.

Lara and Steve broke their kiss and looked down at Molly. They laughed, wrapping their arms around her, pulling her closer to them. The reluctance Molly had seen earlier in Steve's countenance was now gone. Like her and her mother, he was filled with laughter. His eyes glittered and his mouth was wider than she'd ever seen it. He had been joyful many times when he was full of Scotch, but never quite like this.

"Everything's going to be all right," he said, kissing Molly's cheek, then kissing Lara's. "Yeah, everything's going to be all right."

Lara, agreeing, tilted her head back to let the sun toast her face, and she sang, "Everything's going to be all right, all right. Everything's going to be all right, all right . . ."

Then her words were cut off as Steve's mouth covered hers, and again Molly watched, feeling her insides inflate with wonderful happiness.

She buried her face against her mother's shoulder, then

her stepfather's. She giggled as the wonderful, wonderful sensation grew. There seemed to be no end to it. She certainly hoped there'd be no end to it.

She pulled her head back and caught a glimpse of a flower bud on a low-lying plant. A slit opened, like an eye. It watched her for a short moment, then closed.

Molly laughed at it. She didn't care. She felt too wonderful.

19

After supper Molly went to her room and fell into a dreamless sleep. The day spent in the garden had exhausted her. She awakened to darkness and looked at the luminous digital clock on the nightstand; it was 2:32 in the morning. She turned around, pulled the covers closer to her chin and tried to sleep some more, but she was wide awake now.

She kept thinking about the garden on the south side of the house. The happiness she had experienced was gone but not forgotten. She found herself wishing for another experience like that. Somewhere in the back region of her mind she knew something was terribly wrong, even wicked. She remembered seeing bizarre eyes in the garden —or something hideous like eyes. She remembered the cold tremor when she had been certain the tall plant was watching her, but this was lost in the remembrance of countless waves of happiness.

She wanted to be happy like that again—now.

Throwing the covers aside, Molly slipped into her pink furry slippers and peered out the window. At first she saw only featureless darkness, then gradually stars reached her eyes. The more she stared, the more she saw. It was a matter of waiting for the eyes to adjust. She discerned the treetops, which were blacker than the sky, and she discerned the garden, which was blacker than the ground.

Then clouds, more gray than black, separated like a theater curtain to reveal a white moon.

And the moon revealed five white flowers.

Molly's gaze locked on them while her mind squealed with delight at the blossoms' return. They're night flowers, she realized. Moon flowers. If she wanted to see them at a closer range, to smell and touch them, she would have to do it at night, not wait till morning as she'd done yesterday.

But the pale light of the moon seemed awfully cold and unfriendly. The ground at night was another world, a foreign world that she knew nothing about, a place where she did not belong. All the plants were dark, except for the white flowers, and all, without exception, were still. Even the treetops at the yard's border did not move, something which was unnatural and unnerving so near the ocean. It was well past 2:00, and as far as she could remember, she had never been awake at this time.

The world was alien at this hour, probably as alien, cold and still as the landscape of the moon, she thought, tucking her hands under her armpits to keep warm. She knew she should go back to bed and try to fall asleep, but something wouldn't let her.

The flowers held her captive with their beauty—and something else. A part of her tried to define what this something was, but another part only wanted to enjoy it.

She moved closer to the window. She looked down, and the flowers looked up. The lily-colored petals were stretched wide, and shadowy features gradually became evident, like the smeary stains on the surface of the moon. Faces materialized. First came small pairs of smudges—the eyes; then elongated smears appeared beneath them—the mouths. Some were straight, some curved downward, and some reached upward. One smear separated, closed into a single line, then separated again, as though yawning—or silently conversing.

Molly stared at this particular flower, raptly fascinated with its "mouth." It reminded her of an old horror movie she'd seen, about a severed head that kept mouthing words that no one could hear but could sense. That mouth never stopped; it kept going and going, like a fish's. The flower chilled her, but she kept her gaze riveted to it.

The memory of the joy she had found in the garden the previous day grew more intense, the temptation to recapture it steadily irresistible. The wall of glass was no longer able to weaken the potent attraction the flowers exuded.

She studied the flowers longingly for another moment, then she turned from the window and slipped into a robe. Tying the sash tightly at the waist, she left the room, closing the door softly after her. On tiptoe she descended the long staircase, then paused at the foot of it.

Outside, the air was cold and damp. At the front entrance a breeze hit her, ruffling the hem of her robe and chilling her, but on the south lawn there was stillness. The damp smell of salt and seaweed was strong. Molly pulled the robe tighter at the neck, then padded across the yard toward the garden.

The five white flowers, almost fluorescent and ghostly in the dark, seemed to be waiting for her. Of course this was only her imagination, for flowers did not wait for people. They had no brains, no emotions, she told herself. They weren't aware of her presence.

Yet they were watching her carefully.

But this was impossible. Her imagination was getting out of control, as usual. Flowers did not have eyes.

Then she remembered the eyes she had seen in the flower buds earlier, and she remembered the faces in the white flowers. She couldn't see them in the blossoms that were close to her, but in one that was the farthest away she could—or thought she could—discern a face. It was the one with the moving mouth—moving, moving, never stopping.

She felt a great need to approach the plant, and she gave in to it. As she drew near, the facial features began to blur, then disappear altogether. When she turned around to look at the other end of the garden, she saw another face on a flower that was, again, at the farthest end.

She was tempted to return to the opposite side of the garden but was certain this face would also fade as she approached it. So from this small distance she studied the smeary features, watched the shadowy lips move and tried to read them, but the mouth did not form definite words; it just opened and closed ceaselessly.

But in her mind she could hear something from this flower—a whisper, soft and slow. At length she returned to the plant. As she grew nearer, the sound faded, as if she were walking away from it rather than toward it. She stopped in the middle of the garden, looked at the white flower ahead of her, then at the one she had just left. She could see faint features on both of them now, and both were moving their mouths, mindlessly and mechanically.

Both whispered something unintelligently in her mind. She concentrated, trying to make out the words, but for a while it seemed as though she were listening to an unfamiliar language. Then she heard, or rather sensed her name. Then familiar words began to float through her mind, like leaves riding a stream.

Wish . . . Molly . . . Any . . . Wish . . .

Molly strained to pick up more words, but only the same ones returned.

Molly . . . Any . . . Wish . . .

The girl moved closer to the flower ahead of her, hoping the proximity would help clarify more words.

Any . . . Wish . . . Wish . . . Any . . .

Slowly, she dropped to her knees, and the flower was level with her face. She stared deeply into its round, pale blossom. The facial features eluded her again, but she gently touched the petals to be certain none were there. The flower was warm, thin and silky to the touch. So delicate, she thought. But where had the face gone? And the voice? That had eluded her, too. It had grown fainter, and it seemed to come from behind her, which was strange, considering her hearing could never distinguish directions before this.

Then again, it was her mind that heard the whispering, not her ears. She was aware of this, aware that this was all unnatural and possibly dangerous, but she didn't care. She wanted to be near these pretty flowers; she loved the way their faces eluded her like a rainbow, and the way their windlike voices teased and played games with her. She loved the air that surrounded this garden. That euphoric sensation she had experienced the afternoon before was back, gradually intoxicating her.

She returned to the middle of the garden, the point where the features could be seen on both flowers and their murmurs heard the clearest. She was now light-headed, feeling weightless.

Molly . . . Wish . . . Any . . . Make . . .

Make . . . Any . . . Wish . . . Molly . . .

Molly's hands rose to cover her lips in wonder and surprise. Were the flowers urging her to make a wish?

She giggled into her hands, feeling like a girl who had just been asked to dance with a handsome boy. Me? A wish for me?

Molly . . . Wish . . . Any . . .

But why? she suddenly wondered. What had she done to deserve a wish?

Grateful . . . Molly . . . Grateful . . .

The girl frowned, not certain if she understood.

The flowers, as though aware of her confusion, whispered, *Molly . . . Planted us . . . Grateful . . .*

Of course! the girl suddenly realized. The flowers wanted to show her their appreciation for planting their seeds. Otherwise, they'd still be in that old dusty box in the old dusty cellar. She had actually done them a great favor, had given them life.

It was no wonder they wanted to pay her back.

Molly . . . Wish . . . Any . . .

They were insisting. She experienced a surge of warmth, a feeling that one gets when finding a friend.

Molly . . . Grateful . . .

Molly . . . Wish . . . Any . . .

She stared at one moving mouth, then the other, as she concentrated on a wish. There were many things she would like to have or do. She would love to see her mother and stepfather be happier together. She would love to have Dinah back. She would love to have a lot of pretty clothes.

And she would love to be able to hear better.

Make . . . Any . . . Wish . . . Molly . . .

"To hear," she suddenly blurted. Then she pressed her hands harder against her mouth and waited breathlessly, her eyes widening and watching the five white blossoms with hope. The stillness and silence deepened. The moon brightened.

Then she heard leaves rustling in the trees.

She spun toward the sound, her hands and mouth dropping. She listened intently. She heard a faint rhythmic roar and frowned in perplexity. Gradually it occurred to her what the sound could be—the surf.

She never had heard this before and was surprised at how hypnotic and peaceful the crashing of waves sounded. Tears brimmed her eyes while she grinned with incredulous delight. She was tempted to run to the east lawn where the ocean was, but she didn't want to leave the garden. The night flowers still had a strange hold on her.

Without moving, she listened to other sounds. A dog barked in a neighboring property. A lone car sped by the house. An airplane roared overhead.

I can hear! Molly's mind cried with disbelief as she watched the plane's red blinking lights glide across the black sky.

I can hear! I can hear!

Tears spilled down her face, but she made no effort to wipe them away. She was too busy creating her own sounds. She swished the hem of her robe repeatedly. Then she raked her fingers through the soil, loving the scratching noise they made. Then she scratched her head, then an itch on her face.

What beautiful sounds!

She began to hum, then sang a sour verse from "On Top of Old Smokey." She was surprised at how loud she was. She sang another verse, much softer this time.

And then she kissed all the white flowers, repeatedly thanking them in her mind. Then she listened for more sounds and made more sounds.

When the sun rose, pushing aside the darkness, and the white flowers folded inward against the morning light, Molly fell asleep, the smile never fading from her face.

Molly awakened to the touch of her mother's hand on her shoulder. She was surprised to find herself in the garden, with foliage all around her, the pale blue sky and her mother's face above her. She pushed herself up to a sitting position and rubbed the sleep from her eyes. Her tongue felt fuzzy, like some of the plants surrounding her.

"What on earth are you doing sleeping out here?" Lara asked.

Molly looked at her, trying to remember. "Moon flowers," she said as it came to her. "They were out last night, and . . ." She growned as she strained to recall the rest. Gradually the memory of her evening in the garden became vivid, and disappointment became a heavy ache inside her. She had lost her hearing. She could see the border of trees, see wind rustling their leaves, but she couldn't hear them. And she couldn't hear the ocean either.

Maybe it had only been a dream.

"What about the moon flowers, sweetheart?" she read on her mother's lips.

"They bloomed again," she answered miserably, not wanting to talk about them. She rose to her feet and slapped dirt and leaves from her robe. A small cloud of brown dust billowed, then drifted into nothingness. She was still tired. "Gonna go to bed," she mumbled, kissing her mother's cheek and heading toward the house.

Lara held her still for a moment. "You had me worried," she said, betraying a trace of anger. "I looked into your room and found you gone. You've no idea how that scared me, Molly."

"I'm sorry, Mom. I saw the flowers from my room and came out here to look at 'em. They only come out at night. And then—" she shrugged apologetically "—I fell asleep."

Lara stared at her, as though trying to decide whether or not to remain angry with her. At length she released her arm and sighed, "Go to your room and get a decent rest."

"I will, Mom," she promised, heading once more for the house. En route she found herself wondering what was worse—to wake up frightened because of bad dreams, or wake up disappointed because of a good dream?

When she reached her room she looked out the window, down at the garden. Morning dew made it sparkle emerald-like in the morning sun. Her mother was looking at the tall plant, the one she suspected was a sunflower. Molly watched her for a long moment, waiting for her to do something besides stare at the plant, but her mother never moved. At length Molly grew tired of watching and waiting. She climbed into her bed and instantly fell asleep.

Everyone was listening to her, and she was talking freely. When she was done, she listened to her friends, and there were many. They all talked at once, some with hands fluttering and covering their lips, some with faces averted, and one even had his back to her. But none of this mattered; she could hear them all so clearly, every consonant and every vowel. Conversing with them was so easy. Not once did she strain to hear, and not once did she ask anyone to repeat.

Then the phone rang, its ring surprisingly loud and shrill. She picked up the receiver and heard another clear voice. A girl was telling a joke, and when she reached the punch line Molly didn't have to fake laughter as she usually did, for she had followed the joke easily and had caught every word. It felt so wonderful not to ask the girl to say the punch line again, although, like most joke tellers, half the line was swallowed with haste and laughter.

When Molly told a joke in return, it felt good not to worry about her t's and g's, or wonder if anyone was laughing at her speech impediment instead of her joke.

After laughter (the good kind) filled her ear, Molly hung up. This was a mistake, for after the receiver made a distinct click as it made contact with the phone, there was silence.

And it was this silence that awakened Molly with a jolt.

Now the sun was beginning to vanish, streaking the lower sky with pink and salmon tendrils. Today had been warm and humid, and tomorrow would be the same. Molly lay on her bed and stared up at the ceiling for a while, straining to hear the sound of the ocean, but it eluded her. She had heard it only last night, and would probably never hear it again. The disappointment began to hurt, creating a painful lump in her throat, but when her chin began to quiver, she angrily bolted upright on the bed.

She was feeling sorry for herself, and this was something she did not want to do. She had accepted her handicap a long time ago. She had accepted and adjusted, so why was she feeling so bad now? If anything, she knew she should be glad that she'd been given a chance to hear so many things for one night. Some people never got a chance like that.

Maybe tonight, a voice inside her suddenly said.

Tonight what?

Tonight you'd be able to hear again, tonight when the flowers bloom.

Molly felt hope stir within her, and she tried to kill it before it grew out of control.

She went to the window, and was surprised to find her mother still in the garden, which was now dark with shadows. The vining plants were near her feet, looking like snakes silently watching her, readying to strike as their ends tilted upward in her direction. Other plants seemed to be turned toward her also, watching and waiting. But Lara seemed unaware of her surroundings, only aware of the tall plant, which she kept close to her nostrils.

Then Molly's gaze slid magnetically to one of the night flowers. It was beginning to unfurl, promising to be large and splendid again.

"Maybe tonight," a voice repeated. This time it was her own.

20

When Steve pushed the empty glass away from him and ordered another Scotch, the bartender promptly gave him a fresh drink and regarded him a few minutes as he wiped the gleaming bar top with a white cloth. Then he said, "How's it going at The Four Winds?"

Steve looked at him through hazy eyes. At first all he saw was a dark mustache before the rest of the face slowly came into focus. He burped, then leaned forward. "Eh?"

"The Four Winds, Steve," the bartender repeated patiently. He knew Steve quite well now, for Steve had been coming into the lounge regularly these past few weeks. This was his halfway stop between the restaurant in Massachusetts and his house in Rhode Island. Sometimes he would be sullen and silent, but mostly he'd be sullen and voluble after his first drink. "How's the restaurant doing?"

The restaurant? Steve had to think a moment. The business hadn't been on his mind lately. He remembered the long drive to the place, but he never went in. He stayed in the parking lot for a spell, then turned around and started homeward, never bothering to get out of the car. He had just needed to drive and relax, and then he would stop here, to relax some more.

"Rest'rant fine," he answered at last, swirling the ice

in his glass with a small, hollow stirrer before discarding the latter onto a blood-red cocktail napkin. Behind him came soft laughter from a young couple at a table. It was Tuesday night and the lounge was nearly empty.

"The wife and I were there a few days ago," the bartender said. "Had a great meal. Food's superb. Service, too."

"Yeah. Hey, thanks." Steve's tongue was suddenly thick as he tried to sound grateful for the compliment.

The bartender nodded, tacitly saying "You're welcome," then retreated to the other end of the bar, sensing that Steve was in the sullen and silent mood tonight.

Steve stared into his drink. An illuminated Budweiser sign on a wall above a shelf of bottles made the whiskey gleam reddish. Normally a compliment regarding his restaurant would have flattered him, but now it seemed completely unimportant. His interest in the business had slipped into a faraway nook in the back of his mind, perhaps never to find its way back to the front again.

Something else dominated all his thoughts—the garden. It reminded him of an oasis, the way it was tall and thick in the middle of an expansive, flat lawn. It didn't belong there. It was alien, and it had sprung up all of a sudden. When Steve had come home yesterday and followed the sound of hysterical laughter, he was surprised to find the garden on the south lawn. It had made him realize how distracted he'd been. Certainly he should have seen the garden before, but he knew the reason he hadn't was that he had let his aversion toward the house make him ignore anything that was connected to it—even his own family.

He had blocked everything out, concentrating on the restaurant or letting alcohol dull the disturbing thoughts. And he had succeeded. He knew he had promised Lara he'd see a psychiatrist and had even made an appointment, but the appointment had slipped his mind. Now he'd have to make another, but he told himself there was plenty of time for that. He still had his business to think about first.

But now all he could think about was that crazy garden.

It spooked him, just like the house did.

It had surprised him when he first saw the garden, then he began to admire it but didn't know why, especially since nothing was in bloom. He remembered a strange feeling washing over him as he watched his wife and her daughter laugh so joyously. He felt their happiness and wanted nothing more at that moment than to join them. He'd never been as happy as he was when he was with them in that strange plot of paradise, and he remembered the disappointment he felt when the sun went away and the garden's green foliage couldn't be seen anymore. Exhausted, he and his family had retired to the house. This morning he had been tempted to return to the garden, but some of the enchantment was lost and the unease had wormed its way back into him, especially when he happened to glance at the cellar door and was reminded of the ancient, dark room below. Kissing his wife, he had hurried out of the house and begun the long drive to his restaurant. As he gained distance, the garden's magic grew weaker—and magic, he was now certain, was what it was.

It was dark magic, the magic that was perpetually seeping out of the cellar, like black smoke fouling the land and air surrounding the house.

Where had that garden come from? Had it sprouted from the ground for no reason at all? Then he vaguely remembered that Molly had admitted planting the garden, but where on earth—or hell—had she got the seeds?

From the cellar, idiot! From that hole you call a room, from where you got that ring that tried to eat your finger, from where you found that piece of mirror in which you watched yourself die!

That's where the seeds came from.

"Christ," he muttered.

Steve wearily held his head in his hands, as though

endeavoring to still his thoughts.

"Want another, Steve?"

Steve looked at the bartender, then at his glass. He was surprised to find it empty. He had drunk it without realizing, so preoccupied had he been with his thoughts. Dropping his hands, he began to shake his head in refusal. He really should go back to the house and urge his family to stay away from the garden, but then again, maybe the next drink would succeed in calming him.

His head began to nod. Just one more, he decided, then he'd go home. Maybe burn the garden, and then burn the fucking house along with it.

"Yeah, one for the road," he said, and slid his empty glass toward the bartender.

The tall flower had begun to open. While Molly slept in her bedroom, Lara reveled in the faint scent that the plant exuded and found herself trying to identify the fragrance. She hadn't noticed it at first, had only stared at the bud in irresistible fascination. She even tried to understand the reason for this attraction but couldn't, and in the end gave up and allowed herself to enjoy the plant. All she cared about was that it made her happy, made her insides swell, made her warm with a strange glow, and made her forget about anything else. Gradually, the scent grew more noticeable, especially as the flower began to unfurl with a slowness that escaped the eye.

The sun rose to its zenith, then declined, but this went unnoticed. Lara continued to sniff the plant, like someone afflicted with a sinus cold would inhale a glob of Vicks VapoRub melting in a bowl of hot water. She leaned forward, drew in the scent, stepped back to exhale, then leaned forward again. She did this repeatedly—all day. She didn't want to stop, for the faint smell was sweet and warm, filling her lungs and head with euphoria.

As the flower opened, she could see it was not at all as she had thought it would be. It was as large as a sunflower, but if anything, it resembled an orchid. The petals were soft and silky, and the color was the blue of a bleached sky. It was a delicate flower, and Lara found herself reluctant to touch it, lest its frail petals rip. She let only her face come near it.

At noon her stomach had grumbled with hunger, but she ignored it and eventually the pangs went away. Now she found herself hungry again. In a daze, she looked over at the western horizon and was surprised to find the sun sinking out of sight. Then, as though sensing someone was watching her, she turned toward the house and spotted her daughter in the window. She lifted her arm to wave, but it felt strangely detached. So much concentration was needed to make it rise, let alone turn the hand from side to side in a wave, that she let the arm drop. She returned to the flower.

She inhaled, exhaled. Happiness flooded her, then left her. She inhaled again, keeping the sensation inside her as long as possible, then released it.

Her stomach growled persistently, and the sensation she'd been getting from the flower began to weaken. She hadn't eaten all day and knew she really should grab a sandwich or something. Her foggy brain realized that Molly probably hadn't eaten today either. What kind of a mother was she to neglect her child like this?

But she didn't want to leave the flower. It would be like leaving a warm bed on a frosty morning. So the only solution, it seemed, was to take the flower with her.

She had not wanted to even touch the plant, but as she continued to inhale and admire it, the blossom seemed to be urging her to claim it. It was not a voice that she could hear, but something she could sense. The repeated in-halation had made the plant a part of herself, filling her body and mind with its existence.

Tentatively, she touched the stem beneath the flower, not knowing what to expect, perhaps a reaction of some kind. When she received none, she touched the plant with both hands, hesitated a moment, then twisted the flower and several inches of stem free from the plant. Again she half-expected a remonstrative reaction, but the flower opened wider, a sign of welcome if anything.

Holding the blossom close to her nostrils, she moved trancelike toward the house. The flower, so wide, concealed most of her face, letting her see the way ahead of her only whenever she lifted her head. In dreamy slowness she eventually reached her destination. Her heels clacked hollowly on the kitchen's tiled floor, a sound that seemed to come from a great distance. She could not feel her feet touching the floor, so it never occurred to her that it was she who was producing the sound.

As of its own volition, her hand opened the refrigerator. Then she glanced inside, made a quick decision, and pulled out a dish of leftover meat loaf. Next, while keeping her face buried in the flower, she took a loaf of bread from the breadbox and mechanically prepared a sandwich.

"Mom?"

The voice sounded faraway and vaguely familiar. Lara lifted her head and thought about what she had heard. Where had it come from? Whose voice was it?

"Mom?"

She turned around but when she saw the girl in the doorway, she didn't recognize her—not at first.

"Hello," she said uncertainly.

"Why are you lookin' ad me like thad?"

The girl talked funny, the voice thick as though speaking with a mouthful. Then something connected in Lara's head, as if someone or something had finally found a neglected electrical plug lying around in her brain and slipped it into one of the myriad outlets. The girl that talked so strangely was Molly, her daughter.

"Looking at you like what, dear?" she said as she lowered her face into the open flower.

"I don'd know—"

"Your t's, your t's, your t's, dear," Lara reminded, her voice sounding like a muffled echo within the petals. "How many times do I have to tell you?"

Molly didn't answer, so Lara looked up. Through her haze she saw that her daughter seemed to be in a daze as well. The girl was staring at her, but seemed deep in thought.

"Hungry?" Lara asked.

She blinked. "Huh?"

"Hungry, dear? Are you hungry?"

Molly's gaze slowly dropped to the meat loaf sandwich on the kitchen counter. She stared at it a moment, then something clicked in her head. "Yeah, I'm hungry."

"Sit down," the mother in Lara automatically ordered. As the girl obeyed, Lara prepared a second sandwich, clumsily using one hand while she held the flower close to her face with the other.

"Pretty flower, Mom."

"Yes."

There was silence, but it was not an awkward one. Molly drifted off into a thoughtful trance, and Lara drifted off into one of her own. She gave a sandwich to Molly, then taking her own, she sat opposite her. Wordlessly, they ate, barely tasting their food.

When Molly was done, she said, "I can't wait for tonight."

"That was . . . very good . . . dear." She paused as she sniffed the flower.

"What?"

"Your t's. You did . . . them all correctly."

"Oh." The girl smiled, but the smile was ghostly. "I concentrated."

"Good . . . very good."

Molly turned toward a window. There was no sunlight spilling into the room, but there wasn't darkness behind the glass either. She looked at a clock on the wall. It was a little after 5:00. "What time does it get dark?"

"Hmm?"

"Dark, Mom. What time does it get dark?"

Without rising from the chair, Lara turned toward the window. She stared out into the gray-purplish dusk for a brief moment, then inhaled the flower, this time keeping her face hidden for a long while.

"Mom?"

"Mmmmm."

"Mom!"

Groggily, Lara lifted her face. The intrusion annoyed her. "What, child?"

"What time does it get dark?"

"Oh." She looked toward the window again. "Steve should be home by now," she dully realized.

"What time does it—"

"But I don't . . . care. Do you . . . care?"

"Time, Mom. What time?"

"How should I . . . know?"

Molly stared at her. "Does it smell pretty?"

"What, dear?"

"The flower. What does it smell like?"

Lara thought about it. "Actually dear, there's not much of a smell . . . It's faint."

"Then why do you keep sniffing it?"

Lara thought about this. "Actually dear, I'm not too . . . sure." She lost herself to the flower again, and when she raised her head, she added, "I get a lovely feeling when I sniff it. Yes, lovely." She smiled dreamily.

The kitchen began to waver, as though the entire room were submerged under clear water, but this sensation neither alarmed her nor made her ill. Instead, it made her feel as though she and everything around her were floating. It was a lovely feeling.

"Mom?"

Lara emitted a petulant sigh. She really wished she could be alone. She loved her daughter very dearly, but at times like this . . .

"Your face, Mom," Molly went on, looking closely at her.

"What's wrong with my face?" she demanded, at the same instant hiding inside the flower.

"Let me see."

After another irritable sigh, she exposed her face for the girl to inspect. It was becoming more and more difficult to pull away from the warm, silky petals. "Well, dear?"

"You're bleeding, Mom."

"What?" It was a simple statement she had heard, but the meaning failed to penetrate. Rather than make an effort to grasp it, she shrugged indifferently and hid her face.

"Mom! You're *bleeding*, Mom!" Molly began shaking her shoulder.

"Please let me alone, dear!" she snapped, not bothering to look up.

"Look in a mirror."

She ignored her, hoping the girl would go away—which for a little while, she did.

Molly couldn't stop thinking about the night flowers. She kept glancing out the kitchen window, each time hoping she'd find complete darkness outside, but the world beyond the window panes was still gray, more light than dark. Between these impatient glances she watched her mother with mild concern.

When she saw the blood, there was a spark of alarm, then she looked out the window again and momentarily forgot about her mother. When she spotted the blood the second time, the alarm inside of her was stronger and longer. Her mother's pretty face was unnaturally pale, and blood was oozing from a raw sore below one of the nostrils. Like a bleeding cold sore, she thought. Then her gaze returned to the window.

It was a little darker now, wasn't it? The night flowers would soon be fully open, or maybe they already were. There were no windows in the kitchen that looked out onto the south garden, so she hurried out of the room to find a window that did.

She sped toward the library and peered out there, pushing aside heavy, velvet drapes. If she craned her neck she could see a glimpse of the garden—and two of the night flowers. They were half-open. Soon they would be ready for her!

She stood motionless at the window, as though waiting for dusk to deepen. Then she remembered her mother, and the alarm released another spark inside her. She had mentioned something about a mirror. She had wanted her mother to look into one.

So Molly rushed toward the nearest bathroom, found a gilded hand mirror, and raced back into the kitchen with it.

"Leave me . . . alone," her mother moaned when she shook her shoulder. The pale blue flower that hid her face seemed to have grown larger since Molly had left the room.

"Look, Mom, look!" She shook her mother harder, holding the mirror before her.

At length Lara pulled her face away and peered through small, glazed eyes into the mirror. A thin smear of blood ran from below one nostril down to her chin, and the sore from which it bled was the size of a dime and shredded, as though it had been chewed. Now that the flower was not absorbing the wound anymore, the blood bubbled forth and trickled bright red, passing her chin and streaking her neck.

"It's eating your face, Mom."

But Lara didn't seem to care. It was as if she were looking at another person in the mirror, a stranger, and Molly experienced a similar detachment. It was not her mother she was looking at. It was a stranger to her, too, and it was a stranger that did not concern her.

Lara bowed her head to the open flower.

Molly put the hand mirror down on the kitchen table and went to the window.

It was getting darker and darker.

21

The moon was a brilliant sphere, almost full, and stars were everywhere in the black sky. Never had Molly seen so many at once. It was as though every star in the universe had decided to shine through tonight to watch something very special, something that they knew would soon happen.

And Molly was confident that it would be very special. Hands deep in her jeans' pockets, she waited among the five night flowers, which appeared as big and luminous as the moon itself. She shivered when a cool breeze blew in from the ocean, snaked its way around the house, and fanned her face. Then, as quickly as it had come, it was gone, replaced by a lifeless stillness.

She turned the volume of her hearing aid all the way up, then waited.

The stillness continued, the white moonlight spotlighting her, but nothing happened.

Molly felt a lump grow in her throat as disappointment filled her. She had waited all day for this. She strained to listen to the sound of the ocean pounding against the big rocks on the east side of the property, but she heard nothing. Had she dreamed about this last night? Had nothing at all happened here in the garden?

She fought back a strong urge to cry. She'd wait 15 more minutes, then if nothing happened, she'd go back into the house and forget about it.

But somehow, deep inside, she knew her experience in the garden had not been a dream—unless she was dreaming right this very minute. She could sense something, something unnatural in the air. It reminded her of the feeling in the cellar. No, it was not a dream; it was real. The disappointment that had saddened her began to fade, and she was again confident that something would happen tonight.

She was going to hear again tonight.

Another breeze wormed its way toward her, this one colder than the first. Her teeth chattered, and her hands dug deeper into her pockets. Then she heard—sensed—a voice. It whispered the same sibilant words that had filled her mind the previous night.

Wish . . . Molly . . . Any . . . Make . . .

"Same wish!" she cried out loud, relieved and elated that she was given another chance. "I wanna hear again."

There was a soft, dry laugh, and Molly wasn't sure if it was friendly or not. But when she heard leaves rustling in the trees, she gave the laugh no further thought. She stared at the black treetops, saw them sway in the wind that was beginning to blow frequently, and listened. The rustling was incredibly loud.

Then she heard the ocean. It sounded much louder than it did the night before. It was an angry sound, yet to her it was beautiful. This time she gave in to an urge to run to the ocean. As she ran toward the east side, to her amazement she found herself able to hear each step whenever her foot slammed down on the ground.

She laughed, swirled around in the grass, then ran again toward the waist-high wall that separated the lawn from the rocky shore. When she at last reached her destination she found herself pressing her hands against her ears; to her added astonishment and delight the noise was deafening.

She laughed again, but the laughter was lost amidst the violent roar of the surf. She could not see much of the water below, only the whitecaps and sprays as they slammed and swirled around the boulders. The turbulence was all directly below her, but farther out the water seemed incongruously tranquil, deep black except for the pale path on the surface cast by the moon.

Molly withdrew her hands from her ears for a moment. The roar filled her head, and she quickly covered her ears again. The sound did not really hurt. In fact, she enjoyed the incredible loudness, but it would take some getting used to.

She stared in awe at the violent foam around the rocks for a while, letting the angry sound seep into her ears a little at a time, then she withdrew from the wall, suddenly impatient to hear other sounds. She ran to the north side of the house.

Dropping her hands from her ears, she distinctly heard her footfalls again. They were louder, booming drumlike in the air. Were you supposed to hear the sound of your feet hitting the grass like this? There was so much she didn't know about the hearing world, and her heart thundered in her chest in eagerness to learn more.

She halted before the north garden. The sole artichoke-like plant was concealed in shadow. Only the outline of its bulk could been seen, which was now as large as she was, but she could hear it! It was *crr-rreeeaking* as it was growing.

But that was not all that was creaking. The house behind her was making the same kind of sound. Because it was old? she wondered, spinning around toward it. Did old people creak too, when their bones got too stiff to move freely?

She moved her own arm to find out, bending it several times at the elbow. There was a faint pop, but no creak. Then, shrugging, she raced toward the west side. She wanted to hear as many sounds as possible, and she knew she only had the night in which to do it. The morning sun would take her hearing away, and the night flowers might never give her another wish.

A loud windy noise made her gasp and skid to a halt.

The sound had been a powerful whoosh, and it had come from . . . from the road. A car?

Molly's hand covered her lips in disbelief, then she laughed into it. It was all so incredible! She never knew a passing car even made a sound, let alone such a loud one. It had sounded like a train had passed through—not that she had ever heard one, of course. It was what she had imagined it'd be like.

She ran to the driveway and squealed with delight when the heels of her shoes hit the hard pavement. Slap-slap! She jumped down on it. Slap. Slap. Slap-slap. She then began to tap dance on it. Tap-tap. Slap. Tap. Tap. Tap-tap. Slap.

"Ta-dah!" She dropped to her knees and spread her arms, Al Jolson fashion. She imagined the applause, but it was really the ocean she was hearing. Even on this side of the house it was deafening. Then another car sped past, and the noise made her emit another gasp, startling her as though someone had flung a bucketful of icy water on her. Also, the noise had actually hurt and made her head fill up with eerie pressure.

It sure was gonna take some getting used to.

But at least she could hear, and that's what was important. Later, in the morning, she'd remember everything she had heard tonight, but the pain she would forget.

Deciding there were no more sounds to be heard outside, she went into the house. There was a bunch of things she wanted to hear—water from the faucet, the ticking of the grandfather clock, her mother's voice.

A sound resembling a gunshot exploded in her ear, and she cried out, pressing her palms against her ears. She pivoted to see what she had heard, but saw only the front door. She had shut the massive door but had thought she'd done so easily, not slamming it. Now she could hear the leaded glass surrounding the doorframe twang with tension. Still holding her ears, Molly held her breath, expecting the glass to shatter, but the twanging ceased.

When it stopped completely, Molly lowered her hands and exhaled with relief. She found that she could still hear the ocean, although now the sound was comfortably muffled.

Did people normally hear things this loudly? She wasn't sure if she liked having to hear like this. She wished she could turn her hearing down. Her feet touching down on the carpet sounded the same as when they had walked on the grass. It didn't seem to matter how gentle she was.

She lifted her hands to block her ears again.

The house was in darkness, but unlike all the other darkness she had known, this one was filled with sounds—bad sounds—and none of them recognizable. The closest to her was an annoying snipping noise, causing her to imagine a giant pair of scissors cutting away at something. She groped for a light switch, her hand making a horrible rubbery sound as her palm swept the wall. When it finally found it and flipped the switch, a sharp crackle filled the air, sounding as though lightning had struck. She emitted a cry, then fell back against a wall.

Too loud, too loud!

How can people stand this?

Gotta get used to it.

She wasn't sure if she ever would, or even if she'd want to. She leaned against the wall again, waited until her heart was reasonably calm, then pushed herself away. The strange scissorlike sound she heard, she now saw, were not snips but rather ticks of the grandfather clock. Tick . . . tick . . . tick . . .

No tocks, she noted, only ticks.

And not soft as she'd thought they'd be, but loud, much too loud. No longer interested in finding as much noise as possible in the house, she went in search of her mother. She wanted to hear her voice, for she was confident that it would be unlike all these other sounds and be beautiful and soothing.

But Molly couldn't run, for the slamming footfalls

would hurt her ears. Was it like this when a blind person suddenly found himself able to see? Did everything seem too bright, so bright that his eyes hurt? Was this like that?

Moving carefully, as though walking on a floor made of fragile glass, Molly looked into many rooms. She called out for her mother, but quickly gave this up. It seemed no matter how softly she whispered, it would pierce her ears with knifelike sharpness.

After looking into all the rooms downstairs, she started up the stairs, each step creaking raucously under her.

She paused halfway, needing a respite from the creaking sound, but other noises penetrated her hands and filled her head—the ticking of clocks, the wind rattling the windows, her own loud breathing. Even the sound of her heart bothered her, for it seemed to be hammering its way out of her chest. Then, of course, there was the never-changing, forever angry ocean, crashing and crashing.

Molly began to whimper.

No, she'd never get used to it. She didn't like this at all. She wanted the peaceful silence back.

Drawing in a deep breath, she forced herself to finish the flight of stairs. She wanted her mother desperately, wanted to bury her face in her warm chest and muffle, if not block out completely, all these horrible sounds.

She moved slowly down the hall, then began to turn the door knob to her mother's bedroom. The knob squeaked and Molly winced, then she pushed the door inward, steeling herself against the grating creak that she knew would come.

At last she found her mother, standing in the middle of the room in the dark. Molly could see her shadowy form and could see that she wasn't moving. A long minute passed, and still there was no motion. Molly opened her mouth to call out to her mother, then changed her mind. She didn't want to hear her own voice, didn't want to make any noise at all, if possible.

She searched for the light switch, carefully avoiding contact with the wall. When her hand found the switch, she decided against flipping it, remembering the loud knifelike crackle she had heard in the foyer. She feared it would be louder and more painful this time. She let her hand drop and watched her mother in silence.

Eyes adjusting to the gloom, she could see her mother more clearly, and still her mother did not move. Alarm coursed through her as she wondered if the other was possibly dead. Then she realized that a dead person could not stand up like this on her own. Could she?

She became aware of her mother's breathing, and once she was aware of this, it became unmistakable and progressively louder. Every intake of breath and exhalation was distinct, prolonged and raspy. Yes, her mother was still alive, but why was she so deathly still?

Molly swallowed, although her mouth was dry, and got ready to speak in the softest voice possible. "Mom?"

The sound vibrated in her skull, echoing maddeningly as though trapped wihin. She clutched her head, but of course it did no good. She stared at her mother, hoping she had at least elicited a response, but her mother remained motionless. Now Molly could make out the dark form perfectly. The woman's head was bent forward, and in her hand was the big flower, which was raised to her face. She was still smelling the flower, Molly realized with amazement, then felt a chill. She wished her mother would move, would lift her head back or something.

"Mom?" she repeated, now more concerned about her mother than about hurting her own ears.

The woman did not respond, as though unaware of Molly's presence. Molly then ran to her and shook her, but it was like shaking a corpse—lifeless, except for the breathing.

"Mom! Mom!"

Hot pain pierced her ears and head, but she fought determinedly to ignore it. She continued to shake her mother, over and over, but it was useless. Her mother's head remained bent over the flower.

Molly ran back to the light switch and flipped it. She

heard the sharp snap, but her panic muted it. She spun around toward her mother.

The overhead light starkly illuminated Lara. The first thing Molly noticed was the arms, thin and pale, prompting her to wonder why she'd never noticed before how frail they were. Then she noticed the flower at the end of these arms, and she gasped at its size. It reminded her of a large mixing bowl. Inside this bowl was her mother's face, and on its sides and down the pale arms were streaks of red.

Blood?

Molly gawked, not certain of what she was seeing. The flower was not a bleached blue anymore, but had changed to an angry purple. *And what makes purple, children?* The voice of Mr. Alberts, her first grade teacher, suddenly came to mind. She could see his condescending smile as he cradled the blackboard pointer in the crook of one arm. *Blue and red, Mr. Alberts,* the classroom replied in tandem.

Blue from the flower. Red from . . . blood. Mix 'em together and you'd get . . .

Slowly, Lara lifted her face from the flower. Then, she turned her head mechanically toward Molly and smiled.

A sudden gust of wind slammed against a window, rattling the glass and the girl's head.

"Mom?" she whispered, hugging herself tighter. Her throat constricted and for an instant she was certain she'd never breathe again. Then air rushed in and out of her lungs frantically. "Mom, stop it!"

But the woman stared blankly at her, keeping that hideous grin. Her face was potted with bloody sores, looking as if a rat had feasted on it.

"Hello . . . sweet . . . heart," she replied thickly and slowly, as though drugged. Molly stumbled backward, pressing her hands against her ears. Then her mother returned to the flower, sinking her face into its greedy petals.

"No, Mom. No." Molly reached out for the flower, wanting to snatch it away from her, but her mother with unexpected swiftness slipped away from her and was soon at the other end of the room.

From this distance Lara watched her. The smile was still there, as though death had frozen it, but the eyes glared with fury. "Stay . . . away," she hissed.

"Mom, please." Molly reached out, but her mother recoiled, her back against a wall.

"Stay . . . away."

"Mom—"

The woman offered her face to the flower again. When she lifted it to keep a watchful eye on Molly, blood poured from a fresh wound. She seemed unaware of it streaming down her neck and staining the front of her white cotton blouse. It was either this, or she simply did not care.

"Mom, the flower is hurting your face. Stop it, Mom. Stop it." Molly would have screamed the words, but she was afraid the sound would hurt too much. She made another attempt to snatch the flower, but her mother swung toward her and shrieked.

"Away, child!"

Molly bit back a cry, clutched her skull and fell to her knees. Too loud, too loud. God help me, please! Too loud!

She began to cry, not knowing how much more of this she could take. She had never thought that sounds could be so painful. Why hadn't anyone told her? Otherwise she'd never have made the wish.

Then she heard another horrible noise—a deafening slam. There were thunderous footfalls racing up the stairs, sounds that should have been distant but seemed to be inside her head.

Stop! she sobbed. Too loud. Stop.

The door to the room flung open and crashed against the wall. Molly screamed, feeling as though her head had just exploded.

Through her haze of pain she saw Steve gawking at her, then she followed his gaze as it swung toward her mother. Pale and bloody, Lara grinned at Steve, then dipped her face into the dripping blossom.

"Jesus Christ," Steve said, and Molly whimpered, wishing he hadn't spoken so loudly.

He rushed toward his wife, while Molly doubled over on the floor, hands over her head, muffling the sound in any way she could.

"Lara!" he shouted, gripping the woman's shoulders and shaking her. "What did you do?"

The flower fell from Lara's hand and fluttered to the floor. Lara fought to retrieve it, but Steve held her in his grip.

"Let me go!" she demanded. "Damn you! Let me go!"

"Your face!"

"Stop!" Molly cried. "Please, stop!" She was going to lose her mind; she could feel it. She felt like a glass that was vibrating from the noise, and any minute now the glass was going to shatter.

Steve swung toward her. "What's the matter with you?" He released his wife, who immediately scrambled for the flower, and kneeled before Molly.

"What's the matter?" he repeated.

Too loud, too loud, she almost replied, but suddenly her mind knew the real answer, knew what really was the matter. "The garden!" she cried, forcing herself to unfold and sit upright.

"What about the—" He stopped in midsentence as his attention returned to his wife. She was kneeling on the floor, her face in the flower. "What the hell is going on?"

"Don't yell," Molly pleaded, then repeated, "The garden. Id's the garden thad's doin' this."

Steve, confused, glanced frantically at his wife, then back at her. "I don't under—"

Molly grabbed his hand, struggled to her feet, and pulled him toward the door. "The garden," she said again.

He hesitated to follow her, but she was determined. She kept pulling until he gave in.

Outside, noises attacked her everywhere. Molly buried her face against Steve's shirt, like an ostrich in sand, but nothing seemed to help. Steve pushed her away from him and forced her to look up at his face.

"What's wrong?" he enunciated each word. She knew he thought she needed to read his lips, but it was different now. She could hear without seeing—and it was all because of the garden.

"The garden," she said for the umpteenth time. At last they reached it. The five white flowers watched them, seemingly guileless with their delicacy.

"What about it?"

"Id-Id hurdin' me . . . hurdin' Mom."

"How?" He frowned at her, as though wondering if he should be rushing her to a state hospital rather than wasting time out here with a bunch of flowers.

She wished she didn't have to explain, wished he could somehow make all the noise go away. Holding her head with both hands, she began to whimper, then sob.

"Hey, honey, don't cry. Don't cry."

"Godda get rid of id!" she abruptly realized, then in a frenzy started pulling at the plants. Some ripped easily from the soil, but others, including the night flowers, clung to it. "Help me!" she pleaded with Steve.

"Why? Wha—"

"Help me!"

He blinked in confusion, glancing back at the house, and apparently wondering if he should return to his wife, then succumbed to Molly's pleas and helped yank the plants out of the soil.

But he, too, wasn't strong enough to remove the night flowers.

Molly could hear them laugh now. Their laughter was everywhere, even inside her head, and their laughter was cruel and wicked.

God, help! she prayed. Help me, please!

Then it occurred to her to burn the garden. In an

explosion of hope, she cried out to Steve, "A fire!"

"What?"

"Burn id!"

"But—"

"You godda burn id! You godda!"

Once more he blinked indecisively. His breath reeked of whiskey but his eyes were not glazed with alcohol. They were wide and alert, darting back and forth from the garden to the house, where his wife was. He was beginning to understand.

Please, please, Molly sobbed, not sure if she had said the words aloud or screamed them inside her head. She could still hear the laughter rising in pitch, and soon, she was certain, she was going to lose her mind.

Steve watched her face with growing alarm, then he bolted for the shed on the east lawn. Not wanting to be alone, Molly ran behind him, stumbling as she endeavored to keep up with him. The sibilant laughter followed.

When they reached the shed, Steve unhooked the unlocked padlock, and the metal clanged in Molly's ears like the jangle of giant chains. She moaned, but she forced herself to endure the sound, telling herself it would soon be over. She had an idea what Steve was doing, what he was looking for.

Steve threw open the door and rushed inside the gloom. Molly held back, for he was knocking things aside in his hasty search. Molly bit her lip, fighting back sobs and wails.

After what seemed like an hour rather than minutes, Steve emerged from the shed's darkness, carrying a red and yellow gasoline can. Then without exchanging any words, the pair rushed back to the south side.

The laughter rose in volume, but when Steve began dousing the plants, glistening them darkly in the moonlight, the pitch changed to shrieks.

"Ooooow," Molly cried. The shrieks were inside her, crowding her mind, pushing outward against her skull.

Steve threw a match.

Whooooosh!

Molly thought her head had finally erupted like the top of a volcanic mountain, before realizing it was the gasoline that had made the noise. Heat and the oily smell of fuel filled the night air, momentarily reddening it with orange-yellow flames. Then the roar of the fire made her bolt from the scene. She couldn't stand it anymore! Too loud!

She heard grating screams and knew it was the plants. Was this how it was in hell? Was this the sound of tormented souls burning in the eternal fire?

She ran around the house, as though she, herself, were on fire. She pressed her hands against her ears, painfully crushing them, pushing them against her skull. She ran around and around, pressing and pressing.

Eventually the loud roar and cackles stopped, as well as the shrieks and wails. Molly was on the west side when she became aware of this. She glimpsed a car on the street speeding by—but she didn't hear it. Everything was back to normal.

Molly ran to Steve, sobbing with relief. There was a dizzying buzz in her head, but she knew this would soon go away. She crumpled in Steve's arms and began to weep convulsively. She felt his hand stroke her hair, endeavoring to soothe her.

"Everything's all right now, hon," he said. "Everything's all right."

He gave her a handkerchief and she wiped her eyes and nose with it. Sniffing back and hiccuping the remaining tears, she looked at the garden. The fire was dying, and the plants were gone, already reduced to ashes.

She cuddled against ther stepfather and sighed again with relief. She could hear no sounds, only feel the beating of Steve's heart and his breath as it fanned the top of her head. Thank you, God, her mind said gratefully.

At last there was peaceful silence.

Part IV: The North Garden

22

Lara heard soft voices, giggles and rapid conversation, then rubbery footsteps on the tiled floor. A metal cart trundled past. She heard a cheerful "Good morning," then heard an indistinct grunt in reply, which sounded male and old. She became aware of odors and found herself identifying them—Lysol, rubbing alcohol, and urine—and before she opened her eyes, she knew she was in a hospital.

Through a fog she saw two faces looking down at her but didn't recognize them until they spoke.

"Mom?"

"Honey?"

She smiled at them, or thought she did, for her face felt numb and stiff as though it were packed with plaster. She withdrew her hand from under a blanket and extended it toward her beautiful family, the two most wonderful people in her life. Her eyes filled with tears. She wasn't certain why she was emotional or felt a need to cry, but she felt as though she'd been on a long journey and had just come back. She felt her husband's warm hand touch hers. Weakly, she gripped it as hard as she could, but it was useless; she couldn't hold on. She closed her eyes and drifted back to from where she'd come.

When she returned, it was to a new face, black and male, a face she'd never seen before. She closed her eyes, willing it to go away, but when she reopened her eyes, it was still there. It was smiling at her, and its eyes were dark and warm. A friend, her groggy mind thought. Then she saw the pale blue shirt rolled up at the sleeves and the tie loose around the neck, and she knew this was a professional man, and the smile and gleaming eyes had fooled her. He was being polite, not friendly.

"Who. . . ?" she began curiously. She tried to push herself up to a sitting position, but found herself too weak and groggy.

"Mrs. Ludden," he said nodding courteously, "I'm Detective Davis from the police department. If I may, I would like to ask you a few questions."

"Sure." Her voice sounded small and uncertain. She had no idea what this man wanted to know, and she had no idea why she was in this hospital bed. She tried to remember what had happened before she came here, but she could only recall disjointed, dreamlike things. She remembered a flower, her daughter shaking her, her husband holding her, a siren wailing, red lights spinning around and around.

"Mrs. Ludden?"

"Oh . . . I'm sorry," she apologized, giving him the attention he politely demanded. Again she tried to sit upright, and this time with the detective's help she succeeded, for he had pressed the button that elevated the top half of the bed. "Thank you," she said when she was in a comfortable position.

"My pleasure, Mrs. Ludden." He nodded and smiled. "I'd appreciate anything you wish to tell me about the night of . . . ah, your misfortune."

Lara frowned. "Misfortune?"

He pointedly let his gaze roam over her face until she lifted her hand to touch it. She found most of it covered with bandages, but somehow wasn't surprised. Her subconscious must have already known this.

"Certainly you remember something," the detective said, his gaze now focused on her eyes, patiently waiting.

But she couldn't remember very much. "Only the

flower," she said out loud.

"Flower, Mrs. Ludden?"

"Yes," she replied slowly. "It was so lovely. Blue, like your shirt and . . . and . . ." Her memory was failing her.

"What kind of flower was it?"

The image of the plant floated ghostlike in her mind. She could see its delicate petals opening until it resembled a bowl. Then it faded. She had never seen a flower like that before. "I don't know," she said.

"A rose, perhaps, Mrs. Ludden? Or a gardenia? Or—"

"I said I didn't know."

"I understand."

No, you don't, Lara thought, but said nothing.

After a pause, he went on. "What does this flower bring to mind, Mrs. Ludden?"

"I was . . ." She concentrated, but it was as if she were trying to remember details of a dream she just had. She knew something was eluding her. "I was . . . admiring it. Yes, I remember that. It was so lovely and . . . and . . ."

"Do you remember injuring your face at all, Mrs. Ludden?" He interrupted, apparently deciding he'd been patient long enough, though still managing to keep his voice and countenance pleasant.

"No, I don't remember hurting my face," she said, again touching it. She felt no pain, only the rough fabric of a bandage. Was she ugly now? Had she done irreparable damage to her face? Where was the doctor? Why hadn't he told her what was wrong with her face?

Then she remembered that a doctor had examined her. The moment had been lost in the confusion of other moments, and now the doctor's face floated to the surface. The doctor had been a man with gray, wiry hair and heavy eyebrows, reminding her of Groucho Marx. He even had a tendency to roll his eyes, which twinkled warmly. The only thing missing was the cigar at the corner of his mouth. Yes, she remembered him vividly now. He had assured her that she would be fine, that only minor cosmetic surgery would be required. She had relaxed, believing him, and drifted off to sleep.

"Do you remember anything, Mrs. Ludden?" Detective Davis demanded gently, pulling her out of her reverie.

"The doctor said I'll be all right."

"Yes, he did. Many of the wounds are superficial, but what I would like for you to tell me is how you got them."

Still touching her bandages, Lara spotted the hand mirror on the table next to the bed and reached for it. The detective, the gentleman that he was, reached for the mirror himself and gave it to her.

"Thank you."

"My pleasure, Mrs. Ludden."

Lara looked into the mirror, and again a fragment of memory was dislodged, rising to the surface. She had seen herself in this mirror already and had cried, while the doctor had assured her there was nothing to cry about. The patchwork of bandages which made her face look like a hideous quilt made it seem worse than it actually was. Sighing, she handed the mirror back to the detective.

"Please put it back."

"My pleasure, Mrs. Ludden."

Lara gave him a weak smile; the plastic politeness was becoming infectious.

"Do you remember how you hurt yourself?" he asked again. "Do you remember anything at all?"

"The flower," she repeated, for it was the only thing that came to her mind. "The flower."

The detective's countenance hardened as he fought to maintain civility and patience. "Do you recall having a squabble with your husband? A struggle, perhaps?"

"No."

"You sure?"

"Why? Are you implying that Steve did this?"

"My profession demands that I be impartial, Mrs. Ludden. I am merely trying to help you refresh your memory, nothing more."

"Steve would never hurt me!"

"I do not know the man, so of course I've no way of knowing this."

"Well, if you did know him, you would know that he'd never—"

"Then what did hurt you, Mrs. Ludden?"

Lara's mouth remained open, although she didn't finish her sentence. She desperately tried to remember, but the flower seemed to be the only answer. "Flower," she whispered once more.

"Very well, the flower then. What about it? Please elaborate."

She stared at the black man, her face wrinkling as she concentrated. "I think . . . I think it had enchanted me. Yes, I think that's what happened. It blocked everything out."

"Drugs, perhaps?" he suggested quietly.

"What?"

He didn't repeat the suggestion, for he was certain she had heard him.

"I don't think any drugs were involved, Mr. . . . ." She had forgotten his surname.

"Davis. Gregory Davis. But, of course, you can call me—"

"Mr. Davis, I hesitate to take aspirin, so I really don't believe drugs are responsible for this memory blockage."

"Drugs that you weren't aware of, maybe?"

"What do you mean?"

"Perhaps someone slipped something in, let's say, your drink or your food."

"But why? And who?"

The detective remained silent, deliberately letting the questions linger. Then Steve entered the room carrying roses and baby's breath, the stems of which were wrapped in dark green tissue.

"More flowers," the detective quipped.

But the sarcasm was lost on Steve as he looked into Davis's smiling face and the deceiving brown eyes.

"The husband, I presume?" he said, and when Steve

nodded affirmatively, he extended a hand. The men shook, then Steve stepped toward the bed and gave Lara the flowers. She accepted them, somewhat reluctantly, while the detective reached for his sports jacket which he had draped over a chair. Shrugging into it, he said, "I'll leave you two to yourselves now. Good day, Mr. and Mrs. Ludden."

When he was gone, Steve said, "Is something wrong with the flowers, hon?"

"No, no, they're lovely. It's just that . . ." She put the roses and baby's breath aside on the bed table. "I'm a little uneasy . . . about flowers."

Steve leaned over and kissed her forehead, and when he saw that she was smiling, he kissed the smile. "I love you," he whispered.

"And I love you."

He gave her another kiss, a longer one, then pulled a chair up close to the bed and sat in it. "You're remembering?" he said.

"Yes, but not too much. How long have I been in here?"

"Only a day and a half."

"Oh." She felt as if she'd been here much longer, especially since her memory was so foggy.

"Everything's going to be all right now," Steve assured her. "The doctor said only minor surgery will be needed. There will be some small scars, but nothing to be alarmed about."

"Yes, I remember the doctor." After a pause, she asked, "Was I on drugs, Steve? Was that why I was under for so long, why I can't remember everything?"

"The doctor is running some tests. He can't understand why you were in such a groggy state. He's puzzled. The wounds were superficial and—"

"Why was I in that state, Steve?" she demanded. She pulled the blanket up over her shoulders, for the room seemed suddenly chilly.

"You tell me," he replied quietly.

Again, only one answer floated to the surface. "The flower."

"Where did it come from?"

"The garden. Molly's garden."

"And where did she get—"

"Where is she now?"

"What?"

"Where's Molly?"

"Relax, hon," Steve urged gently. "Molly's in the lobby. I told her I wanted to see you alone for a little while, to talk to you about this."

"Is everything all right with her?"

"Yes. She's a little shaken up, and so am I. I wanted to see what you knew about this garden stuff before I talked to her."

Two nurses passed by the room, squeals of laughter trailing after them. Lara waited until the sound faded, using the moment to think.

She said, "She planted the gardens almost as soon as we moved into the house. I remember I was glad that she'd found herself a little hobby."

"What made her start? Where did she get the plants?"

"From seeds, I imagine."

"And where did she get the seeds?"

The rapidity of his questions and the intense look on his face disturbed her. "I don't know, dear. She never told me."

"How many gardens did she plant?"

"I'm not sure."

"But it was more than one?"

"Yes." Gradually her mind recalled the garden in which all the flowers, save the colors, were identical. Those flowers had been lovely, too, and they had reminded her of soldiers, the way they were in perfect rows. Whatever had happened to them?

"Two gardens, as far as I know," she said at length. "I haven't been outside on the grounds much."

"Well, I've burnt one of them, and Molly has been too

upset to talk about it. But I am going to have her talk about it,'' he added adamantly, as though expecting Lara to protest.

But Lara was trying to understand what had happened to her. So much of it did not make sense. "What did I do to my face?" she asked. "How did it happen? What happened, Steve?"

"I'm not sure. I think the flower . . ." His voice trailed off.

"The flower did it?"

He said nothing, then gave her a faint nod.

"But . . . but how?"

Again he hesitated to reply. "Magic."

Lara stared at him. He was serious, for his eyes were flat and his mouth was pulled back in a tight, grim line. A muscle pulsed at his temple. Two days ago she would have reminded him to see a psychiatrist, but now . . .

She was beginning to believe him.

Nothing else made sense.

She looked away from him. "It's over now," she said. "Everything will be back to normal."

"We're moving out of that house." It was a firm statement, leaving no room for argument.

She looked back at him, then said quietly, "All right."

Surprise flickered in his eyes, since he hadn't expected her to agree so easily. "It'll be best, honey," he said after a long silence.

"I know," she whispered, then smiled when his warm lips kissed hers. Magic, she thought. Kisses were magic. Love was magic. Magic did exist, and there were all kinds of magic. Beautiful magic—and ugly magic.

But they did exist. Yes, they did.

Later, when Molly came into the room, Lara smiled and spread out her arms, but the girl seemed hesitant to fall into them. "I'm sorry, Mom," she said, and Lara could see the grief and guilt in her eyes and pouting mouth.

"Sweetheart, don't blame yourself. I'm going to be all right."

Molly didn't seem to believe her, but she came closer, hugged her and kissed her cheek, finding a spot that was free of bandage. Magic, Lara thought again, then closed her eyes. She was tired and could feel herself beginning to drift away. Beautiful magic, sweet magic . . .

She never heard her husband and daughter leave the room.

Detective Davis was waiting for Steve and Molly at the gate of the big house. Steve stifled a groan as he pulled his Cutlass into the driveway while the detective's silver Toyota Hatchback followed. Questions, questions, he thought miserably. Will there be no end to them? The police had come around yesterday, and now it was the detective's turn.

"Who's that?" Molly asked, turning to look out the rear window.

"Cop," he replied, then braked the car and killed the engine. He waited until the black investigator was at the car door looking in, nodding courteously at him, then he got out.

"I'm Detective Davis, Mr. Ludden. We already met at—"

"I remember."

"If it isn't too much of an inconvenience, I would like to ask you and this young lady here a few questions. I promise not to consume too much of your time."

"Shoot."

The detective gave him another polite nod, mutely thanking him for his cooperation. "May we go outside?"

Steve shrugged, then led the way to the front entrance. When they were seated in the living room, the detective complimented him on the house, then came to the point.

"Exactly what happened, Mr. Ludden?"

"I was not here for most of it."

"I see. Mind telling me where you were?"

"Does it matter? I don't understand what all this is about. There's no crime involved here."

"To put it bluntly, Mr. Ludden, your wife's condition

was found to be rather puzzling, to say the least. Of
course, you have the right not to tell us anything, but we
are trying to understand what happened. Rat bites were
ruled out. Chemicals are being questioned—''

"You think I tried to kill my wife? Is that it?" Steve's
voice rose incredulously.

"I'm an objective man, Mr. Ludden. I don't make any
conclusions until I am certain of all the facts."

"Facts!" Steve spat out the word with disgust. "You
wouldn't believe 'em if I gave them to you."

"I might, Mr. Ludden." The detective gave him a
shrug and a raised brow, as though to say, "Try me."

Steve leaned back against the sofa as he tried to decide
how much he should tell. He thought of pouring himself
a glass of Scotch, then changed his mind. He might talk
too freely.

For a protracted moment the men's eyes locked.
Would he believe me? Steve wondered. Or would he, as
Lara had first done, insist that he seek psychiatric aid?

Did it matter whether or not the detective believed
him?

At length, Steve said, "The flower did it."

The detective was nonplussed. His countenance said,
as though the words had been distinctly uttered, "What is
this, some kind of a sick joke?" Then the dark face
slowly hardened. With anger? With controlled patience?

"I knew you wouldn't believe me," Steve reminded
him.

"Your wife claims the very same thing," the detective
said, ignoring the remark. "Now please tell me, Mr.
Ludden. How is it possible for a flower to harm Mrs.
Ludden the way it did?"

"I don't know." Again he was tempted to pour
himself a drink and again forced himself not to think
about it. He'd wait until after the detective was gone.

"But you do know that the flower was responsible?"

Steve said nothing.

"Does this flower have *teeth*?" Mockery was in his
polite voice.

"Didn't look."

"May I see this incredible flower, Mr. Ludden?"

"It's gone. It withered away."

"Oh." The one word sounded smug. "Are there any remains, any evidence of its existence?"

"It withered away in one of the bedrooms. No one picked it up because . . ." His mouth was so goddamn dry!

The detective leaned closer, and his voice was suddenly gentle. "Because what, Mr. Ludden?"

Steve licked his lower lips. "It was covered with blood."

The detective leaned back again, his face once more hard with that controlled anger or patience. "I see. The flower was dripping with it, wasn't it?"

"What? . . . Uh, yes."

"May I see the bedroom where this flower had withered away?"

"Sure," he said, rising to his feet. He willed himself to ignore the panic that was stirring inside him like a frenetic animal in a cage made of thin glass. Had he said too much? Would the detective get the men in white after him?

In the bedroom where Lara had spent most of the evening with the flower, the two men stood before the blood stains on the ancient Indian rug. Molly had slipped into her own room, having given up trying to follow the men's discussion.

"Would you mind if I sent someone down to take a sample of this stain?"

Steve shrugged, seeing no sense in objecting. He wasn't even sure if he was at liberty to object, and besides, he had nothing to hide.

"And these . . . dust particles, too," the man added, noticing a tiny heap of reddish-brown powder. Then, with an amicable smile that Steve was beginning to dislike immensely because of its insincerity, he stepped away from the spot where the flower had been dropped and said, "I would appreciate a few words with the girl.

Molly is her name, am I correct?"

"Why do you wish to speak with her?"

"She was present most of the time, was she not? You said you were away, though you failed to say where. Care to inform me now?"

"I was at work at my restaurant. Then I stopped for a few drinks. No crime, I hope," he finished sarcastically.

The detective merely maintained his smile. Then he walked to the door. "The girl, if you don't mind?" he requested laconically.

Steve sighed, then led the man to Molly's room. He banged vigorously on the door until Molly heard and felt the knocking. "Detective whatever-his-name would like to ask you a few questions."

Molly's eyes were filled with uncertainty. She looked over at the black man and nodded. Her hands were deep in the pockets of her jeans, but through the fabric her fingers could be seen moving nervously.

"My, Molly, you're a pretty girl, aren't you?" The detective turned on his charm to the fullest, but it didn't seem to ease her.

"Thank you," she said, then waited for the questions.

"She's still upset about what happened to her mother," Steve explained.

"Very understandable." The detective nodded, keeping his eyes and smile on Molly. "I won't be too long. I just want to know what happened to your mother. I want your own words," he said, then he seemed to brace himself, praying the girl's answer would be different.

But the girl disappointed him. "I don't know."

"But you were here, weren't you, sweetheart?"

"Yes, but . . . but . . . ." Tears began to rush to her eyes, which were already reddish from previous crying.

"Easy now," the detective said soothingly. "You can take all the time in the world you want."

"But I don'd know whad happened!" she cried, then ran back into her room to bury her face in the pillow on her bed.

"Sorry," Steve said to the detective, not meaning it.

"Understandable," he repeated, this time to mask his disappointment. Then he extended his hand. "Thank you for your cooperation, Mr. Ludden. If you'd so kindly direct me to a phone, I'll call someone to come down to scrape a sample from the rug, then I'll be on my way."

Steve led him to a phone in the library, where the detective brazenly closed the door on him and kept his voice low and indistinct as he talked into the receiver. When the man was finally done and gone, Steve relaxed, his muscles loosening with relief. Then he poured himself a glass of Scotch.

As he drank, he paced restlessly. His eyes swept the floral silk walls, the paneled fireplaces, the antiques that were everywhere. The house was so old and ancient. There was so much about it that he didn't know—and didn't want to know. He should have burned this fucking house down along with the garden!

He was suddenly filled with an urge to fling his glass into the fireplace, but fought it. People only did that in soap operas, he told himself. Then, when he was certain the urge had passed, he emptied his glass and poured himself another drink.

"Where did the flowers come from?" Steve demanded of Molly, two hours later. He was on his fourth drink, and a young man already had come, scraped some of the dried blood off the rug, taken a sample of the reddish-brown powder, then left. No more than five words had been exchanged, and the young man had been as polite and clinical as the black detective had been.

Molly cringed against the headboard of her bed as his whiskey breath fanned her. "The . . . the garden."

"What did that flower do to her face, Molly? Try to eat it?"

"I don'd know . . . I don'd know . . ." Tears ran down her cheeks. She swept them away with the back of her hand, but they kept coming. "I don'd know."

"Don't cry. Please, don't cry. We're not going to get

anywhere if you keep doing that. I've been waiting for you to be more calm, but you're going to have to tell me the truth sooner or later."

"I . . . don'd . . . know."

Steve cupped the girl's chin and gently but firmly forced her to look up at him. "You're trying to block everything out, Molly," he said slowly so that she could catch every word, "but I can't let you do that, not with the way your mother is right now. Do you realize that if I hadn't come back here when I did, it could've been too late for your mother? She could have been scarred beyond help, or worse, she could have died, Molly. Bled to death."

The girl tried to wrench her face free, but when she realized he was not going to let her go until he was finished, she stopped.

"The cop believes I'm trying to cover something up," he went on. "He's suspicious because he can't understand how a flower can physically hurt anyone. But I know that anything beyond understanding is possible in this house. So tell me how this garden came about. Tell me the truth."

"I-I . . ." She swallowed, wiped away more tears, then spoke carefully, "I planted it about two months ago when we first got here."

"But with what? Seeds? Little plants already started?"

"Seeds."

"Where did you get them?"

"I found them."

"Where?"

"The cellar."

Steve found himself speechless, as though the girl had slapped him. He had expected something like this, that the cellar would be connected, but to actually hear it . . .

"Oh Christ," he groaned, feeling the haze that the drinks had given him disperse, as though an icy wind had blown it away.

Molly watched him with large, red-rimmed eyes.

"Where in the cellar?" he said after a long silence.

"In the wall, behind a stone."

"What were they in?" He released his grip on her chin, sensing that force was no longer needed for her to cooperate. "How many were there?"

She told him about the metal box they were in and about the four separate cloth bags; then, as though suddenly remembering, she mentioned the red flash that had flared and died when the stone was removed from the wall and again when the metal box was opened.

"A seal of some kind had been broken," was the only explanation he could think of. Molly had probably released something that had been dormant for a long time. "How old did this box of seeds look?"

Molly seemed uncertain as to how to answer this. "Old," she simply replied. "How old can seeds last before they're not good anymore?"

How old, indeed, he thought. Then he remembered learning in school something about three lotus seeds that had been recovered in the early fifties. They had been found buried in a neolithic canoe under a peat bog somewhere near Tokyo. Two of those seeds had germinated and developed flowers—even though the seeds were 2,000 years old!

But the conditions had been right for those seeds, an inner voice reminded him. The peat bog had helped preserved them, just as something had preserved the seeds Molly had found.

Magic had preserved them.

"Christ," he muttered again.

Molly was still watching him, and his fear was infectiously filling her. "What . . . what did I do?"

"Show me the gardens," he abruptly commanded, ignoring her question and jumping to his feet.

Haltingly, Molly obeyed. She climbed off the bed, wiped away a tear that had trickled slowly and was near the edge of her jaw, then led her stepfather to the south garden, which was now nothing but a charred plot of earth.

"Your mother told me you had planted more than one

garden," Steve told her. Wordlessly she led him to the remains of the west garden. Here, all the identical stems in uniform rows were brown and brittle. A strong gust of wind from the ocean would soon crumble them into dry flakes and blow them away.

"They grew at the same time," she told him. "Except for the colors, they all looked alike, and they died at the same time in one day. Just like that," she said, but didn't snap her fingers to demonstrate. Her eyes were fixed on his face, as though hoping he would have all the answers.

"Did they do anything strange?"

She thought about it for a moment, then shook her head. "No. They had a nice smell, but I got sick of it after a while."

"You sure?"

She gave this additional thought, then once more shook her head, this time firmly. "Yeah, I'm sure."

But Steve wasn't convinced, especially since the same batch of seeds that had produced hellish plants in the other gardens was used in this one. "Plant anything else?" he asked.

Molly led him to the east side. "But nothing grew here." Dandelions and crab grass were beginning to cover the soil that had turned crusty and lumpy.

"Nothing strange here either?" he asked pointedly, his voice demanding the truth.

"Nothing except . . ." Her voice trailed away.

"Yes?"

"The bugs that ate Dinah."

It took Steve a moment to realize who Dinah was, then it gradually occurred to him it was his mother's cat that the girl had adopted and renamed herself. Until now he hadn't been aware of its absence.

"What ate Dinah?"

"The little bugs that were living under the dirt." Molly's eyes looked away from him, obviously not wanting to talk about it.

Now it was coming back to him. He remembered something about a swarm of insects, but he hadn't given it serious thought. He had shut himself out from anything that was connected to this house. He had wanted no part of it and had left it all for Lara, since it was she who wanted to stay here so much.

"But I don't think it had anything to do with the seeds," Molly said, moving away from the weedy plot.

But Steve didn't agree with her. He felt confident that the seeds had everything to do with it. "How did the bugs eat Dinah, Molly?"

Her eyes continued to dart everywhere but on him and the plot of ground. Her chin began to quiver, and Steve realized it was painful for her to talk about her cat, but he had to know.

"How?" he demanded.

"They . . . they just did. There were millions of 'em. And they just . . . swallowed her."

Steve stared at the clumps of crab grass and dandelions. Ordinary weeds. Ordinary dirt. It was hard to believe that something so hideous had happened here. Correction! It was *easy* to believe. Anything could happen around here, anything. The laws of nature were not obeyed here.

"They're gone now," Molly said of the swarm. Steve was surprised to find that she had moved away from him and was at the edge of the lawn. "There's another garden."

"Jesus, how many are there?"

But she didn't hear him, already heading toward the north lawn. He followed her at a distance and stopped close behind her, before a greenish-brown growth that seemed to be a cross between a giant artichoke and a walnut. It was somewhere between five and six feet in length, four feet in width, and four feet in height. Together, he and Molly stared at this monstrosity in silence.

"What are we going to do with it?" Molly said eventually, turning to him. Turning for help, he thought. Turning when it was probably too fucking late.

The giant growth rocked slightly. Had it done so by

itself, or had a breeze caused it, a breeze that had escaped him? Then the walnut-shaped plant was motionless, causing him to wonder if he had only imagined its movement.

What are we going to do with it?

His first thought was to destroy it; it was the only sensible thing to do. But how? Then came an onslaught of questions that, like a sudden cold gust, chilled him. What if the growth blows up like a barrel of gasoline? What if he awakens something horrible as he tries to destroy it? What if he starts something that can't be stopped or controlled?

He was dealing with something he knew nothing about.

He thought of touching it, wondering if it was heavy or light, warm or cool, but he couldn't bring himself to move closer, let alone make physical contact with it.

It rocked again, almost imperceptibly. It tilted to one side, then to the other. Steve took a backward step, and Molly did the same. Then she gave him another desperate look.

"When your mother gets home, we're going to get the hell out of here," he suddenly told her, his voice harsh. "That's what we're going to do. Now, are there any more gardens?"

Molly shook her head.

"Good!" he snapped, then started toward the house. Molly, not wanting to be left alone with the huge plant, ran to catch up with him. He could tell that she needed to be comforted, to be held. The girl was undoubtedly petrified and miserable with guilt, but he couldn't bring himself to console her. And why the hell should he?

After all, she was the one who planted the damn seeds in the first place!

23

"The blood sample matches Lara Ludden's all right, Greg, and you've got dried-up, crumbled flower petals. An orchid is my guess."

"That's it?" Detective Gregory Davis groaned, disappointed with the news from the forensic lab.

"What were you expecting?" the young male voice asked over the phone.

Something I didn't already know, Davis replied to himself. Out loud, he asked, "Any trace of acids or anything like that?"

"No. None."

"Are you certain it's an orchid?"

"No. It's just a guess, but we can find out, if you want."

Davis mulled over this. Was he wasting his and the lab's time on this half-assed case? Nobody was pressing charges, especially not Lara Ludden who, he was intuitively certain, had been physically abused by her husband. He was certain it was Steve who had messed up her face. It wasn't that Davis cared all that much for Lara's safety. After all, if the lady wanted to protect a husband who was beating her, that was her business. Violence was probably a turn-on for her, for both of them. A lot of folks associated violence with love. A lot of folks were whacky like that. But the reason he hadn't dismissed the case as a domestic squabble was that his curiosity had been piqued. *How* did the Ludden guy fuck up his wife's face?

But no answers came from the hospital, and it looked like none would be coming from the lab guys either.

"Greg?"

"Eh?" He felt as though someone had just awakened him from a deep sleep. "Oh yeah. Listen, don't bother. I don't give a fuck what kind of flower it was. I don't give a fuck what happens to that couple, either. If the lady doesn't want to talk, then there's nothing I can do. So forget it, and thanks anyway."

"Y'sure?"

"Yeah. I got more important things to do."

He hung up the phone and leaned back in his swivel chair, lacing his fingers behind his head. He glanced at his tidy desk, then swung his body toward the window that overlooked Main Street. It was 2:00 o'clock in the afternoon and not much was happening.

Not much ever happens in this hick town, he thought, sighing. He then swiveled back toward his desk. No memos. No messages on the answering machine. No appointments. Nothing. Dead and dull.

This job was not at all as exciting or hectic or grisly as he had expected it to be when he first took it, a little over a year ago. Christ, he had seen more action when he was a traffic cop.

Sighing again, he rested his head against the desk, making a pillow with his arms, and took a nap. This was something he did almost every afternoon now.

There was nothing better to do.

Lara came home the next morning. Her face was still swathed in bandages, and Molly, at the sight of her, became tearful. No matter how much she was told that she was not at fault, she could not be convinced otherwise.

"The doctor is going to remove the bandages next

week," Lara said, "and I'm going to look almost as good as new."

"Almost?" Molly had caught the one word that made a difference. She and her mother were on the latter's bed. Steve was in the doorway, silently watching them. Gray, dreary light filled the room, since outside the sky was cloudy with the promise of violent rain.

"There will be tiny scars, sweetheart." Lara gave Molly an oh-well-what-can-you-do shrug and lopsided smile. "But if I find them, well, too ugly, I'll have plastic surgery done. Nothing that can't be fixed."

"You're not mad at me, Mom?"

"Of course not! Now, I want you to stop punishing yourself like this. If this is anybody's fault, it's mine."

"But it was *my* fault!" Molly insisted. "*I* planted that flower, Mom."

Sighing, Laura pulled her daughter into her arms and held her tightly against her. She wished there was something she could do or say that would rid the girl of her guilt. "I'm going to be all right, sweetheart. I'm going to be all right."

"I didn't know they were bad seeds, Mom."

"I realize that."

"And now," she hiccuped tearfully, " 'cause of me, we're going to have to leave."

Lara looked over at Steve in the doorway. He had spent most of the day packing things into cardboard boxes. He had already called the real estate agent and put the house on the market. Tomorrow they would go back to their old apartment, for it was still theirs, the lease not up until September. Now Steve was mutely warning her not to go back on this agreement.

"We haven't been happy here," she said to Molly, keeping her gaze fixed on her husband. "This house hasn't been good to us, so I guess it's best that we leave."

Molly looked up at her, trying to catch every word. She sniffed back her tears. "What's the matter with this house, Mom? Are there ghosts here?"

"Steve knows more about it than I do. He was brought up here."

Molly looked over at her stepfather, and her eyes echoed the question.

"There's something here," he answered curtly and then was gone.

Lara and Molly stared at the now empty doorway. Then Molly buried her face against her mother's breasts. "He's mad at me." Though muffled, her voice sounded distinctly heartbroken. "He hates me."

"Now, you know that's not true."

"He hates me for starting the garden."

"No, sweetheart, no." She rocked her gently in her arms. "Nobody hates you. Nobody could ever hate you."

The words, she knew, were lost on the girl, but she hoped the softness of her voice and gentle rocking motions would tranquilize her.

"Nobody hates you, sweetheart. Nobody," she repeated, now almost humming the words. She closed her eyes and continued to rock her child, slowly beginning to sway with her. "Everybody loves you, sweetheart. Everybody."

Rain began to fall, softly hitting the windows. It was a cozy, warm feeling to listen to the raindrops and to hold her child so closely, especially when the child began to relax and fall asleep.

"Yes, everybody loves you," she crooned: "Everybody."

It was cozy and warm.

Then the sky darkened, and the rain began to fall harder.

It was early afternoon when Molly awoke. The rain had dimmed her mother's bedroom to such a degree that the lamp was needed to see anything clearly. When the room was illuminated with soft yellow light, she threw back a patchwork comforter that her mother had spread over her before leaving the room, and quickly felt the damp chill in the air. She looked over at the windows. The rain was beating at the dark panes with alarming intensity. The light from the room reflected the angry streaks of rain, making the panes resemble blank canvases that had been savagely slashed with a blade or scalpel.

Molly peered out a window and saw the angry sky and turbulent ocean. Was this a hurricane or just a bad summer storm? Not certain which, she took a step back, afraid the window might explode inwardly into her face. The wind seemed powerful enough. Then her gaze swept toward another window on the north side. Lightning flashed, fleetingly illuminating the room with ghostly light, then seconds later she felt the rumble of thunder.

It's a summer storm, not a hurricane, she decided. As far as she knew, there was no lightning and thunder in a hurricane, but this realization did not appease her in any way. The storm raging outside still seemed too violent and dangerous.

Careful not to move too close, for she still feared the possibility of shattered glass, she looked down at the garden. Lightning streaked the rolling, charcoal sky again. Molly jumped back, but not before she caught a glimpse of what the rain was doing to the walnut-shaped plant in the garden.

It was washing away the scaly covering, softening and reshaping the plant.

Molly wanted another glimpse to be sure, but try as she might, she couldn't muster enough courage to return to the window. She started downstairs to look for her mother; she didn't want to be alone any more than she had to.

As Molly went through the living room and the dining room she became aware, for the first time, of the house's true size. A monster was the word that jumped into her mind—an old monster, like a dinosaur, or maybe more like a dragon, which she thought was more vicious and dangerous. The monster had been sleeping and was now, very slowly, waking up. Soon, very soon, it was going to be fully awake and it was going to . . . attack?

Molly peeked into the kitchen and saw Steve at the large stove, stirring something in a large saucepan. She could see the steam rising and smell the spicy aroma of spaghetti sauce.

"Spaghetti and meatballs," Steve told her as he heard her opening the door. "Your favorite, right?"

"Yeah." She was starving, too, but her hunger was not her main concern now. "Where's Mom?"

He shrugged uncertainly. "Somewhere in the house, packing." Then he turned his face away from her and resumed stirring the tomato sauce. Molly slipped away from the kitchen and continued searching for her mother.

She found her in the music room, sitting at the Steinway piano, staring at the keys while one finger occasionally pressed them. From the way she sat, one elbow on the top of the piano, one hand resting against her head while the other hand played idly, Molly could tell she was deep in thought—and sad. Standing in the doorway, Molly listened to the faint plunks, but all the notes sounded the same to her. Then she joined her mother at the piano bench.

Lara was surprised to see her and gave her a weak smile. Molly said nothing, only watched her mother's long, tapered fingers push down the ivory keys.

She just wanted to be close to her, to forget about . . . the stirring dragon.

Lara gave her another wan smile, and Molly returned it.

"I remember wishing to play the piano when I was your age," Lara said.

"You had a piano?"

"No, but I remember wanting one so very much."

"Why?"

"Oh, I don't know. I guess I thought that if I had a piano and could play it well, it would make me somebody. Classy, I guess."

Molly frowned, not sure if she understood.

"I guess I always wanted something classy, to pretend I was sophisticated when I wasn't. I guess that's why I wanted to keep this house so much. It's classy and sophisticated."

Her fingers stopped, then withdrew from the keys and rested on her lap. She looked over at Molly and gave her another one of those sad smiles. "I'm sorry," she whispered.

Molly's frown deepened. "Why?"

"None of this would have happened if I hadn't been determined to stay here. My memory's coming back, and now I remember how frightened you were that night. I remember you screaming, holding your head as if you were in a great deal of pain."

"Everything got loud, Mom. I could hear that night, but I didn't like it. It was too loud. It hurt."

Lara stared at her, surprised and confused.

"The night flowers did it, Mom," Molly said, then explained how she had heard the ocean, the wind, and her booming footfalls on the grass and carpet.

"Oh God," Lara cried softly, then squeezed her eyes shut. She either seemed to be praying or was struggling to control her sanity. When she reopened her eyes, she said, "It is so hard to believe, Molly, so hard, but I think Steve's been right all along. There's something unnatural here."

Mother and daughter looked at each other in silence; the former betraying relief that minimal damage had resulted and that soon it would be over and behind them, and the latter betraying dread that the dragon was still stirring and the worst was yet to come.

Then Steve's yell broke through the silence. "Dinner's ready, wherever everybody is!"

Lara blinked, wrapped an arm around Molly and led her away from the piano. "I'm famished. I was supposed to do some packing," she said as they walked toward the dining room. "Now I'll have to wait until after dinner."

The mahogany dining room table looked foolishly oversized with only three plates at one end. Again Molly was reminded of the size of the house—the monster and the dragon.

The family sat at the table and began to eat. The spaghetti was delicious, and though there were a lot of mushrooms in the sauce, just the way she liked it, Molly soon found herself not as hungry as she thought she was. Her eyes continued to dart toward the long, dark windows. She could see the golden reflection of the dining room chandelier and the angry, seemingly luminous streaks of rain on the glass.

"Raining hard," Lara remarked, also looking up at the windows.

"Heavy gale winds," Steve said, following their gaze. "It's expected to last for most of the evening, but they're predicting sunny and dry weather for tomorrow."

"That's good," Lara said half-heartedly. Losing interest in the rain, she looked away from the windows and concentrated on her food. Face tight from the bandages, she took small bites. But after three forkfuls of wound spaghetti, she wiped her lips with a napkin and sat back.

"I'm afraid I haven't the appetite I thought I had."

"Me, too," Molly said.

"And to think I made enough to feed an army." Steve groaned, shaking his head.

But the rueful complaint was lost on Lara, for she was already deep in thought, sipping her coffee. After a lengthy silence, she said, "I still can't believe it. It's so hard to believe it all."

"Believe what, hon?"

She turned to look at him, but her eyes did not seem to see him. "That something wicked surrounds this place, that—"

"Let's not talk about it!" he interrupted sharply. Suddenly losing his appetite as well, he set his fork down and pushed his plate away. In a softer voice, he said, "When we leave, we are going to forget about this place. We are going to pretend it never existed."

"When are we going to leave?" Molly wanted to

know. She, too, was eager to have this house behind her, to forget its existence.

"Well, we're just about done packing, aren't we, hon?" He glanced at Lara, expecting her to confirm this, but she still had the faraway look in her eyes. "Sometime tomorrow, I hope," he said, looking back at Molly.

"Can you leave the house with nobody in it?"

"Sure. Why not? The real estate agent will have a key, and she can come here to show the house whenever anyone is interested in seeing it."

"Think somebody will buy it?"

"Hope so. Wouldn't like to be stuck with it."

Molly thought of asking if he had told the real estate people that something bad was in the house, but decided not to. Like her stepfather, she didn't want to talk about it. She glanced at the windows again. The violent rain still made her uneasy, made her wonder if the windows would keep the fury back, keep it from rushing into the house.

"So you think it was responsible for Shelly's death?" Lara suddenly asked, surprising Steve.

"What was responsible?"

"The . . . house."

He hesitated only briefly. "Yes."

"How?"

"I don't know, but I'm sure it was."

Lara, saying nothing, fell into another thoughtful trance. Then there was a sound at the front entrance, two rooms away. Molly didn't hear it, but Lara turned her head sharply in that direction, her reverie shattered, and Steve rose from the table.

"What on earth was that?" Lara's hand rose to her lips.

"Sounds like something fell against the door," Steve said, standing but not moving.

"A limb from a tree, you think?"

"Maybe." He then began to move toward the foyer.

In her mind's eye, Molly saw the dragon open its second eye. It was completely awake now, and it was waiting.

"No!" she cried.

Steve and Lara turned toward her in surprise.

"What's wrong, sweetheart?" Lara asked.

But Molly wasn't sure what was wrong. She had bad feelings, but were they imaginary? She stared silently at her mother, not knowing how to express her fears.

Steve waited for a moment, and when it was apparent that Molly wasn't going to say anything more, he continued toward the front entrance.

"I-I'm scared, Mom!" she finally blurted out.

"But it's only a limb, I'm sure." Lara got up from the table and turned to follow her husband.

"Mom!"

She stopped, surprised to find her daughter so frightened. "Sweetheart, we have to see what or who is at the door."

Molly wanted to yell "No!" again, but it was obvious that her mother wasn't going to listen. So she reached for her hand, not wanting to be left alone. She knew she was behaving like a baby, but she didn't care.

Lara smiled to console her. "Come on, we'll see together." Hand in hand they walked through two rooms toward the spacious foyer.

Steve was at the big oak door when they reached him, his hand already on the brass handle. Molly tensed, holding her breath as she and her mother waited, keeping a small distance from him. He glanced over his shoulder at them, but his face was blank. Then he opened the door.

A violent gust of wind rushed in, whipping leaves and rain into the house. Molly let out a cry and tried to pull back into another room, taking her mother with her, but her mother firmly held onto her hand, keeping her at her side. Then Molly realized it was only the wind and rain that had frightened her, and her outcry quickly turned to an embarrassed laugh.

"A limb, isn't it, dear?" Lara said, craning her neck to see past her husband who was blocking the entrance way, obstructing her view.

Steve did not answer. He was looking down at something on the stoop.

"Dear, what is it?"

This time he heard her. "A man."

"What?"

But Steve had stepped outside and was on his knees. Lara, now apprehensive, gripped Molly's hand, painfully crushing it. She inched closer, unwittingly pulling the girl along with her.

When they were close enough, they saw the man. Lara gawked for a stunned moment, then swept in front of Molly to block her view, but it was too late. Molly had seen that the man was naked.

It had only been a fleeting instance, but it was long enough to burn a permanent image in Molly's mind. The man was in a crouched position on the concrete steps, his shoulders hunched forward, his thin arms between his legs, and his knees drawn to his chest. He was hunched in a ball, protecting himself from the harsh, unrelenting rain. He was skeletal, bones at the joints knobby, pushing against skin that was moon white, glistening wetly from the storm. He was sickly and shivering, looking up at Steve, his face pleading for his aid.

But it was his eyes that made Molly uneasy. They were a startling contrast to the paleness of his skin and thin, tawny hair. They were vivid spots of color. Green. Grass green. Plant green.

"I think it'd be a good idea if you went to your room, sweetheart," her mother said.

"Don't . . . don't let him in, Mom."

"Molly," she warned in a low voice, "you're being rude."

"Don't let—"

"Please go to your room," she repeated. Her tone, although still a whisper, was firmer. "Steve and I will handle this."

Molly began to step aside to steal another peek. Maybe if she saw the man's eyes again she'd see that they were not unusual. A lot of people had green eyes. But her mother moved along with her, keeping the view hidden.

"He's naked, Molly," she said, "and I don't want you to see him."

Molly hesitated. She wanted to plead with her mother not to let the man into the house. She had bad feelings, very bad feelings, but she could tell it would be useless. She went upstairs.

But instead of going to her room, she went to her mother's. Here she looked out the window that overlooked the north garden. It was too dark to see anything clearly. She could vaguely make out the bulk of the huge, walnut-shaped plant, but when lightning lit the sky and ground, she clearly saw it.

The plant had collapsed inwardly. It was as if something inside it, like air from a deflated balloon, had escaped.

24

After recovering from the shock of seeing a naked man at her doorstep, Lara began to feel pity toward this stranger. She moved closer until she was directly behind her husband, who remained on his knees, bent over the sickly man.

"What's the matter?" she heard Steve ask him, his voice uncertain and barely audible in the wrathful wind and rain.

The stranger's green eyes looked at him, then up at Lara. They were pleading for help, and they were the saddest eyes Lara had ever seen—and they were weakening, like a pair of flashlights with waning batteries. This man was dying.

"Who are you?" Steve tried again to make him speak.

The stranger focused his gaze on him, then worked his colorless lips to speak, but no sounds came forth. He swallowed, then tried again.

"I-I am cold," he said at length, his voice hoarse as though it had been an extremely long time since he had last spoken. "And perhaps feverish as well. Please be kind enough to welcome me into your home."

His eyes widened for an instant, punctuating the plea, then they dropped as if suddenly hopeless.

Steve looked over at Lara, wondering what to do, but she was just as uncertain as he. "Who are you?" he repeated, turning back to the stranger.

"My mind is failing me." His pitiful eyes looked back up at him, huge with grief, regret and hope. "My memory eludes me. I cannot remember the name that had been mine. I remember only the terrible event."

"Event?" Steve echoed the word.

"The ship sank in this storm. Oh, please be kind. Please welcome me into your home," he pleaded again.

Lara experienced another rush of pity for this man. She was ready to pull him inside, at least into the foyer so that everyone could be sheltered from the cold downpour, but Steve had more questions.

"Where are your clothes?"

"Clothes?"

"You are naked."

The man seemed unaware of this until now. His eyes dropped, as though to ponder, to concentrate, to remember, then they rose once more to meet Steve's. "Please try to understand that my memory is faulty. However, I do recall removing a garment to stem a wound."

"You're wounded?"

Again the stranger was silent as he tried to think of a reply. His lips worked soundlessly for a moment, then he said, "A colleague on the ship was wounded, sir. It was a fatal wound, I regret to say."

"I see." But Steve's tone clearly betrayed doubt. "Maybe I better call the police."

"Police?" the stranger questioned, as though the word was foreign.

"Yes, police. Is there any reason why I shouldn't call them?"

"I am cold, sir. I seek only warmth and rest. That is all I beseech of you, sir, and you, also, madam," he added, turning his eyes to Lara.

"Oh, Steve, let him in," she said, feeling her heart reach out to the man. "We're all going to catch pneumonia staying out here."

"But honey," Steve said in a low voice so that only she

might hear, "this man could be dangerous."

"This man needs help. Can't you see that?"

"The police can help him."

"Yes, I suppose they can, but please, let's get in and out of the rain!"

"I don't know." Steve was still doubtful.

"If he dies from exposure, it'll be on your conscience."

"I am cold," the man repeated again. "Please welcome me into your . . ." His voice trailed off, as though too weak to finish.

"Steve, please," Lara implored. "This man is sick. Can't you see that? We can't just leave him out here like this."

Steve looked at the man for a minute more, then he gently held him at the elbow and helped him to his feet. The man swayed, as though dizzy, but Lara hurried to his other side to steady him. Hands on each arm and elbow, he walked on wobbly legs into the foyer.

"I'll get a blanket," Lara said, then hurriedly closed the big door and went up the stairs toward one of the bedrooms. Within seconds she was back, carrying a navy blue woolen blanket. She draped this over the man's frail shoulders, not only warming him but hiding his nakedness. He thanked her with his huge, expressive eyes and pulled the blanket closer to him. Lara noticed his long, bony fingers and wondered when he had last eaten.

She asked him this, but he seemed too weak to answer.

"I'll warm up a bowl of soup," she said. "Take him to one of the bedrooms. This man is cold, tired, and hungry."

"I should call the police is what I should do," Steve muttered, but he took Lara's suggestion and helped the man mount the stairs.

"No police," the man said in a pleading voice. "They will ask too many questions. I am too weary, sir, but tomorrow I shall be stronger. Yes, tomorrow I shall be stronger."

Lara watched as he and her husband ascended the

steps. The stranger moved as though every joint were too stiff and every muscle too flaccid. Like a marionette, she thought. If Steve should let go, the man would collapse in a heap.

When the men could no longer be seen, she went into the kitchen and made Lipton chicken soup, but when she brought the soup to the room upstairs, she found the stranger already in bed, sleeping.

"Guess he's more tired than hungry," Steve said.

Lara set the steaming soup down on the nightstand and stared at the man. He looked so frail and under-nourished. His skin was whiter than anyone's she had ever seen, prompting her to wonder when he had last been out in the sun.

"Think he'll be all right?" she asked Steve softly so as not to awaken the man.

"Not exactly a picture of health," Steve said, "but he wouldn't let me call a doctor, either. Told me to wait until tomorrow. He just wanted to rest. Said that it exhausted him just to reach the door to this house."

"Think he crawled to it?"

"Just about."

"But from where, do you suppose? From the shore?"

"He did mention something about a ship sinking."

"My God."

"Where do you think he came from?"

"I don't know. He talked . . . so formal, so strange."

The couple fell silent. They watched the small man breathe peacefully as he slept. Outside, the wind whined and the rain slapped at the windows.

"What do you think we should do?" Steve asked after a long while.

"Do? Why, we keep him here until he's stronger, of course."

"You think that's wise?"

"You're not *afraid* of him, are you?"

"I want to leave tomorrow," he reminded her. "As soon as possible."

Lara looked at her husband, as though unable to

believe how insensitive and callous he was. "My God, Steve, how can you think of throwing this man out? And how can you be afraid of him? Look at him, for God's sake! Look at how sick he is! God, he's not even half your size!"

"Honey, I don't care if he's half my size. He's a stranger, and I don't like the way he suddenly appeared at our—"

"Shhh!" Lara sharply shushed him. The man had stirred, and for a moment it seemed like he would wake up. "Let's leave the room," she suggested, and before Steve could respond she was tiptoeing out into the hallway. When Steve joined her, she softly closed the door.

"This is not a good idea, honey," he insisted.

"How can he possibly harm us?"

"He could be deceiving us."

Lara's mouth opened, about to question this, but Molly suddenly stepped out of her room and ran toward her. "Sweetheart, what's wrong?"

"Id's a pland!" she cried.

"You're talking too fast. We can't understand you."

"It's a plant, Mom."

"What is, dear?"

"That—that man!" She pointed at the door that Lara had just closed.

"Come on, let's go downstairs," Lara suggested. "If we're going to talk, let's do it where we won't disturb anyone."

When the family was in the living room, Lara said to Molly, "Now what is this nonsense about the man being a plant?"

Molly told her about the north garden and the large plant that had deflated at the same time the man had appeared at the door.

"But I'm sure that's only a coincidence," Lara said. "The rain must have destroyed the plant in the garden. Certainly you don't think the man was inside it, as if it were some kind of an egg?"

Molly said nothing, but her silence told Lara that she did.

"But that's . . . absurd!"

"Absurd like a plant eating your face?" Steve said.

"That's . . . that's . . ."

"Different?" Steve lifted one brow.

Lara's mouth formed the word "Yes" but never uttered it. Was it truly different? she wondered. Was it possible, no matter how farfetched it seemed, that the man upstairs was hatched from . . .

"But we can't just throw the man out," she said. "Not in this weather."

"We should kill it!" Molly said.

"Don't be silly. We can't just kill an innocent man. Right, dear?" She turned to her husband, but he had walked into the library and, judging from the sound of tinkling ice cubes and glass, was making himself a drink. Damn him! she thought. Whenever the going gets tough, the weakling drinks!

"Steve!" she called, and sure enough he reappeared with a crystal glass half-filled with amber liquid. "Must you?"

"Yes, I must." And as if to prove this, he took a long swallow.

"Why must you always play the Good Samaritan?" he demanded, his voice betraying disgust. "Every stray animal that ever came to you, you took in. You even lost an apartment because of this."

"Well, I'm sorry," she snapped sarcastically, "but I happen to find it difficult to turn anyone or anything away that wants help."

"And my sister," he went on, as though she hadn't spoken, "you wanted to take her back, nurse her back to health, although she had turned into an uncontrollable lunatic. Why the hell do you do these things? Do you like living dangerously? Is that it?"

"No, it's not. I just can't *not* help people, Steve."

"You missed your calling, then. You should have been a nurse."

"We can't just throw the man out," Lara said again, ignoring the remark. "And we certainly can't kill him. We could be wrong. Has that ever occurred to you? We could be wrong. He could be completely harmless." When no one made any comment, she added, "Well, it's true. We have to find out more about him."

"Yeah, right, hon," he replied flatly. Suddenly he was more concerned with his drink than with anything she had to say. He stared at the glass, then took another sizable gulp.

"Steve!" she said sharply.

"What?"

"Don't . . . don't shut me off with a stupid drink!"

The remark penetrated slowly, then he spun toward her, nearly spilling his drink in the abrupt swivel. His eyes were ablaze with a fury that she had never seen in him before, a fury that she hadn't realized was even in him. She recoiled under the wrathful gaze, seizing her daughter's hand and pulling her closer, instinctively protecting her from a man who had unexpectedly turned into a beast.

"I have to shut you off," he snarled, "because otherwise I'd go insane! There is no pleasing you. You always go against me, and you never let up until you have your way!"

"That's not true," she countered weakly.

"It is true! I didn't want to stay here. *You* did. And because *you* did, we stayed! So you can blame yourself for everything that happened here. Even Shelly's death!"

"Steve, that's unfair!"

"Unfair my ass! And *you*!" He turned on Molly. "If you hadn't been so goddamn nosy, you wouldn't have gone into the cellar, and you wouldn't have found those fucking seeds!"

"Steve, your language . . ."

He ignored her, still glaring at the girl who was pushing hard against Lara, as though to escape inside her. "So you have no one to blame but yourself for the gardens you planted! Damn both of you!" Then he swung around and threw the glass against the wall, where the glass shattered into countless shards and the liquid sprayed against the wall, ceiling and carpet.

"Steve, stop it!" Lara screamed, clutching her daughter who was now sobbing with fright. She couldn't believe what he had done.

"*You stop it!*" he yelled back. Then in frustration because there was nothing in his hands for him to throw or drink or hit, he clenched them into fists, let the anger shake him, color his face until it was an ugly raspberry shade, then he stormed out of the room.

"That's it!" Lara screamed after him, not caring that it'd be better and wiser if she remained silent. "Run away! Run away! You . . . you bastard!"

A door slammed, and she knew it was the final punctuation of the last sentence. It was over.

She began to cry, and Molly cried with her.

From a window in the dining room Molly watched the red taillights of the Cutlass fade as the car left the long driveway. She felt the cold tightness in her belly intensify. Now that her stepfather was gone there was more space in the house. The house had become even a bigger monster.

Clutching her elbows as she hugged herself, she turned away from the window and watched her mother who was at the table, deep in thought, sipping cold coffee. Her hand, holding the cup, trembled, and regret was evident in her eyes and in the way she nibbled at her lower lip. Regret that she had made Steve angry and leave? Molly wondered. Or regret that she had ever married him in the first place?

"Mom?"

Lara looked up. Her eyes were red-rimmed, yet she tried to mask her grief with a smile. "Yes, sweetheart?"

"What are we going to do?"

"What do you mean?"

"Steve won't be here to help us."

"We don't need any help."

"But Mom—" She stopped, for her belly was actually

beginning to hurt her; it was so cold, so tight. She willed herself to be calmer, then she tried again. "There's a . . . monster upstairs."

Lara sighed, then drained her cup. "You don't know that for sure."

"But the garden—"

"Coincidence, I told you."

Molly, aware that she'd never convince her mother otherwise, changed the subject. "When will Steve come back?"

"I don't know."

"Where did he go?"

Lara didn't answer, but Molly could tell that she was holding back. So she waited, and after a while Lara said, "To get drunk, I'm sure. That's what he does when things don't go his way. Childish, isn't he?"

"But he will be back, won't he?" she asked, ignoring the question.

"Eventually, yes, but he won't be much good, anyway. He'll be drunk, barely able to walk or talk."

"He won't be able to help us?"

"We don't need his help!" Lara snapped, then immediately regretted the outburst. "I'm sorry. I didn't mean to snap at you like that."

Molly gave her a small nod, indicating that it was all right. "Are we still going to leave tomorrow?" she asked hopefully.

"I don't know. We can't very well leave without your stepfather."

"Oh."

"I thought you loved this house, sweetheart."

Molly looked at her, at the bandages, and felt the usual surge of guilt and the cold tremor along her spine as she remembered the large flower that had cupped her mother's face.

She said, "Not anymore."

Lara knocked softly on the door. She did not want to disturb the man if he was sleeping, but if he wasn't she wanted to talk with him, to learn more about him. Then, and only then, would she make a decision whether or not to summon the police and have the stranger removed from the house.

She knocked again, her knuckles scarcely touching the wooden door. She was ready to give up and was turning to leave when she heard the man's faint, hoarse voice.

"Is anyone there?"

"It's me, Lara," she said through the door. "May I come in? I would like to talk with you."

After a brief pause, she heard, "Certainly, madam."

Lara opened the door, suddenly feeling bashful and uncertain. Or was it trepidation she was experiencing? She paused halfway between the bed and the door, her hands folded behind her back. She gave him a smile, but the smile was more awkward than warm. The man, clad in a pair of Steve's pajamas, pushed himself up to a sitting position on the bed. He seemed better already. His face was still a sickly, bloodless white, but his eyes somehow seemed to compensate for this; they seemed energetic, alert, even healthy.

He smiled at her, and she was surprised to find no teeth in the gaping mouth. The man looked young, somewhere in his late twenties or early thirties. Too young to have no teeth, she thought.

"About what do you wish to converse with me, madam?" he asked.

He sounded so proper. Where did he come from? England? France? She detected a slight accent, but mostly his words were flat monotones, dull, almost robotlike.

"Madam?" He was waiting for an answer.

There was no sign of impatience, only polite endurance. "I'm sorry. I didn't mean to stare at you like this. And please, don't call me madam. It sounds so . . . so old."

"Whatever you wish, er—"

"Lara. Call me Lara."

"Very well . . . Lara." He smiled at her, this time

keeping his lips together. His eyes twinkled, reminding her of green grass glistening with morning dew. Charming, she decided.

"I would like to know more about you, that's all," she said, still feeling awkward and bashful. "After all, you are a stranger in my home, and I don't even know your name, let alone where you came from."

"Very understandable." His eyelids dropped a fraction, and his smile softened. He withdrew his long, thin arms from under the covers and rested them on his chest. He watched her for a silent minute through lazy hooded eyes, eyes that she found admirably intelligent. He's like a worldly professor, she thought.

He said, "I wish I could inform you of my name, but I am afraid my memory will not permit it."

"You think it's from that ship accident?"

"I do not recall anything prior to the dreadful event."

"You must have amnesia," she said.

He didn't answer but only searched her face with that langorous scrutiny of his.

"Maybe I should call a doctor."

"Perhaps later, but I beg of you, not at present. I feel too disoriented, too confused. You must understand that I wish to regain more control before I speak with any authoritative figure."

"But a doctor would help you regain control," Lara pointed out.

"Please . . . Lara," he implored. "Respect my wishes."

"Well . . ." she said uncertainly.

"Please."

Lara sighed, acquiescing. How could this man possibly hurt her? He was ill, thin and weak. He was harmless, harmless as a . . . flower?

She swiftly pushed the thought from her mind, as though it were a speck of dirt. This was a man before her, a human being, and it would be inhumane to throw a human being out into a storm, just because he didn't want to see a doctor.

"But later you must see one," she said. "In the morning."

"Perhaps," he agreed. Then, when he saw that she wasn't going to say anything more of the matter, he said, "Please sit on the bed. You appear to be in discomfort standing before me."

"I don't intend to stay too—"

"Please . . . Lara."

She hesitated, then sat at the foot of the bed, smiling awkwardly at him.

"Do you have additional questions you wish to ask of me?" he said.

"Well, I came here hoping to refresh your memory, if possible, but I can see I'm not going to be able to do this."

"There are some things I can remember, but I'm afraid they are only confusing fragments. And they are frustrating, I must say. I am confident that I shall recall everything in the future, hopefully soon."

"Maybe I can help you dislodge a few things," she suggested.

"I would be grateful."

"Well . . ." Lara paused, searching her mind for questions with possibilities. It was like trying to decide what combination of numbers would unlock a safe. There were countless combinations, as well as countless questions. "Do you remember having a wife?"

"Wife?"

"A girlfriend? Mate?" Maybe he's gay, she suddenly thought, then added, "A partner?"

"Partner?" He weighed the word, hooding his emerald eyes some more. He was still looking at her, but she wasn't certain if he was actually seeing her or was lost in thought. "Ah yes," he said after a long while, "I seem to recall a partner. Actually, assistant perhaps would be a better word. Ah yes," he said again, a smile of amusement spreading slowly across his pallid face. "Now what was his name? Kyles? Wiles? . . . Miles! Yes, that was it. Miles. Ah, he was such a foolish man."

"He was your assistant?" Lara spoke softly, as though afraid his memory would scurry back to the dark recesses where it had been hiding, like a mole or groundhog.

"Yes, he was my assistant."

"What did you do?"

"I cannot remember, but I do recall Miles. I can see his very face in my mind. I can recall that he used to incense me so, yet I felt fondness for the man. And I can remember something I had done to him, for he needed to be corrected at times. Friday was our day to fast, feasting on bread only, but Miles could not fast, I eventually learned. He had stealthily dined on things other than bread on this day. Therefore, to correct him, I let him put a black pudding in his mouth, but did not let him bite it nor take it out. After I allowed others to see him in this humiliating situation, I released it. Ah, it is so vivid. His face was as red as a rose, but he learned well. His master taught him well."

"I don't think I understand."

"Fragments, madam—forgive me—Lara. Only fragments come to my mind."

"You were a master?"

"I recall my assistant addressing me as such."

Lara felt uneasy, and now knew it was not due to shyness. Had she made a mistake coming in here to question him? Was she dealing with something or someone beyond her scope, something or someone that should be left alone? This man seemed to be talking as though he had come from another time period, not just another country.

"Was this assistant black?" she asked, thinking of slavery during the Civil War period.

"Pardon?"

"Never mind. It doesn't matter."

"You are upset. I can see it in your eyes."

"No, no, I'm all right."

"Oh, but it is not all right, Lara. What have I said that upset you so? Please do tell."

Lara hesitated, but his eyes urged her to express what

was troubling her. She looked away from him, then back. "Assistant and master," she began slowly. "They sound . . . I don't know . . . dated."

"Ah, now I understand. But Lara, I've already informed you. I am remembering only fragments, perhaps fragments from a book I have read. Yes?"

"I suppose."

"Please, do not let anything I say upset you. Otherwise I will have no alternative but to be silent."

"Oh, please don't do that," Lara said, realizing the harm she could cause him. She had managed to get him to open up to her, so it would be cruel and possibly damaging to make him stop now. "What else do you remember?"

"More about Miles, but . . . I am not certain if you wish to hear of it."

"Yes, I do want to hear it." When he made no attempt to speak, she added, "Please."

"Well . . ." he said, leaning back against the headboard and closing his eyes, "I remember that I had struck him dumb for the space of a whole month. He did not speak. He did not disobey or betray me after that."

"How did you do that?" Lara whispered. What did he mean he "struck him dumb?" What kind of man was she dealing with here?

The rain slapping against the house suddenly seemed louder and more vicious, and the air seemed not only colder, but damper.

The man slowly opened his eyes and peered deeply into hers. He seemed suddenly aware that he had said too much. "How did I strike him dumb, you wish to know?"

"Yes."

He stared into her eyes, not speaking for a lengthy moment. Only the rain and wind broke the silence. Then he pulled his gaze away from her and said in a flat voice, "Perhaps I only fancied rendering a person dumb. Perhaps I had been an imaginative person or an avid reader, and I am merely recounting something I had read. Forgive me, for I can see I have upset you again."

Lara contemplated denying this, but knew she'd never sound convincing. "But your name . . . can you remember it now?"

"I am afraid not."

She couldn't tell if he was lying. He had answered too quickly, without bothering to give the question any thought. "And can't you remember where you came from? Where your boat or ship came from?"

He sighed, shaking his head. "I'm tired. Please, no more questions."

With regret, Lara realized she had pushed him too far. "I'm sorry," she apologized. "I'll leave you alone to rest."

When she reached the door, he said, "Lara, I am very grateful."

The statement surprised her. "What?"

"Your compassion and concern is immensely appreciated."

Lara found herself speechless but also found a warm glow deep inside her. Yes, this man was charming—disturbingly mysterious less than a second ago, but charming once again. One would have to have the heart of a witch to send him away. "Oh, it was nothing," she said finally, then ópened the door.

"And Lara?"

"Yes?"

"Perhaps in the morning I shall be fortunate to remember who I am."

"That will be nice."

He smiled, then wearily closed his eyes. "Good evening," he said barely audibly, drifting off to sleep.

"Good night," she whispered in reply. She watched him, again thinking how charming he was. Then she closed the door and retreated quietly from the room.

She could not stop wondering who he was and where he came from.

25

Molly slept clutching her red, plastic flashlight. She did this for two reasons—to sweep the room with light whenever she felt someone was in her room, and to use it as a weapon if necessary, for it felt like a small baseball bat in her hand. It gave her a sense of security, although she wasn't sure if she'd have the courage to use it, and having the stranger in the house made her uneasy.

She was positive that this stranger came from the north garden, from that deflated plant which now looked like a large greenish-brown cloth that had been tossed in a heap. It was lumpy, somewhat bunched, but mostly flat. Before this it had been plump and firmly shaped, like an egg with scales.

Molly woke up intermittently throughout the night. Now gray, fuzzy light was paling the darkness, and the furniture gradually began to take form. She lay in the bed for a long while, watching a highboy across the room grow clearer and clearer until the details of the ornate brass handles could be seen. When the hazy light was no longer dreary but sharp and bright, she climbed out of bed, leaving the flashlight on the nightstand, and wiggled into her robe. She didn't want to be alone anymore.

Moving as quietly as possible, she stepped out into the hallway and started toward her mother's room. En route, she paused at the stranger's door and placed her palm against the wood. There seemed to be no movement coming from the other side. Was the stranger asleep?

She lingered at the closed door, then proceeded toward her mother's room. She thought of knocking on her mother's door, then changed her mind, afraid it would awaken the stranger. So she opened the door a crack and peeked inside.

Lara was asleep. The blankets were twisted and bunched, suggesting that she too had a restless night. Molly found herself not wanting to disturb her, in case she had just fallen asleep. She closed the door softly, then went downstairs. Maybe she would find Steve. Maybe he was back and was now making breakfast. She could stay with him for a while.

She found him sleeping on the sofa in the library, his frame too big for the small furniture. He was in a fetal position, his knees bent to fit. His hair was matted, as though he hadn't combed it in weeks, and his jaw was shadowy with unshaven stubble. He was snoring, for she could see his parted mouth inhale and exhale. The air around him reeked of whiskey and vomit, and on the floor beside the sofa was a bottle of Cutty Sark, its contents almost gone. This was not the Prince Charming who had married her mother.

Molly didn't want to awaken him, knowing he would only be miserable with a hangover, but she didn't want to be alone either. So she sat in the wing chair near the cold fireplace and flipped through a book about Early American furniture. Frequently her eyes went to the open door, expecting to find the stranger entering the room, but this never happened. Eventually she grew bored and put the book aside. She headed for the kitchen, deciding she'd make herself a bowl of cereal and return to the library to eat it.

But when she reached the kitchen she found the stranger in it. Her first instinct was to pivot and run, but what she saw held her transfixed. Clad in blue pajamas that were several sizes too big, the man was at the sink with his back to her, and his head was tilted far back as he drank water from a plastic tumbler. It was the rapidity and eagerness in the way he drank that stupefied and gradually chilled her. The water gushed from the faucet, and he repeatedly filled the tumbler. He drank and drank, not caring when the water missed his mouth and ran down his cheek and neck, drenching the collar.

Molly began to count the times he filled the tumbler and drank. One . . . two . . . three . . .

Nobody drank this much, she thought incredulously. Nobody was ever this thirsty.

Four . . . five . . .

When it seemed as if he would never stop, he suddenly turned the faucet off, set the tumbler down on the counter and turned toward her—as though he knew all along she'd been standing there. He stared at her for a moment, then opened his toothless mouth and smiled.

She shrank away from him and ran back into the library.

She shook Steve, but couldn't wake him up. He grunted and listlessly waved her away, as though she were a pesty housefly. She shook him harder, but it was no use. Finally she selected a new book, this one about stars and planets, and again sat in the wing chair. As she turned the pages of the large book with myriad colorful illustrations and photos, she kept her eyes on the door.

An hour passed slowly, and finally Molly mustered up courage to leave the chair and the room. Her mother, she thought, should be getting up about now. Maybe she would feel safer with her than her stepfather. She was beginning to believe that her mother was the stronger of the two.

Haltingly, she peeked around the corner into the formal dining room. Seeing no sign of the stranger, she then darted across the long room toward the door that opened to the living room and the spacious foyer. As she ran she found herself wondering why she was so frightened. Even if her belief that the stranger came from the garden was true, he was still someone or something sickly and scrawny. How could he hurt her? He seemed so weak.

But still he frightened her.

She found the living room and the foyer empty, too. She bolted for the stairs, skipping steps as she raced toward her mother's room. She knew she was probably overreacting, behaving as though something were actually chasing her, but she couldn't help it. She didn't want the stranger to be anywhere near her. She didn't want to see him drinking like that again, pouring gallons of water down his throat without pausing to swallow. And she didn't want to look into those horrible green eyes again either—eyes that seemed to know too much, eyes that made her feel dumb, small and afraid.

She ran into her mother's room and nearly slammed the door after her. She would have leaped onto the bed, but her mother, awake, was looking at her strangely.

"Sweetheart, what's wrong?"

"Mom, when are we leaving?" she said, ignoring the question with one of her own.

"I don't know. It all depends on Steve. For all I know he's probably still out."

"He's sleeping in the library."

Lara's lips tightened and her nostrils flared, but she said nothing. Instead, she got up and slipped into a robe.

Molly looked out a window, then cried out, "There he is!"

Lara jumped, her hand reaching for her chest, as though instinctively to still her heart. "My God, Molly, don't yell like that."

"But there he is, Mom!"

Lara joined her at the window and looked out. Standing in the middle of the lawn was the stranger, his head angled toward the sun which was a glaring eye in a cloudless, bleached sky. A seagull hovered in his line of view, then flapped away in the direction of the ocean.

"What is he doing, Mom?"

"Enjoying the sun, what else?"

But Molly felt certain it was more than this. She couldn't see his face, but she had a gut feeling that his eyes were open. "He's looking at the sun, Mom."

"Now why do you say that? Can you see him?"

"No, but . . ." But what? Why was she so sure that he was staring at the sun? Because he's a plant! He's drinking the sunlight like the way he drank the water.

She felt her mother's hand on hers, gently pulling her away from the window.

"Come on, sweetheart, let's have some breakfast," she said. "And then we'll see how the nice man is doing, see if he can remember his name now."

"No!"

"No what, dear?"

"Don't go near the man, Mom. Please."

"Sweetheart, you're not still afraid of him, are you?"

Molly didn't answer, not wanting her mother to see what a baby she was. Then fear and truth took hold, and she nodded.

Lara sighed, then hugged her. "Nothing to be afraid of. He's a sick man, and he's going through a difficult time right now. He doesn't even know who he is. He has amnesia, I'm sure. I would have called a doctor, but he made me promise to wait, and I was afraid that if I didn't respect his wishes he would have a setback. Now we wouldn't want that on our conscience, would we?"

Molly said nothing.

"But, of course, if he's still stubborn today, I'll call," she went on. "I thought it would be best if he had a good night's rest, that's all. Now come on and stop worrying. He's not going to hurt you. I simply wouldn't let him."

"But, Mom, he came from the garden!" Molly wailed.

"We have no way of knowing that for sure. I admit he is somewhat creepy looking, but he doesn't at all look like a flower or a plant. Now does he?"

"No, but . . ."

"He looks like a man. Right?"

"Yes, but . . ."

"How can I throw a man out, sweetheart? Particularly one who is weak and sick? Would you?"

The girl gave this some thought, shook her head

slowly, then added, "But it's not a man, Mom."

"For the hundredth time, we are not sure about this. Now, are you hungry for breakfast?" she asked, swiftly changing the subject.

"Mom . . ."

She was gone, stepping out into the hallway, the hem of her long robe billowing as she moved. It was clear that she didn't want to discuss the man anymore.

Molly looked out the window again. The stranger hadn't even moved. He was motionless, and his head was still angled toward the sun. Molly watched him, transfixed, feeling safe since she was so far away from him. Then, as before in the kitchen, he sensed her scrutiny and slowly turned toward her. She cried out in surprise and horror—surprise that he again had known she was behind him, and horror when she saw that his eyes were open wide and turned inward so that only the whites were revealed.

Jumping back, Molly tripped over her feet, fell onto her backside, emitted another cry, then scrambled up and bolted out of the room.

"Mom!"

She found her on the stairs. "Sweetheart, please calm down," Lara urged, waiting for Molly to catch up.

"He saw me!"

"And?"

"His eyes were white."

Lara looked at her thoughtfully, as though trying to decide if this was something to be concerned about or something that was the product of an overworked imagination. "I'll call a doctor after I have a talk with him," she said at length. Once more she headed toward the kitchen.

"Mom, how come you don't believe me?"

"About what? About the man being some kind of plant?"

Molly nodded. "The other plants were weird," she reminded her.

"Yes, I know, but this man hasn't really done anything

unusual. Until then, I simply have to treat him like a human being. I could not ignore him—or, heaven forbid, destroy him. He came here pleading for shelter, and I don't think I'd ever be able to live with myself if I didn't help him."

"Steve believes," Molly said.

"Yes, I know."

Molly caught the sad regret in her voice. She waited, expecting more to be said, but her mother's chin rose suddenly and her mouth tightened, as though trying to maintain control.

When they passed the library door, Molly said, "Maybe Steve's up now."

"It doesn't matter if he is or not."

In the kitchen Molly sat in the breakfast nook and silently watched her mother prepare cereal for both of them.

"You still mad at him?" she asked when her mother sat down opposite her.

"Disappointed is a better word."

Molly mulled over this as she chewed corn flakes. "What's gonna happen when we go back to the apartment?"

"I'm not too sure, but, of course, you and I will always be together."

There was a long silence as Molly absently played with her food, twirling her spoon around and around in the cereal and milk, creating a diminutive whirlpool. "What happened, Mom?"

Lara sighed. "Oh, I don't know, but . . ." Her eyes filled with tears and she paused to pull them back. ". . . I don't like what he has become. And I certainly don't like the way he behaved last night—especially toward you. He had no reason to yell at you like that."

"I think I know why." When her mother didn't answer, she explained. "I think he's scared, Mom—like me."

"But that gives him no reason to drink the way he does and shut us off."

"Guess not."

"Well, you and I talk about our problems," Lara said pointedly, "just like we're doing right now, but I have to force him most of the time to talk. That's why you and I get along so well, sweetheart. We talk."

The rest of the meal was eaten in silence. Molly forced herself to eat two more spoonfuls, then she asked to be excused from the table.

When she left the kitchen, she found herself again glancing nervously around her, expecting to see the stranger hiding in one of the hundreds of shadows that dimmed the big house. She agreed with her mother that they were close, and it was because they talked to each other a lot. But sometimes her mother didn't always listen—like now. There seemed to be no way to make her believe that the stranger was not a sickly man—was not even a man! But Steve already believed. Maybe if she went to him, he would listen and do something.

When she opened the door to the library, her stepfather looked up at her from the sofa, his eyes bloodshot and belligerent. Molly contemplated slipping back out of the room, but he was silently waiting for her to explain her presence. He pushed himself up to a sitting position, then leaned forward, resting his elbows on his knees and his head in his hands.

He groaned, then snapped at her, "What do you want?"

Molly found herself too timid to answer. Instead, she gawked at his wrinkled clothes, his messy hair, and a chalky streak below one corner of his mouth where he had drooled while he slept.

"Whadda you want?" he growled again, annoyed at the way she was staring at him.

Molly kept close to the door behind her, one hand still on the heavy brass handle. She could run out if he got too grouchy. "I . . . I . . ."

"I what?"

Her mouth opened and stayed that way. Why was he yelling at her like that? Why was he so mad at her?

Steve, realizing he was scaring the girl, sighed and pulled his wrathful gaze away from her. "Sorry," he mumbled, then rubbed his temples, apparently to soothe the throbbing headache that drinking had given him.

Molly let go of the handle and haltingly moved closer to him. When she was a few inches away, she said, "You godda help, Steve."

"Oh yeah?"

"Please."

He searched her face, then leaned back against the sofa and closed his eyes. He blew out foul air and Molly found herself fighting the instinct to avert her head from the stale, sour smell of his breath. When he opened his eyes again, she saw how weary and miserable he was.

"How can I help?" he said.

"We godda ded rid of the man."

"Godda ded?" he mimicked.

Molly felt a sharp stab in her stomach. It was one she had experienced countless times, especially at school when kids made fun of her. No matter how many times she felt this, she never got used to it. The pain was still as sharp as the first time someone had mocked her.

Wordlessly, she turned to leave, but when she reached the door, she felt Steve's hand on her shoulder. With his other hand he pushed shut the door that she had begun to open. Then he gently forced her to face him.

"I'm sorry," he said. "I'm in a lousy mood. I didn't mean to yell at you or make fun of you. Sorry," he said again.

Molly relaxed, but that sharp pain was still in her stomach; she knew it would not go away for a long while. It never did.

Seeing that he had calmed her down somewhat, he returned to the sofa and plopped heavily into it. "So how do you want me to get rid of the man?"

"I don't know." She was hoping he would have the answer.

"Well?"

"But he's not . . . normal," she said.

"We don't know that for sure."

"You sound just like Mom now!"

"Well, it's the truth."

Molly started to tell him about all the water the stranger had drunk and the way he had stared at the sun, then she changed her mind. Normal people drank water and basked in the sun. There was nothing strange about this—except that she was certain, deep in her belly, that this was different. This wasn't normal. But how could she tell her stepfather this and make him believe in this uneasy feeling she was having?

He was staring at her, and suddenly she was certain he could read her thoughts. "Why didn't you leave well enough alone?" he said at length.

"You mean about the seeds?"

"Yes, the seeds. You had no business down in that cellar."

Molly remained silent, since there was nothing she could say to make everything right again. It was too late; she had gone down in the cellar, had found the seeds, and had planted them.

He continued to stare at her, and she found herself wanting to escape from the room again. He was blaming her for everything, and he was disgusted with her, maybe even filled with hatred toward her. All this was obvious in his bloodshot eyes.

"I never wanted to come back to this goddamn house," he said quietly, yet vehemently. "When I had moved out of here to go to college, I made a vow never to return. That's how much I hated this house. But my sister, damn her, kept calling me back, saying I was breaking Mom's heart. She made me feel so damn guilty, so I forced myself to come back—now and then. And your mother—damn her, too!—she had to live here. Damn her! Damn all of them!"

Molly still remained silent.

"And you hate this house, too," he said. "You hate it because you did the same thing that I did. You went into that room in the cellar and you poked around where you shouldn't have poked. You became aware of the evil that was hiding there, right?''

Gulping, she nodded.

He gave a short contemptuous laugh, then he locked her gaze with his. He reminded her of a madman, as one corner of his mouth curved into a cruel sneer.

"We both should have stayed out of that fucking cellar!" he hissed, then he noticed the bottle of Cutty Sark lying on its side near his feet. "Ah-hah!" he exclaimed, snatching the bottle. "The only remedy for a hangover," he muttered, unscrewing the cap.

"No. Don't drink," Molly pleaded.

"Gotta," he said, tilting the bottle to his lips. "If we want to do something about that creature you grew, I gotta get rid of this nasty hangover."

And before she could say anything further, he drained the bottle.

26

"What are we going to do?" Molly whispered as Steve sat with his head in his hands, his elbows on his knees.

He didn't answer for a long while, and judging from the way his hands kept rubbing his face and messing his hair even more, she knew the whiskey wasn't curing his hangover as he had said it would. Finally, just when she thought her question had been ignored, he lifted his head toward her and said, "First we have to be sure that he is what we think he is. Then we'll go from there."

"How are we going to be sure?"

"Well," he said slowly, "we'll ask him some questions and . . . and . . ." his eyes roamed the room, as though in search of something ". . . we'll *nick* him!"

"Huh?"

"Yes, that's what we'll do," he declared, not hearing her. He stared unseeingly at an old watercolor painting on the wall behind her, and she could see that he was lost in thought. She waited patiently and curiously for him to say what was on his mind.

Eventually his gaze swept back toward her. "I'll use a razor blade," he said, still speaking slowly and pensively. "I'll make it look like an accident. I'll pretend I'm packing my shaving equipment, and I'll just innocently nick him."

Molly frowned, then lifted and dropped her shoulders,

not understanding what nicking the stranger would do.

"To see if he bleeds like you and I," he clarified.

"Oh."

Suddenly she wasn't sure if this was a good idea.

"What's the matter?" Steve asked, seeing the doubt on her face. "You changing your mind?"

"You won't hurt him, will you?"

He gave her a short laugh, as though unable to believe what she had said. "Hey, you're the one who wanted to get rid of him, remember?"

"I know, but—"

"But what, damnit?"

"I don't want him to bleed a lot, I guess."

"Oh, you're squeamish, eh?"

She looked down at the floor, saying nothing. It was true; she *was* squeamish. The sight of blood usually made her nauseated and sick, but that wasn't the reason. In fact, she didn't even know why she was suddenly feeling uneasy. It was one thing to want to get rid of somebody, but another to actually go ahead and do it.

"Hey, I'm only going to nick him, not cut him to pieces," he reminded her. "This is just a test."

"What are we going to do after—"

"After we find that he's actually one of the pea pod people? Then we'll let the police handle it."

But Molly didn't believe it would be that simple. It wouldn't be simple at all.

Hesitantly, Molly followed him as he went into a bathroom, carrying an empty shoe box. She watched him in silence as he filled it with items from the medicine cabinet. When he dropped his plastic razor into it, he winked at her and said, "Teflon blade for an extra smooth shave."

His eyes glinted and his lopsided grin was filled with sarcasm. Molly wanted to plead with him to be more serious, but as he looked away from her she saw a change in his expression. The mask had slipped and gone was the mocking grin. Now a nerve was pulsing at his temple, betraying the tension he was apparently under.

"Gotta take a leak, if you don't mind," he suddenly said, embarrassing her. Wordlessly, she left the room and waited outside the door.

A minute later he came out. The shoe box, now full, was in his hands. Together they searched for the stranger, peering out several windows to see if he was still outside absorbing the sun. Then they headed upstairs toward his room. As they reached the room, they found Lara leaving it.

Her visage hardened the instant she saw Steve, and Steve automatically averted his face. There was a frosty moment of silence, and Molly found herself wishing desperately for something romantic to happen. This was a perfect time to ask for forgiveness, a time to kiss and make up, but the moment grew colder, then abruptly ended.

"What's that?" Lara asked of the shoe box in Steve's hands.

"Stuff from the medicine cabinet," he answered, then added, "I've more to pack."

"Oh. Yes, I've still things to pack, too." When Steve didn't comment, she added, "He still doesn't know his name."

"Is that so?"

"He still refuses to see a doctor," she went on, although his response was cool and indifferent. "He said he'd leave right away if I didn't promise not to call."

"Let him leave."

"But the man is sick."

Steve shrugged. "Then call."

"But I'm afraid it might cause more harm than good. What if he has a setback and leaves?" Her face softened with worry.

"Why do you care so much? He's only a stranger, for Christ's sake!"

"I can't help it. I just care, that's all! Not everybody

is—'' She stopped abruptly, not wanting to finish, not wanting a scene.

"As heartless? Is that what you were going to say . . . Ms. Nightingale?"

Lara searched his face, then something collapsed in her eyes.

"Steve?"

"Yeah?"

She opened her mouth to say something, but suddenly lacked the courage to utter the words. Slowly, she closed her mouth and shook her head. "Never mind." She passed them and hurried down the hall.

Steve watched her leave, then knocked on the stranger's door and, without bothering to wait for a reply, went in.

Molly remained in the doorway, too timid to follow.

Feigning concern, Steve walked over to the bed and set the box of cosmetics and medical supplies on a cherry table near it. The stranger's eyes were closed, but when Steve came near, they sprung open and locked on him. The suddenness startled Steve, but he quickly composed himself with a smile.

"How're you doing?"

The man nodded, indicating he was fine. He looked much better than the last time Steve had seen him, but the skin still had that sickly, bloodless color.

"Need something to drink or eat—anything?"

The man shook his head, then his eyes slid toward Molly in the doorway. He could see the tension in the girl's face. He looked back over to Steve, as though expecting an explanation.

"That's Molly, my stepdaughter," Steve said amicably. "She's a little nervous about having a stranger in the house."

The man said nothing, and an awkward silence ensued. Steve made an effort to widen his smile, but it seemed to have reached its limit, for it began to falter.

"We still know nothing about you, so you *are* a stranger," he said.

"It is returning," the man finally answered, his voice dry and faint.

"Returning?"

"My memory."

"Hey, that's great. Do you remember your name?"

The man stared at him, and Steve distinctly felt that he was being analyzed. This man did know his name, but the question was whether or not to reveal it, whether or not to trust Steve. At length he said, "No."

"But you almost had it, huh?" Steve said, although he suspected this wasn't true at all. The man knew who he was but for some reason did not want to disclose his identity. "Well, I'm sure it'll come to you soon."

There was another awkward pause.

"I don't know if Lara—that's my wife—told you," Steve went on, after clearing his throat, "but we're in the process of moving out. In fact, we were to be out of this house today. So, uh, I guess you know what that means."

The man said nothing, and Steve fought an instinct to sigh audibly.

"It means," he continued, "you can't stay here after today."

Again it appeared that the man would keep his silence, then he opened his toothless mouth, briefly repulsing Steve with sour, stagnant breath, and said, "I will leave as well, of course."

"Maybe you should see a doctor."

Once more he received silence.

"Well, I just wanted to see how you were doing." Steve reached for the box and held it in his arms. Now, he thought as he inwardly braced himself, it's showtime, folks!

Feigning clumsiness, he dropped the box. "Shit!" he muttered as the contents spilled out onto the bed and floor. "They always said I was a klutz." He retrieved most of the items and threw them back into the box, which he kept on the bed. When he reached for the razor he let it slip out of his hand and fall onto the stranger's bare arm. "Oops!" He made another attempt to retrieve it, and as he did this he let the sharp blade scrape the arm before he picked it up.

"Aw Christ, sorry!" he exclaimed, hoping he sounded genuinely contrite. Then he threw the razor into the box.

Molly took a step back, partly concealing herself behind the doorframe, as though not certain if she wanted to witness this. The stranger looked at her in confusion, then he followed Steve's gaze and saw the cut on his arm. It was thin, but deep. The man moved his arm, and the lips of the cut gaped widely. But there was no blood!

Molly and Steve stared, and the man, in turn, stared at them.

Then a greenish-yellow viscid liquid began to ooze out of the wound. Pus? Steve wondered, then decided it wasn't. It was too thick and syrupy.

The man lifted his arm to slide it beneath the covers and hide it, and as he moved, the cut opened and closed like a mouth, drooling more of the sickening stuff. It reminded Steve of green molasses, sap.

Christ.

Arm hidden, the man then stared evenly at him, challenging him. Steve felt cold and tingly. Slowly, he backed away from the bed. Behind him he heard Molly flee down the hallway and stairs.

When he reached the door, he stopped and studied the man on the bed, then whispered, "What are you?"

But the man, as before, remained silent.

What do you want? The question popped into Steve's mind, but he was too stunned to utter it. Then came another question. What to do? Certainly he and his family couldn't stay here with this . . . this thing!

Yes, what to do?

Steve's eyes moved jerkily to the box that was still on

the bed. He contemplated retrieving it, then changed his mind. Fuck it! The important thing to do was get the hell out of this house—now!

Without another word, he turned and hurried out of the room.

The man closed his eyes. Every time he did this, the memories became vivid. He could remember so much now, and most of the memories were sorrowful, memories of things that he wished he could change. He could remember that night, so long ago, centuries ago, when he had fought so strenuously to keep death at bay. He remembered how weak he'd been, and how grateful when the spirit had materialized in that stone cell. He'd been too dazed, too close to death to discern the apparition clearly, but he thought he had suffered enough for his sins. That had been why he had believed the spirit before him on his death bed was holy, not demonical, but he had been mistaken and now would regret it.

A devil had appeared and offered him another life, for it knew that the life that was drawing to a finish had been one of grief and frustration. He had held the secret of the universe but had abused it and had spent the final years in isolation and repentance. The offer had been immensely tempting, and he had succumbed to it. He had been deceived. He truly had believed a divine spirit had made the offer with kindness, but it was not, he could see now, that way at all.

He had unwittingly made a pact with a devil.

The man opened his eyes, and some of the horrible images receded into the darkness where the memories dwelled. He stared at the crystal light fixture, knowing what it was although electricity did not exist in his time. But he had the knowledge of the universe now. He had gone into another level and was now back. He had thought, on his return, he would bring with him so much knowledge, so much wisdom, and that he would share them this time because previously the world had not been ready. But he was not certain if the world was even prepared now.

The man named Steve had left him with doubt.

Another life awaited him, and he had so much more wisdom this time. He had been scorned by many because of his knowledge, especially of his Art. When the spirit had tempted him with another chance, with perhaps a more fulfilling life, his first thought had been that he would be comfortable in a future society and be able to enjoy it. He had been ahead of himself in the other life, but in a future life he might fit just fine.

Ah yes, the temptation had been too immense to ignore.

But now again, he feared he was ahead of himself. The world was still too ignorant. He would not be at liberty to share his wisdom. He now had knowledge of the grave, and he had merged with earth's two life-forms—flora and fauna.

Was the world ready for someone like him?

He certainly saw that Steve and the girl were not.

So what was he to do now?

The man closed his eyes again, feeling a need to weep, but there were no tears. In the darkness behind his lids the memories rushed back.

You cannot, my dear friar, remain much longer in this condition. Certainly you are aware that you are near the end.

The voice had belonged to a mist, vaguely shaped to resemble a human, but there had been no features about the head, only a grayish sphere. He saw the mouth move, saw the body waver, but it had all been so hazy—something that he had blamed on his feverish condition.

But the voice—oh, that was distinct and unmistakable.

"I did not summon you," the friar had said. "I destroyed the books years ago. I no longer use my art. So please, vanish and let me be."

You are dying, Friar Roger.

"Of that I am aware."

And if it is your desire, you may return.

"Why, do tell, would I wish to return?"

You are unhappy, Friar Bacon. Your life has been filled with woes and frustrations. You have punished yourself with guilt. You have blamed yourself for needless deaths and blamed it on your art. It is too late to start life anew, but only this life, friar. I could grant you another.

"Another life?"

Yes.

"But . . . I do not understand. How will you do this?"

I will recreate you.

"You are a divine spirit, are you not?" the friar exclaimed in a surge of excitement and incredulity, then fell back onto his bed as waves of dizziness swept over him. He felt himself leaving rapidly. It would only be a matter of days before death would claim him—perhaps only hours.

I will recreate you, the spirit said again. *But it would not be you alone. You must agree to share the rebirth.*

"Is that all? To share the rebirth?"

That is all. Is the agreement satisfactory, friar?

"Satisfactory? Why, it is incredible. When shall I return?"

Certainly you do not wish to return to this century nor to the next and suffer once more in a dim society. Therefore, the seeds will be protected and when ample time has passed they will be planted, and you will rise from the soil.

"Incredible," the friar repeated.

Then I presume the pact is made?

"Yes, oh yes," he had said.

Now the man opened his eyes once again and focused them on the light fixture. He hated that word—pact. It made him cold, angry and frustrated. Pact. He knew now what he had done, and perhaps he deserved being tricked the way he had.

Pact.

In his first life he should have never amused himself with the arts of conjuration and necromancy. He should have never tried to outwit Satan when he did, that night so long ago at the crossroads.

Pact.

Now he was back. He was given another life to live, but after this . . .

He groaned. He had made a horrible mistake.

He had made a pact with the devil, and this time he would not win.

27

Steve found Lara in the kitchen, sipping tea. Molly was with her, a glass of untouched milk in front of her. Both looked up quickly when he entered, and both, he noted, looked troubled, even frightened.

"We're getting the hell out of here!" he commanded. He expected his wife and the girl to jump obediently, but instead they stared at him, their eyes still betraying uncertainty and fear. Molly got up from her chair and stood near her mother, who wrapped an arm around her waist.

"Did you hear what I said?" Steve's voice rose. "Let's get a move on. Let's get out of here!"

"You're acting as though the house's on fire," Lara said, but her voice was weak, barely audible.

Steve glared at her, then turned his attention to Molly. "You saw it, didn't you?" When she didn't answer and only pressed closer to her mother, he repeated, "Didn't you?"

Her head moved in a slow, faint nod, but it was Lara who answered. "Maybe he has some kind of blood disorder."

"You didn't see—"

"Molly told me, and obviously something's wrong with his blood, Steve."

"He doesn't have any blood. That's what's wrong!"

"But we don't know that for sure."

Steve gaped at her. He couldn't believe this woman! Half her face had been eaten away—and she still didn't believe! "Christ!" he exploded. "How much fucking proof do you need?"

"Steve, please, let's not have another scene."

For a moment Steve found himself speechless, glancing incredulously at her, at Molly, then back at her. "Well, what the hell do you suggest we do, huh?"

"Definitely call a doctor. Have him test the man," Lara said. Her voice was calm, but her hand holding the cup of tea trembled, betraying her.

"And how do we get him to a doctor?"

"Maybe we can have a doctor come here."

"House calls went out with hula hoops, Lara."

"Maybe if we tell the doctor it's an emergency."

"Not we, Lara. *You!*" he clarified.

"Steve—"

"I'm leaving, leaving for once and for all!"

"Steve—"

"For fucking good, damnit! You can have this house! It's all yours! You can do whatever you want with it. From now on count me out of your life!"

"Steve, please, let's not go through this again."

But it was too late; Steve could no longer control himself. Something inside him had let go. "Get yourself a lawyer and contact me at the restaurant. Goodbye, Lara."

"Steve, don't be like this. That man needs help. We can't just get up and leave—"

"I said good-bye." He turned to leave the room.

"Steve!"

He ignored her cry. A small part of him wanted to return to the kitchen, to urge her to forget everything he had said, but the larger part wanted to cut loose and detach himself from this house. He had certainly endured it long enough.

"Steve!" Lara followed him to the door, then stopped.

He stormed across the dining room, heading toward the stairs in the foyer.

"Steve, don't leave me! Steve, I love you."

There was a sob, then he was out of hearing range. He partly hoped Lara would continue after him, but intuitively he knew she was too proud to do so. The kitchen door was her limit, and she would not go beyond it. If he wanted a reconciliation, he would have to go back himself. Though he wanted to, his body moved on its own volition.

He went up to his bedroom to pack his clothes.

The man was tired, but he did not want to close his eyes. Doing this would make the memories too vivid. He wished to enjoy only the present—his new life—and he wished to make this life as long as possible, because after this . . .

His eyelids drooped. Already the memories were filling his mind. They were rushing inexorably like an avalanche toward him, rushing from that deep darkness, appearing suddenly out of nowhere. Eternity. Horrible, black eternity.

His eyelids dropped. Darkness. Eternity.

And he abhorred it. When he had died and floated from his body, he thought he would be drawn toward peace. Darkness surrounded him and for a while peace did as well, but eventually this peace faded, and loneliness and boredom prevailed. He had hoped for a change and desperately prayed for it, but no one heard him. The divine spirit ignored him. He was alone and did not have a voice that he could hear, so the silence was as complete as the darkness. Only his thoughts had amused him, but that eventually grew infrequent and jaded.

He knew there would have been peace if there had been no awareness, but he was aware of his loneliness, aware of the darkness and silence. Although he no longer was trapped inside a body, he nevertheless felt trapped inside something, inside eternity. He would be here in this darkness forever. On and on and on.

Along with the silence and darkness was something else, and it was this that caused him to realize there would never be peace, that he was not where the holy spirits dwelled. In the silence and darkness there was a ceaseless stream of black emotions, filtering through his soul, like ink coloring water, slowly darkening it until it was as black as the surrounding darkness. There were so many emotions feeding him—frustration, resentment, anger, hate, a constant and eternal flow.

He found himself eagerly waiting for the time he would return and rise from the soil. When at last that time came, he felt a powerful, magnetic pull; he knew the seed had been sown, and he was seeping into it. There was confusion, a strange spinning, whirling sensation. Something, he knew was happening, was beginning. Then there was blissful nothingness as his seed germinated. It was not like the horrible eternity, for there was no awareness. Then finally he awakened and felt the wonderful, warm sunshine once again and the moist, smooth rain.

Life.

He was immensely relieved that he was now no longer in that endless void. This was a respite, and he was determined to have this respite be as lengthy as possible, because he knew that after his new life there would be only darkness, silence and discontentment again—forever.

He also knew that Steve and his family would endeavor to ruin or destroy his respite. Therefore, to prevent this, he would have to destroy them first.

Because of the black emotions that had flowed unrelentlessly through him, he was easily capable of anything vile. Yes, he definitely would have to destroy them first.

Steve was inside the walk-in closet when he heard the footsteps behind him. It's Lara, he thought. She has swallowed her pride and is going to plead with him to reconsider, which was fine, but he was not going to give in about the house or about that creature staying here. He was moving out—now!

But it wasn't Lara he had heard.

Pulling a shirt off a hanger, he turned to throw it in a suitcase that was open on the floor. That was when he saw the pale man in the doorway. Something chilly gripped him, but he quickly told himself there was nothing to fear. This man could not harm him. He was weak. He was sickly. He was—

"Where are you going, Steve?" The voice was low as a whisper, but dry and grating as rusty metal. "That is the correct name, is it not?"

Steve swallowed, then nodded. "Yeah, Steve it is. I'm packing." Then, as though to prove this, he turned toward the clothes rod for another shirt. He forced himself to move with ease and affect calmness. "You should still be in bed, shouldn't you?"

"You did not answer my first inquiry."

"Oh, what was that?"

"Where are you going?"

Steve, this time, folded his shirt before placing it in the suitcase, giving him a moment to think. "My wife and I are having problems. And I'm—" he shrugged "—splitting."

"Splitting?"

"Yeah, Separating."

The man frowned, then the lines in his face smoothed, as though he'd decided the confusion did not matter. "But I still do not know where you are going."

Reaching for another shirt, he said, "Back to Massachusetts. I've a business there, and I'll find myself another apartment."

"No." The word was quiet but firm.

"What?"

"I cannot permit you to leave."

Steve stared at him, absently bunching the shirt that he had started to fold in his hands. "I-I don't think you're in any position to tell me what to—"

"You, undoubtedly, will inform others."

"What?"

"I wish to live another full life."

"Look, I don't know what you're talking about, but I've packing to do. So, if you don't mind—"

The door behind the creature slammed shut, and Steve wasn't sure if a draft had done this or the creature had reached behind itself for the knob. The 40-watt bulb on the closet ceiling was not enough light; it left too many shadows from the clothes and the two men in the confined space. And it left an eerie yellowish color on the creature's face. The eyes, with lack of light illuminating them, were more black than green, like one of those flies that swarmed over garbage on the beach, he thought. Black and shiny with a tint of green.

"Open the door."

But the man did not move.

Steve let the shirt in his hand drop into the suitcase, then he reached for the door himself. Its knob twisted, but the door wouldn't open. He twisted the knob harder, then pushed against the door. Still it refused to budge. Was something against it on the other side? There was no lock, so what else could it be? He slammed his shoulder against the door, but the door remained solid, unyielding.

Then he turned toward the man, who was silently watching him—and he knew. Nothing was on the other side of the door. This man had somehow slammed it shut and was keeping it shut. There was a force at work here, and the force had trapped him.

"Let me out of here," he hissed, fighting panic. This man is frail, he reminded himself. He is sick. He is weak.

"I said let me out of here!"

The man remained silent, staring at him with those black, greenish eyes. Then the shadows around him seemed to darken, and the light seemed to fade. Steve's eyes shot to the light bulb on the ceiling. The light was waning and waxing, as though something invisible were sucking, then exhaling it. Soon, he knew with a chilling dread, the light would go out completely.

"Stop it!" he demanded, but the words scarcely passed his lips. The man continued to stare at him, not moving.

"What are you doing?" Steve's voice was stronger this time "Why are you doing this?"

"You already know the reason," the man answered at last. "You will inform others."

"Inform them of what?"

"Of what I am."

"I don't even know what you are, for Christ's sake!" His voice was rising with the panic. Stay calm, he told himself.

Suddenly an image of himself gasping and struggling to stay alive appeared in his mind. It was the image he had seen in the piece of glass that had shown him his death.

Had the time now arrived?

"Look, just let me go," he pleaded. "I don't know what you are, and I don't care what you are."

"You are aware that I am not like you. You will inform others, and I will be examined. I will be discovered, and because I am beyond anyone's comprehension I will be feared, and I will be destroyed."

"No, not necessarily."

"Yes." The man's head bowed confidently. "I foresee another lifetime of ostracism and condemnation in a benighted world. I must prevent this from happening. I wish for a long life, a wonderful life this time, because after this, there will be . . . nothing. You must understand."

"I won't tell anything. I swear. Just let me out of here and I'll get in my car and you'll never see or hear from me again. I'll be out of your life."

"Car?"

"Yes, car. Automobile, like . . . like a boat on wheels. It'll take me away very fast, and I'll be out of your life," he repeated emphatically. "You won't have to worry about me."

"Will the woman and girl be with you in this car?"

"No, I'm going alone. I've already told you, we're separated. We had words; we're no longer a family."

The man mulled over this.

"Now please, let me go," Steve pleaded.

But the man was motionless once again, and the light bulb on the ceiling was dimming rapidly now. Light faded almost to complete darkness, then returned weakly. In sickening dread Steve watched the man's bloodless face disappear and reappear, like a hideous moon on a cloudy night.

Then the light went out for the final time.

Noooo, Steve voicelessly cried. Never had he seen such complete darkness. It was even darker than the horrible cellar, where this creature came from in the first place.

Nooo. He felt like a child again, petrified like a child. He threw himself against the door, then threw himself again. Pain seared through his body as it battered the hard wood, but the door would not break open.

Panting, he swung around to where he knew the man was standing. He could not see him, not even a vague outline, but he could smell his putrid breath. Rotting vegetation, he thought.

"What are you going to do?"

Only silence answered him. If it weren't for the foul breath, Steve would have been certain he was alone in the closet. He tried again to force open the door.

"C'mon, damnit, come on!"

Then he swung around again toward the invisible man. The breath was stronger now, and the air seemed warmer —or was it himself, working up to a full-fledged panic?

"Look," he strained to make his voice even and threatening, "if you don't open this door now, I'll make you regret it."

There was another long silence, then an amused "Regret?"

"Yes."

The man laughed, quite softly, yet it unnerved Steve. He might be bigger and stronger, but only in the physical sense. This man was stronger in another sense—a sense that was incomparable and incomprehensible.

Steve pressed his back against the door. With the back of his hand he wiped the sweat off his forehead, then above his lips. He was waiting for something to happen, but there was only silence and that nauseating smell.

What was this man going to do?

He could feel the green-black eyes on him, and he wondered if these eyes could actually see him.

Steve squared his shoulders and lifted his chin, but he knew he would not fool this man—creature—with the way he was sweating so profusely.

Minutes elapsed, and he waited. Certainly *something* would happen. Something must be planned. Steve began to breathe heavily. Was he hyperventilating? On the verge of hysteria?

No, he was a man, for Christ's sake! He was strong. He would not fall apart.

But you always fall apart, an inner voice pointed out, and you always run away. Now you're locked in and can't run away.

Steve wiped the trickling sweat off his face again. He closed his eyes and tried to concentrate on his breathing, to curb it.

His chest rose and fell laboriously.

He reopened his eyes. Maybe if he talked . . .

"Why . . . I mean, what are you?"

No answer.

"Do you remember your name?"

"Yes."

"And?"

Again the silence, and Steve groaned in frustration. How long were they going to stay in here and what was going to happen? He was confident something would, but what?

"Roger Bacon."

"What?" He wasn't sure if he heard anything, let alone right. When the name wasn't repeated, he said uncertainly, "Did you say Roger Bacon?"

"Indeed, I did."

The sweat on Steve's face cooled, chilling him. "The famous monk?"

"I became famous?"

"H-how come you're back as . . . as . . . ."

"The devil's cruel trick," the friar hissed with surprising ferocity. He fouled the air with his thick breath. "I was deceived. I had foolishly believed I would return as I was. Now these demons shall have the final laugh, because I shall belong to them, perhaps deservingly, for I had outwitted and incensed them at times. But . . ." he paused, letting the one word linger " . . . I shall relish this new life, nevertheless. No one shall mar or destroy it."

The sentence was uttered with resolve and unmistakable bitterness. Steve remembered reading that this friar was a good man, a man who had tormented himself with guilt for dabbling in the art of necromancy and the conjuration of spirits, but here, unseen before him, was someone or something exuding resentment, hate and silent fury without any guilt. Where did these negative emotions come from?

"Rumor has it that you burned all your magic," Steve said.

"It was not magic!" the man corrected sharply. "It only appears as such because so many are ignorant. It is an art. It takes skill and wisdom to perfect what you so foolishly call magic."

"But didn't you burn them before—"

"Before I passed on to that other level, to that black void?" he finished caustically. "I thought I had destroyed the harmful items. I had destroyed *Key of Solomon, Picatrix* and *Canon*. I had cleansed my chambers of so many objects, so many books, so much equipment, but there had been thieves among us. Scholars had stolen my studies and robbed me of several possessions. Above all, I suspect Miles, my assistant, had betrayed me. He was one fool who could never be trusted. Why I kept him as my assistant I will never know, but I had several times caught him conjuring up spirits and perusing my studies."

Steve suddenly wanted to know about the mirror, certain that it had belonged to this ex-friar. "What did you do with the mirror? And the ring? How did they find their way over here?"

"The mirror?"

"It . . . it forecasted death."

"Ah yes, it was this glass that had caused me so much grief. I had destroyed it into hundreds of shards, so I doubt very much if we are speaking of the same, despicable glass."

"I only found a shard."

There was silence, then a contemptuous snort. "My assistant, no doubt. Apparently he had taken a shard for himself after I had smashed the glass. I wonder how much else he took for himself and passed on to his descendants."

"The seeds," Steve reminded him.

"Of course, the seeds. Then, indeed, it was Miles who had taken the shard and the ring—I had several, in fact. It was to Miles that I had given the seeds. The despicable spirit that had beguiled me had removed skin from my breast and with it created a seed. I did not know that other living cells, another life form, would be added to my own. If I had . . . Never mind, it no longer matters."

Steve stared in the direction of the man, wishing he could see him. He waited for him to say more, but nothing else was proffered. A long silence ensued, broken only by his own laborious breathing and the man's, which were long, strange pulls of inhalation, without the sounds of exhalation.

What did this mean?

"C'mon, let me out of here," he pleaded. "You don't have to worry about me telling anyone about you. To be truthful, who on earth would ever believe me?"

No answer came forth, only that eerie sucking sound.

"Please."

Nothing. What was he sucking, anyway? The air?

Then it hit him! He had guessed right. Bacon was sucking in air—*his* air. Hadn't he heard somewhere that a plant could rob a person of air if confined together in a small space? He could almost hear his eighth grade biology teacher's droning voice: "Plants can ameliorate the air, and then only if they are placed in strong light.

However, flowers and other nongreen parts, as well as green leaves left in darkness, use up oxygen just as animals do."

Left in darkness!

So that was why the light bulb went out.

Now there was a contest for the air in the closet, and judging from the sound of Bacon's voluminous pull of air, he would win.

Already Steve could feel a difference. The air was thinner, and he was having difficulty breathing. He had thought this was because of his rising panic, but now knew it was more than this.

He was suffocating in here.

"Stop . . . stop it!" he gasped.

Bacon inhaled deeply and noisily in reply.

Steve spun toward the door again, banging at it with his fist, but he was weak now and knew the house was too big for Lara to hear him, especially if she was downstairs somewhere.

Then he turned toward Bacon. "Damn you, stop it!" He clenched his hand into a fist and swung into the darkness. He punched empty air. Then he heard the deep inhalation near his left ear. He pivoted in that direction and swung again. Nothing. With an eruption of renewed panic, he realized that Bacon could see him after all. That was why he was able to dodge his punches.

"Damn, damn!" He kept swinging and kept missing.

Then an unbidden image of himself gasping filled his mind again. This, he knew with cold certainly, was the moment he had seen in the shard of glass.

He was going to die, exactly as he had witnessed it.

He reached for his neck and clawed at it, then he dropped to his knees. His lungs were swelling and burning, yet he could not get enough air, for it was thinning, thinning . . . and thinning.

28

Something bothered him as he left the closet. His hazy mind, which was not as keen as it used to be, was trying to tell him something. It was as if a warning light were flashing in the distance, and he had to sit on the bed to concentrate.

Slowly it came to him. The boat on wheels. What had the man called it?

Again he concentrated, rubbing both hands against his skull, relaxing the brain within it. No, his mind this time was not as alert, as alive. It was sluggish.

He sighed, but he did not cease to concentrate. Then the word finally surfaced. Car. The man had called it a car, and he had said it would take him away very fast.

As he continued to massage his head, he reasoned this car could take the woman and girl away, also. The woman and girl could escape from here. They, like the man, would leave and inform others of his existence, and the others would return and search for him, capture him, study him, and in the end—what?

He did not want to find out. He must prevent this, for he wished to walk among men inconspicuously, to observe his new world but not *be* observed. Therefore, he must find this car. He must not let the woman and girl get away.

Moving to the window, he peered out at the ocean. He

saw birds swooping toward the water, but no boats on
wheels. Then he left the room and stole down the stairs.
He heard Lara's voice from the distant room and was
thankful for that; this meant the woman was preoccupied
and might not hear his footsteps. He opened the heavy
front door as quietly as possible and stepped outside. Sun
warmed and fed him, and he paused for a long moment,
tilting his face upward. Then he closed the door softly
behind him and looked about.

Where was the boat on wheels?

As soon as the question was formed he knew the
answer. Almost directly in front of him was a metallic
object, and it was sitting on wheels. Curiously, he walked
toward it, then ran his hand across its smooth surface. He
found the door, briefly experimented with the silver
handle until he heard a click. Then he opened the door
and climbed inside. There was another wheel. He stared
at it for a moment without touching it. Would this wheel
activate the boat? He would have to be careful, he knew.
There were so many things that were unfamiliar to him,
so many things he would have to learn.

But after he was rid of the woman and the girl he
would be able to tread slowly. He was strong enough now
to begin his new life. He would move away from this
house and land, and he would explore. He would live a
long, long life. He would savor it immensely, and he
would not think beyond this. But first the car, then the
woman and the girl.

He touched the wheel. It moved a fraction of an inch,
then clicked and refused to move again. He frowned,
then concentrated. Energy, he mused, produces motion,
and in his short stay in the house he had observed that the
same form of energy that surrounded and flowed through
him in the other level was used commonly here. Electricity.

He willed himself to generate the energy needed, and
he laughed disdainfully as he remembered that this would
have been declared magic and evil in his past. Wizards

and witches had been believed to smite people and objects with ragged, blinding bolts. Now he was capable of doing exactly that.

He ran his hands over the plastic wheel, across the top of the dashboard, then down its panel. There was a sharp crackle, then a roar as the vehicle erupted to life. The sudden noise startled him, then pleased him. He experimented with the wheel again and ran his other hand over the dials, switches and levers in front of him. He tested the protruding objects on the floor with his feet. The "boat" roared again, but it did not move. Then he noted a sticklike object protruding from the right side of the wheel. He worked at this, and eventually succeeded in jerking the vehicle forward.

He headed toward the house, and instinctively his hand let go of the wheel and his foot withdrew from the part that made the car roar. The vehicle lurched forward, then he noticed the wheel was moving. He touched it once more and felt it pull under his hand. He turned it and discovered the vehicle moved with him.

Slowly and spasmodically, he drove to the side of the house. He wanted to conceal the vehicle in the ocean but was not sure how to accomplish this. He feared he may not leap out in time and would plunge with the vehicle. He had found the device near his foot that would make him stop, and when he spotted the thick growth of rhododendrons and azaleas he headed for it. He paused here, experimented with the dials and switches again, and soon found how to stifle the roar.

Then he sat back against the seat and laughed quietly, pleased with himself. Yes, he thought, there would be plenty to learn, but he would tread slowly and carefully.

He climbed out of the vehicle and fluffed up the shrubs that surrounded it. The sides were concealed, but the roof was exposed, glinting under the sun. He tore several branches off a shrub and placed them over the bare metal, then he stepped back to appraise his work. One could detect something was among the rhododendrons and azaleas, but from the house—maybe not. Maybe the woman and the girl would never notice.

He laughed quietly again, then tilted his face toward the sun. He smiled as he absorbed its wonderful rays and closed his eyes.

Memories rushed forward. Black eternity.

He quickly reopened his eyes, scowling. Now he knew why the demonical spirit had given him a second chance. It wanted to torment him. It had shown him the infinite horror that was ahead of him, and it was now showing him what was temporary.

But, he reminded himself, temporary could be a long time—if he were careful. Already he had the boat with the wheels out of the way, and now he would concentrate solely on the woman and the girl. He would take his time and be careful.

He lingered under the sun, and when he felt strong and refreshed, he turned toward the house.

Lara fought to keep Steve's words from sinking in. Only words, she told herself, only words without meaning.

Lara squeezed her eyes shut, but it was useless. She knew Steve meant everything he'd said. It was over.

"Mom?"

She opened her eyes and was surprised to find them filled with tears. Embarrassed to have her daughter see her like this, she quickly wiped them and managed a smile. "Yes, sweetheart?"

"You okay?" Molly's face was filled with concern as she looked up at her, and it was this look that made Lara gush more tears.

"Oh, sweetheart, of course I'm okay," she lied, wiping her eyes first with her finger, then the back of her hand. "Perhaps it's better this way."

"Go ahead, Mom. Cry. They say it's good to cry."

"Oh, sweetheart . . ." She sighed, then gave in to the advice. She let the tears flow, occasionally dabbing her eyes with a tissue that Molly had fetched from the kitchen counter for her. When her eyes were finally dry, she pushed the box of tissues away and sat at the kitchen table. With eyes red and puffy while most of her face was concealed behind bandages, she gestured for Molly to sit on her lap. It had been such a long time since she'd done that.

Molly hesitated only briefly. Although she was almost as tall as her mother now, she was still a child, and right now she needed to be comforted. They both needed to be comforted.

"He'll come back, Mom," Molly said, wrapping her arms around her mother's neck and snuggling close to her.

"Even if he does, I don't think I'll take him back."

"How come?"

Lara thought about it for a moment. "He runs away from problems and doesn't work them out. I don't like that in a person, and I don't think we'll ever get anywhere that way. I think . . . I think you and I will have to move on."

"But don't you love him?"

Again there was a long thoughtful pause, "I thought I did."

Molly looked at her, and slowly her big eyes began to fill with water. "I liked him a lot, Mom."

"I know you did, but some things . . . well, they just can't be helped."

Molly wiped her eyes with her hand, then leaned her head against Lara's shoulder.

"My baby," Lara whispered. "It's you I love so much." She rested her cheek against the softness of her daughter's hair, and some of the ache melted. As long as she had her child, she told herself, everything would be all right. She had survived this far, so there was no reason why she couldn't continue to survive.

She began to hum and soon was actually feeling peaceful. Then she heard the car engine roar and sputter outside. She tensed. Was Steve leaving? But why was the engine making so much noise? Was it because Steve was still angry and this was his immature way of showing it? Then she relaxed and stroked Molly's silky hair. Let him leave, she thought. She didn't care. She would move on. She and Molly would move on and on and on.

When there was silence, she went over to the window that looked out onto the driveway. The car was gone. There was a cutting stab in her heart, but she told herself it was indignation. How dare he leave her and Molly—and the poor man upstairs—stranded!

Molly joined her at the window. "What's wrong, Mom?" she asked, apparently sensing that something was.

Lara thought of making up a lie, not wanting to alarm her, then decided against it. So far she had been honest and frank, so why stop now? "Steve has left us. The car . . . he took it."

"He left us stranded?"

"When he runs, he *runs,*" Lara muttered bitterly. "Obviously he doesn't care who he leaves behind."

"What?" Lara's voice had been too low for the girl to catch.

"Nothing. It's not important. What is important, though, is that you not worry about us being stranded. There's always a taxi, you know."

Molly said nothing. Lara then moved away from the window and willed herself to think about the sick man. No blood, Steve had said. Was that true? Now how could anyone possibly survive without blood? Or was this man some kind of creature as her husband—correction: ex-husband—had suggested?

As she pondered this, her hand rose to the coarse bandage on her face. Nothing was absurd, was it? A flower did harm her face, didn't it? But although she had evidence, it all seemed so unreal and dreamlike. She just couldn't be as certain as Steve was.

But a doctor could decide. He would be certain.

She remembered the promise she had made to the nameless man, but that, she realized, was no longer important. A doctor was needed—as soon as possible. If there was a setback, then it would be the doctor's problem; he would take care of it.

In the living room she flipped through a phone book, found the number she wanted and began dialing. Molly watched her from the doorway, her eyes focused on her lips.

There were two rings, then a nasal feminine voice answered. "Doctor Carrington's office. May I help you?"

"If possible, I would like to speak with the doctor."

"I'm afraid he's busy at the moment, ma'am."

"When would be the best time to speak with him then?"

"If you wish to make an appointment," the secretary said clinically, ignoring the question, "just tell me your name and the problem."

"But I wish for the doctor to make a house call."

"He doesn't make house calls, ma'am. Only in extreme emergencies."

"This . . . this is an emergency."

There was a pause. Lara knew she had failed to convince the woman on the other end of the line.

"Please let me speak with the doctor," she pleaded.

There was another pause. "One moment please."

A minute later a deep masculine voice said, "Doctor Carrington speaking."

For a fleeting instant Lara's mind drew a blank. What to say? How to convince this man it was extremely important to make a house call? She drew a deep breath and sat down. "Dr. Carrington," she said, forcing herself to take her time, "I've a man here that I think you should see. He's a stranger and he doesn't remember his name."

"Fine, my secretary will gladly arrange an appointment."

"No, you don't understand. I would like for you to examine him here at the house."

"I'm sorry, ma'am, but there is simply no time. I've patients here at the office and at two hospitals. I'm sorry," he said again.

"But this man refuses to see a doctor. I feel he definitely needs to be checked, and I don't have a car."

"I'm sorry."

"I'll gladly pay whatever—"

"I'm too busy," the doctor said coldly, and she knew she had affronted him.

"Please, Dr. Carrington," she implored. "Make an exception. It's important that you see him."

The doctor emitted an audible sigh, a sign that told Lara he was relenting. She closed her eyes with relief.

"Today would be impossible," the doctor said after a long pause.

"Tonight?"

"Tomorrow. Around eight."

He was not giving her a choice. She had wanted him to come sooner. "That would be fine," she said, masking the disappointment in her voice. She gave him the address of the house, then added, "Thank you, doctor."

The man grunted in her ear, then hung up. Lara lowered the receiver, then looked over at her daughter who was still in the doorway. "Tomorrow," she said needlessly.

"Can we leave him here and let the doctor see him alone? I-I'm afraid."

"But *I'm* here."

"I know, Mom, but I'm still—"

"We'll be leaving soon, sweetheart," Lara promised. She left the chair and hugged the girl. "Very soon."

"Tomorrow? After the doctor leaves?"

"Yes."

"For good?"

"For good."

Molly's large fearful eyes absorbed her face, seeking

reassurance. Lara could hear the grandfather's clock in the foyer, ticking softly yet distinctly.

Seconds passed.

"Mom?"

"Yes, sweetheart?"

"I don't want to sleep alone tonight."

Lara knocked on the door. When she heard no sound coming from the other side, she knocked again, then listened with her ear pressed against the door. Still she heard nothing. She had wanted to tell the man that a doctor would be coming to see him the next morning.

"Sir?" she called, knocking again, this time much louder.

No response.

Lara debated whether or not to peek in the room. Was the man in there? Had he left without her knowing? Was he sleeping? Or was he . . . dead?

Her hand gripped the glass knob. She turned it, then hesitated, thinking she had no right to do this. This would be an invasion of the man's privacy. He could be naked.

But I've already seen him naked, she reminded herself, and I should be able to enter any room I please.

She opened the door.

He was in bed, still wearing Steve's blue pajamas.

She watched him silently, suddenly feeling very foolish. Until now she hadn't realized how tense she was, how afraid to open the door. The man before her was sound asleep, looking as peaceful and harmless as a newborn. She even had an urge to kiss his forehead and wish him pleasant dreams.

How on earth could Steve and Molly be afraid of him?

Deciding not to tell him about the doctor, she quietly retreated from the room. Maybe it would be best if he didn't know. If he reacted unfavorably, the doctor would know how to handle him much better than she ever could.

She closed the door.

He opened his eyes. He had closed them when the woman entered the room. He had felt her watching him and had contemplated on how best to be rid of her. The temptation to reach for her throat had been strong, but he had fought it. He had reminded himself to tread slowly. Carefully.

He closed his eyes.

"Don't you usually take your hearing aid off, sweet-heart?" Lara asked as Molly reached over for the lamp. They were in Molly's bed, and it was nighttime.

"I'm going to keep it on tonight." In one hand she clutched the flashlight.

"But why?"

"I might hear something."

"And the flashlight?"

"In case I want to see in the dark." She paused, then added, "I don't like the dark and silence no more."

"Oh, sweetheart, you're scaring yourself needlessly. Nothing is going to happen to you. That man is gentle. He wouldn't hurt you."

Molly said nothing, but she obviously wasn't convinced. She held the flashlight close to her, like a child clutching a doll.

Lara sighed, then kissed her forehead. "Good night."

"Night, Mom." Stretching again for the lamp, she plunged the room into darkness.

The bed was small, and Lara found it difficult to fall asleep. Also, her mind refused to rest. She found herself thinking about Steve, wondering where he was sleeping tonight. Was it at the restaurant? Or was it at the apartment in Massachusetts? Was he to live there while she lived here? But didn't he know that she didn't want this house without him?

She tossed and turned, and Molly grunted each time she did this. Lara then forced herself to lie still. Minutes passed interminably, then hours, and still she found herself unable to sleep.

Gradually she began to think about spending the rest of the night in her own room. She could always return early in the morning, before Molly even woke up. Molly would never know, she told herself, for she was now snoring softly beside her, sleeping soundly.

And, of course, what she didn't know . . .

Gently, Lara slid out of bed and tiptoed from the room.

29

The smell woke Molly up. She tried to ignore it, telling herself it wasn't real, that it was something she had dreamed, but the smell wouldn't go away. If anything, it grew stronger and more repugnant.

Staring up at the darkness, she began to wonder what was making this awful odor, and where it was coming from. Deep down she knew the answer, but she was unwilling to admit it.

Was there something smelly out in the ocean? Was it the smell of dead fish? Was it from one of those colored tides she had heard her mother talk about once? It had something to do with dead things in the water.

Or was the smell from something else, something that had nothing to do with the ocean?

Molly, still staring up at the dark ceiling of her room, reached for her mother, but her hand touched only the bare sheet. Her mother was gone!

Molly tensed and held her breath.

The smell was stronger now. It seemed to be all around her, closing in like some kind of horrible fog. It was a sour smell, a smell of something that had gone bad, like a garbage can in hot weather, reeking of wilted vegetables and sweaty meat. It was the smell of rot.

Mom, she cried silently.

She closed her eyes, hoping the odor would go away,

but it only grew worse.

Mom, please.

Now she could feel warm air on her face. Her eyes sprung open, and she clutched her flashlight tighter against her. Whatever was making the smell, she knew, was only inches away from her, and if she beamed her flashlight directly in front of her, she would see what it was. But she couldn't muster up enough courage to do this.

"Mom." This time she whimpered the name out loud.

If only she could hear better. The silence was frightening her, and the darkness was too dark, for she couldn't make out anything in the room. She reached out again for her mother, letting her right hand grope the mattress while her body remained stiff.

Where did she go?

Why did she go?

Mom, where are you?

Fear was paralyzing her. Her mind began to scream at her to snap on the light. Maybe she would see nothing, and then the smell and that warm air would go away. But her hand wouldn't listen. A thumb was on the plastic switch of the flashlight, ready to slide it up—up for ON, down for OFF—but it was frozen like the rest of her.

She didn't want to see. She was too afraid, afraid that it would be. . .

Something brushed against the bed, and she felt the mattress quiver.

The light, her mind demanded again. Turn on the light and you'll know!

Molly held her breath, positioned the flashlight directly in front of her, then silently counted: one . . . two . . .

Three!

Yellow light illuminated a white face with glistening green-black eyes. It hovered, disembodied, like a shining moon in the dark. It blinked once at the sudden flare of light, then stared grimly down at her. It was the man that she suspected had come from the north garden, and he was here to—what—kill her?

The hard, stern expression seemed to confirm this. He moved closer toward her, then stopped. His eyes locked with hers, continuing to mesmerize her with terror. Then his head slowly began to lean toward her.

The face descended closer and closer.

The man's toothless mouth was slightly open, and through the gap the sour stench leaked, like a garbage can with a lid that was half on, she thought numbly. What made him smell like that? What was inside him?

His face paused and expelled more foul breath on her, making her gag, then it tilted to the side, parting its lips wider. Molly stared up into the yawning mouth, into a black cavern, then the trance shattered and panic erupted. *He's gonna kiss me!*

She screamed. Then out of the darkness his hands appeared at her shoulders and pinned her against the mattress. She squirmed, screaming louder.

"Mom! Mom-mieee! Help! Mommieeee!"

She continued to wiggle and thrash, but it was useless. The man's mouth covered hers, muffling the screams. Now not only could she smell the fetid odor that emanated from him, but she could taste it as well. Rot and evil was everywhere, consuming her.

Lara heard the scream and bolted upright on her bed. For a fleeting instant she wondered if she had only dreamed the sound, then it filled the air again, chilling and panicking her. She threw back the covers and raced across the dark room to where she knew the door was. When she reached the hallway she groped for the light switch without decreasing her frenetic pace.

She heard another scream. It was unmistakably Molly's.

"Coming, baby! Coming!"

She reached Molly's room and found the door ajar. A wedge of light from the hallway spilled into this room, dimly illuminating a hunched form over the bed. Lara pushed the door open wider and reached inside for the light switch. At the same time, as the overhead light flooded the room, she shouted, "Get away from her!"

The man, as though too intent with what he was doing, did not move. Molly struggled under him, grunting and gasping.

"Away from her!" Lara screamed, then bolted toward him. She pulled at the back of his pajama top in a frantic attempt to yank him off her daughter. She heard the fabric rip, yet she continued to pull. When she realized she wasn't getting anywhere, she began to pummel his back, determined to break it, if anything, but it was like hammering on a concrete surface.

"Damn you!" she cried. "Leave my baby alone! Do you hear me! Leave her alone!"

She seized a handful of his hair and yanked with all her might. To her relief, he finally yielded. His head snapped back with her hand, his mouth gaping, his eyes bulging. There was a low, almost inaudible growl, betraying anger for the intrusion. Then slowly, the man's face turned in Lara's hand toward her and glowered.

Molly coughed, gagged, then coughed again.

"Run!" Lara ordered. But the girl hesitated, not wanting to leave her. "Run, I said!"

The girl looked at the man, back at her, then ran out of the room.

Lara let go of the man's hair. It had felt as dry and fuzzy as lichen. Then she took a step back, for the man was still glaring at her, his mouth parted, fouling the air with rancid breath.

"W-what were you doing?" she stammered, taking another backward step, then another. Suddenly this wasn't a frail, sickly man anymore. This was a rabid creature, panting and glaring like a wolf. Lara was afraid to turn her back on him. "Get out of here!" she commanded when he didn't answer.

He moved toward her, slowly and steadily. She backed into the wall.

"Look, if you don't . . . if you don't leave, I'm going to call the police." He kept coming. "Did you hear me? I'm going to call—"

She broke for the door and slammed it shut behind her, hoping the separation would at least briefly stall him. Then she raced down the hall and stairs.

"Molly!" she cried. "Where are you?"

The girl made no reply. Probably couldn't hear her, Lara realized in a rush of panic. She wanted desperately to find her and run away from the house. Seeing that man bent over her daughter, like some kind of vampire, had blasted all doubts from her mind. Why hadn't she listened to Steve and Molly? Now she was certain that the man she had thought to be so harmless was extremely dangerous.

"Molly!" she shouted at the top of her lungs.

She ran into the dining room, into the kitchen, into the library. Then in a sudden burst of alarm she rushed back toward the stairs in the foyer. It occurred to her the girl could be in one of the upstairs bedrooms, and the man could easily find her before she did!

"Molly!" she screamed again and again. Then she cursed herself. What on earth was the matter with her, shouting like this? Molly was practically deaf, but that man wasn't. She was only helping him find her.

Biting down on her lower lip, almost drawing blood, she rushed up the stairs, stumbling on several steps in her haste and panic. She pushed open the door to the first bedroom, quickly scanned the room, then proceeded to the next, not bothering to close the door. The second room proved to be equally vacant. This one was an old nursery, perhaps when Steve and Shelly were infants. Now it was gray with dust and cobwebs, and the air was exceptionally warm and stale. Undoubtedly it had been a long time since anyone even opened the door to this room, let alone a window.

Lara fled toward the third room, her late mother-in-law's. Here it was disturbingly quiet, as though Death, having claimed the old woman, still lingered, waiting for another victim. The silence was too thick.

"Molly," she whispered, just to break this silence.

Then she headed for Shelly's room, then her own. This

house is too big, she thought in an explosion of frustration. Steve's been right all along. The house is too damn big—and too damn frightening. Too many rooms. Too many *dead* rooms!

She gave her own room a quick glance, then noticed the closet door was ajar. Could the girl be in there? God, there were dozens of closets in this house. She could be in any one of them!

Lara started for the closet, but when her hand reached the knob to pull the door open, she heard a noise behind her. She spun around and gasped in surprise at the figure entering the room. It was the sickly man, only now he didn't look so sickly. He was walking toward her with confident strides, his bony chin tilted upward and his glittering eyes cast downward, as though he were many feet taller than he actually was. He moved with a purpose, and there was no vestige of doubt that he wouldn't achieve his purpose.

"Get away from me!" she hissed, her back to the closet door, her hand sliding off the knob. She felt a rush of panic as she realized she was trapped, that the man was blocking the entrance. If she wanted to flee the room she would have to get past him.

"Please get away," she said again, this time pleading.

But he continued to move toward her.

She contemplated hiding in the closet, then quickly reminded herself she would only be cornered. Then she frantically looked about, searching for something that could be used as a weapon. Her eyes spotted a porcelain water pitcher on top of the dresser and seized it. It wasn't a gun or knife, but at least it was something.

"C-Come any closer and I'll—I'll—"

He laughed, a laugh that came from deep inside him and passed through unsmiling lips. In long fluid steps he reached her and with one firm hand pushed her against the closet door, closing and clicking it shut. The shove reminded her of how deceivingly strong he was, drowning her with panic.

He pinned her to the closet door with his one hand. She

slammed the pitcher against the side of his head, and the porcelain cracked. She hit him again, harder, and this time the pitcher shattered; it could have been made of thin glass for the little good it did. The man winced but never let go of his hand against her shoulder. Instead, he pressed his other hand against her other shoulder, pinning her even more.

She let go of the pitcher handle, which was all that was left, and it fell with a soft clink to join its broken remains on the floor. "Let go! Let go of me!" She tried to wrench herself from him. When that failed, she kneed him in the groin. As with the pitcher, he winced but kept her pinned to the closet door. She slammed her knee into him a second time, and the result was even more ineffectual; he didn't even flinch. Then, with growing panic, she realized why the man was not reacting as expected. It was simple —almost laughable. *He wasn't a man.*

"Why are you doing this?" she asked.

He didn't answer. Instead, he pressed firmly against her, and his body repulsed her. It was not a normal body; it was spongy and pliable. With her nails she dug into his forearm, and the nails sank in easily, like sinking into cheese. If she had wanted, she knew she could sink her fingers up to her knuckles into this "flesh."

She fought for control. "W-What are you going to do?" Her voice cracked.

In answer, his face came closer. His lips parted.

In a burst of determination, she gave him a violent shove, and this time succeeded in freeing herself from him. He stumbled back in surprise, and she bolted past him, speeding toward the door. She felt his hand on the back of her nightgown, but before he could grasp it firmly she gave her body a violent wrench and shot forward.

She ran down the hall. She was certain he was close in pursuit, but she didn't dare look back. Blood pounded in her ears, and her heart hammered violently.

She raced down the first half of the stairs, then fell

down the rest. At the bottom she rested momentarily in a crumpled heap.

She tried to jump back up on her feet, but searing pain was everywhere in her body. Her back, her ribs, her shoulder—

Something crashed down on her, flattening her. She screamed, knowing instantly what it was. She twisted under the horrible weight, reaching out for something to pull her out from under, but her hands only found the edge of the old Indian rug, which slid uselessly toward her.

"Off!" she sobbed. "Get off!"

He flipped her over, letting her look up at him.

"No!"

The green eyes glared down at her. The nose was long and sharp, now flaring at the nostrils, and the mouth was a thin line opening more and more.

What is he going to do? Rape me?

With every strength she had, she fought him. She heaved, hoping to throw him off her. Then she frantically rocked from side to side. He wasn't heavy, probably not weighing more than 110, but he was incredibly strong.

"Please . . ." she sobbed.

His mouth covered hers. She bit his lips, and as before, there was no reaction. She whimpered, still thrashing and bucking vainly under him. At first his hideous kiss was dry, then she felt something viscid seep from his mouth and wet her clenched lips. She struggled to avert her head, but he managed to follow no matter which way she turned. His mouth adamantly remained over hers.

Then she felt something push its way between her lips, forcing them apart. It felt like a tongue, yet it didn't. It was too wide, too thick, and too slippery. The sticky substance that she'd felt on her lips was now seeping into her. It tasted horribly bitter and she tried to spit it back out, but her mouth was plugged.

God, where are you? Help me!

Then she heard deep sucking sounds, and she knew

what was happening. He was pulling air out of her, pulling air like a vampire would pull blood, and there wasn't anything she could do about it. She was pinned under him, at his mercy.

Her feet kicked, and her arms, which were free only from the elbows down, flailed. Soon these slowed down, like dying fish out of water. The face above her began to blur and dim. Her lungs felt hot, swollen and ready to erupt. She knew it would only be a matter of seconds now. She was slipping fast, and there was nothing to grab.

Far, far away she heard her daughter. It was a frantic voice, a voice that was too loud and guttural. *Slow down, sweetheart. Remember your t's and g's.*

"Police? You dodda ded down here! He's killing my mom!"

Lara's body shuddered, then sighed, then the man on top of her calmly rose to his feet and turned toward the living room, toward the girl on the phone.

30

Molly didn't hear him, but she saw his shadow on the rug approaching her from behind. She spun around and was stunned to find him so close. Her hand let go of the phone receiver, letting it clunk to the floor while its base remained on the table. Then she backed away from him, bumped into an armchair and skirted it, her eyes never leaving him.

He was a monster. There was no doubt about it now. She had seen him kill her mother. He had been like some kind of giant bird over her, like the one you'd see dining on a dead dog or raccoon on the side of the road. And her mother's legs, which were all she could see from the living room, hadn't moved in the end. They hadn't moved at all.

Molly tried not to let this sink in. Instead, she concentrated on the man—monster—before her. He walked like a robot, she numbly reflected. He was programmed to—

"Go away!" Her voice was weak, a moan. She paused behind a rocking chair, momentarily feeling secure that something was between them. Then she moved away from the chair and toward the door that led to the foyer. She wanted to see her mother. Maybe she wasn't dead. Maybe she had just fainted.

"Away!" She waved the man off, as though he were a

mad dog inching toward her. His eyes glared, certainly resembling a canine's, and his lips were open in an eerie snarl, as though to bare the teeth that he didn't have.

Molly kept to the wall, expecting him to pounce on her at any moment, but the man moved forward only when she moved away. What would happen if she stopped? Would he do the same? Or would he take the chance to jump her?

Not wanting to find out, she continued to move along the wall and around the furniture that hugged it. She intended to break into a run, hoping she'd be faster if he should chase her.

Through the door she could see a glimpse of her mother. It was the legs again that were in view—her unmoving legs. Keeping her eyes on the man, Molly inched her way toward the foyer.

"Away!" she repeated.

Walking backwards she entered the foyer. She thought of closing the door to the living room, then decided against it. There was not enough time to lock the door; he only would rush forward to stop her. She would just check on her mother, then she would bolt.

She would outrun him. She would have to.

The back of her feet bumped into her mother's body. She and her heart stopped. Then, remembering to keep moving, she stepped over the body and looked down.

The first thing she saw was the thick transparant substance over her mother's lips and chin. It was yellowish and gleamed wetly under the foyer's chandelier. It was like—her mind searched for the right words—like ectoplasm, like pus.

Then she saw that the eyes were closed. She desperately wanted to touch her mother, but she knew if she did this, the man would touch *her*. She had to keep moving.

She quickly looked at her mother's chest, hoping to see it rise and fall, but as she took backward steps she wasn't sure if the movement was in her mother's chest or in herself.

"Mom?" she cried, so desperately wanting to awaken her.

It was the man who answered. "Do not be afraid, little girl."

"Away!" she demanded, her voice cracking.

He extended a hand, long fingers splayed, and repeated, "Please do not be afraid."

"You killed my mother!"

"I will not hurt you."

"You hurt my mother. You killed her."

"Do not be afraid."

Not only did he walk like a robot, she thought suddenly, but he talked like one. He was repetitious, and he spoke in a monotone. It was time for her to break into a run, since she could sense that he was ready to attack, but she was reluctant to leave her mother behind.

"Do not be afraid," he said for the fourth time. He, too, stepped over Lara's inert body.

Run! Run now!

She glanced sideways at the front door, then back at the man. She knew it was dark outside. Maybe she could outrun and lose him, then she could call the police from the nearest neighbor. Which was what? Acres and acres away. A quarter of a mile?

"Please, little girl. I will not hurt—"

She bolted for the door, but felt a strange tug, as though something was pulling her back. She fought the sensation, reached the door, gave the handle a violent turn, then pulled at it. The door would not open.

It's locked! Why is it locked?

She jiggled at the handle, yanking at it again. Then she caught the man's horrible stench and ran away from the door, passing him. For an instant she stood in the foyer, wondering where to go next. As she asked herself the question, she thought of the kitchen door. She made a dash for it. Behind her, the man followed at a leisurely pace, as though he knew he did not have to hurry, that he would catch up in the end.

Molly felt another tug, and once more she resisted, wrenching her shoulders as though to free invisible hands that were endeavoring to still her.

The outside door in the kitchen would not open either.

Molly felt panic take hold. Tears began to fill her eyes, blurring her vision, and her chin trembled. Why are the doors locked? Did the horrible man do this? How did he do it?

Magic, dummy!

Molly found herself paralyzed with terror. Tears drenched her cheeks. This was all her fault. Her cat had died because of her. Her stepfather left because of what she had done. And her mother was dead because of her. There was no doubt about it; it was all her fault because she had planted those stupid seeds. Now she wished she could somehow start all over again.

The man entered the room and moved mechanically toward her.

"Away!" She waved frantically at him, ineffectually shooing him. "Away! Away!"

He did not listen. He was soon halfway across the kitchen. What was she going to do now? There seemed to be only one answer, and that was to run. But as she prepared herself to do this, her eyes spotted the cutlery set on the counter. There were about a half a dozen knives sheathed in a slanted, wooden block holder leaving only the handles, also wooden, exposed. Judging from the size of the handles, she knew some of the knives were big. They would be perfect for . . .

She hesitated, then ran toward the cutlery. Using both hands she reached for the two largest handles and pulled them out of the case. Then she spun around, holding the instruments like a cowboy drawing two pistols, and confronted the man.

The knives felt surprisingly heavy in her hands, and the blades were brand new, shining like mirrors. Noboby probably ever used them, except maybe on Thanksgiving to carve turkeys, but she was going to use them now.

The man paused, his dark eyes flashing hesitantly, then

they dulled, and he proceeded toward tne girl.

Molly gripped the knives' thick wooden handles tighter, suddenly not sure if she would have the nerve to use them.

Her hands shook, blurring the twin blades. She was almost petrified out of her mind, and she had a sudden urge to pee.

"Away!" she sobbed. "Away . . ."

Paralyzed, she watched the man ignore her plea and advance closer in slow, dreamlike movements. Her mind screamed at her to run again, but her legs were like jelly; she knew she could never run without falling. And she knew that if she fell, the man would leap on top of her, exactly as he had done to her mother. If that happened, she would not have a chance. It was better this way—standing firmly on her feet, weapons in hands.

But could she actually kill him? She wasn't too sure if she could go that far. Maybe she could if she had a gun. It was one thing to pull a trigger, but another to thrust blades through skin and muscle. It would take much more effort, more strength—mental as well as physical.

The knives in her hands continued to shake. He's not human, she reminded herself. He's just a vegetable, and it's okay to kill a vegetable. It wouldn't be the same as killing a man.

He was now two arms' lengths away. This was her last chance to run. It was either this or thrust her hands forward and let him have it in the belly.

He was one arm's length away. His nauseating breath fanned her face. Stop! Stop! I'm gonna do it if you don't stop!

She squeezed her eyes shut and twisted her head to the side, as though to separate this part of her from the rest. One hand shot forward, felt resistance, then with added pressure shot forward again, this time with slippery ease. The other hand swung blindly. Again there was resistance, but her hand kept swinging and whacking, as though determined to break through something—which it soon did.

Molly opened her eye, then the other. The man had stopped advancing toward her. A knife protruded from his stomach, but it was not this that the man was looking down at—it was at his left hand, which had been cleanly severed and was lying on the tiled floor. He stared, stunned. There was no blood, and for an instant Molly was certain she was dreaming. In real life the man would be bleeding.

Then she remembered. He wasn't human.

She broke into a run, stumbling on weak legs. She sped through rooms, then frantically tried the front door again. For one wonderful moment it gave and her hand pulled back the door, then it slammed shut, throwing her forward with it. She cried out, startled, then shot a glance over her shoulder, knowing beforehand what she would see.

The man was glaring at her, once more advancing steadily and calmly toward her. The knife was still buried in his belly, its wooden handle preceding him. The hand-less extremity was now dripping the thick translucent stuff that she had seen coating her mother's lips and chin.

"I will not hurt you, little girl," he intoned.

Liar! her mind screamed at him. How dumb did he think she was? He had killed her mother, and he would now kill her.

Then she thought of the windows. She could escape through one of them. She could use a chair to smash the glass, like they did in movies. Then she thought of something else.

She bolted past the man, thankful that she was at least faster than he, and seized a fistful of stick matches from the wrought iron dispenser near the fireplace in the living room. These she tucked inside her panties, for her night-shirt had no pockets, then with her free hands she grabbed the back of a Windsor chair and dragged it toward a window. Taking a deep breath, as though to draw in strength, she lifted the chair by its back and swung it with all her might toward the window.

Glass exploded. Instinctively Molly jumped back,

dropping the chair and throwing her hands over her face. Then she looked behind her to assure herself that the man was not near. She saw him just as he entered the room. Like a robot, she thought again. He did not speed up or slow down.

She then quickly surveyed the window. Long, dangerous shards were clinging to the frame, so she lifted the chair again and slammed it against the window once more. This time the way was clear. Tossing the chair aside, she then climbed through the window. She cut her sleeveless arm on a piece of glass that had failed to break loose. She experienced another tugging sensation from the man, but she refused to let this deter her. When she landed on an evergreen shrub she quickly scrambled to her feet and ran toward the garden shed.

As always, the door was unlocked. She flung it open, relieved that the man was not yet close enough to use his powers on the door. Glancing back at the house she could vaguely see him climbing through the window that she had shattered. The night was cloudy, and the moon was a faint, foggy sphere.

She hurried inside and began groping for something in the inky interior. Her hands knocked aside garden tools and clay flowerpots. Stumbling over a fertilizer spreader, she fell to her knees and bit back a cry of agony, then looked over at the open door, praying that she still had time. Outside it was a shade lighter, and through the doorway she could see the man coming toward the shed. Nothing was going to stop him, she knew. Nothing except. . .

Now on her hands and knees she crawled across the wooden floor, which felt gritty and powdery with dirt, chemical fertilizer and dust. She sneezed but did not pause in her search. Her hands touched the wheels of a lawnmower and a garden cart. Then at last she found what she was looking for—the gasoline can.

She lifted the container and could feel the liquid slosh inside. It was half empty, but it was more than enough. Now the problem was how to douse the man with the

gasoline. She could never throw the liquid at him through
the spigot at the top of the can. She would have to use
something else. But what?

Frantically, she began groping again, wishing she had
thought of bringing along her flashlight. As she searched
with her hands, she looked frequently at the door behind
her. Finally, she found a coffee can filled with nails, bolts
and screws. She dumped out the contents and scrambled
back to the gasoline can.

She sneezed again. Then on her knees, she carefully
poured the gasoline into the coffee can, stopping now
and then to be sure that the spigot was in line with the
mouth of the can. Also, she dipped her finger inside to
test its level. Eventually, after what felt like long minutes
instead of seconds, the can was full. Once more she
glanced at the door; he was near the shed now.

The smell of gasoline was everywhere, warm and thick.
It even made the sweat on her face and body seem oily.
Maybe she shouldn't go through with this; maybe she'd
blow up, too.

But when she saw the man in the doorway, she knew it
was too late. She was cornered now; there was nothing
left to do except continue.

Careful not to spill the gasoline and repeatedly
reminding herself to be calm, she waited for the man to
walk up to her.

"I will not hurt you, little girl."

She hid the can behind her, not sure of how keen his
eyesight was in the dark. She couldn't see his face, but
she could make out the outline of his bulk, black against
black. She held her breath, then when she believed he was
close enough she threw the gasoline in the direction of his
face.

She expected a scream, but he only stopped, stunned,
reacting the way he had done moments earlier in the
kitchen. He seemed suddenly uncertain. Molly, however,
acted quickly. She pulled out a match that was tucked
inside her underpants and grated its bulbous tip against
the rough floor planks.

The match did not ignite.

She tried again, harder. The thin wooden stick snapped. Frantically, she reached for another match and in her haste dropped the others. She struck the match against the floor, over and over. Still nothing. She discarded the match and searched the floor for another. She found one and once more endeavored to light a flame.

She felt a hand on the back of her nightgown, bunching it, readying to pull her up. In a frenzy she struck the match across the floor. Come on, come on, come on!

The hand was strong; it began to pull upward.

Please! . . . Come on!

A flame erupted at the end of the match, orange and brilliant in a black, infinite sea, and Molly cried out with relief. Then with a violent wrench she freed herself, feeling the nightshirt rip as the man held on. She fell backwards against a garden cart from the sudden release, but amazingly the match, which she managed to hold aloft, was still burning. Then he came for her.

It was the handless arm that she saw in the faint glow of the match. It reached for her, as though by instinct. Where the hand had been severed there was nothing, but at the wrist were two clumps with a number of wriggling, wormlike appendages protruding from them. Two miniature hands had begun to sprout, like a tree trunk sprouting branches, Molly thought crazily.

She threw a match at the man's face.

For a terrifying instant she thought it was over—for her. The match, in transit through the air, went out. Molly scrambled away as far and fast as she could, no longer knowing where the other dropped matches were. The man, she was certain, would find her before she'd find them. Then the man's head ignited.

Molly bolted for the door, and she didn't look back until she was outside and could feel the cool air around her. Only the man's head burned at first, looking like an eerie jack-o'-lantern, since it was so orange and bright. It spun around and around, then the fire began to lose its globular form and spread downward.

"Noooo!" she heard him wail, surprised that he could speak while engulfed in flames. "Not now! Not fair!"

He staggered and bumped into a wall; that, too, caught afire.

"Too soon! Not fair! Too soooooon!"

Molly watched in horrified fascination as he burned.

"Tooooo sooooooooon . . ."

What was too soon? Or had she, as usual, heard wrong? Suddenly she felt a sudden urge to extinguish the fire. She didn't like the way the man was thrashing. She could almost feel his agony, as though she herself were on fire.

The man spun around and around, screaming again. Or was it only the lingering echo from the last cry? Molly watched the shed turn into a furious bonfire, feeling the heat on her face. She could still see the man stumbling and spinning inside, and she shuddered, wishing he'd stop, wishing he wouldn't suffer so much. She took a backward step, then another. Finally the man fell and stopped moving. She stared a moment longer, and when it was certain that he was no longer alive, she snapped out of her trance and fled toward the house to call the police and fire department.

Inside, she stopped short at the sight of her mother lying motionless on the carpet in the foyer. She let out a sob and dropped to her knees. "Mom? . . . Mom, please wake up."

Tears burned her eyes, then she remembered why she had come back into the house. Fighting back the tears, she forced herself to leave her mother's side and go into the living room to use a phone.

Finding a directory she looked up the number for the fire department, then she made the call. The man on the other end said something after she told him to come right away, but she couldn't make it out. She gave him the address, urged him to hurry, then hung up. Next, she called the ambulance. Maybe her mother wasn't dead. Maybe the doctors and nurses could save her. Then she ran into the kitchen, thinking a cold, wet cloth on the forehead might help revive her mother. She'd seen them do this hundreds of times in movies and on TV.

She ran a dish towel under the faucet, wondering if the water was supposed to be hot instead of cold. After the towel was soaked she turned around, then froze. The towel fell from her hand with a heavy, soft plop. On the floor was the creature's severed hand, but it was different now; it had grown things from the fingers and out of the severed end.

Molly gawked at it, not sure what she was seeing. The things looked like long strands of yellowish-brown hair, curling at the tips. Roots?

The girl made a wide berth around it, but when she reached the door she stopped. That hand was alive, she realized. She couldn't ignore it. What if . . . what if it grew and became another creature?

She couldn't leave it lying there on the floor. She would have to get rid of it, kill it.

Molly turned to look at the hand again. How was she going to move it? Then her eyes swept toward the knife that had cut off the hand. It was lying two feet away. She could use this to carry the hand; that way she wouldn't have to touch it.

Drawing in a deep breath to steel herself, she picked up the heavy chef's knife, then impaled the hand with the utensil. The blade went in easy. She lifted the knife with the hideous hand attached, the gossamer strands floating and swaying like hair in water, and ran outside.

She would burn it and kill it like the creature it belonged to, but before she reached the flaming shed, she felt the strands curl around her wrist. With a gasp she let go of the knife, but it was too late. The knife and the attached hand fell only a few inches from her own hand, for the strands clinging to her wrist kept them aloft.

Molly frantically clawed at the strands with her other

hand. She pulled and yanked, but they clung to her. Then to her horror she saw that they were extending, coiling upward like diminutive snakes toward her elbow.

"Nooooo!" she screamed. She dropped to her knees and repeatedly slammed her hand and forearm against the ground, trying to squash the growing strands. She could feel them tightening their grips on her. "Noooo!"

They slithered round and round, spiraling toward her upper arm and shoulder. Over and over she cried for help, filling the air with her screams. She went back to clawing and pulling, but it was like trying to break apart nylon strings. Was this how she was going to die?

Was she going to be tangled to death? Squeezed to death?

Maybe the ambulance would come in time, she suddenly thought. Then the strands wormed toward her neck, and she knew in an explosion of panic that there was no time. She would have to do something now, or else—

"God, help! Please, please help!"

Her eyes fell on the dangling knife. Of course! She could cut the strands!

In a frenzy she began to twist and pull at the instrument. Adrenaline rushed through her, and soon she was able to free the knife from the creature's hand. She sawed at the strands.

She felt strands slither and coil around her neck. In another second they were going to strangle her. She had to hurry. There was no time.

She sawed faster, but the strands were tough. If only the knife was sharper . . .

She gripped the severed hand as firmly as she could, while with her other hand she sawed and sawed. At last she succeeded in cutting the roots that protruded from the severed end but she was only half done, for there were just as many strands growing from the fingers and thumb.

She could feel their grip tightening on her neck.

Desperately she sawed.

God, please, I don't want to die.

She could feel herself slipping, getting dizzy, getting weaker.

She sawed and sawed and . . .

At last the strands broke free! Sobbing with relief, Molly tore at the coiled roots on her neck, loosening them until she could breathe again. She speared the creature's hand with the knife, ran with it toward the burning shed, and flung it as deep as she could into the fire. Then she collapsed on the ground.

Her body shook with violent sobs for long minutes. She hugged herself as she knelt on the grass, but she could not stop the trembling. Never had she been so frightened, and never had she felt such relief. It was over. At last the horror was over!

Then she remembered that her mother was dead.

There was a sudden, painful tightness in her heart, as though something had brutally squeezed it. She jumped up and ran back to the house for the second time that night. Her mother was in the exact same position. She hadn't moved.

Why wasn't the ambulance here yet?

Molly stared at her mother's inert body, as though trying to will it to move. When that failed, she fell to the floor and began shaking her. "Mom? Wake up! Please wake up!"

Lara's head rocked limply from side to side.

"Oh Mom, please."

She shook harder.

Guilt and grief hit her with sudden, violent force. She doubled over as though something deadly had attacked her in the stomach. Her body shook again with sobs, this time more violent and convulsive.

It was all her fault, all of it. She should have known there would be danger when she had seen the red stream of light escaping from the box of seeds. Right then and there she should have known she was fooling around with something evil. But no, she had let curiosity take over.

And curiosity had killed . . .

"Mom!" she wailed. "Mom . . . I'm s-sor-ry," she hiccuped as her eyes and nose ran.

The tears made the foyer as well as her mother blurr. She did not bother to wipe her eyes. The walls and stairs began to move. The floor moved. Her mother moved.

Molly's heart accelerated.

She stared at her mother, hope soaring. Had her mother really moved? She wiped her eyes frantically, staring harder.

Move, Mom. Oh please, Mom. Move!

But there was only stillness. Then . . .

The eyes fluttered beneath the closed lids.

"Mom!"

They opened.

"*Mom!*"

The eyes looked up at her, and Molly broke into the widest smile she'd ever made in her life. "Mom, Mom, Mom!"

Lara blinked, then weakly lifted a hand to stroke the girl's air. "Sweet . . . heart," she whispered.

Molly hugged her, so fiercely that the woman cried out.

"I'm sorry."

"Shush, sweetheart. You're . . . you're crying." She sounded surprised.

"I thoughd you were dead."

"Your t's . . . Remember your t's."

Molly swallowed, nodding readily and beginning again. "I thought you were—"

"I wouldn't die on you," she interrupted softly. "Now wipe your eyes."

Molly obeyed, using the back of her hand. Then, sniffling and still grinning, she leaned her head against her mother's breasts. She felt wonderfully warm and safe and alive. Thank you, God, she said silently. Never had she felt so relieved, so happy, so very grateful.

She was still on the floor, in her mother's arms, when the ambulance and firemen arrived.

Epilogue

Lara looked up from the morning paper and over at her daughter sitting across from her. They were at the kitchen table in a new apartment. Lara could have had returned to the old apartment, the one they had kept vacant while they lived in the big house in Rhode Island, but her late husband could not be forgotten there. There were too many memories. Living in that apartment would have been like living in the past.

Sometimes the past would rush back and cripple her with grief. It would strike without warning. She would be drying the dishes, a glass that had been in her hand would slip and crash to the floor, and she would not notice it until after several minutes had passed. Or she would be at work, at the counter of a women's boutique where she was a clerk, and suddenly she would find herself looking vacantly at her employer or a customer who had been trying to penetrate her daze. Or she'd be reading a mystery novel, something that she did almost every night now, and find that she'd turned pages but couldn't recall a word she had read. It would be Steve she had thought about. She still loved him so very much, and now that he was gone she wished she'd been more tolerant of his weaknesses. She wished she had helped him and had tried harder to communicate with him.

But he was gone now, and she was determined to move

onward. She could never bring him back, no matter how much she wished she could.

Now Molly was reading the comics, unaware of Lara's gaze. The sun was behind her, streaming in through the window, highlighting the girl's pineapple-colored hair. Lara smiled inwardly. It had been a year since that horrible summer, and finally Molly was recovering. When Steve's body had been found in the closet, the girl had become hysterical, certain that his death had been her fault. It had taken months and numerous sessions before the doctor could convince her that she was blameless. Now, at last, she was coming along nicely and she was learning to do what Lara had learned many, many years ago—to move forward and shed the past like a skin.

Lara took a sip of her coffee and turned the page of the paper. A heading at the bottom caught her attention:

UNIDENTIFIED FLOWERS FOUND GROWING IN HOME

Mrs. Gail Garrett claimed that flowering plants had sprouted from her bathroom commode and sink. A botanist investigated the claim but made no comment. Mrs. Garrett, however, stated that she had heard the scientist mutter that this, indeed, was quite unusual when he saw the flowers, and that he had taken samples for tests . . .

The words began to swim before Lara's eyes. She again looked up at her daughter who was still engrossed in the comics. "Molly?" The girl did not hear her, so she rapped her knuckles against the tabletop until she had her attention.

"Yes, Mom?"

Lara swallowed. "I know . . . I know you don't like to talk about last summer, sweetheart," she said slowly, "but do you remember throwing any seeds down a toilet or sink in that house?"

The question surprised her. Molly thought about this for a moment, then said, "I remember throwing away some flowers down the toilet because I couldn't stand the smell of them."

Lara could feel the blood leave her face. Was there a connection? Had those flowers produced seeds, germinated in the town sewer, and then . . .

"Why, Mom?" the girl asked, frowning.

"Oh . . . no reason." Lara forced herself to smile. There seemed to be no sense in telling the girl. Lord knew she had suffered enough guilt. And she had been doing so well recently, had been practicing her list of words, and was at last beginning to speak with ease and, best of all, confidence.

Besides, Lara told herself, maybe she was getting all upset for nothing. Maybe the flowers that Molly had thrown away and the flowers that the woman had found were not related at all. It was only a coincidence that the town was the same, only a coincidence.

Move forward. Forget the past.

"No reason," she said again, shaking her head dismissively. Then she forced herself to turn to another page and read about something else.

BONE-CHILLING HORROR
FROM EDMUND PLANTE

SEED OF EVIL. A savage union with a strange man left Patty, a divorced mother of two, with a child she couldn't bring herself to abort—or love. He looked like a normal boy, but when "accidents" began to happen—murderous, violent occurrences—Patty knew that this child was nothing less than the spawn of the devil.

___2581-7 $3.95US/$4.95CAN

TRANSFORMATION. Sally Martin was changing. Her body had become pale and bloated, her lustrous hair had fallen out, her jaundiced eyes were no longer able to bear sunlight. Meanwhile, ripening inside her, a hideous pulsing organism was waiting to burst upon an unsuspecting world, infecting all it touched.

___2490-X $3.95US/$4.95CAN

OBELISK
AN ANCIENT TERROR TO CHILL THE MARROW OF YOUR BONES
by Ehren M. Ehly

Trapped in the hot, fetid darkness of an ancient Egyptian tomb, Steve Harrison was suddenly assaulted by bizarre and horrific images of a past he had never known. Even when he returned to New York, he found himself driven by strange cravings and erotic desires he couldn't explain; his girl friend suddenly feared for her life and that of her unborn child. Steve Harrison only had one chance to restore his deteriorating body and cleanse his diseased mind—a final confrontation with incredible forces of evil, this time in Central Park, this time in the shadow of the forbidding. . .

OBELISK

____2612-0 $3.95US/$4.95CAN